pd

DEEPER IN THE WOOD SOUNDED THE MEASURED RING OF AXES.

A Country Christmas.

Kitty's Class Day
And Other Stories

By

Louisa M. Alcott

Author of "Little Women," etc.

Originally published under the title
"PROVERB STORIES"

GROSSET & DUNLAP
PUBLISHERS   NEW YORK

Published by arrangement with Little, Brown and Company

PREFACE

———◆———

BEING forbidden to write anything at present
I have collected various waifs and strays to ap-
pease the young people who clamor for more,
forgetting that mortal brains need rest.

As many girls have asked to see what sort of
tales Jo March wrote at the beginning of her
career, I have added " The Baron's Gloves," as a
sample of the romantic rubbish which paid so well
once upon a time. If it shows them what *not* to
write it will not have been rescued from oblivion
in vain.

L. M. ALCOTT.

CONTENTS

PROVERB STORIES

———◆———

KITTY'S CLASS DAY

"A stitch in time saves nine."

"O PRIS, Pris, I'm really going! Here's the invitation — rough paper — Chapel — spreads — Lyceum Hall — everything splendid; and Jack to take care of me!"

As Kitty burst into the room and performed a rapturous *pas seul,* waving the cards over her head, sister Priscilla looked up from her work with a smile of satisfaction on her quiet face.

"Who invites you, dear?"

"Why, Jack, of course, — dear old cousin Jack. Nobody else ever thinks of me, or cares whether I have a bit of pleasure now and then. Isn't he kind? Mayn't I go? and, O Pris, what *shall* I wear?"

Kitty paused suddenly, as if the last all-important question had a solemnizing effect upon both mind and body.

"Why, your white muslin, silk sacque, and new hat, of course," began Pris with an air of surprise. But Kitty broke in impetuously, —

"I'll never wear that old muslin again; it's

full of darns, up to my knees, and all out of
fashion. So is my sacque; and as for my hat,
though it does well enough here, it would be
absurd for Class Day."

"You don't expect an entirely new suit for
this occasion, — do you?" asked Pris, anxiously.

"Yes, I do, and I'll tell you how I mean to
get it. I've planned everything; for, though I
hardly dreamed of going, I amused myself by
thinking how I could manage if I *did* get invited."

"Let us hear." And Pris took up her work
with an air of resignation.

"First, my dress," began Kitty, perching herself on the arm of the sofa, and entering into the
subject with enthusiasm. "I've got the ten dollars grandpa sent me, and with eight of it I'm
going to buy Lizzie King's organdie muslin.
She got it in Paris; but her aunt providentially
— no, unfortunately — died; so she can't wear
it, and wants to get rid of it. She is bigger than
I am, you know; so there is enough for a little
mantle or sacque, for it isn't made up. The
skirt is cut off and gored, with a splendid
train —"

"My dear, you don't mean you are going
to wear one of those absurd, new-fashioned
dresses?" exclaimed Pris, lifting hands and eyes.

"I do! Nothing would induce me to go to
Class Day without a train. It's been the desire
of my heart to have one, and now I *will*, if I

never have another gown to my back!" returned
Kitty, with immense decision.

Pris shook her head, and said, "Go on!" as
if prepared for any extravagance after that.

"We can make it ourselves," continued Kitty,
"and trim it with the same. It's white with
blue stripes and daisies in the stripes; the loveliest thing you ever saw, and can't be got here.
So simple, yet distingué, I know you'll like it.
Next, my bonnet," — here the solemnity of
Kitty's face and manner was charming to behold.
"I shall make it out of one of my new illusion
undersleeves. I've never worn them; and the
puffed part will be a plenty for a little fly-away
bonnet of the latest style. I've got blue ribbons
to tie it with, and have only to look up some
daisies for the inside. With my extra two dollars I shall buy my gloves, and pay my fares, —
and there I am, all complete."

She looked so happy, so pretty, and full of
girlish satisfaction, that sister Pris could n't bear
to disturb the little plan, much as she disapproved
of it. They were poor, and every penny had to
be counted. There were plenty of neighbors to
gossip and criticise, and plenty of friends to
make disagreeable remarks on any unusual extravagance. Pris saw things with the prudent
eyes of thirty, but Kitty with the romantic eyes
of seventeen; and the elder sister, in the kindness of her heart, had no wish to sadden life to
those bright young eyes, or deny the child a

harmless pleasure. She sewed thoughtfully for a minute, then looked up, saying, with the smile that always assured Kitty the day was won, —

" Get your things together, and we will see what can be done. But remember, dear, that it is both bad taste and bad economy for poor people to try to ape the rich."

" You 're a perfect angel, Pris; so don't moralize. I 'll run and get the dress, and we 'll begin at once, for there is much to do, and only two days to do it in." And Kitty skipped away, singing " Lauriger Horatius," at the top of her voice.

Priscilla soon found that the girl's head was completely turned by the advice and example of certain fashionable young neighbors. It was in vain for Pris to remonstrate and warn.

" Just this once let me do as others do, and thoroughly enjoy myself," pleaded Kitty; and Pris yielded, saying to herself, " She shall have her wish, and if she learns a lesson, neither time nor money will be lost."

So they snipped and sewed, and planned and pieced, going through all the alternations of despair and triumph, worry and satisfaction, which women undergo when a new suit is under way. Company kept coming, for news of Kitty's expedition had flown abroad, and her young friends must just run in to hear about it, and ask what she was going to wear; while Kitty was so glad and proud to tell, and show, and enjoy her little

triumph that many half hours were wasted, and
the second day found much still to do.

The lovely muslin did n't hold out, and Kitty
sacrificed the waist to the train, for a train she
must have or the whole thing would be an utter
failure. A little sacque was eked out, however,
and when the frills were on, it was " ravishing,"
as Kitty said, with a sigh of mingled delight and
fatigue. The gored skirt was a fearful job, as
any one who has ever plunged into the mysteries
will testify; and before the facing, even experienced Pris quailed.

The bonnet also was a trial, for when the lace
was on, it was discovered that the ribbons did n't
match the dress. Here was a catastrophe! Kitty
frantically rummaged the house, the shops, the
stores of her friends, and rummaged in vain.
There was no time to send to the city, and despair
was about to fall on Kitty, when Pris rescued
her by quietly making one of the small sacrifices
which were easy to her because her life was
spent for others. Some one suggested a strip of
blue illusion, — and that could be got; but, alas!
Kitty had no money, for the gloves were already
bought. Pris heard the lamentations, and giving
up fresh ribbons for herself, pulled her sister out
of a slough of despond with two yards of
" heavenly tulle."

" Now the daisies; and oh, dear me, not one
can I find in this poverty-stricken town," sighed
Kitty, prinking at the glass, and fervently hop-

ing that nothing would happen to her complexion over night.

"I see plenty just like those on your dress," answered Pris, nodding toward the meadow full of young whiteweed.

"Pris, you're a treasure! I'll wear real ones; they keep well, I know, and are so common I can refresh my bonnet anywhere. It's a splendid idea."

Away rushed Kitty to return with an apron full of American daisies. A pretty cluster was soon fastened just over the left-hand frizzle of bright hair, and the little bonnet was complete.

"Now, Pris, tell me how I look," cried Kitty, as she swept into the room late that afternoon in full gala costume.

It would have been impossible for the primmest, the sourest, or the most sensible creature in the world to say that it wasn't a pretty sight. The long train, the big chignon, the apology for a bonnet, were all ridiculous, — no one could deny that, — but youth, beauty, and a happy heart made even those absurdities charming. The erect young figure gave an air to the crisp folds of the delicate dress; the bright eyes and fresh cheeks under the lace rosette made one forget its size; and the rippling brown hair won admiration in spite of the ugly bunch which disfigured the girl's head. The little jacket set "divinely," the new gloves were as immaculate as white kids could be, and to crown all, Lizzie

King, in a burst of generosity, lent Kitty the blue and white Paris sunshade which she could n't use herself.

" Now I could die content; I'm perfect in all respects, and I know Jack won't be ashamed of me. I really owe it to him to look my best, you know, and that 's why I 'm so particular," said Kitty, in an apologetic tone, as she began to lay away her finery.

" I hope you will enjoy every minute of the time, deary. Don't forget to finish running up the facing; I 've basted it carefully, and would do it if my head did n't ache so, I really can't hold it up any longer," answered Pris, who had worked like a disinterested bee, while Kitty had flown about like a distracted butterfly.

" Go and lie down, you dear, kind soul, and don't think of my nonsense again," said Kitty, feeling remorseful, till Pris was comfortably asleep, when she went to her room and revelled in her finery till bedtime. So absorbed was she in learning to manage her train gracefully, that she forgot the facing till very late. Then, being worn out with work and worry, she did, what girls are too apt to do, stuck a pin here and there, and, trusting to Priscilla's careful bastings, left it as it was, retiring to dream of a certain Horace Fletcher, whose aristocratic elegance had made a deep impression upon her during the few evenings she had seen him.

Nothing could have been lovelier than the

morning, and few hearts happier than Kitty's,
as she arrayed herself with the utmost care, and
waited in solemn state for the carriage; for
muslin trains and dewy roads were incompatible,
and one luxury brought another.

" My goodness, where did she get that stylish
suit? " whispered Miss Smith to Miss Jones, as
Kitty floated into the station with all sail set, finding it impossible to resist the temptation to aston-
ish certain young ladies who had snubbed her in
times past, which snubs had rankled, and were
now avenged.

" I looked everywhere for a muslin for to-day
and could n't find any I liked, so I was forced to
wear my mauve silk," observed Miss Smith,
complacently settling the silvery folds of her
dress.

" It 's very pretty, but one ruins a silk at Class
Day, you know. I thought this organdie would
be more comfortable and appropriate this warm
day. A friend brought it from Paris, and it 's
like one the Princess of Wales wore at the great
flower-show this year," returned Kitty, with the
air of a young lady who had all her dresses
from Paris, and was intimately acquainted with
the royal family.

" Those girls " were entirely extinguished by
this stroke, and had n't a word to say for themselves, while Kitty casually mentioned Horace
Fletcher, Lyceum Hall, and Cousin Jack, for *they*

had only a little Freshman brother to boast of, and were *not* going to Lyceum Hall.

As she stepped out of the cars at Cambridge, Jack opened his honest blue eyes and indulged in a low whistle of astonishment; for if there was anything he especially hated, it was the trains, chignons and tiny bonnets then in fashion. He was very fond of Kitty, and prided himself on being able to show his friends a girl who was charming, and yet not over-dressed.

" She has made a regular guy of herself; I won't tell her so, and the dear little soul shall have a jolly time in spite of her fuss and feathers. But I do wish she had let her hair alone and worn that pretty hat of hers."

As this thought passed through Jack's mind he smiled and bowed and made his way among the crowd, whispering as he drew his cousin's arm through his own, —

" Why, Kitty, you're got up regardless of expense, are n't you? I 'm so glad you came, we 'll have a rousing good time, and you shall see all the fun."

" Oh, thank you, Jack! Do I look nice, really? I tried to be a credit to you and Pris, and I did have such a job of it. I 'll make you laugh over it some time. A carriage for me? Bless us, how fine we are!" and Kitty stepped in, feeling that only one thing more was needed to make her cup overflow. That one thing was speedily vouch-

safed, for before her skirts were smoothly settled,
Jack called out, in his hearty way, —

"How are you, Fletcher? If you are bound
for Chapel I 'll take you up."

"Thanks; good-morning, Miss Heath."

It was all done in an instant, and the next thing
Kitty knew she was rolling away with the elegant
Horace sitting opposite. How little it takes to
make a young girl happy! A pretty dress, sunshine, and somebody opposite, and they are blest.
Kitty's face glowed and dimpled with pleasure
as she glanced about her, especially when *she,*
sitting in state with two gentlemen all to herself,
passed "those girls" walking in the dust with a
beardless boy; she felt that she could forgive past
slights, and did so with a magnanimous smile and
bow.

Both Jack and Fletcher had graduated the year
before, but still took an interest in their old
haunts, and patronized the fellows who were not
yet through the mill, at least the Seniors and
Juniors; of Sophs and Freshs they were sub-
limely unconscious. Greeted by frequent slaps on
the shoulder, and hearty "How are you, old
fellows," they piloted Kitty to a seat in the chapel.
An excellent place, but the girl's satisfaction was
marred by Fletcher's desertion, and she could not
see anything attractive about the dashing young
lady in the pink bonnet to whom he devoted himself, "because she was a stranger," Kitty said.

Everybody knows what goes on in the Chapel,

after the fight and scramble are over. The rustle
and buzz, the music, the oratory and the poem,
during which the men cheer and the girls simper;
the professors yawn, and the poet's friends pro-
nounce him a second Longfellow. Then the closing flourishes, the grand crush, and general scat-
tering.

Then the fun really begins, as far as the young
folks are concerned. *They* don't mind swarming
up and down stairs in a solid phalanx; they can
enjoy half a dozen courses of salad, ice and
strawberries, with stout gentlemen crushing their
feet, anxious mammas sticking sharp elbows into
their sides, and absent-minded tutors walking
over them. They can flirt vigorously in a torrid
atmosphere of dinner, dust, and din; can smile
with hot coffee running down their backs, small
avalanches of ice-cream descending upon their
best bonnets, and sandwiches, butter-side down,
reposing on their delicate silks. They know that
it is a costly rapture, but they carefully refrain
from thinking of the morrow, and energetically
illustrate the Yankee maxim which bids us enjoy
ourselves in our early bloom.

Kitty did have "a rousing good time;" for
Jack was devoted, taking her everywhere, showing her everything, feeding and fanning her, and
festooning her train with untiring patience. How
many forcible expressions he mentally indulged
in as he walked on that unlucky train we will not
record; he smiled and skipped and talked of

treading on flowers in a way that would have
charmed Kitty, if some one else had not been
hovering about "The Daisy," as Fletcher called
her.

After he returned, she neglected Jack, who
took it coolly, and was never in the way unless
she wanted him. For the first time in her life,
Kitty deliberately flirted. The little coquetries,
which are as natural to a gay young girl as her
laughter, were all in full play, and had she gone
no further no harm would have been done. But,
excited by the example of those about her, Kitty
tried to enact the fashionable young lady, and,
like most novices, she overdid the part. Quite
forgetting her cousin, she tossed her head, twirled
her fan, gave affected little shrieks at college
jokes, and talked college slang in a way that con-
vulsed Fletcher, who enjoyed the fun immensely.

Jack saw it all, shook his head and said nothing; but his face grew rather sober as he watched
Kitty, flushed, dishevelled, and breathless, whirling round Lyceum Hall, on the arm of Fletcher,
who danced divinely, as all the girls agreed. Jack
had proposed going, but Kitty had frowned, so he
fell back, leaving her to listen and laugh, blush
and shrink a little at her partner's flowery compliments and admiring glances.

"If she stands that long she 's not the girl I
took her for," thought Jack, beginning to lose
patience. "She does n't look like my little Kitty,
and somehow I don't feel half so fond and proud

of her as usual. I know one thing, *my* daughters shall never be seen knocking about in that style."

As if the thought suggested the act, Jack suddenly assumed an air of paternal authority, and, arresting his cousin as she was about to begin again, he said, in a tone she had never heard before, —

"I promised Pris to take care of you, so I shall carry you off to rest, and put yourself to rights after this game of romps. I advise you to do the same, Fletcher, or give your friend in the pink bonnet a turn."

Kitty took Jack's arm pettishly, but glanced over her shoulder with such an inviting smile that Fletcher followed, feeling very much like a top, in danger of tumbling down the instant he stopped spinning. As she came out Kitty's face cleared, and, assuming her sprightliest air, she spread her plumage and prepared to descend with effect, for a party of uninvited *peris* stood at the gate of this Paradise casting longing glances at the forbidden splendors within. Slowly, that all might see her, Kitty sailed down, with Horace, the debonair, in her wake, and was just thinking to herself, "Those girls won't get over this very soon, I fancy," when all in one moment she heard Fletcher exclaim, wrathfully, "Hang the flounces!" she saw a very glossy black hat come skipping down the steps, felt a violent twitch backward, and, to save herself from a fall, sat

down on the lower step with most undignified
haste.

It was impossible for the bystanders to help
laughing, for there was Fletcher hopping wildly
about, with one foot nicely caught in a muslin
loop, and there sat Kitty longing to run away and
hide herself, yet perfectly helpless, while every
one tittered. Miss Jones and Miss Smith laughed
shrilly, and the despised little Freshman completed her mortification, by a feeble joke about
Kitty Heath's new man-trap. It was only an instant, but it seemed an hour before Fletcher freed
her, and snatching up the dusty beaver, left her
with a flushed countenance and an abrupt bow.

If it had n't been for Jack, Kitty would have
burst into tears then and there, so terrible was
the sense of humiliation which oppressed her.
For his sake she controlled herself, and, bundling
up her torn train, set her teeth, stared straight
before her, and let him lead her in dead silence
to a friend's room near by. There he locked the
door, and began to comfort her by making light
of the little mishap. But Kitty cried so tragically, that he was at his wit's end, till the ludicrous side of the affair struck her, and she began
to laugh hysterically. With a vague idea that
vigorous treatment was best for that feminine
ailment, Jack was about to empty the contents of
an ice-pitcher over her, when she arrested him,
by exclaiming, incoherently, —

"Oh, don't! — it was so funny! — how can

you laugh, you cruel boy? — I'm disgraced, forever — take me home to Pris, oh, take me home
to Pris!"

"I will, my dear, I will; but first let me right
you up a bit; you look as if you had been hazed,
upon my life you do;" and Jack laughed in spite
of himself at the wretched little object before
him, for dust, dancing, and the downfall produced a ruinous spectacle.

That broke Kitty's heart; and, spreading her
hands before her face, she was about to cry again,
when the sad sight which met her eyes dispelled
the gathering tears. The new gloves were both
split up the middle and very dirty with clutching
at the steps as she went down.

"Never mind, you can wash them," said Jack,
soothingly.

"I paid a dollar and a half for them, and they
can't be washed," groaned Kitty.

"Oh, hang the gloves! I meant your hands,"
cried Jack, trying to keep sober.

"No matter for my hands, I mourn my gloves.
But I won't cry any more, for my head aches now
so I can hardly see." And Kitty threw off her
bonnet, as if even that airy trifle hurt her.

Seeing how pale she looked, Jack tenderly
suggested a rest on the old sofa, and a wet handkerchief on her hot forehead, while he got the
good landlady to send her up a cup of tea. As
Kitty rose to comply she glanced at her dress,
and, clasping her hands, exclaimed, tragically, —

" The facing, the fatal facing! That made all the mischief, for if I 'd sewed it last night it would n't have ripped to-day; if it had n't ripped Fletcher would n't have got his foot in it, I should n't have made an object of myself, he would n't have gone off in a rage, and — who knows what might have happened?"

" Bless the what 's-its-name if it has settled him," cried Jack. " He is a contemptible fellow not to stay and help you out of the scrape he got you into. Follow his lead and don't trouble yourself about him."

" Well, he *was* rather absurd to-day, I allow; but he *has* got handsome eyes and hands, and he *does* dance like an angel," sighed Kitty, as she pinned up the treacherous loop which had brought destruction to her little castle in the air.

" Handsome eyes, white hands, and angelic feet don't make a man. Wait till you can do better, Kit."

With an odd, grave look, that rather startled Kitty, Jack vanished, to return presently with a comfortable cup of tea and a motherly old lady to help repair damages and soothe her by the foolish little purrings and pattings so grateful to female nerves after a flurry.

" I 'll come back and take you out to see the dance round the tree when you 've had a bit of a rest," said Jack, vibrating between door and sofa as if it was n't easy to get away.

" Oh, I could n't," cried Kitty, with a shudder

at the bare idea of meeting any one. "I can't
be seen again to-night; let me stay here till my
train goes."

"I thought it had gone, already," said Jack,
with an irrepressible twinkle of the eye that
glanced at the draggled dress sweeping the floor.

"How *can* you joke about it!" and the girl's
reproachful eyes filled with tears of shame. "I
know I've been very silly, Jack, but I've had my
punishment, and I don't need any more. To feel
that you despise me is worse than all the rest."

She ended with a little sob, and turned her face
away to hide the trembling of her lips. At that,
Jack flushed up, his eyes shone, and he stooped
suddenly as if to make some impetuous reply.
But, remembering the old lady (who, by the by,
was discreetly looking out of the window), he
put his hands in his pockets and strolled out of
the room.

"I've lost them both by this day's folly,"
thought Kitty, as Mrs. Brown departed with the
teacup. "I don't care for Fletcher, for I dare
say he didn't mean half he said, and I was only
flattered because he is rich and handsome and the
girls glorify him. But I shall miss Jack, for I've
known and loved him all my life. How good
he's been to me to-day! so patient, careful, and
kind, though he must have been ashamed of me.
I know he didn't like my dress; but he never
said a word and stood by me through everything.
Oh, I wish I'd minded Pris! then he would have

respected me, at least; I wonder if he ever will,
again? "

Following a sudden impulse, Kitty sprang up,
locked the door, and then proceeded to destroy
all her little vanities as far as possible. She
smoothed out her crimps with a wet and ruthless
hand; fastened up her pretty hair in the simple
way Jack liked; gave her once cherished bonnet
a spiteful shake, as she put it on, and utterly extinguished it with a big blue veil. She looped up
her dress, leaving no vestige of the now hateful
train, and did herself up uncompromisingly in the
Quakerish gray shawl Pris had insisted on her
taking for the evening. Then she surveyed herself with pensive satisfaction, saying, in the tone
of one bent on resolutely mortifying the flesh, —

" Neat but not gaudy; I 'm a fright, but I deserve it, and it 's better than being a peacock."

Kitty had time to feel a little friendless and
forlorn, sitting there alone as twilight fell, and
amused herself by wondering if Fletcher would
come to inquire about her, or show any further
interest in her; yet when the sound of a manly
tramp approached, she trembled lest it should be
the victim of the fatal facing. The door opened,
and with a sigh of relief she saw Jack come in,
bearing a pair of new gloves in one hand and a
great bouquet of June roses in the other.

" How good of you to bring me these! They
are more refreshing than oceans of tea. You
know what I like, Jack; thank you very much."

cried Kitty, sniffing at her roses with grateful rapture.

"And you know what I like," returned Jack, with an approving glance at the altered figure before him.

"I'll never do so any more," murmured Kitty, wondering why she felt bashful all of a sudden, when it was only cousin Jack.

"Now put on your gloves, dear, and come out and hear the music; your train does n't go for two hours yet, and you must n't mope here all that time," said Jack, offering his second gift.

"How did you know my size?" asked Kitty, putting on the gloves in a hurry; for though Jack had called her "dear" for years, the little word had a new sound to-night.

"I guessed, — no, I did n't, I had the old ones with me; they are no good now, are they?" and too honest to lie, Jack tried to speak carelessly, though he turned red in the dusk, well knowing that the dirty little gloves were folded away in his left breast-pocket at that identical moment.

"Oh, dear, no! these fit nicely. I 'm ready, if you don't mind going with such a fright," said Kitty, forgetting her dread of seeing people in her desire to get away from that room, because for the first time in her life she was n't at ease with Jack.

"I think I like the little gray moth better than the fine butterfly," returned Jack, who, in spite of his invitation, seemed to find "moping" rather pleasant.

"You are a rainy-day friend, and he is n't," said Kitty, softly, as she drew him away.

Jack's only answer was to lay his hand on the little white glove resting so confidingly on his arm, and, keeping it there, they roamed away into the summer twilight.

Something had happened to the evening and the place, for both seemed suddenly endowed with uncommon beauty and interest. The dingy old houses might have been fairy palaces, for anything they saw to the contrary; the dusty walks, the trampled grass, were regular Elysian fields to them, and the music was the music of the spheres, though they found themselves "Right in the middle of the boom, jing, jing." For both had made a little discovery, — no, not a little one, the greatest and sweetest man and woman can make. In the sharp twinge of jealousy which the sight of Kitty's flirtation with Fletcher gave him, and the delight he found in her after conduct, Jack discovered how much he loved her. In the shame, gratitude, and half sweet, half bitter emotion that filled her heart, Kitty felt that to her Jack would never be "only cousin Jack" any more. All the vanity, coquetry, selfishness, and ill-temper of the day seemed magnified to heinous sins, for now her only thought was, "seeing these faults, he *can't* care for me. Oh, I wish I was a better girl!"

She did not say " for his sake," but in the new humility, the ardent wish to be all that a woman should be, little Kitty proved how true her love was, and might have said with Portia, —

> " For myself alone, I would not be
> Ambitious in my wish ; but, for you,
> I would be trebled twenty times myself ;
> A thousand times more fair,
> Ten thousand times more rich."

All about them other pairs were wandering under the patriarchal elms, enjoying music, starlight, balmy winds, and all the luxuries of the season. If the band had played

> " Oh, there 's nothing half so sweet in life
> As love's young dream — "

it is my private opinion that it would have suited the audience to a T. Being principally composed of elderly gentlemen with large families, they had not that fine sense of the fitness of things so charming to see, and tooted and banged away with waltzes and marches, quite regardless of the flocks of Romeos and Juliets philandering all about them.

Under cover of a popular medley, Kitty overheard Fletcher quizzing her for the amusement of Miss Pinkbonnet, who was evidently making up for lost time. It was feeble wit, but it put the finishing stroke to Kitty's vanity, and she dropped

a tear in her blue tissue retreat, and clung to
Jack, feeling that she had never valued him half
enough.   She hoped he did n't hear the gossip
going on at the other side of the tree near which
they stood; but he did, for his hand involuntarily
doubled itself up into a very dangerous-looking
fist, and he darted such fiery glances at the
speaker, that, if the thing had been possible,
Fletcher's ambrosial curls would have been
scorched off his head.

"Never mind, and don't get angry, Jack.
They are right about one thing, — the daisies in
my bonnet *were* real, and I *could n't* afford any
others.   I don't care much, only Pris worked so
hard to get me ready I hate to have my things
made fun of."

"He is n't worth a thrashing, so we 'll let it
pass this time," said Jack, irefully, yet privately
resolving to have it out with Fletcher by and by.

"Why, Kitty, I thought the real daisies the
prettiest things about your dress.   Don't throw
them away.   I 'll wear them just to show that
noodle that I prefer nature to art;" and Jack
gallantly stuck the faded posy in his button-hole,
while Kitty treasured up the hint so kindly given
for future use.

If a clock with great want of tact had n't insisted on telling them that it was getting late,
Kitty never would have got home, for both the
young people felt inclined to loiter about arm in
arm through the sweet summer night forever.

Jack had meant to say something before she went, and was immensely surprised to find the chance lost for the present. He wanted to go home with her and free his mind; but a neighborly old gentleman having been engaged as escort, there would have been very little satisfaction in a travelling trio; so he gave it up. He was very silent as they walked to the station with Dr. Dodd trudging behind them. Kitty thought he was tired, perhaps glad to be rid of her, and meekly accepted her fate. But as the train approached, she gave his hand an impulsive squeeze, and said very gratefully, —

"Jack, I can't thank you enough for your kindness to your silly little cousin; but I never shall forget it, and if I ever can return it in any way, I will with all my heart."

Jack looked down at the young face almost pathetic now with weariness, humility, and pain, yet very sweet, with that new shyness in the loving eyes, and, stooping suddenly, he kissed it, whispering in a tone that made the girl's heart flutter, —

"I 'll tell you how you may return it 'with all your heart,' by and by. Good-night, my Kitty."

"Have you had a good time, dear?" asked Pris, as her sister appeared an hour later.

"Don't I look as if I had?" and, throwing off her wraps, Kitty revolved slowly before her that she might behold every portion of the wreck. "My gown is all dust, crumple, and rags, my bonnet perfectly limp and flat, and my gloves are ruined; I 've broken Lizzie's parasol, made a spectacle of myself, and wasted money, time, and temper; yet my Class Day is n't a failure, for Jack is the dearest boy in the world, and I 'm very, very happy!"

Pris looked at her a minute, then opened her arms without a word, and Kitty forgot all her little troubles in one great joy.

When Miss Smith and Miss Jones called a few days after to tell her that Mr. Fletcher was going abroad, the amiable creatures were entirely routed by finding Jack there in a most unmistakable situation. He blandly wished Horace " bon voyage," and regretted that he would n't be there to the wedding in October. Kitty devoted herself to blushing beautifully, and darning many rents in a short daisy muslin skirt, " which I intend to wear a great deal, because Jack likes it, and so do I," she said, with a demure look at her lover, who laughed as if that was the best joke of the season.

AUNT KIPP

"Children and fools speak the truth."

I

"WHAT'S that sigh for, Polly dear?"
"I'm tired, mother, tired of working and waiting. If I'm ever going
to have any fun, I want it *now* while I can enjoy
it."

"You should n't wait another hour if I could
have my way; but you know how helpless I
am;" and poor Mrs. Snow sighed dolefully, as
she glanced about the dingy room and pretty
Mary turning her faded gown for the second
time.

"If Aunt Kipp would give us the money she
is always talking about, instead of waiting till
she dies, we should be *so* comfortable. She is a
dreadful bore, for she lives in such terror of
dropping dead with her heart-complaint that she
does n't take any pleasure in life herself or let
any one else; so the sooner she goes the better
for all of us," said Polly, in a desperate tone; for
things looked very black to her just then.

"My dear, don't say that," began her mother,
mildly shocked; but a bluff little voice broke in
with the forcible remark, —

" She's everlastingly telling me never to put off till to-morrow what can be done to-day; next time she comes I'll remind her of that, and ask her, if she is going to die, why she does n't do it?"

" Toady! you're a wicked, disrespectful boy; never let me hear you say such a thing again about your dear Aunt Kipp."

" She is n't dear! You know we all hate her, and you are more afraid of her than you are of spiders, — so now."

The young personage whose proper name had been corrupted into Toady, was a small boy of ten or eleven, apple-cheeked, round-eyed, and curly-headed; arrayed in well-worn, gray knick-erbockers, profusely adorned with paint, glue, and shreds of cotton. Perched on a high stool, at an isolated table in a state of chaos, he was absorbed in making a boat, entirely oblivious of the racking tooth-ache which had been his excuse for staying from school. As cool, saucy, hard-handed, and soft-hearted a little specimen of young America was Toady as you would care to see; a tyrant at home, a rebel at school, a sworn foe to law, order, and Aunt Kipp. This young person was regarded as a reprobate by all but his mother, sister, and sister's sweetheart, Van Bahr Lamb. Having been, through much anguish of flesh and spirit, taught that lying was a deadly sin, Toady rushed to the other extreme, and bolted out the truth, the whole truth and nothing but the truth, at all times and places, with a startling abruptness that brought wrath and dismay upon his friends and relatives.

"It's wicked to fib; you've whipped that into me and you can't rub it out," he was wont to say, with vivid recollection of the past tingling in the chubby portions of his frame.

"Mind your chips, Toady, and take care what you say to Aunt Kipp, or you'll be as poor as a little rat all the days of your life," said Polly, warningly.

"I don't want her old money, and I'll tell her so if she bothers me about it. I shall go into business with Van and take care of the whole lot; so don't you preach, Polly," returned Toady, with as much dignity as was compatible with a great dab of glue on the end of his snub nose.

"Mother, did aunt say anything about coming this week?" asked Polly, after a pause of intense thought over a breadth with three darns, two spots, and a burn.

"Yes; she wrote that she was too feeble to come at present, as she had such dreadful palpitations she didn't dare stir from her room. So we are quite safe for the next week at least, and — bless my soul, there she is now!"

Mrs. Snow clasped her hands with a gesture of dismay, and sat as if transfixed by the spectacle of a ponderous lady, in an awe-inspiring bonnet, who came walking slowly down the street. Polly gave a groan, and pulled a bright ribbon from her hair. Toady muttered, "Oh, bother!" and vainly attempted to polish up his countenance with a fragmentary pocket-handkerchief.

"Nothing but salt fish for dinner," wailed Mrs. Snow, as the shadow of the coming event fell upon her.

"Van will make a fool of himself, and ruin everything," sighed Polly, glancing at the ring on her finger.

"I know she'll kiss me; she never *will* let a fellow alone," growled Toady, scowling darkly.

The garden gate clashed, dust flew from the door-mat, a heavy step echoed in the hall, an imperious voice called "Sophy!" and Aunt Kipp entered with a flourish of trumpets, for Toady blew a blast through his fingers which made the bows totter on her bonnet.

"My dear aunt, I'm very glad to see you," murmured Mrs. Snow, advancing with a smile of welcome; for though as weak as water gruel, she was as kind-hearted a little woman as ever lived.

"What a fib that was!" said Toady, *sotto voce*.

"We were just saying we were afraid you would n't" — began Mary, when a warning, "Mind now, Polly," caused her to stop short and busy herself with the newcomer's bag and umbrella.

"I changed my mind. Theodore, come and kiss me," answered Aunt Kipp, briefly.

"Yes 'm," was the plaintive reply, and, closing his eyes, Toady awaited his fate with fortitude.

But the dreaded salute did not come, for Aunt Kipp exclaimed in alarm, —

"Mercy on us! has the boy got the plague?"

"No 'm, it 's paint, and dirt, and glue, and it *won't* come off," said Toady, stroking his variegated countenance with grateful admiration for the stains that saved him.

"Go and wash this moment, sir. Thank Heaven, *I 've* got no boys," cried Aunt Kipp, as if boys were some virulent disease which she had narrowly escaped.

With a hasty peck at the lips of her two elder relatives, the old lady seated herself, and slowly removed the awful bonnet, which in shape and hue much resembled a hearse hung with black crape.

"I 'm glad you are better," said Mary, reverently receiving the funereal head-gear.

"I 'm *not* better," cut in Aunt Kipp. "I 'm worse, much worse; my days are numbered; I stand on the brink of the tomb, and may drop at any moment."

Toady's face was a study, as he glanced up at the old lady's florid countenance, down at the floor, as if in search of the above-mentioned "brink," and looked unaffectedly anxious to see her drop. "Why don't you, then?" was on his lips; but a frown from Polly restrained him, and

he sat himself down on the rug to contemplate
the corpulent victim.

"Have a cup of tea, aunt?" said Mrs. Snow.

"I will."

"Lie down and rest a little," suggested Polly.

"I won't."

"Can we do anything for you?" said both.

"Take my things away, and have dinner
early."

Both departed to perform these behests, and,
leaning back in her chair, Aunt Kipp reposed.

"I say, what's a bore?" asked Toady from
the rug, where he sat rocking meditatively to and
fro, holding on by his shoe-strings.

"It's a kind of a pig, very fierce, and folks
are afraid of 'em," said Aunt Kipp, whose knowledge of Natural History was limited.

"Good for Polly! so you are!" sung out the
boy, with the hearty child's laugh so pleasant to
most ears.

"What do you mean, sir?" demanded the old
lady, irefully poking at him with her umbrella.

"Why, Polly said you were a bore," explained
Toady, with artless frankness. "You *are* fat,
you know, and fierce sometimes, and folks are
afraid of you. Good, was n't it?"

"Very! Mary is a nice, grateful, respectful,
loving niece, and I shan't forget her, she may
depend on that," and Aunt Kipp laughed grimly.

"May she? well, that's jolly now. She was

afraid you would n't give her the money; so I 'll
tell her it 's all right;" and innocent Toady
nodded approvingly.

"Oh, she expects some of my money, does
she?"

"Course she does; ain't you always saying
you 'll remember us in your will, because father
was your favorite nephew, and all that? I 'll tell
you a secret, if you won't let Polly know I spoke
first. You 'll find it out to-night, for you 'd see
Van and she were sweethearts in a minute."

"Sweethearts?" cried Aunt Kipp, turning red
in the face.

"Yes 'm. Van settled it last week, and Polly 's
been so happy ever since. Mother likes it, and *I*
like it, for I 'm fond of Van, though I do call him
Baa-baa, because he looks like a sheep. We all
like it, and we 'd all say so, if we were not afraid
of you. Mother and Polly, I mean; of course
we men don't mind, but we don't want a fuss.
You won't make one, will you, now?"

Anything more expressive of brotherly good-
will, persuasive frankness, and a placid consciousness of having "fixed it," than Toady's
dirty little face, it would be hard to find. Aunt
Kipp eyed him so fiercely that even before she
spoke a dim suspicion that something was wrong
began to dawn on his too-confiding soul.

"*I* don't like it, and I 'll put a stop to it. I
won't have any ridiculous baa-baas in my family.

If Mary counts on my money to begin house-keeping with, she 'll find herself mistaken; for not one penny shall she have, married or single, and you may tell her so."

Toady was so taken aback by this explosion that he let go his shoe-strings, fell over with a crash, and lay flat, with shovel and tongs spread upon him like a pall. In rushed Mrs. Snow and Polly, to find the boy's spirits quite quenched, for once, and Aunt Kipp in a towering passion. It all came out in one overwhelming flood of words, and Toady fled from the storm to wander round the house, a prey to the deepest remorse. The meekness of that boy at dinner-time was so angelic that Mrs. Snow would have feared speedy translation for him, if she had not been very angry. Polly's red eyes, and Aunt Kipp's griffinesque expression of countenance, weighed upon his soul so heavily, that even roly-poly pudding failed to assuage his trouble, and, taking his mother into the china-closet, he anxiously inquired " if it was all up with Polly? "

" I 'm afraid so, for aunt vows she will make a new will to-morrow, and leave every penny to the Charitable Rag-bag Society," sighed Mrs. Snow.

" I did n't mean to do it, I truly did n't! I thought I 'd just ' give her a hint,' as you say. She looked all right, and laughed when I told her about being a bore, and I thought she liked it. If she was a man, I 'd thrash her for making

Polly cry;" and Toady shook his fist at Aunt
Kipp's umbrella, which was an immense relief
to his perturbed spirit.

"Bless the boy! I do believe he would!"
cried Mrs. Snow, watching the little turkey-cock
with maternal pride. "You can't do that: so
just be careful and not make any more mischief,
dear."

"I'll try, mother; but I'm always getting
into scrapes with Aunt Kipp. She's worse than
measles, any day, — such an old aggrawater!
Van's coming this afternoon, won't he make her
pleasant again?"

"Oh, dear, no! He will probably make things
ten times worse, he's so bashful and queer. I'm
afraid our last chance is gone, deary, and we
must rub along as we have done."

One sniff of emotion burst from Toady, and
for a moment he laid his head in the knife-
tray, overcome with disappointment and regret.
But scorning to yield to unmanly tears, he was
soon himself again. Thrusting his beloved jackknife, with three blades and a file, into Polly's
hand, he whispered, brokenly, —

"Keep it forever 'n' ever; I'm awful sorry!"
Then, feeling that the magnitude of this sacrifice
atoned for everything, he went to watch for Van,
— the forlorn hope to which he now clung.

II

"SOPHY, I'm surprised at your want of judgment. Do you really mean to let your girl marry this Lamb? Why, the man's a fool!" began Aunt Kipp, after dinner, by way of opening a pleasant conversation with her relatives.

"Dear me, aunt! how can you know that, when you never saw him?" mildly returned Mrs. Snow.

"I've heard of him, and that's enough for me. I've a deal of penetration in judging character, and I tell you Van Bahr Lamb is a fool."

The amiable old lady thought this would rouse Polly, against whom her anger still burned hotly. But Polly also possessed penetration; and, well knowing that contradiction would delight Aunt Kipp, she completely took the wind out of her sails, by coolly remarking, —

"I like fools."

"Bless my heart! what does the girl mean?" ejaculated Aunt Kipp.

"Just what I say. If Van is a fool, I prefer simpletons to wiseacres. I know he is shy and awkward, and does absurd things now and then.

But I also know that he has the kindest heart
that ever was; is unselfish, faithful and loving;
that he took good care of his old parents till
they died, and never thought of himself while
they needed him. He loves me dearly; will wait
for me a dozen years, if I say so, and work all
his days to make me happy. He's a help and
comfort to mother, a good friend to Toady, and
I love and respect and am proud of him, though
you do say he is a fool," cried Polly heartily.

"And you insist on marrying him?" demanded Aunt Kipp.

"Yes, I do."

"Then I wish a carriage immediately," was
the somewhat irrelevant reply.

"Why, aunt, you don't mean to go so soon?"
cried Mrs. Snow, with a reproachful glance at
the rebellious Polly.

"Far from it. I wish to see Judge Banks
about altering my will," was the awful answer.

Polly's face fell; her mother gave a despairing sigh; Toady, who had hovered about the
door, uttered a suppressed whistle of dismay;
and Mrs. Kipp looked about her with vengeful
satisfaction.

"Get the big carryall and old Bob, so the boy
can drive, and all of you come; the trip will
do you good."

It was like Aunt Kipp to invite her poor rela-
tions to go and "nip their own noses off," as
she elegantly expressed it. It was a party of

pleasure that just suited her, for all the fun was on her side. She grew affable at once, was quite pressing in her invitation, regretted that Sophy was too busy to go, praised Polly's hat; and professed herself quite satisfied with "that dear boy" for a driver. The "dear boy" distorted his young countenance frightfully behind her back, but found a balm for every wound in the delight of being commander of the expedition.

The big carryall appeared, and, with much creaking and swaying Mrs. Kipp was got into the back seat, where the big bonnet gloomed like a thunder-cloud. Polly, in a high state of indignation, which only made her look ten times prettier, sat in front with Toady, who was a sight to see as he drove off with his short legs planted against the boot, his elbows squared, and the big whip scientifically cracking now and then. Away they went, leaving poor Mrs. Snow to bewail herself dismally after she had smiled and nodded them out of sight.

"Don't go over any bridges or railroad crossings or by any saw-mills," said the old lady, as if the town could be suddenly remodelled to suit her taste.

"Yes 'm," returned Toady, with a crack which would have done honor to a French postilion.

It was a fine day, and the young people would have enjoyed the ride in spite of the breakers ahead, if Aunt Kipp had n't entertained the girl with a glowing account of the splendors of her own wedding, and aggravated the boy by frequent pokes and directions in the art of driving, of which she was of course, profoundly ignorant. Polly could n't restrain a tear or two, in thinking of her own poor little prospects, and Toady was goaded to desperation.

"I'll give her a regular shaking up; it'll make her hold her tongue and do her good," he said to himself, as a stony hill sloped temptingly before him.

A sly chuck, and some mysterious manœuvre with the reins, and Bob started off at a brisk trot, as if he objected to the old lady as much as her mischievous little nephew.

"Hold him in! Keep a taut rein! Lord 'a mercy, he's running away!" shrieked Aunt Kipp, or tried to shriek, for the bouncing and bumping jerked the words out of her mouth with ludicrous incoherency.

"I am holding him, but he *will* go," said Toady, with a wicked triumph in his eye as he glanced back at Polly.

The next minute the words were quite true; for, as he spoke, two or three distracted hens flew squalling over the wall and scattered about, under, over, and before the horse, as only distracted hens could do. It was too much for Bob's nerves; and, taking matters into his own hands, or feet, rather, he broke into a run, and rattled the old lady over the stones with a velocity which left her speechless.

Polly laughed, and Toady chuckled, as they caught glimpses of the awful bonnet vibrating wildly in the background, and felt the frantic clutchings of the old lady's hands. But both grew sober as a shrill car-whistle sounded not far off; and Bob, as if possessed by an evil spirit, turned suddenly into the road that led to the railroad crossing.

"That will do, Toady; now pull up, for we can't get over in time," said Polly, glancing anxiously toward the rapidly approaching puffs of white smoke.

"I can't, Polly, — I really can't," cried the boy, tugging with all his might, and beginning to look scared.

Polly lent her aid; but Bob scarcely seemed to feel it, for he had been a racer once, and when his blood was up he was hard to handle. His own good sense might have checked him, if Aunt Kipp had n't unfortunately recovered her voice at this crisis, and uttered a succession of the shrillest screams that ever saluted mortal ears. With a snort and a bound Bob dashed straight on toward the crossing, as the train appeared round the bend.

"Let me out! Let me out! Jump! Jump!" shrieked Aunt Kipp, thrusting her head out of the window, while she fumbled madly for the door-handle.

"O Toady, save us! save us!" gasped Polly, losing her presence of mind, and dropping the reins to cling to her brother, with a woman's instinctive faith in the stronger sex.

But Toady held on manfully, though his arms were nearly pulled off, for "Never say die," was his motto, and the plucky little lad would n't show fear before the women.

"Don't howl; we 'll do it! Hi, Bob!" and with a savage slash of the whip, an exciting cry, a terrible reeling and rattling, they *did* do it; for Bob cleared the track at a breakneck pace, just in time for the train to sweep swiftly by behind them.

Aunt Kipp dropped in a heap, Polly looked up at her brother, with a look which he never forgot; and Toady tried to say, stoutly, "It 's all right!" with lips that were white and dry in spite of himself.

"We shall smash up at the bridge," he muttered, as they tore through the town, where every one obligingly shouted, waved their hats, and danced about on the sidewalks, doing nothing but add to Bob's fright and the party's danger. But Toady was wrong, — they did not smash up at the bridge; for, before they reached the perilous spot, one man had the sense to fly straight at the horse's head and hold on till the momentary check enabled others to lend a hand.

The instant they were safe, Polly, like a regular heroine, threw herself into the arms of her dishevelled preserver, who of course was Van, and would have refreshed herself with hysterics

if the sight of Toady had n't steadied her. The
boy sat as stiff and rigid as a wooden figure till
they took the reins from him; then all the
strength seemed to go out of him, and he leaned
against his sister, as white and trembling as she,
whispering with an irrepressible sob, —

"O Polly, was n't it horrid? Tell mother I
stood by you like a man. Do tell her that!"

If any one had had time or heart to laugh,
they certainly would have done it when, after
much groping, heaving, and hoisting, Mrs. Kipp
was extricated and restored to consciousness;
for a more ludicrously deplorable spectacle was
seldom seen. Quite unhurt, though much
shaken, the old lady insisted on believing herself
to be dying, and kept the town in a ferment till
three doctors had pronounced her perfectly well
able to go home. Then the perversity of her
nature induced her to comply, that she might
have the satisfaction of dying on the way, and
proving herself in the right.

Unfortunately she did not expire, but, having
safely arrived, went to bed in high dudgeon, and
led Polly and her mother a sad life of it for two
weary days. Having heard of Toady's gallant
behavior, she solemnly ordered him up to receive her blessing. But the sight of Aunt Kipp's
rubicund visage, surrounded by the stiff frills of
an immense nightcap, caused the irreverent boy
to explode with laughter in his handkerchief,
and to be hustled away by his mother before

Aunt Kipp discovered the true cause of his con-
vulsed appearance.

"Ah! poor dear, his feelings are too much
for him. He sees my doom in my face, and is
overcome by what you refuse to believe. I shan't
forget that boy's devotion. Now leave me to the
meditations befitting these solemn hours."

Mrs. Snow retired, and Aunt Kipp tried to
sleep; but the murmur of voices, and the sound
of stifled laughter in the next room disturbed
her repose.

"They are rejoicing over my approaching end,
knowing that I have n't changed my will. Mer-
cenary creatures, don't exult too soon! there's
time yet," she muttered; and presently, unable
to control her curiosity, she crept out of bed to
listen and peep through the keyhole.

Van Bahr Lamb did look rather like a sheep.
He had a blond curly head, a long face, pale,
mild eyes, a plaintive voice, and a general expression of innocent timidity strongly suggestive
of animated mutton. But Baa-baa was a
"trump," as Toady emphatically declared, and
though every one laughed at him, every one
liked him, and that is more than can be said of
many saints and sages. He adored Polly, was
dutifully kind to her mother, and had stood by
T. Snow, Jr., in many an hour of tribulation
with fraternal fidelity. Though he had long
blushed, sighed, and cast sheep's eyes at the idol
of his affections, only till lately had he dared to

bleat forth his passion. Polly loved him because she could n't help it; but she was proud, and would n't marry till Aunt Kipp's money was hers, or at least a sure prospect of it; and now even the prospect of a prospect was destroyed by that irrepressible Toady. They were talking of this as the old lady suspected, and of course the following conversation afforded her intense satisfaction.

" It 's a shame to torment us as she does, knowing how poor we are and how happy a little of her money would make us. I 'm tired of being a slave to a cruel old woman just because she 's rich. If it was not for mother, I declare I 'd wash my hands of her entirely, and do the best I could for myself."

" Hooray for Polly! I always said let her money go and be jolly without it," cried Toady, who, in his character of wounded hero, reposed with a lordly air on the sofa, enjoying the fragrance of the opodeldoc with which his strained wrists were bandaged.

" It 's on your account, children, that I bear with aunt's temper as I do. I don't want anything for myself, but I really think she owes it to your dear father, who was devoted to her while he lived, to provide for his children when he could n't;" after which remarkably spirited speech for her, Mrs. Snow dropped a tear, and stitched away on a small trouser-leg which was suffering from a complicated compound fracture.

"Don't you worry about me, mother; I'll take care of myself and you too," remarked Toady, with the cheery belief in impossibilities which makes youth so charming.

"Now, Van, tell us what to do, for things have come to such a pass that we must either break away altogether or be galley-slaves as long as Aunt Kipp lives," said Polly, who was a good deal excited about the matter.

"Well, really, my dear, I don't know," hesitated Van, who did know what *he* wanted, but thought it might be selfish to urge it. "Have you tried to soften your aunt's heart?" he asked, after a moment's meditation.

"Good gracious, Van, she hasn't got any," cried Polly, who firmly believed it.

"It's hossified," thoughtfully remarked Toady, quite unconscious of any approach to a joke till every one giggled.

"You've had hossification enough for one while, my lad," laughed Van. "Well, Polly, if the old lady has no heart you'd better let her go, for people without hearts are not worth much."

"That's a beautiful remark, Van, and a wise one. I just wish she could hear you make it, for she called you a fool," said Polly, irefully.

"Did she? Well, I don't mind, I'm used to it," returned Van, placidly; and so he was, for Polly called him a goose every day of her life, and he enjoyed it immensely.

"Then you think, dear, if we stopped worrying about aunt and her money, and worked instead of waiting, that we should n't be any poorer and might be a great deal happier than we are now?" asked Polly, making a pretty little tableau as she put her hand through Van's arm and looked up at him with as much love, respect, and reliance as if he had been six feet tall, with the face of an Apollo and the manners of a Chesterfield.

"Yes, my dear, I do, for it has troubled me a good deal to see you so badgered by that very uncomfortable old lady. Independence is a very nice thing, and poverty is n't half as bad as this sort of slavery. But you are not going to be poor, nor worry about anything. We 'll just be married and take mother and Toady home and be as jolly as grigs, and never think of Mrs. K. again, — unless she loses her fortune, or gets sick, or comes to grief in any way. We 'd lend her a hand then, would n't we, Polly?" and Van's mild face was pleasant to behold as he made the kindly proposition.

"Well, we 'd think of it," said Polly, trying not to relent, but feeling that she was going very fast.

"Let 's do it!" cried Toady, fired with the thought of privy conspiracy and rebellion. "Mother would be so comfortable with Polly, and I 'd help Van in the store, when I 've learned that confounded multiplication table," he added with a groan; "and if Aunt Kipp comes a visiting, we'll just say 'Not at home,' and let her trot off again."

"It sounds very nice, but aunt will be dreadfully offended and I don't wish to be ungrateful," said Mrs. Snow, brightening visibly.

"There's no ingratitude about it," cried Van. "She might have done everything to make you love, and respect, and admire her, and been a happy, useful, motherly, old soul; but she didn't choose to, and now she must take the consequences. No one cares for her, because she cares for nobody; her money's the plague of her life, and not a single heart will ache when she dies."

"Poor Aunt Kipp!" said Polly, softly.

Mrs. Snow echoed the words, and for a moment all thought pitifully of the woman whose life had given so little happiness, whose age had won so little reverence, and whose death would cause so little regret. Even Toady had a kind thought for her, as he broke the silence, saying soberly, —

"You'd better put tails on my jackets, mother; then the next time we get run away with, Aunt Kipp will have something to hold on by."

It was impossible to help laughing at the recollection of the old lady clutching at the boy till he had hardly a button left, and at the paternal air with which he now proposed a much-desired change of costume, as if intent on Aunt Kipp's future accommodation.

Under cover of the laugh, the old lady stole back to bed, wide awake, and with subjects enough to meditate upon now. The shaking up had certainly done her good, for somehow the few virtues she possessed came to the surface, and the mental shower-bath just received had produced a salutary change. Polly would n't have doubted her aunt's possession of a heart, if she could have known the pain and loneliness that made it ache, as the old woman crept away; and Toady would n't have laughed if he had seen the tears on the face, between the big frills, as Aunt Kipp laid it on the pillow, muttering, drearily, —

"I might have been a happy, useful woman, but I did n't choose to, and now it 's too late."

It *was* too late to be all she might have been, for the work of seventy selfish years could n't be undone in a minute. But with regret, rose the sincere wish to earn a little love before the end came, and the old perversity gave a relish to the reformation, for even while she resolved to do the just and generous thing, she said to herself, —

"They say I 've got no heart; I 'll show 'em that I have: they don't want my money; I 'll *make* 'em take it: they turn their backs on me; I 'll just render myself so useful and agreeable that they can't do without me."

III

AUNT KIPP sat bolt upright in the parlor, hemming a small handkerchief, adorned with a red ship, surrounded by a border of green monkeys. Toady suspected that this elegant article of dress was intended for him, and yearned to possess it; so, taking advantage of his mother's and Polly's absence, he strolled into the room, and, seating himself on a high, hard chair, folded his hands, crossed his legs, and asked for a story with the thirsting-for-knowledge air which little boys wear in the moral story-books.

Now Aunt Kipp had one soft place in her heart, though it *was* partially ossified, as she very truly declared, and Toady was enshrined therein. She thought there never was such a child, and loved him as she had done his father before him, though the rack would n't have forced her to confess it. She scolded, snubbed, and predicted he 'd come to a bad end in public; but she forgave his naughtiest pranks, always brought him something when she came, and privately intended to make his future comfortable

with half of her fortune. There was a dash and
daring, a generosity and integrity, about the little fellow, that charmed her. Sophy was weak
and low-spirited, Polly pretty and headstrong,
and Aunt Kipp did n't think much of either of
them; but Toady defied, distracted, and delighted her, and to Toady she clung, as the one
sunshiny thing in her sour, selfish old age.

When he made his demure request, she looked
at him, and her eyes began to twinkle, for the
child's purpose was plainly seen in the loving
glances cast upon the pictorial pocket-handkerchief.

"A story? Yes, I 'll tell you one about a
little boy who had a kind old — ahem! —
grandma. She was rich, and had n't made up
her mind who she 'd leave her money to. She
was fond of the boy, — a deal fonder than he
deserved, — for he was as mischievous a monkey as any that ever lived in a tree, with a curly
tail. He put pepper in her snuff-box," — here
Toady turned scarlet, — "he cut up her best
frisette to make a mane for his rocking-horse,"
— Toady opened his mouth impulsively, but
shut it again without betraying himself — "he
repeated rude things to her, and called her 'an
old aggrewater,'" — here Toady wriggled in his
chair, and gave a little gasp.

"If you are tired I won't go on," observed
Aunt Kipp, mildly.

"I 'm not tired, 'm; it 's a very interesting

story," replied Toady, with a gravity that nearly upset the old lady.

"Well, in spite of all this, that kind, good, forgiving grandma left that bad boy twenty thousand dollars when she died. What do you think of that?" asked Aunt Kipp, pausing suddenly with her sharp eye on him.

"I — I think she was a regular dear," cried Toady, holding on to the chair with both hands, as if that climax rather took him off his legs.

"And what did the boy do about it?" continued Aunt Kipp, curiously.

"He bought a velocipede, and gave his sister half, and paid his mother's rent, and put a splendid marble cherakin over the old lady, and had a jolly good time, and —"

"What in the world is a cherakin?" laughed Aunt Kipp, as Toady paused for breath.

"Why, don't you know? It's a angel crying, or pointing up, or flapping his wings. They have them over graves; and I'll give you the biggest one I can find when you die. But I'm not in a *very* great hurry to have you."

"Thankee, dear; I'm in no hurry, myself. But, Toady, the boy did wrong in giving his sister half; she didn't deserve *any*; and the grandma left word she wasn't to have a penny of it."

"Really?" cried the boy, with a troubled face.

"Yes, really. If he gave her any he lost it all; the old lady said so. Now what do you think?" asked Aunt Kipp, who found it impossible to pardon Polly, — perhaps because she was young, and pretty, and much beloved.

Toady's eyes kindled, and his red cheeks grew redder still, as he cried out defiantly, —

"I think she was a selfish pig, — don't you?"

"No, I don't, sir; and I'm sure that little boy wasn't such a fool as to lose the money. He minded his grandma's wishes, and kept it all."

"No, he didn't," roared Toady, tumbling off his chair in great excitement. "He just threw it out a winder, and smashed the old cherakin all to bits."

Aunt Kipp dropped her work with a shrill squeak, for she thought the boy was dangerous, as he stood before her, sparring away at nothing as the only vent for his indignation.

"It isn't an interesting story," he cried; "and I won't hear any more; and I won't have your money if I mayn't go halves with Polly; and I'll work to earn more than that, and we'll all be jolly together, and you may give your twenty thousand to the old rag-bags, and so I tell you, Aunt Kipp."

"Why, Toady, my boy, what's the matter?" cried a mild voice at the door, as young Lamb came trotting up to the rescue.

"Never you mind, Baa-baa; I shan't do it; and it's a mean shame Polly can't have half; then she could marry you and be so happy," blub-

bered Toady, running to try to hide his tears
of disappointment in the coat-skirts of his friend.

"Mr. Lamb, I suppose you *are* that misguided
young man?" said Aunt Kipp, as if it was a personal insult to herself.

"Van Bahr Lamb, ma'am, if you please. Yes,
thank you," murmured Baa-Baa, bowing, blushing, and rumpling his curly fleece in bashful
trepidation.

"Don't thank me," cried the old lady. "I'm
not going to give you anything, — far from it.
I object to you altogether. What business have
you to come courting my niece?"

"Because I love her, ma'am," returned Van,
with unexpected spirit.

"No, you don't; you want her money, or
rather my money. She depends on it; but you'll
both be disappointed, for she won't have a penny
of it," cried Aunt Kipp, who, in spite of her
good resolutions, found it impossible to be amiable all at once.

"I'm glad of it!" burst out Van, indignant
at her accusation. "I didn't want Polly for the
money; I always doubted if she got it; and I
never wished her to make herself a slave to any-
body. I've got enough for all, if we're careful;
and when my share of the Van Bahr property
comes, we shall live in clover."

"What's that? What property are you talking of?" demanded Aunt Kipp, pricking up her
ears.

"The great Van Bahr estate, ma'am. There has been a long lawsuit about it, but it's nearly settled, and there isn't much doubt that we shall get it. I am the last of our branch, and my share will be a large one."

"Oh, indeed! I wish you joy," said Aunt Kipp, with sudden affability; for she adored wealth, like a few other persons in the world. "But suppose you don't get it, how then?"

"Then I shall try to be contented with my salary of two thousand, and make Polly as happy as I can. Money doesn't *always* make people happy or agreeable, I find." And Van looked at Aunt Kipp in a way that would have made her hair stand erect if she had possessed any. She stared at him a moment, then, obeying one of the odd whims that made an irascible weathercock of her, she said, abruptly, —

"If you had capital should you go into business for yourself, Mr. Lambkin?"

"Yes, ma'am, at once," replied Van, promptly.

"Suppose you lost the Van Bahr money, and some one offered you a tidy little sum to start with, would you take it?"

"It would depend upon who made the offer, ma'am," said Van, looking more like a sheep than ever, as he stood staring in blank surprise.

"Suppose it was me, wouldn't you take it?" asked Aunt Kipp, blandly, for the new fancy pleased her.

"No, thank you, ma'am," said Van, decidedly.

"And why not, pray?" cried the old lady, with a shrillness that made him jump, and Toady back to the door precipitately.

"Because, if you'll excuse my speaking plainly, I think you owe anything you may have to spare to your niece, Mrs. Snow;" and, having freed his mind, Van joined Toady, ready to fly if necessary.

"You're an idiot, sir," began Aunt Kipp, in a rage again.

"Thank you, ma'am." And Van actually laughed and bowed in return for the compliment.

"Hold your tongue, sir," snapped the old lady. "You're a fool and Sophy is another. She's no strength of mind, no sense about anything; and would make ducks and drakes of my money in less than no time if I gave it to her, as I've thought of doing."

"Mrs. Kipp, you forget who you are speaking to. Mrs. Snow's sons love and respect her if you don't, and they won't hear anything untrue or unkind said of a good woman, a devoted mother, and an almost friendless widow."

Van wasn't a dignified man at all, but as he said that with a sudden flash of his mild eyes, there was something in his face and manner that daunted Aunt Kipp more than the small fist belligerently shaken at her from behind the sofa. The poor old soul was cross, and worried, and ashamed of herself, and being as feeble-minded

as Sophy in many respects, she suddenly burst
into tears, and, covering her face with the gay
handkerchief, cried as if bent on floating the
red ship in a sea of salt water without delay.

" I 'm a poor, lonely, abused old woman," she
moaned, with a green monkey at each eye. " No
one loves me, or minds me, or thanks me when
I want to help 'em. My money 's only a worry-
ment and a burden, and I don't know what to
do with it, for people I don't want to leave it
to ought to have it, and people I do like won't
take it. Oh, deary me, what *shall* I do! what
shall I do!"

" Shall I tell you, ma'am?" asked Van, gently, for, though she was a very provoking old
lady, he pitied and wished to help her.

A nod and a gurgle seemed to give consent,
and, boldly advancing, Van said, with blush and
a stammer, but a very hearty voice, —

" I think, ma'am, if you 'd do the right thing
with your money you 'd be at ease and find it
saved a deal of worry all round. Give it to Mrs.
Snow; she deserves it, poor lady, for she 's had
a hard time, and done her duty faithfully. Don't
wait till you are — that is, till you — well, till
you in point of fact die, ma'am. Give it now,
and enjoy the happiness it will make. Give it
kindly, let them see you 're glad to do it, and I
am sure you 'll find them grateful; I 'm sure you
won't be lonely any more, or feel that you are
not loved and thanked. Try it, ma'am, just try

it," cried Van, getting excited by the picture
he drew. "And I give you my word I'll do
my best to respect and love you like a son,
ma'am."

He knew that he was promising a great deal,
but for Polly's sake he felt that he could make
even that Herculean effort. Aunt Kipp was surprised and touched; but the contrary old lady
could n't make up her mind to yield so soon, and
would n't have done it if Toady had n't taken
her by storm. Having a truly masculine horror
of tears, a very tender heart under his tailless
jacket, and being much "tumbled up and down
in his own mind" by the events of the week, the
poor little lad felt nerved to attempt any novel
enterprise, even that of voluntarily embracing
Aunt Kipp. First a grimy little hand came on
her shoulder, as she sat sniffing behind the handkerchief; then, peeping out, she saw an apple-
cheeked face very near her own, with eyes full
of pity, penitence, and affection; and then she
heard a choky little voice say earnestly, —

"Don't cry, aunty; I'm sorry I was rude.
Please be good to Mother and Polly, and I'll
love and take care of you, and stand by you all
my life. Yes, I'll — I'll *kiss* you, I will, by
George!" And with one promiscuous plunge
the Spartan boy cast himself into her arms.

That finished Aunt Kipp; she hugged him
close, and cried out with a salute that went off
like a pistol-shot, —

" Oh, my dear, my dear! this is better than a dozen cherakins! "

When Toady emerged, somewhat flushed and tumbled, Mrs. Snow, Polly, and Van were looking on with faces full of wonder, doubt, and satisfaction.   To be an object of interest was agreeable to Aunt Kipp; and, as her old heart was really softened, she met them with a gracious smile, and extended the olive-branch generally.

" Sophy, I shall give my money to *you* at once and entirely, only asking that you 'll let me stay with you when Polly 's gone. I 'll do my best to be agreeable, and you 'll bear with me because I 'm a cranky, solitary old woman, and I loved your husband."

Mrs. Snow hugged her on the spot, and gushed, of course, murmuring thanks, welcomes, and promises in one grateful burst.

" Polly, I forgive you; I consent to your marriage, and will provide your wedding finery. Mr. Lamb, you are not a fool, but a very excellent young man. I thank you for saving my life, and I wish you well with all my heart. You need n't say anything. I 'm far from strong, and all this agitation is shortening my life."

Polly and Van shook her hand heartily, and beamed upon each other like a pair of infatuated turtle-doves with good prospects.

" Toady, you are as near an angel as a boy can be. Put a name to whatever you most wish for in the world, and it's yours," said Aunt Kipp, dramatically waving the rest away.

With his short legs wide apart, his hands behind him, and his rosy face as round and radiant as a rising sun, Toady stood before the fire surveying the scene with the air of a man who has successfully carried through a difficult and dangerous undertaking, and wasn't proud. His face brightened, then fell, as he heaved a sigh, and answered, with a shake of his curly head, —

"You can't give me what I want most. There are three things, and I've got to wait for them all."

"Gracious me, what are they?" cried the old lady, good-naturedly, for she felt better already.

"A mustache, a beaver, *and* a sweetheart," answered Toady, with his eyes fixed wistfully on Baa-baa, who possessed all these blessings, and was particularly enjoying the latter at that moment.

How Aunt Kipp did laugh at this early budding of romance in her pet! And all the rest joined her, for Toady's sentimental air was irresistible.

"You precocious chick! I dare say you will have them all before we know where we are. Never mind, deary; you shall have my little watch, and the silver-headed cane with a *boar's* head on it," answered the old lady, in high good-humor. "You needn't blush, dear; I don't bear malice; so let's forget and forgive. I shall settle things to-morrow, and have a free mind. You are welcome to my money, and I hope I shall live to see you all enjoy it."

So she did; for she lived to see Sophy plump, cheery, and care-free; Polly surrounded by a flock of Lambkins; Van in possession of a generous slice of the Van Bahr fortune; Toady revelling in the objects of his desire; and, best of all, she lived to find that it is never too late to make oneself useful, happy, and beloved.

PSYCHE'S ART

" Handsome is that handsome does."

I

ONCE upon a time there raged in a certain city one of those fashionable epidemics which occasionally attack our youthful population. It was n't the music mania, nor gymnastic convulsions, nor that wide-spread malady, croquet. Neither was it one of the new dances which, like a tarantula-bite, set every one a twirling, nor stage madness, nor yet that American lecturing influenza which yearly sweeps over the land. No, it was a new disease called the Art fever, and it attacked the young women of the community with great violence.

Nothing but time could cure it, and it ran its course to the dismay, amusement, or edification of the beholders, for its victims did all manner of queer things in their delirium. They besieged potteries for clay, drove Italian plaster-workers out of their wits with unexecutable orders, got neuralgia and rheumatism sketching perched on fences and trees like artistic hens, and caused a rise in the price of bread, paper, and charcoal, by their ardor in crayoning. They

covered canvas with the expedition of scene-
painters, had classes, lectures, receptions, and
exhibitions, made models of each other, and rendered their walls hideous with bad likenesses
of all their friends.   Their conversation ceased
to be intelligible to the uninitiated, and they prat-
tled prettily of " chiaro oscuro, French sauce, re-
fraction of the angle of the eye, seventh spinus
process, depth and juiciness of color, tender
touch, and a good tone."   Even in dress the
artistic disorder was visible; some cast aside
crinoline altogether, and stalked about with a
severe simplicity of outline worthy of Flaxman.
Others flushed themselves with scarlet, that no
landscape which they adorned should be without some touch of Turner's favorite tint.   Some
were *blue* in every sense of the word, and the
heads of all were adorned with classic braids,
curls tied Hebe-wise, or hair dressed à la hurri-
cane.

It was found impossible to keep them safe at
home, and, as the fever grew, these harmless
maniacs invaded the sacred retreats where artists of the other sex did congregate, startling
those anchorites with visions of large-eyed damsels bearing portfolios in hands delicately be-
grimed with crayon, chalk, and clay, gliding
through the corridors hitherto haunted only by
shabby paletots, shadowy hats, and cigar smoke.
This irruption was borne with manly fortitude,
not to say cheerfulness, for studio doors stood

hospitably open as the fair invaders passed, and
studies from life were generously offered them
in glimpses of picturesque gentlemen posed before easels, brooding over master-pieces in "a
divine despair," or attitudinizing upon couches
as if exhausted by the soarings of genius.

An atmosphere of romance began to pervade
the old buildings when the girls came, and nature and art took turns. There were peepings
and whisperings, much stifled laughter and
whisking in and out; not to mention the acci-
dental rencontres, small services, and eye tele-
grams, which somewhat lightened the severe
studies of all parties.

Half a dozen young victims of this malady
met daily in one of the cells of a great art
beehive called "Raphael's Rooms," and devoted
their shining hours to modelling fancy heads,
gossiping the while; for the poor things found
the road to fame rather dull and dusty without
such verbal sprinklings.

"Psyche Dean, you 've had an adventure! I
see it in your face; so tell it at once, for we are
as stupid as owls here to-day," cried one of the
sisterhood, as a bright-eyed girl entered with
some precipitation.

"I dropped my portfolio, and a man picked
it up, that's all," replied Psyche, hurrying on
her gray linen pinafore.

"That won't do; I know something interesting happened, for you 've been blushing, and you

look brisker than usual this morning," said the
first speaker, polishing off the massive nose of
her Homer.

" It was n't anything," began Psyche a little
reluctantly. " I was coming up in a hurry when
I ran against a man coming down in a hurry.
My portfolio slipped, and my papers went flying
all about the landing. Of course we both
laughed and begged pardon, and I began to pick
them up, but he would n't let me; so I held the
book while he collected the sketches. I saw him
glance at them as he did so, and that made me
blush, for they are wretched things, you know."

" Not a bit of it; they are capital, and you
are a regular genius, as we all agree," cut in
the Homeric Miss Cutter.

" Never tell people they are geniuses unless
you wish to spoil them," returned Psyche severely. " Well, when the portfolio was put to
rights I was going on, but he fell to picking up
a little bunch of violets I had dropped; you
know I always wear a posy into town to give
me inspiration. I did n't care for the dusty
flowers, and told him so, and hurried away before any one came. At the top of the stairs I
peeped over the railing, and there he was, gathering up every one of those half-dead violets as
carefully as if they had been tea-roses."

" Psyche Dean, you have met your fate this
day ! " exclaimed a third damsel, with straw-
colored tresses, and a good deal of weedy shrub-

bery in her hat, which gave an Ophelia-like expression to her sentimental countenance.

Psyche frowned and shook her head, as if half sorry she had told her little story.

"Was he handsome?" asked Miss Larkins, the believer in fate.

"I did n't particularly observe."

"It was the red-headed man, whom we call Titian: he 's always on the stairs."

"No, it was n't; his hair was brown and curly," cried Psyche, innocently falling into the trap.

"Like Peerybingle's baby when its cap was taken off," quoted Miss Dickenson, who pined to drop the last two letters of her name.

"Was it Murillo, the black-eyed one?" asked the fair Cutter, for the girls had a name for all the attitudinizers and promenaders whom they oftenest met.

"No, he had gray eyes, and very fine ones they were too," answered Psyche, adding, as if to herself, "he looked as I imagine Michael Angelo might have looked when young."

"Had he a broken nose, like the great Mike?" asked an irreverent damsel.

"If he had, no one would mind it, for his head is splendid; he took his hat off, so I had a fine view. He is n't handsome, but he 'll *do* something," said Psyche, prophetically, as she recalled the strong, ambitious face which she had often observed, but never mentioned before.

"Well, dear, considering that you did n't 'particularly look' at the man, you 've given us a very good idea of his appearance. We 'll call him Michael Angelo, and he shall be your idol. I prefer stout old Rembrandt myself, and Larkie adores that dandified Raphael," said the lively Cutter, slapping away at Homer's bald pate energetically, as she spoke.

"Raphael is a dear, but Rubens is more to my taste now," returned Miss Larkins. "He was in the hall yesterday talking with Sir Joshua, who had his inevitable umbrella, like a true Englishman. Just as I came up, the umbrella fell right before me. I started back; Sir Joshua laughed, but Rubens said, 'Deuce take it!' and caught up the umbrella, giving me a never-to-be-forgotten look. It was perfectly thrilling."

"Which, — the umbrella, the speech, or the look?" asked Psyche, who was not sentimental.

"Ah, you have no soul for art in nature, and nature in art," sighed the amber-tressed Larkins. "I have, for I feed upon a glance, a tint, a curve, with exquisite delight. Rubens is adorable (*as a study*); that lustrous eye, that night of hair, that sumptuous cheek, are perfect. He only needs a cloak, lace collar, and slouching hat to be the genuine thing."

"This is n't the genuine thing by any means. What *does* it need?" said Psyche, looking with a despondent air at the head on her stand.

Many would have pronounced it a clever thing; the nose was strictly Greek, the chin curved upward gracefully, the mouth was sweetly haughty, the brow classically smooth and low, and the breezy hair well done. But something was wanting; Psyche felt that, and could have taken her Venus by the dimpled shoulders, and given her a hearty shake, if that would have put strength and spirit into the lifeless face.

" Now *I* am perfectly satisfied with my Apollo, though you all insist that it is the image of Theodore Smythe. He says so himself, and assures me it will make a sensation when we exhibit," remarked Miss Larkins, complacently caressing the ambrosial locks of her Smythified Phebus.

" What shall you do if it does not?" asked Miss Cutter, with elegance.

" I shall feel that I have mistaken my sphere, shall drop my tools, veil my bust, and cast myself into the arms of Nature, since Art rejects me; " replied Miss Larkins, with a tragic gesture and an expression which strongly suggested that in her eyes nature meant Theodore.

" She must have capacious arms if she is to receive all Art's rejected admirers. Shall I be one of them? "

Psyche put the question to herself as she turned to work, but somehow ambitious aspirations were not in a flourishing condition that morning; her heart was not in tune, and head

and hands sympathized. Nothing went well, for certain neglected home-duties had dogged her into town, and now worried her more than dust, or heat, or the ceaseless clatter of tongues. Tom, Dick, and Harry's unmended hose persisted in dancing a spectral jig before her mental eye, mother's querulous complaints spoilt the song she hummed to cheer herself, and little May's wistful face put the goddess of beauty entirely out of countenance.

"It's no use; I can't work till the clay is wet again. Where is Giovanni?" she asked, throwing down her tools with a petulant gesture and a dejected air.

"He is probably playing truant in the empty upper rooms, as usual. I can't wait for him any longer, so I'm doing his work myself," answered Miss Dickenson, who was tenderly winding a wet bandage round her Juno's face, one side of which was so much plumper than the other that it looked as if the Queen of Olympus was being hydropathically treated for a severe fit of ague.

"I'll go and find the little scamp; a run will do me good; so will a breath of air and a view of the park from the upper windows."

Doffing her apron, Psyche strolled away up an unfrequented staircase to the empty apartments, which seemed to be too high even for the lovers of High Art. On the western side they were shady and cool, and, leaning from one

of the windows, Psyche watched the feathery
tree-tops ruffled by the balmy wind, that brought
spring odors from the hills, lying green and
sunny far away. Silence and solitude were such
pleasant companions that the girl forgot herself,
till a shrill whistle disturbed her day-dreams, and
reminded her what she came for. Following the
sound she found the little Italian errand-boy
busily uncovering a clay model which stood in
the middle of a scantily furnished room near by.

"He is not here; come and look; it is greatly
beautiful," cried Giovanni, beckoning with an
air of importance.

Psyche did look and speedily forgot both her
errand and herself. It was the figure of a man,
standing erect, and looking straight before him
with a wonderfully lifelike expression. It was
neither a mythological nor a historical character,
Psyche thought, and was glad of it, being tired
to death of gods and heroes. She soon ceased
to wonder what it was, feeling only the inde-
scribable charm of something higher than beauty.
Small as her knowledge was, she could see and
enjoy the power visible in every part of it; the
accurate anatomy of the vigorous limbs, the
grace of the pose, the strength and spirit in the
countenance, clay though it was. A majestic
figure, but the spell lay in the face, which, while
it suggested the divine, was full of human truth
and tenderness, for pain and passion seemed to
have passed over it, and a humility half pathetic,

a courage half heroic seemed to have been born
from some great loss or woe.

How long she stood there Psyche did not
know. Giovanni went away unseen, to fill his
water-pail, and in the silence she just stood and
looked. Her eyes kindled, her color rose, despondency and discontent vanished, and her soul
was in her face, for she loved beauty passionately, and all that was best and truest in her did
honor to the genius of the unknown worker.

"If I could do a thing like that, I'd die
happy!" she exclaimed impetuously, as a feeling
of despair came over her at the thought of her
own poor attempts.

"Who did it, Giovanni?" she asked, still looking up at the grand face with unsatisfied eyes.

"Paul Gage."

It was not the boy's voice, and, with a start,
Psyche turned to see her Michael Angelo, standing in the doorway, attentively observing her.
Being too full of artless admiration to think of
herself just yet, she neither blushed nor apolo-
gized, but looked straight at him, saying heartily, —

"You have done a wonderful piece of work,
and I envy you more than I can tell!"

The enthusiasm in her face, the frankness of
her manner, seemed to please him, for there was
no affectation about either. He gave her a keen,
kind glance out of the "fine gray eyes," a little
bow, and a grateful smile, saying quietly, —

"Then my Adam is not a failure in spite of his fall?"

Psyche turned from the sculptor to his model with increased admiration in her face, and earnestness in her voice, as she exclaimed delighted, —

"Adam! I might have known it was he. O sir, you have indeed succeeded, for you have given that figure the power and pathos of the first man who sinned and suffered, and began again."

"Then I am satisfied." That was all he said, but the look he gave his work was a very eloquent one, for it betrayed that he had paid the price of success in patience and privation, labor and hope.

"What can one do to learn your secret?" asked the girl wistfully, for there was nothing in the man's manner to disturb her self-forgetful mood, but much to foster it, because to the solitary worker this confiding guest was as welcome as the doves who often hopped in at his window.

"Work and wait, and meantime feed heart, soul, and imagination with the best food one can get," he answered slowly, finding it impossible to give a receipt for genius.

"I can work and wait a long time to gain my end; but I don't know where to find the food you speak of?" she answered, looking at him like a hungry child.

"I wish I could tell you, but each needs different fare, and each must look for it in different places."

The kindly tone and the sympathizing look, as well as the lines in his forehead, and a few gray hairs among the brown, gave Psyche courage to say more.

"I love beauty so much that I not only want to possess it myself, but to gain the power of seeing it in all things, and the art of reproducing it with truth. I have tried very hard to do it, but something is wanting; and in spite of my intense desire I never get on."

As she spoke the girl's eyes filled and fell in spite of herself, and turning a little with sudden shamefacedness she saw, lying on the table beside her among other scraps in manuscript and print, the well-known lines, —

> "I slept, and dreamed that life was beauty;
> I woke, and found that life was duty.
> Was thy dream then a shadowy lie?
> Toil on, sad heart, courageously,
> And thou shalt find thy dream to be
> A noonday light and truth to thee."

She knew them at a glance, had read them many times, but now they came home to her with sudden force, and, seeing that his eye had followed hers, she said in her impulsive fashion. —

"Is doing one's duty a good way to feed heart, soul, and imagination?"

As if he had caught a glimpse of what was going on in her mind, Paul answered emphatically, —

"Excellent; for if one is good, one is happy, and if happy, one can work well. Moulding character is the highest sort of sculpture, and all of us should learn that art before we touch clay or marble."

He spoke with the energy of a man who believed what he said, and did his best to be worthy of the rich gift bestowed upon him. The sight of her violets in a glass of water, and Giovanni staring at her with round eyes, suddenly recalled Psyche to a sense of the proprieties which she had been innocently outraging for the last ten minutes. A sort of panic seized her; she blushed deeply, retreated precipitately to the door, and vanished, murmuring thanks and apologies as she went.

"Did you find him? I thought you had forgotten," said Miss Dickenson, now hard at work.

"Yes, I found him. No, I shall not forget," returned Psyche, thinking of Gage, not Giovanni.

She stood before her work eying it intently for several minutes; then, with an expression of great contempt for the whole thing, she suddenly tilted her cherished Venus on to the floor, gave the classical face a finishing crunch, and

put on her hat in a decisive manner, saying
briefly to the dismayed damsels, —

"Good-by, girls; I shan't come any more,
for I 'm going to work at home hereafter."

II

THE prospect of pursuing artistic studies at home was not brilliant, as one may imagine when I mention that Psyche's father was a painfully prosaic man, wrapt in flannel, so to speak; for his woollen mills left him no time for anything but sleep, food, and newspapers. Mrs. Dean was one of those exasperating women who pervade their mansions like a domestic steam-engine one week and take to their sofas the next, absorbed by fidgets and foot-stoves, shawls and lamentations. There were three riotous and robust young brothers, whom it is unnecessary to describe except by stating that they were *boys* in the broadest sense of that delightful word. There was a feeble little sister, whose patient, suffering face demanded constant love and care to mitigate the weariness of a life of pain. And last, but not least by any means, there were two Irish ladies, who, with the best intentions imaginable, produced a universal state of topsy-turviness when left to themselves for a moment.

But being very much in earnest about doing

her duty, not because it *was* her duty, but as a means toward an end, Psyche fell to work with a will, hoping to serve both masters at once. So she might have done, perhaps, if flesh and blood had been as plastic as clay, but the live models were so exacting in their demands upon her time and strength, that the poor statues went to the wall. Sculpture and sewing, calls and crayons, Ruskin and receipt-books, did n't work well together, and poor Psyche found duties and desires desperately antagonistic. Take a day as a sample.

" The washing and ironing are well over, thank goodness, mother quiet, the boys out of the way, and May comfortable, so I 'll indulge myself in a blissful day after my own heart," Psyche said, as she shut herself into her little studio, and prepared to enjoy a few hours of hard study and happy day-dreams.

With a book on her lap, and her own round white arm going through all manner of queer evolutions, she was placidly repeating, "Deltoides, Biceps, Triceps, Pronator, Supinator, Palmanis, Flexor carpi ulnaris — "

" Here 's Flexis what-you-call-ums for you," interrupted a voice, which began in a shrill falsetto and ended in a gruff bass, as a flushed, dusty, long-legged boy burst in, with a bleeding hand obligingly extended for inspection.

" Mercy on us, Harry! what have you done to yourself now? Split your fingers witn

cricket-ball again?" cried Psyche, as her arms
went up and her book went down.

"I just thrashed one of the fellows because
he got mad and said father was going to fail."

"O Harry, is he?"

"Of course he is n't! It's hard times for
every one, but father will pull through all right.
No use to try and explain it all; girls can't
understand business; so you just tie me up, and
don't worry," was the characteristic reply of the
young man, who, being three years her junior,
of course treated the weaker vessel with lordly
condescension.

"What a dreadful wound! I hope nothing
is broken, for I have n't studied the hand much
yet, and may do mischief doing it up," said
Psyche, examining the great grimy paw with
tender solicitude.

"Much good your biceps, and deltoids, and
things do you, if you can't right up a little cut
like that," squeaked the ungrateful hero.

"I'm not going to be a surgeon, thank
heaven; I intend to make perfect hands and
arms, not mend damaged ones," retorted Psyche,
in a dignified tone, somewhat marred by a great
piece of court-plaster on her tongue.

"I should say a surgeon could improve *that*
perfect thing, if he did n't die a-laughing before
he began," growled Harry, pointing with a
scornful grin at a clay arm humpy with muscles,
all carefully developed in the wrong places.

"Don't sneer, Hal, for you don't know anything about it. Wait a few years and see if you 're not proud of me."

"Sculp away and do something, then I 'll hurrah for your mud-pies like a good one;" with which cheering promise the youth left, having effectually disturbed his sister's peaceful mood.

Anxious thoughts of her father rendered "biceps, deltoids, and things" uninteresting, and hoping to compose her mind, she took up The Old Painters and went on with the story of Claude Lorraine. She had just reached the tender scene where, —

"Calista gazed with enthusiasm, while she looked like a being of heaven rather than earth. 'My friend,' she cried, 'I read in thy picture thy immortality!' As she spoke, her head sunk upon his bosom, and it was several moments before Claude perceived that he supported a lifeless form."

"How sweet!" said Psyche, with a romantic sigh.

"Faith, and swate it is, thin!" echoed Katy, whose red head had just appeared round the half opened door. "It 's gingy-bread I 'm making the day, miss, and will I be puttin' purlash or sallyrathis into it, if ye plase?"

"Purlash, by all means," returned the girl, keeping her countenance, fearing to enrage Katy by a laugh; for the angry passions of the red-haired one rose more quickly than her bread.

As she departed with alacrity to add a spoonful of starch and a pinch of whiting to her cake, Psyche, feeling better for her story and her smile, put on her bib and paper cap and fell to work on the deformed arm. An hour of bliss, then came a ring at the door-bell, followed by Biddy to announce callers, and add that as "the mistress was in her bed, miss must go and take care of 'em." Whereat "miss" cast down her tools in despair, threw her cap one way, her bib another, and went in to her guests with anything but a rapturous welcome.

Dinner being accomplished after much rushing up and down stairs with trays and messages for Mrs. Dean, Psyche fled again to her studio, ordering no one to approach under pain of a scolding. All went well till, going in search of something, she found her little sister sitting on the floor with her cheek against the studio door.

"I did n't mean to be naughty, Sy, but mother is asleep, and the boys all gone, so I just came to be near you; it 's so lonely everywhere," she said, apologetically, as she lifted up the heavy head that always ached.

"The boys are very thoughtless. Come in and stay with me; you are such a mouse you won't disturb me. Would n't you like to play be a model and let me draw your arm, and tell you all about the nice little bones and muscles?" asked Psyche, who had the fever very strong upon her just then.

May did n't look as if the proposed amusement overwhelmed her with delight, but meekly
consented to be perched upon a high stool with
one arm propped up by a dropsical plaster
cherub, while Psyche drew busily, feeling that
duty and pleasure were being delightfully combined.

"Can't you hold your arm still, child? It
shakes so I can't get it right," she said, rather
impatiently.

"No, it will tremble 'cause it's weak. I try
hard, Sy, but there does n't seem to be much
strongness in me lately."

"That's better; keep it so a few minutes and
I'll be done," cried the artist, forgetting that a
few minutes may seem ages.

"My arm is so thin you can see the bunches
nicely, — can't you?"

"Yes, dear."

Psyche glanced up at the wasted limb, and
when she drew again there was a blur before
her eyes for a minute.

"I wish I was as fat as this white boy; but
I get thinner every day somehow, and pretty
soon there won't be any of me left but my little
bones," said the child, looking at the winged
cherub with sorrowful envy.

"Don't, my darling; don't say that," cried
Psyche, dropping her work with a sudden pang
at her heart. "I'm a sinful, selfish girl to keep
you here! you're weak for want of air; come

out and see the chickens, and pick dandelions, and have a good romp with the boys."

The weak arms were strong enough to clasp Psyche's neck, and the tired face brightened beautifully as the child exclaimed, with grateful delight, —

"Oh, I'd like it very much! I wanted to go dreadfully; but everybody is so busy all the time. I don't want to play, Sy; but just to lie on the grass with my head in your lap while you tell stories and draw me pretty things as you used to."

The studio was deserted all that afternoon, for Psyche sat in the orchard drawing squirrels on the wall, pert robins hopping by, buttercups and mosses, elves and angels; while May lay contentedly enjoying sun and air, sisterly care, and the "pretty things" she loved so well. Psyche did not find the task a hard one; for this time her heart was in it, and if she needed any reward she surely found it; for the little face on her knee lost its weary look, and the peace and beauty of nature soothed her own troubled spirit, cheered her heart, and did her more good than hours of solitary study.

Finding, much to her own surprise, that her fancy was teeming with lovely conceits, she did hope for a quiet evening. But mother wanted a bit of gossip, father must have his papers read to him, the boys had lessons and rips and grievances to be attended to, May's lullaby could not

be forgotten, and the maids had to be looked
after, lest burly " cousins " should be hidden in
the boiler, or lucifer matches among the shavings. So Psyche's day ended, leaving her very
tired, rather discouraged, and almost heart-sick
with the shadow of a coming sorrow.

All summer she did her best, but accomplished
very little, as she thought; yet this was the
teaching she most needed, and in time she came
to see it. In the autumn May died, whispering,
with her arms about her sister's neck, —

" You make me so happy, Sy, I would n't mind
the pain if I could stay a little longer. But if
I can't, good-by, dear, good-by."

Her last look and word and kiss were all for
Psyche, who felt then with grateful tears that
her summer had not been wasted; for the smile
upon the little dead face was more to her than
any marble perfection her hands could have
carved.

In the solemn pause which death makes in
every family, Psyche said, with the sweet self-
forgetfulness of a strong yet tender nature, —

" I must not think of myself, but try to comfort them;" and with this resolution she gave
herself heart and soul to duty, never thinking
of reward.

A busy, anxious, humdrum winter, for, as
Harry said, " it was hard times for every one."
Mr. Dean grew gray with the weight of business
cares about which he never spoke; Mrs. Dean,

laboring under the delusion that an invalid was
a necessary appendage to the family, installed
herself in the place the child's death left vacant,
and the boys needed much comforting, for the
poor lads never knew how much they loved " the
baby" till the little chair stood empty. All
turned to Sy for help and consolation, and her
strength seemed to increase with the demand
upon it. Patience and cheerfulness, courage and
skill came at her call like good fairies who had
bided their time. Housekeeping ceased to be
hateful, and peace reigned in parlor and kitchen
while Mrs. Dean, shrouded in shawls, read
Hahnemann's Lesser Writings on her sofa. Mr.
Dean sometimes forgot his mills when a bright
face came to meet him, a gentle hand smoothed
the wrinkles out of his anxious forehead, and
a daughterly heart sympathized with all his
cares. The boys found home very pleasant with
Sy always there ready to " lend a hand," whether
it was to make fancy ties, help conjugate " a
confounded verb," pull candy, or sing sweetly
in the twilight when all thought of little May
and grew quiet.

The studio door remained locked till her
brothers begged Psyche to open it and make a
bust of the child. A flush of joy swept over her
face at the request, and her patient eyes grew
bright and eager, as a thirsty traveller's might
at the sight or sound of water. Then it faded
as she shook her head, saying with a regretful

sigh, " I 'm afraid I 've lost the little skill I ever had."

But she tried, and with great wonder and delight discovered that she could work as she had never done before. She thought the newly found power lay in her longing to see the little face again; for it grew like magic under her loving hands, while every tender memory, sweet thought, and devout hope she had ever cherished, seemed to lend their aid. But when it was done and welcomed with tears and smiles, and praise more precious than any the world could give, then Psyche said within herself, like one who saw light at last, —

" He was right; doing one's duty *is* the way to feed heart, soul, and imagination; for if one is good, one is happy, and if happy, one can work well."

III

"SHE broke her head and went home to come no more," was Giovanni's somewhat startling answer when Paul asked about Psyche, finding that he no longer met her on the stairs or in the halls. He understood what the boy meant, and with an approving nod turned to his work again, saying, "I like that! If there is any power in her, she has taken the right way to find it out, I suspect."

How she prospered he never asked; for, though he met her more than once that year, the interviews were brief ones in street, concert-room, or picture-gallery, and she carefully avoided speaking of herself. But, possessing the gifted eyes which can look below the surface of things, he detected in the girl's face something better than beauty, though each time he saw it, it looked older and more thoughtful, often anxious and sad.

"She is getting on," he said to himself with a cordial satisfaction which gave his manner a friendliness as grateful to Psyche as his wise reticence.

Adam was finished at last, proved a genuine success, and Paul heartily enjoyed the well-earned reward for years of honest work. One blithe May morning, he slipped early into the art-gallery, where the statue now stood, to look at his creation with paternal pride. He was quite alone with the stately figure that shone white against the purple draperies and seemed to offer him a voiceless welcome from its marble lips. He gave it one loving look, and then forgot it, for at the feet of his Adam lay a handful of wild violets, with the dew still on them. A sudden smile broke over his face as he took them up, with the thought, " She has been here and found my work good."

For several moments he stood thoughtfully turning the flowers to and fro in his hands; then, as if deciding some question within himself, he said, still smiling, —

" It is just a year since she went home; she must have accomplished something in that time; I 'll take the violets as a sign that I may go and ask her what."

He knew she lived just out of the city, between the river and the mills, and as he left the streets behind him, he found more violets blooming all along the way like flowery guides to lead him right. Greener grew the road, balmier blew the wind, and blither sang the birds, as he went on, enjoying his holiday with the zest of a boy, until he reached a most attractive little path

winding away across the fields. The gate swung
invitingly open, and all the ground before it was
blue with violets. Still following their guidance
he took the narrow path, till, coming to a mossy
stone beside a brook, he sat down to listen to
the blackbirds singing deliciously in the willows
over head. Close by the stone, half hidden in
the grass lay a little book, and, taking it up he
found it was a pocket-diary. No name appeared
on the fly-leaf, and, turning the pages to find
some clue to its owner, he read here and there
enough to give him glimpses into an innocent
and earnest heart which seemed to be learning
some hard lesson patiently. Only near the end
did he find the clue in words of his own, spoken
long ago, and a name. Then, though longing
intensely to know more, he shut the little book
and went on, showing by his altered face that
the simple record of a girl's life had touched
him deeply.

Soon an old house appeared nestling to the
hillside with the river shining in the low green
meadows just before it.

"She lives there," he said, with as much cer-
tainty as if the pansies by the door-stone spelt
her name, and, knocking, he asked for Psyche.

"She's gone to town, but I expect her home
every minute. Ask the gentleman to walk in
and wait, Katy," cried a voice from above, where
the whisk of skirts was followed by the appearance of an inquiring eye over the banisters.

The gentleman did walk in, and while he waited looked about him. The room, though very simply furnished, had a good deal of beauty in it, for the pictures were few and well chosen, the books such as never grow old, the music lying on the well-worn piano of the sort which is never out of fashion, and standing somewhat apart was one small statue in a recess full of flowers. Lovely in its simple grace and truth was the figure of a child looking upward as if watching the airy flight of some butterfly which had evidently escaped from the chrysalis still lying in the little hand.

Paul was looking at it with approving eyes when Mrs. Dean appeared with his card in her hand, three shawls on her shoulders, and in her face a somewhat startled expression, as if she expected some novel demonstration from the man whose genius her daughter so much admired.

"I hope Miss Psyche is well," began Paul, with great discrimination if not originality.

The delightfully commonplace remark tranquillized Mrs. Dean at once, and, taking off the upper shawl with a fussy gesture, she settled herself for a chat.

"Yes, thank heaven, Sy is well. I don't know what would become of us if she was n't. It has been a hard and sorrowful year for us with Mr. Dean's business embarrassments, my feeble health, and May's death. I don't know that you were aware of our loss, sir;" and unaffected maternal grief gave sudden dignity to the faded, fretful face of the speaker.

Paul murmured his regrets, understanding better now the pathetic words on a certain tear-stained page of the little book still in his pocket.

"Poor dear, she suffered everything, and it came very hard upon Sy, for the child was n't happy with any one else, and almost lived in her arms," continued Mrs. Dean, dropping the second shawl to get her handkerchief.

"Miss Psyche has not had much time for art-studies this year, I suppose?" said Paul, hoping to arrest the shower, natural as it was.

"How could she with two invalids, the house-keeping, her father and the boys to attend to? No, she gave that up last spring, and though it was a great disappointment to her at the time, she has got over it now, I hope," added her mother, remembering as she spoke that Psyche even now went about the house sometimes pale and silent, with a hungry look in her eyes.

"I am glad to hear it," though a little shadow passed over his face as Paul spoke, for he was too true an artist to believe that any work could be as happy as that which he loved and lived for. "I thought there was much promise in Miss Psyche, and I sincerely believe that time will prove me a true prophet," he said, with mingled regret and hope in his voice, as he glanced about the room, which betrayed the tastes still cherished by the girl.

"I'm afraid ambition isn't good for women; I mean the sort that makes them known by coming before the public in any way. But Sy deserves some reward, I'm sure, and I know she'll have it, for a better daughter never lived."

Here the third shawl was cast off, as if the thought of Psyche, or the presence of a genial guest had touched Mrs. Dean's chilly nature with a comfortable warmth.

Further conversation was interrupted by the avalanche of boys which came tumbling down the front stairs, as Tom, Dick, and Harry shouted in a sort of chorus, —

"Sy, my balloon has got away; lend us a hand at catching him!"

"Sy, I want a lot of paste made, right off."

"Sy, I've split my jacket down the back; come sew me up, there's a dear!"

On beholding a stranger the young gentlemen suddenly lost their voices, found their manners, and with nods and grins took themselves away as quietly as could be expected of six clumping boots and an unlimited quantity of animal spirits in a high state of effervescence. As they trooped off, an unmistakable odor of burnt milk pervaded the air, and the crash of china, followed by an Irish wail, caused Mrs. Dean to clap on her three shawls again and excuse herself in visible trepidation.

Paul laughed quietly to himself, then turned sober and said, "Poor Psyche!" with a sympathetic sigh. He roamed about the room impatiently till the sound of voices drew him to the window to behold the girl coming up the walk with her tired old father leaning on one arm, the other loaded with baskets and bundles, and her hands occupied by a remarkably ugly turtle.

"Here we are!" cried a cheery voice, as they entered without observing the new-comer. "I've done all my errands and had a lovely time. There is Tom's gunpowder, Dick's fish-hooks, and one of Professor Gazzy's famous turtles for Harry. Here are your bundles, mother dear, and, best of all, here's father home in time for a good rest before dinner. I went to the mill and got him."

Psyche spoke as if she had brought a treasure; and so she had, for though Mr. Dean's face usually was about as expressive as the turtle's, it woke and warmed with the affection which his daughter had fostered till no amount of flannel could extinguish it. His big hand patted her cheek very gently as he said, in a tone of fatherly love and pride, —

"My little Sy never forgets old father, does she?"

"Good gracious me, my dear, there's such a mess in the kitchen! Katy's burnt up the pudding, put castor-oil instead of olive in the salad, smashed the best meat-dish, and here's Mr. Gage come to dinner," cried Mrs. Dean in ac-

cents of despair as she tied up her head in a
fourth shawl.

"Oh, I'm so glad; I'll go in and see him
a few minutes, and then I'll come and attend
to everything; so don't worry, mother."

"How did you find me out?" asked Psyche
as she shook hands with her guest and stood
looking up at him with all the old confiding
frankness in her face and manner.

"The violets showed me the way."

She glanced at the posy in his button-hole and
smiled.

"Yes, I gave them to Adam, but I did n't
think you would guess. I enjoyed your work
for an hour to-day, and I have no words strong
enough to express my admiration."

"There is no need of any. Tell me about
yourself; what have you been doing all this
year?" he asked, watching with genuine satisfaction the serene and sunny face before him,
for discontent, anxiety, and sadness were no
longer visible there.

"I've been working and waiting," she began.

"And succeeding, if I may believe what I see
and hear and read," he said, with an expressive
little wave of the book as he laid it down before
her.

"My diary! I did n't know I had lost it.
Where did you find it?"

"By the brook where I stopped to rest. The
moment I saw your name I shut it up. Forgive

me, but I can't ask pardon for reading a few pages of that little gospel of patience, love, and self-denial."

She gave him a reproachful look, and hurried the telltale book out of sight as she said, with a momentary shadow on her face, —

"It has been a hard task; but I think I have learned it, and am just beginning to find that my dream *is* 'a noonday light and truth,' to me."

"Then you do not relinquish your hopes, and lay down your tools?" he asked, with some eagerness.

"Never! I thought at first that I could not serve two masters, but in trying to be faithful to one I find I am nearer and dearer to the other. My cares and duties are growing lighter every day (or I have learned to bear them better), and when my leisure does come I shall know how to use it, for my head is full of ambitious plans, and I feel that I can do something *now*."

All the old enthusiasm shone in her eyes, and a sense of power betrayed itself in voice and gesture as she spoke.

"I believe it," he said heartily. "You have learned the secret, as that proves."

Psyche looked at the childish image as he pointed to it, and into her face there came a motherly expression that made it very sweet.

"That little sister was so dear to me I could not fail to make her lovely, for I put my heart into my work. The year has gone, but I don't regret it, though this is all I have done."

"You forget your three wishes; I think the year has granted them."

"What were they?"

"To possess beauty in yourself, the power of seeing it in all things, and the art of reproducing it with truth."

She colored deeply under the glance which accompanied the threefold compliment, and answered with grateful humility, —

"You are very kind to say so; I wish I could believe it." Then, as if anxious to forget herself, she added rather abruptly, —

"I hear you think of giving your Adam a mate, — have you begun yet?"

"Yes, my design is finished, all but the face."

"I should think you could image Eve's beauty, since you have succeeded so well with Adam's."

"The features perhaps, but not the expression. That is the charm of feminine faces, a charm so subtile that few can catch and keep it. I want a truly womanly face, one that shall be sweet and strong without being either weak or hard. A hopeful, loving, earnest face with a tender touch of motherliness in it, and perhaps the shadow of a grief that has softened but not saddened it."

"It will be hard to find a face like that."

"I don't expect to find it in perfection; but one sometimes sees faces which suggest all this, and in rare moments give glimpses of a lovely possibility."

" I sincerely hope you will find one then," said Psyche, thinking of the dinner.

" Thank you; *I* think I have."

Now, in order that every one may be suited, we will stop here, and leave our readers to finish the story as they like. Those who prefer the good old fashion may believe that the hero and heroine fell in love, were married, and lived happily ever afterward. But those who can conceive of a world outside of a wedding-ring may believe that the friends remained faithful friends all their lives, while Paul won fame and fortune, and Psyche grew beautiful with the beauty of a serene and sunny nature, happy in duties which became pleasures, rich in the art which made life lovely to herself and others, and brought rewards in time.

A COUNTRY CHRISTMAS

"A handful of good life is worth a bushel of learning."

"DEAR EMILY, — I have a brilliant idea, and at once hasten to share it with you. Three weeks ago I came up here to the wilds of Vermont to visit my old aunt, also to get a little quiet and distance in which to survey certain new prospects which have opened before me, and to decide whether I will marry a millionnaire and become a queen of society, or remain 'the charming Miss Vaughan' and wait till the conquering hero comes.

"Aunt Plumy begs me to stay over Christmas, and I have consented, as I always dread the formal dinner with which my guardian celebrates the day.

"My brilliant idea is this. I'm going to make it a real old-fashioned frolic, and won't you come and help me? You will enjoy it immensely I am sure, for Aunt is a character, Cousin Saul worth seeing, and Ruth a far prettier girl than any of the city rose-buds coming out this season. Bring Leonard Randal along with you to take notes for his new books; then it will be fresher and truer than the last, clever as it was.

"The air is delicious up here, society amusing, this old farmhouse full of treasures, and your bosom friend pining to embrace you. Just telegraph yes or no, and we will expect you on Tuesday.   Ever yours,

"SOPHIE VAUGHAN."

"They will both come, for they are as tired of city life and as fond of change as I am," said the writer of the above, as she folded her letter and went to get it posted without delay.

Aunt Plumy was in the great kitchen making pies; a jolly old soul, with a face as ruddy as a winter apple, a cheery voice, and the kindest heart that ever beat under a gingham gown. Pretty Ruth was chopping the mince, and singing so gaily as she worked that the four-and-twenty immortal blackbirds could not have put more music into a pie than she did. Saul was piling wood into the big oven, and Sophie paused a moment on the threshold to look at him, for she always enjoyed the sight of this stalwart cousin, whom she likened to a Norse viking, with his fair hair and beard, keen blue eyes, and six feet of manly height, with shoulders that looked broad and strong enough to bear any burden.

His back was toward her, but he saw her first, and turned his flushed face to meet her, with the sudden lighting up it always showed when she approached.

"I've done it, Aunt; and now I want Saul to post the letter, so we can get a speedy answer."

"Just as soon as I can hitch up, cousin;" and Saul pitched in his last log, looking ready to put a girdle round the earth in less than forty minutes.

"Well, dear, I ain't the least mite of objection, as long as it pleases you. I guess we can stan' it ef your city folks can. I presume to say things will look kind of sing'lar to 'em, but I s'pose that's what they come for. Idle folks do dreadful queer things to amuse 'em;" and Aunt Plumy leaned on the rolling-pin to smile and nod with a shrewd twinkle of her eye, as if she enjoyed the prospect as much as Sophie did.

"I shall be afraid of 'em, but I'll try not to make you ashamed of me," said Ruth, who loved her charming cousin even more than she admired her.

"No fear of that, dear. They will be the awkward ones, and you must set them at ease by just being your simple selves, and treating them as if they were every-day people. Nell is very nice and jolly when she drops her city ways, as she must here. She will enter into the spirit of the fun at once, and I know you'll all like her. Mr. Randal is rather the worse for too much praise and petting, as successful people are apt to be, so a little plain talk and rough work will do him good. He is a true gentleman in

spite of his airs and elegance, and he will take
it all in good part, if you treat him like a man
and not a lion."

" I 'll see to him," said Saul, who had listened
with great interest to the latter part of Sophie's
speech, evidently suspecting a lover, and enjoying the idea of supplying him with a liberal
amount of " plain talk and rough work."

" I 'll keep 'em busy if that 's what they need,
for there will be a sight to do, and we can't get
help easy up here. Our darters don't hire out
much. Work to home till they marry, and don't
go gaddin' 'round gettin' their heads full of foolish notions, and forgettin' all the useful things
their mothers taught 'em."

Aunt Plumy glanced at Ruth as she spoke,
and a sudden color in the girl's cheeks proved
that the words hit certain ambitious fancies of
this pretty daughter of the house of Basset.

" They shall do their parts and not be a
trouble; I 'll see to that, for you certainly are
the dearest aunt in the world to let me take possession of you and yours in this way," cried
Sophie, embracing the old lady with warmth.

Saul wished the embrace could be returned
by proxy, as his mother's hands were too floury
to do more than hover affectionately round the
delicate face that looked so fresh and young
beside her wrinkled one. As it could not be
done, he fled temptation and " hitched up " without delay.

The three women laid their heads together in his absence, and Sophie's plan grew apace, for Ruth longed to see a real novelist and a fine lady, and Aunt Plumy, having plans of her own to further, said " Yes, dear," to every suggestion.

Great was the arranging and adorning that went on that day in the old farmhouse, for Sophie wanted her friends to enjoy this taste of country pleasures, and knew just what additions would be indispensable to their comfort; what simple ornaments would be in keeping with the rustic stage on which she meant to play the part of prima donna.

Next day a telegram arrived accepting the invitation, for both the lady and the lion. They would arrive that afternoon, as little preparation was needed for this impromptu journey, the novelty of which was its chief charm to these *blasé* people.

Saul wanted to get out the double sleigh and span, for he prided himself on his horses, and a fall of snow came most opportunely to beautify the landscape and add a new pleasure to Christmas festivities.

But Sophie declared that the old yellow sleigh, with Punch, the farm-horse, must be used, as she wished everything to be in keeping; and Saul obeyed, thinking he had never seen anything prettier than his cousin when she appeared in his mother's old-fashioned camlet cloak and blue silk pumpkin hood. He looked remarkably well himself in his fur coat, with hair and beard brushed till they shone like spun gold, a fresh color in his cheek, and the sparkle of amusement in his eyes, while excitement gave his usually grave face the animation it needed to be handsome.

Away they jogged in the creaking old sleigh, leaving Ruth to make herself pretty, with a fluttering heart, and Aunt Plumy to dish up a late dinner fit to tempt the most fastidious appetite.

"She has not come for us, and there is not even a stage to take us up. There must be some mistake," said Emily Herrick, as she looked about the shabby little station where they were set down.

"That is the never-to-be-forgotten face of our fair friend, but the bonnet of her grandmother, if my eyes do not deceive me," answered Randal, turning to survey the couple approaching in the rear.

"Sophie Vaughan, what do you mean by making such a guy of yourself?" exclaimed Emily, as she kissed the smiling face in the hood and stared at the quaint cloak.

"I'm dressed for my part, and I intend to keep it up. This is our host, my cousin, Saul Basset. Come to the sleigh at once, he will see to your luggage," said Sophie, painfully conscious of the antiquity of her array as her eyes rested on Emily's pretty hat and mantle, and the masculine elegance of Randal's wraps.

They were hardly tucked in when Saul appeared with a valise in one hand and a large trunk on his shoulder, swinging both on to a wood-sled that stood near by as easily as if they had been hand-bags.

"That is your hero, is it? Well, he looks it, calm and comely, taciturn and tall," said Emily, in a tone of approbation.

"He should have been named Samson or Goliath; though I believe it was the small man who slung things about and turned out the hero in the end," added Randal, surveying the performance with interest and a touch of envy, for much pen work had made his own hands as delicate as a woman's.

"Saul does n't live in a glass house, so stones won't hurt him. Remember sarcasm is forbidden and sincerity the order of the day. You are country folks now, and it will do you good to try their simple, honest ways for a few days."

Sophie had no time to say more, for Saul came up and drove off with the brief remark that the baggage would "be along right away."

Being hungry, cold and tired, the guests were rather silent during the short drive, but Aunt Plumy's hospitable welcome, and the savory fumes of the dinner awaiting them, thawed the ice and won their hearts at once.

"Is n't it nice? Are n't you glad you came?" asked Sophie, as she led her friends into the parlor, which she had redeemed from its primness

by putting bright chintz curtains to the windows,
hemlock boughs over the old portraits, a china
bowl of flowers on the table, and a splendid fire
on the wide hearth.

"It is perfectly jolly, and this is the way I
begin to enjoy myself," answered Emily, sitting
down upon the home-made rug, whose red flannel roses bloomed in a blue list basket.

"If I may add a little smoke to your glorious
fire, it will be quite perfect. Won't Samson join
me?" asked Randal, waiting for permission,
cigar-case in hand.

"He has no small vices, but you may indulge
yours," answered Sophie, from the depths of a
grandmotherly chair.

Emily glanced up at her friend as if she caught
a new tone in her voice, then turned to the fire
again with a wise little nod, as if confiding some
secret to the reflection of herself in the bright
brass andiron.

"His Delilah does not take this form. I wait
with interest to discover if he has one. What
a daisy the sister is. Does she ever speak?"
asked Randal, trying to lounge on the haircloth
sofa, where he was slipping uncomfortably about.

"Oh yes, and sings like a bird. You shall
hear her when she gets over her shyness. But
no trifling, mind you, for it is a jealously
guarded daisy and not to be picked by any idle
hand," said Sophie warningly, as she recalled
Ruth's blushes and Randal's compliments at
dinner.

"I should expect to be annihilated by the big brother if I attempted any but the 'sincerest' admiration and respect. Have no fears on that score, but tell us what is to follow this superb dinner. An apple bee, spinning match, husking party, or primitive pastime of some sort, I have no doubt."

"As you are new to our ways I am going to let you rest this evening. We will sit about the fire and tell stories. Aunt is a master hand at that, and Saul has reminiscences of the war that are well worth hearing if we can only get him to tell them."

"Ah, he was there, was he?"

"Yes, all through it, and is Major Basset, though he likes his plain name best. He fought splendidly and had several wounds, though only a mere boy when he earned his scars and bars. I'm very proud of him for that," and Sophie looked so as she glanced at the photograph of a stripling in uniform set in the place of honor on the high mantel-piece.

"We must stir him up and hear these martial memories. I want some new incidents, and shall book all I can get, if I may."

Here Randal was interrupted by Saul himself, who came in with an armful of wood for the fire.

"Anything more I can do for you, cousin?" he asked, surveying the scene with a rather wistful look.

"Only come and sit with us and talk over war times with Mr. Randal."

"When I've foddered the cattle and done my chores I'd be pleased to. What regiment were you in?" asked Saul, looking down from his lofty height upon the slender gentleman, who answered briefly, —

"In none. I was abroad at the time."

"Sick?"

"No, busy with a novel."

"Took four years to write it?"

"I was obliged to travel and study before I could finish it. These things take more time to work up than outsiders would believe."

"Seems to me our war was a finer story than any you could find in Europe, and the best way to study it would be to fight it out. If you want heroes and heroines you'd have found plenty of 'em there."

"I have no doubt of it, and shall be glad to atone for my seeming neglect of them by hearing about your own exploits, Major."

Randal hoped to turn the conversation gracefully, but Saul was not to be caught, and left the room, saying, with a gleam of fun in his eye, —

"I can't stop now; heroes can wait, pigs can't."

The girls laughed at this sudden descent from the sublime to the ridiculous, and Randal joined them, feeling his condescension had not been unobserved.

As if drawn by the merry sound Aunt Plumy

appeared, and being established in the rocking-chair fell to talking as easily as if she had known her guests for years.

"Laugh away, young folks, that's better for digestion than any of the messes people use. Are you troubled with dyspepsy, dear? You did n't seem to take your vittles very hearty, so I mistrusted you was delicate," she said, looking at Emily, whose pale cheeks and weary eyes told the story of late hours and a gay life.

"I have n't eaten so much for years, I assure you, Mrs. Basset; but it was impossible to taste all your good things. I am not dyspeptic, thank you, but a little seedy and tired, for I've been working rather hard lately."

"Be you a teacher? or have you a 'perfessun,' as they call a trade nowadays?" asked the old lady in a tone of kindly interest, which prevented a laugh at the idea of Emily's being anything but a beauty and a belle. The others kept their countenances with difficulty, and she answered demurely, —

"I have no trade as yet, but I dare say I should be happier if I had."

"Not a doubt on 't, my dear."

"What would you recommend, ma'am?"

"I should say dressmakin' was rather in your line, ain't it? Your clothes is dreadful tasty, and do you credit if you made 'em yourself," and Aunt Plumy surveyed with feminine interest the simple elegance of the travelling dress which was the masterpiece of a French modiste.

"No, ma'am, I don't make my own things, I'm too lazy. It takes so much time and trouble to select them that I have only strength left to wear them."

"Housekeepin' used to be the favorite perfessun in my day. It ain't fashionable now, but it needs a sight of trainin' to be perfect in all that's required, and I've an idee it would be a sight healthier and usefuller than the paintin' and music and fancy work young women do nowadays."

"But every one wants some beauty in their lives, and each one has a different sphere to fill, if one can only find it."

"'Pears to me there's no call for so much art when nater is full of beauty for them that can see and love it. As for 'spears' and so on, I've a notion if each of us did up our own little chores smart and thorough we need n't go wanderin' round to set the world to rights. That's the Lord's job, and I presume to say He can do it without any advice of ourn."

Something in the homely but true words seemed to rebuke the three listeners for wasted lives, and for a moment there was no sound but the crackle of the fire, the brisk click of the old lady's knitting needles, and Ruth's voice singing overhead as she made ready to join the party below.

"To judge by that sweet sound you have done one of your 'chores' very beautifully, Mrs. Bas-

set, and in spite of the follies of our day, succeeded in keeping one girl healthy, happy and
unspoiled," said Emily, looking up into the
peaceful old face with her own lovely one full
of respect and envy.

"I do hope so, for she's my ewe lamb, the
last of four dear little girls; all the rest are in
the burying ground 'side of father. I don't expect to keep her long, and don't ought to regret
when I lose her, for Saul is the best of sons;
but daughters is more to mothers somehow, and
I always yearn over girls that is left without a
broodin' wing to keep 'em safe and warm in this
world of tribulation."

Aunt Plumy laid her hand on Sophie's head
as she spoke, with such a motherly look that
both girls drew nearer, and Randal resolved to
put her in a book without delay.

Presently Saul returned with little Ruth hanging on his arm and shyly nestling near him as
he took the three-cornered leathern chair in the
chimney nook, while she sat on a stool close by.

"Now the circle is complete and the picture
perfect. Don't light the lamps yet, please, but
talk away and let me make a mental study of
you. I seldom find so charming a scene to
paint," said Randal, beginning to enjoy himself
immensely, with a true artist's taste for novelty
and effect.

"Tell us about your book, for we have been
reading it as it comes out in the magazine, and

are much exercised about how it 's going to end,"
began Saul, gallantly throwing himself into the
breach, for a momentary embarrassment fell
upon the women at the idea of sitting for their
portraits before they were ready.

"Do you really read my poor serial up here,
and do me the honor to like it?" asked the novelist, both flattered and amused, for his work
was of the æsthetic sort, microscopic studies of
character, and careful pictures of modern life.

"Sakes alive, why should n't we?" cried Aunt
Plumy. "We have some eddication, though we
ain't very genteel. We 've got a town libry,
kep up by the women mostly, with fairs and tea
parties and so on. We have all the magazines
reg'lar, and Saul reads out the pieces while Ruth
sews and I knit, my eyes bein' poor. Our winter
is long and evenins would be kinder lonesome if
we did n't have novils and newspapers to cheer
'em up."

"I am very glad I can help to beguile them
for you. Now tell me what you honestly think
of my work? Criticism is always valuable, and
I should really like yours, Mrs. Basset," said
Randal, wondering what the good woman would
make of the delicate analysis and worldly wisdom on which he prided himself.

Short work, as Aunt Plumy soon showed him,
for she rather enjoyed freeing her mind at all
times, and decidedly resented the insinuation
that country folk could not appreciate light literature as well as city people.

"I ain't no great of a jedge about anything but nat'ralness of books, and it really does seem as if some of your men and women was dreadful uncomfortable creaters. 'Pears to me it ain't wise to be always pickin' ourselves to pieces and pryin' into things that ought to come gradual by way of experience and the visitations of Providence. Flowers won't blow worth a cent ef you pull 'em open. Better wait and see what they can do alone. I do relish the smart sayins, the odd ways of furrin parts, and the sarcastic slaps at folkses weak spots. But massy knows, we can't live on spice-cake and Charlotte Ruche, and I do feel as if books was more sustainin' ef they was full of every-day people and things, like good bread and butter. Them that goes to the heart and ain't soon forgotten is the kind I hanker for. Mis Terry's books now, and Mis Stowe's, and Dickens's Christmas pieces, — them is real sweet and cheerin', to my mind."

As the blunt old lady paused it was evident she had produced a sensation, for Saul smiled at the fire, Ruth looked dismayed at this assault upon one of her idols, and the young ladies were both astonished and amused at the keenness of the new critic who dared express what they had often felt. Randal, however, was quite composed and laughed good-naturedly, though secretly feeling as if a pail of cold water had been poured over him.

"Many thanks, madam; you have discovered

my weak point with surprising accuracy. But
you see I cannot help 'picking folks to pieces,'
as you have expressed it; that is my gift, and
it has its attractions, as the sale of my books will
testify. People like the 'spice-bread,' and as
that is the only sort my oven will bake, I must
keep on in order to make my living."

"So rumsellers say, but it ain't a good trade
to foller, and I'd chop wood 'fore I'd earn my
livin' harmin' my feller man. 'Pears to me I'd
let my oven cool a spell, and hunt up some
homely, happy folks to write about; folks that
don't borrer trouble and go lookin' for holes in
their neighbors' coats, but take their lives brave
and cheerful; and rememberin' we are all human, have pity on the weak, and try to be as full
of mercy, patience and lovin' kindness as Him
who made us. That sort of a book would do
a heap of good; be real warmin' and strength-
enin', and make them that read it love the man
that wrote it, and remember him when he was
dead and gone."

"I wish I could!" and Randal meant what
he said, for he was as tired of his own style as
a watch-maker might be of the magnifying glass
through which he strains his eyes all day. He
knew that the heart was left out of his work,
and that both mind and soul were growing mor-
bid with dwelling on the faulty, absurd and
metaphysical phases of life and character. He
often threw down his pen and vowed he would

write no more; but he loved ease and the books brought money readily; he was accustomed to the stimulant of praise and missed it as the toper misses his wine, so that which had once been a pleasure to himself and others was fast becoming a burden and a disappointment.

The brief pause which followed his involuntary betrayal of discontent was broken by Ruth, who exclaimed, with a girlish enthusiasm that overpowered girlish bashfulness, —

"*I* think all the novels are splendid! I hope you will write hundreds more, and I shall live to read 'em."

"Bravo, my gentle champion! I promise that I will write one more at least, and have a heroine in it whom your mother will both admire and love," answered Randal, surprised to find how grateful he was for the girl's approval, and how rapidly his trained fancy began to paint the background on which he hoped to copy this fresh, human daisy.

Abashed by her involuntary outburst, Ruth tried to efface herself behind Saul's broad shoulder, and he brought the conversation back to its starting-point by saying in a tone of the most sincere interest, —

"Speaking of the serial, I am very anxious to know how your hero comes out. He is a fine fellow, and I can't decide whether he is going to spoil his life marrying that silly woman, or do something grand and generous, and not be made a fool of."

"Upon my soul, I don't know myself. It is very hard to find new finales. Can't you suggest something, Major? then I shall not be obliged to leave my story without an end, as people complain I am rather fond of doing."

"Well, no, I don't think I've anything to offer. Seems to me it is n't the sensational exploits that show the hero best, but some great sacrifice quietly made by a common sort of man who is noble without knowing it. I saw a good many such during the war, and often wish I could write them down, for it is surprising how much courage, goodness and real piety is stowed away in common folks ready to show when the right time comes."

"Tell us one of them, and I'll bless you for a hint. No one knows the anguish of an author's spirit when he can't ring down the curtain on an effective tableau," said Randal, with a glance at his friends to ask their aid in eliciting an anecdote or reminiscence.

"Tell about the splendid fellow who held the bridge, like Horatius, till help came up. That was a thrilling story, I assure you," answered Sophie, with an inviting smile.

But Saul would not be his own hero, and said briefly:

"Any man can be brave when the battle-fever is on him, and it only takes a little physical courage to dash ahead." He paused a moment, with his eyes on the snowy landscape without, where twilight was deepening; then, as if constrained by the memory that winter scene evoked, he slowly continued, —

"One of the bravest things I ever knew was done by a poor fellow who has been a hero to me ever since, though I only met him that night. It was after one of the big battles of that last winter, and I was knocked over with a broken leg and two or three bullets here and there. Night was coming on, snow falling, and a sharp wind blew over the field where a lot of us lay, dead and alive, waiting for the ambulance to come and pick us up. There was skirmishing going on not far off, and our prospects were rather poor between frost and fire. I was calculating how I'd manage, when I found two poor chaps close by who were worse off, so I braced up and did what I could for them. One had an arm blown away, and kept up a dreadful groaning. The other was shot bad, and bleeding to death for want of help, but never complained. He was nearest, and I liked his pluck, for he spoke cheerful and made me ashamed to growl. Such times make dreadful brutes of men if they haven't something to hold on to, and all three of us were most wild with pain and cold and hunger, for we'd fought all day fasting, when we heard a rumble in the road below, and saw lanterns bobbing round. That meant life to us, and we all tried to holler; two of us were pretty faint. but I managed a good yell, and they heard it.

"'Room for one more. Hard luck, old boys, but we are full and must save the worst wounded first. Take a drink, and hold on till we come back,' says one of them with the stretcher.

"'Here's the one to go,' I says, pointin' out my man, for I saw by the light that he was hard hit.

"'No, that one. He's got more chances than I, or this one; he's young and got a mother; I'll wait,' said the good feller, touchin' my arm, for he'd heard me mutterin' to myself about this dear old lady. We always want mother when we are down, you know."

Saul's eyes turned to the beloved face with a glance of tenderest affection, and Aunt Plumy answered with a dismal groan at the recollection of his need that night, and her absence.

"Well, to be short, the groaning chap was taken, and my man left. I was mad, but there was no time for talk, and the selfish one went off and left that poor feller to run his one chance. I had my rifle, and guessed I could hobble up to use it if need be; so we settled back to wait without much hope of help, everything being in a muddle. And wait we did till morning, for that ambulance did not come back till next day, when most of us were past needing it.

"I'll never forget that night. I dream it all over again as plain as if it was real. Snow, cold, darkness, hunger, thirst, pain, and all round us cries and cursing growing less and less, till at

last only the wind went moaning over that
meadow. It was awful! so lonesome, helpless,
and seemingly God-forsaken. Hour after hour
we lay there side by side under one coat, waiting
to be saved or die, for the wind grew strong and
we grew weak."

Saul drew a long breath, and held his hands
to the fire as if he felt again the sharp suffering
of that night.

"And the man?" asked Emily, softly, as if
reluctant to break the silence.

"He *was* a man! In times like that men talk
like brothers and show what they are. Lying
there, slowly freezing, Joe Cummings told me
about his wife and babies, his old folks waiting
for him, all depending on him, yet all ready to
give him up when he was needed. A plain man,
but honest and true, and loving as a woman; I
soon saw that as he went on talking, half to me
and half to himself, for sometimes he wandered
a little toward the end. I 've read books, heard
sermons, and seen good folks, but nothing ever
came so close or did me so much good as seeing
this man die. He had one chance and gave it
cheerfully. He longed for those he loved, and
let 'em go with a good-by they could n't hear.
He suffered all the pains we most shrink from
without a murmur, and kept my heart warm
while his own was growing cold. It 's no use
trying to tell that part of it; but I heard prayers
that night that meant something, and I saw how

faith could hold a soul up when everything was
gone but God."

Saul stopped there with a sudden huskiness
in his deep voice, and when he went on it was in
the tone of one who speaks of a dear friend.

" Joe grew still by and by, and I thought he
was asleep, for I felt his breath when I tucked
him up, and his hand held on to mine. The cold
sort of numbed me, and I dropped off, too weak
and stupid to think or feel. I never should have
waked up if it had n't been for Joe. When I
came to, it was morning, and I thought I was
dead, for all I could see was that great field of
white mounds, like graves, and a splendid sky
above. Then I looked for Joe, remembering;
but he had put my coat back over me, and lay
stiff and still under the snow that covered him
like a shroud, all except his face. A bit of my
cape had blown over it, and when I took it off
and the sun shone on his dead face, I declare to
you it was so full of heavenly peace I felt as if
that common man had been glorified by God's
light, and rewarded by God's ' Well done.'
That 's all."

No one spoke for a moment, while the women
wiped their eyes, and Saul dropped his as if to
hide something softer than tears.

" It was very noble, very touching. And
you? how did you get off at last? " asked Randal, with real admiration and respect in his usually languid face.

"Crawled off," answered Saul, relapsing into his former brevity of speech.

"Why not before, and save yourself all that misery?"

"Could n't leave Joe."

"Ah, I see; there were two heroes that night."

"Dozens, I 've no doubt. Those were times that made heroes of men, and women, too."

"Tell us more," begged Emily, looking up with an expression none of her admirers ever brought to her face by their softest compliments or wiliest gossip.

"I 've done my part. It 's Mr. Randal's turn now," and Saul drew himself out of the ruddy circle of firelight, as if ashamed of the prominent part he was playing.

Sophie and her friend had often heard Randal talk, for he was an accomplished raconteur, but that night he exerted himself, and was unusually brilliant and entertaining, as if upon his mettle. The Bassets were charmed. They sat late and were very merry, for Aunt Plumy got up a little supper for them, and her cider was as exhilarating as champagne. When they parted for the night and Sophie kissed her aunt, Emily did the same, saying heartily, —

"It seems as if I 'd known you all my life, and this is certainly the most enchanting old place that ever wa'."

"Glad you like it, dear. But it ain't all fun,

as you 'll find out to-morrow when you go to work, for Sophie says you must," answered Mrs. Basset, as her guests trooped away, rashly promising to like everything.

They found it difficult to keep their word when they were called at half past six next morning. Their rooms were warm, however, and they managed to scramble down in time for breakfast, guided by the fragrance of coffee and Aunt Plumy's shrill voice singing the good old hymn —

"Lord, in the morning Thou shalt hear
My voice ascending high."

An open fire blazed on the hearth, for the cooking was done in the lean-to, and the spacious, sunny kitchen was kept in all its old-fashioned perfection, with the wooden settle in a warm nook, the tall clock behind the door, copper and pewter utensils shining on the dresser, old china in the corner closet and a little spinning wheel rescued from the garret by Sophie to adorn the deep window, full of scarlet geraniums, Christmas roses, and white chrysanthemums.

The young lady, in a checked apron and mob-cap, greeted her friends with a dish of buckwheats in one hand, and a pair of cheeks that proved she had been learning to fry these delectable cakes.

"'You do 'keep it up' in earnest, upon my

word; and very becoming it is, dear. But won't
you ruin your complexion and roughen your
hands if you do so much of this new fancy-
work?" asked Emily, much amazed at this novel
freak.

"I like it, and really believe I've found my
proper sphere at last. Domestic life seems so
pleasant to me that I feel as if I'd better keep
it up for the rest of my life," answered Sophie,
making a pretty picture of herself as she cut
great slices of brown bread, with the early sunshine touching her happy face.

"The charming Miss Vaughan in the rôle of
a farmer's wife. I find it difficult to imagine,
and shrink from the thought of the wide-spread
dismay such a fate will produce among her
adorers," added Randal, as he basked in the glow
of the hospitable fire.

"She might do worse; but come to breakfast and do honor to my handiwork," said Sophie, thinking of her worn-out millionaire, and
rather nettled by the satiric smile on Randal's
lips.

"What an appetite early rising gives one. I
feel equal to almost anything, so let me help
wash cups," said Emily, with unusual energy,
when the hearty meal was over and Sophie
began to pick up the dishes as if it was her usual
work.

Ruth went to the window to water the flowers, and Randal followed to make himself agree-

able, remembering her defence of him last night. He was used to admiration from feminine eyes, and flattery from soft lips, but found something new and charming in the innocent delight which showed itself at his approach in blushes more eloquent than words, and shy glances from eyes full of hero-worship.

" I hope you are going to spare me a posy for to-morrow night, since I can be fine in no other way to do honor to the dance Miss Sophie proposes for us," he said, leaning in the bay window to look down on the little girl, with the devoted air he usually wore for pretty women.

" Anything you like! I should be so glad to have you wear my flowers. There will be enough for all, and I've nothing else to give to people who have made me as happy as cousin Sophie and you," answered Ruth, half drowning her great calla as she spoke with grateful warmth.

" You must make her happy by accepting the invitation to go home with her which I heard given last night. A peep at the world would do you good, and be a pleasant change, I think."

" Oh, very pleasant! but would it do me good?" and Ruth looked up with sudden seriousness in her blue eyes, as a child questions an elder, eager, yet wistful.

" Why not?" asked Randal, wondering at the hesitation.

" I might grow discontented with things here

if I saw splendid houses and fine people, I am very happy now, and it would break my heart to lose that happiness, or ever learn to be ashamed of home."

"But don't you long for more pleasure, new scenes and other friends than these?" asked the man, touched by the little creature's loyalty to the things she knew and loved.

"Very often, but mother says when I'm ready they will come, so I wait and try not to be impatient." But Ruth's eyes looked out over the green leaves as if the longing was very strong within her to see more of the unknown world lying beyond the mountains that hemmed her in.

"It is natural for birds to hop out of the nest, so I shall expect to see you over there before long, and ask you how you enjoy your first flight," said Randal, in a paternal tone that had a curious effect on Ruth.

To his surprise, she laughed, then blushed like one of her own roses, and answered with a demure dignity that was very pretty to see.

"I intend to hop soon, but it won't be a very long flight or very far from mother. She can't spare me, and nobody in the world can fill her place to me."

"Bless the child, does she think I'm going to make love to her," thought Randal, much amused, but quite mistaken. Wiser women had thought so when he assumed the caressing air

with which he beguiled them into the little revelations of character he liked to use, as the south
wind makes flowers open their hearts to give up
their odor, then leaves them to carry it elsewhere,
the more welcome for the stolen sweetness.

" Perhaps you are right. The maternal wing
is a safe shelter for confiding little souls like
you, Miss Ruth. You will be as comfortable
here as your flowers in this sunny window," he
said, carelessly pinching geranium leaves, and
ruffling the roses till the pink petals of the larg-
est fluttered to the floor.

As if she instinctively felt and resented something in the man which his act symbolized, the
girl answered quietly, as she went on with her
work, " Yes, if the frost does not touch me, or
careless people spoil me too soon."

Before Randal could reply Aunt Plumy approached like a maternal hen who sees her
chicken in danger.

" Saul is goin' to haul wood after he 's done
his chores, mebbe you 'd like to go along? The
view is good, the roads well broke, and the day
uncommon fine."

" Thanks; it will be delightful, I dare say,"
politely responded the lion, with a secret shudder at the idea of a rural promenade at 8 A. M.
in the winter.

" Come on, then; we 'll feed the stock, and
then I 'll show you how to yoke oxen," said Saul,
with a twinkle in his eye as he led the way, when

his new aide had muffled himself up as if for a polar voyage.

" Now, that's too bad of Saul! He did it on purpose, just to please you, Sophie," cried Ruth presently, and the girls ran to the window to behold Randal bravely following his host with a pail of pigs' food in each hand, and an expression of resigned disgust upon his aristocratic face.

" To what base uses may we come," quoted Emily, as they all nodded and smiled upon the victim as he looked back from the barn-yard, where he was clamorously welcomed by his new charges.

" It is rather a shock at first, but it will do him good, and Saul won't be too hard upon him, I 'm sure," said Sophie, going back to her work, while Ruth turned her best buds to the sun that they might be ready for a peace-offering to-morrow.

There was a merry clatter in the big kitchen for an hour; then Aunt Plumy and her daughter shut themselves up in the pantry to perform some culinary rites, and the young ladies went to inspect certain antique costumes laid forth in Sophie's room.

" You see, Em, I thought it would be appropriate to the house and season to have an old-fashioned dance. Aunt has quantities of ancient finery stowed away, for great-grandfather Bas-set was a fine old gentleman and his family lived

in state. Take your choice of the crimson, blue
or silver-gray damask. Ruth is to wear the
worked muslin and quilted white satin skirt, with
that coquettish hat."

"Being dark, I'll take the red and trim it up
with this fine lace. You must wear the blue and
primrose, with the distracting high-heeled shoes.
Have you any suits for the men?" asked Emily,
throwing herself at once into the all-absorbing
matter of costume.

"A claret velvet coat and vest, silk stockings,
cocked hat and snuff-box for Randal. Nothing
large enough for Saul, so he must wear his uniform. Won't Aunt Plumy be superb in this
plum-colored satin and immense cap?"

A delightful morning was spent in adapting
the faded finery of the past to the blooming
beauty of the present, and time and tongues
flew till the toot of a horn called them down to
dinner.

The girls were amazed to see Randal come
whistling up the road with his trousers tucked
into his boots, blue mittens on his hands, and an
unusual amount of energy in his whole figure,
as he drove the oxen, while Saul laughed at his
vain attempts to guide the bewildered beasts.

"It's immense! The view from the hill is
well worth seeing, for the snow glorifies the
landscape and reminds one of Switzerland. I'm
going to make a sketch of it this afternoon; better come and enjoy the delicious freshness,
young ladies."

Randal was eating with such an appetite that he did not see the glances the girls exchanged as they promised to go.

"Bring home some more winter-green, I want things to be real nice, and we have n't enough for the kitchen," said Ruth, dimpling with girlish delight as she imagined herself dancing under the green garlands in her grandmother's wedding gown.

It was very lovely on the hill, for far as the eye could reach lay the wintry landscape sparkling with the brief beauty of sunshine on virgin snow. Pines sighed overhead, hardy birds flitted to and fro, and in all the trodden spots rose the little spires of evergreen ready for its Christmas duty. Deeper in the wood sounded the measured ring of axes, the crash of falling trees, while the red shirts of the men added color to the scene, and a fresh wind brought the aromatic breath of newly cloven hemlock and pine.

"How beautiful it is! I never knew before what winter woods were like. Did you, Sophie?" asked Emily, sitting on a stump to enjoy the novel pleasure at her ease.

"I 've found out lately; Saul lets me come as often as I like, and this fine air seems to make a new creature of me," answered Sophie, looking about her with sparkling eyes, as if this was a kingdom where she reigned supreme.

"Something is making a new creature of you, that is very evident. I have n't yet discovered whether it is the air or some magic herb among that green stuff you are gathering so diligently;" and Emily laughed to see the color deepen beautifully in her friend's half-averted face.

"Scarlet is the only wear just now, I find. If we are lost like babes in the woods there are plenty of redbreasts to cover us with leaves," and Randal joined Emily's laugh, with a glance at Saul, who had just pulled his coat off.

"You wanted to see this tree go down, so stand from under and I'll show you how it's done," said the farmer, taking up his axe, not unwilling to gratify his guests and display his manly accomplishments at the same time.

It was a fine sight, the stalwart man swinging his axe with magnificent strength and skill, each blow sending a thrill through the stately tree, till its heart was reached and it tottered to its fall. Never pausing for breath Saul shook his yellow mane out of his eyes, and hewed away, while the drops stood on his forehead and his arm ached, as bent on distinguishing himself as if he had been a knight tilting against his rival for his lady's favor.

"I don't know which to admire most, the man or his muscle. One does n't often see such vigor, size and comeliness in these degenerate days," said Randal, mentally booking the fine figure in the red shirt.

"I think we have discovered a rough diamond.

I only wonder if Sophie is going to try and polish it," answered Emily, glancing at her friend, who stood a little apart, watching the rise and fall of the axe as intently as if her fate depended on it.

Down rushed the tree at last, and, leaving them to examine a crow's nest in its branches, Saul went off to his men, as if he found the praises of his prowess rather too much for him.

Randal fell to sketching, the girls to their garland-making, and for a little while the sunny woodland nook was full of lively chat and pleasant laughter, for the air exhilarated them all like wine. Suddenly a man came running from the wood, pale and anxious, saying, as he hastened by for help, " Blasted tree fell on him! Bleed to death before the doctor comes! "

" Who? who? " cried the startled trio.

But the man ran on, with some breathless reply, in which only a name was audible — " Basset."

" The deuce it is! " and Randal dropped his pencil, while the girls sprang up in dismay. Then, with one impulse, they hastened to the distant group, half visible behind the fallen trees and corded wood.

Sophie was there first, and forcing her way through the little crowd of men, saw a red-shirted figure on the ground, crushed and bleeding, and threw herself down beside it with a cry that pierced the hearts of those who heard it.

In the act she saw it was not Saul, and covered her bewildered face as if to hide its joy. A strong arm lifted her, and the familiar voice said cheeringly, —

"I'm all right, dear. Poor Bruce is hurt, but we've sent for help. Better go right home and forget all about it."

"Yes, I will, if I can do nothing;" and Sophie meekly returned to her friends who stood outside the circle over which Saul's head towered, assuring them of his safety.

Hoping they had not seen her agitation, she led Emily away, leaving Randal to give what aid he could and bring them news of the poor wood-chopper's state.

Aunt Plumy produced the "camphire" the moment she saw Sophie's pale face, and made her lie down, while the brave old lady trudged briskly off with bandages and brandy to the scene of action. On her return she brought comfortable news of the man, so the little flurry blew over and was forgotten by all but Sophie, who remained pale and quiet all the evening, tying evergreen as if her life depended on it.

"A good night's sleep will set her up. She ain't used to such things, dear child, and needs cossetin'," said Aunt Plumy, purring over her until she was in her bed, with a hot stone at her feet and a bowl of herb tea to quiet her nerves.

An hour later when Emily went up, she peeped in to see if Sophie was sleeping nicely,

and was surprised to find the invalid wrapped
in a dressing-gown writing busily.

"Last will and testament, or sudden inspiration, dear? How are you? faint or feverish,
delirious or in the dumps! Saul looks so anxious, and Mrs. Basset hushes us all up so, I ca
to bed, leaving Randal to entertain Ruth"

As she spoke Emily saw the pape
in a portfolio, and Sophie rose w

"I was writing letters.
Quite over my foolis
and get your be
the natives t

" So
aw

"Keep an eye on me, girls, for I shall certainly split somewheres or lose my head-piece off when I'm trottin' round. What would my blessed mother say if she could see me rigged out in her best things?" and with a smile and a sigh the old lady departed to look after "the boys," and see that the supper was all right.

Three prettier damsels never tripped down the wide staircase than the brilliant brunette in crimson brocade, the pensive blonde in blue, or the rosy little bride in old muslin and white satin.

A gallant court gentleman met them in the hall with a superb bow, and escorted them to the parlor, where Grandma Basset's ghost was dis-overed dancing with a modern major in full form.

utual admiration and many compliments fol- till other ancient ladies and gentlemen in all manner of queer costumes, and the seemed to wake from its humdrum sudden music and merriment, as if ation had returned to keep its Christ-

fiddler soon struck up the good hen the strangers saw dancing ith mingled mirth and envy; so hearty. The young men, in their grandfathers' knee- and swallow-tail coats, buxom girls who were ness, and danced with

[overlaid rotated text:]

pear awn. sleepy now. Go thank you. w." p that you may dazzle good night;" and Emily went to herself, "Something is goin I must find out what it is before I lea Sophie can't blind me." But Sophie did all the next day, being d fully gay at the dinner, and devoting he the young minister who was invited to distinguished novelist, and evidently b ing neighbor, gladly basked in the smiles o of him. A dashing sleigh- the afternoon, and then great w excitement over the costumes. Aunt Plumy laughed till the her cheeks as the girls com plum-colored gown with i mutton sleeves, and narro scarf hid all deficiencie struck awe into the observer.

such vigor that their high combs stood awry, their furbelows waved wildly, and their cheeks were as red as their breast-knots, or hose.

It was impossible to stand still, and one after the other the city folk yielded to the spell, Randal leading off with Ruth, Sophie swept away by Saul, and Emily being taken possession of by a young giant of eighteen, who spun her around with a boyish impetuosity that took her breath away. Even Aunt Plumy was discovered jigging it alone in the pantry, as if the music was too much for her, and the plates and glasses jingled gaily on the shelves in time to Money Musk and Fishers' Hornpipe.

A pause came at last, however, and fans fluttered, heated brows were wiped, jokes were made, lovers exchanged confidences, and every nook and corner held a man and maid carrying on the sweet game which is never out of fashion. There was a glitter of gold lace in the back entry, and a train of blue and primrose shone in the dim light. There was a richer crimson than that of the geraniums in the deep window, and a dainty shoe tapped the bare floor impatiently as the brilliant black eyes looked everywhere for the court gentleman, while their owner listened to the gruff prattle of an enamored boy. But in the upper hall walked a little white ghost as if waiting for some shadowy companion, and when a dark form appeared ran to take its arm, saying, in a tone of soft satisfaction, —

" I was so afraid you would n't come! "

" Why did you leave me, Ruth? " answered a manly voice in a tone of surprise, though the small hand slipping from the velvet coat-sleeve was replaced as if it was pleasant to feel it there.

A pause, and then the other voice answered demurely, —

" Because I was afraid my head would be turned by the fine things you were saying."

" It is impossible to help saying what one feels to such an artless little creature as you are. It does me good to admire anything so fresh and sweet, and won't harm you."

" It might if — "

" If what, my daisy? "

" I believed it," and a laugh seemed to finish the broken sentence better than the words.

" You may, Ruth, for I do sincerely admire the most genuine girl I have seen for a long time. And walking here with you in your bridal white I was just asking myself if I should not be a happier man with a home of my own and a little wife hanging on my arm than drifting about the world as I do now with only myself to care for."

" I know you would! " and Ruth spoke so earnestly that Randal was both touched and startled, fearing he had ventured too far in a mood of unwonted sentiment, born of the romance of the hour and the sweet frankness of his companion.

"Then you don't think it would be rash for some sweet woman to take me in hand and make me happy, since fame is a failure?"

"Oh, no; it would be easy work if she loved you. I know some one — if I only dared to tell her name."

"Upon my soul, this is cool," and Randal looked down, wondering if the audacious lady on his arm could be shy Ruth.

If he had seen the malicious merriment in her eyes he would have been more humiliated still, but they were modestly averted, and the face under the little hat was full of a soft agitation rather dangerous even to a man of the world.

"She is a captivating little creature, but it is too soon for anything but a mild flirtation. I must delay further innocent revelations or I shall do something rash."

While making this excellent resolution Randal had been pressing the hand upon his arm and gently pacing down the dimly lighted hall with the sound of music in his ears, Ruth's sweetest roses in his button-hole, and a loving little girl beside him, as he thought.

"You shall tell me by and by when we are in town. I am sure you will come, and meanwhile don't forget me."

"I am going in the spring, but I shall not be with Sophie," answered Ruth, in a whisper.

"With whom then? I shall long to see you."

"With my husband. I am to be married in May."

"The deuce you are!" escaped Randal, as he stopped short to stare at his companion, sure she was not in earnest.

But she was, for as he looked the sound of steps coming up the back stairs made her whole face flush and brighten with the unmistakable glow of happy love, and she completed Randal's astonishment by running into the arms of the young minister, saying with an irrepressible laugh, "Oh, John, why did n't you come before?"

The court gentleman was all right in a moment, and the coolest of the three as he offered his congratulations and gracefully retired, leaving the lovers to enjoy the tryst he had delayed. But as he went down stairs his brows were knit, and he slapped the broad railing smartly with his cocked hat as if some irritation must find vent in a more energetic way than merely saying, "Confound the little baggage!" under his breath.

Such an amazing supper came from Aunt Plumy's big pantry that the city guests could not eat for laughing at the queer dishes circulating through the rooms, and copiously partaken of by the hearty young folks.

Doughnuts and cheese, pie and pickles, cider and tea, baked beans and custards, cake and cold turkey, bread and butter, plum pudding and French bonbons, Sophie's contribution.

"May I offer you the native delicacies, and

share your plate? Both are very good, but the
china has run short, and after such vigorous ex-
ercise as you have had you must need refresh-
ment. I'm sure I do!" said Randal, bowing
before Emily with a great blue platter laden
with two doughnuts, two wedges of pumpkin
pie and two spoons.

The smile with which she welcomed him, the
alacrity with which she made room beside her
and seemed to enjoy the supper he brought, was
so soothing to his ruffled spirit that he soon began to feel that there is no friend like an old
friend, that it would not be difficult to name a
sweet woman who would take him in hand and
would make him happy if he cared to ask her,
and he began to think he would by and by, it was
so pleasant to sit in that green corner with waves
of crimson brocade flowing over his feet, and a
fine face softening beautifully under his eyes.

The supper was not romantic, but the situation was, and Emily found that pie ambrosial
food eaten with the man she loved, whose eyes
talked more eloquently than the tongue just then
busy with a doughnut. Ruth kept away, but
glanced at them as she served her company, and
her own happy experience helped her to see that
all was going well in that quarter. Saul and
Sophie emerged from the back entry with shining
countenances, but carefully avoided each other
for the rest of the evening. No one observed
this but Aunt Plumy from the recesses of her

pantry, and she folded her hands as if well content, as she murmured fervently over a pan full of crullers, " Bless the dears! Now I can die happy."

Every one thought Sophie's old-fashioned dress immensely becoming, and several of his former men said to Saul with blunt admiration, " Major, you look to-night as you used to after we 'd gained a big battle."

" I feel as if I had," answered the splendid Major, with eyes much brighter than his buttons, and a heart under them infinitely prouder than when he was promoted on the field of honor, for his Waterloo was won.

There was more dancing, followed by games, in which Aunt Plumy shone pre-eminent, for the supper was off her mind and she could enjoy herself. There were shouts of merriment as the blithe old lady twirled the platter, hunted the squirrel, and went to Jerusalem like a girl of sixteen; her cap in a ruinous condition, and every seam of the purple dress straining like sails in a gale. It was great fun, but at midnight it came to an end, and the young folks, still bubbling over with innocent jollity, went jingling away along the snowy hills, unanimously pronouncing Mrs. Basset's party the best of the season.

" Never had such a good time in my life!" exclaimed Sophie, as the family stood together in the kitchen where the candles among the wreaths were going out, and the floor was strewn with wrecks of past joy.

"I'm proper glad, dear. Now you all go to bed and lay as late as you like to-morrow. I'm so kinder worked up I could n't sleep, so Saul and me will put things to rights without a mite of noise to disturb you;" and Aunt Plumy sent them off with a smile that was a benediction, Sophie thought.

"The dear old soul speaks as if midnight was an unheard-of hour for Christians to be up. What would she say if she knew how we seldom go to bed till dawn in the ball season? I'm so wide awake I've half a mind to pack a little. Randal must go at two, he says, and we shall want his escort," said Emily, as the girls laid away their brocades in the press in Sophie's room.

"I'm not going. Aunt can't spare me, and there is nothing to go for yet," answered Sophie, beginning to take the white chrysanthemums out of her pretty hair.

"My dear child, you will die of ennui up here. Very nice for a week or so, but frightful for a winter. We are going to be very gay, and cannot get on without you," cried Emily dismayed at the suggestion.

"You will have to, for I'm not coming. I am very happy here, and so tired of the frivolous life I lead in town, that I have decided to try a better one," and Sophie's mirror reflected a face full of the sweetest content.

"Have you lost your mind? experienced religion? or any other dreadful thing? You always were odd, but this last freak is the strangest of all. What will your guardian say, and the world?" added Emily in the awe-stricken tone of one who stood in fear of the omnipotent Mrs. Grundy.

"Guardy will be glad to be rid of me, and I don't care that for the world," cried Sophie, snapping her fingers with a joyful sort of recklessness which completed Emily's bewilderment.

"But Mr. Hammond? Are you going to throw away millions, lose your chance of making the best match in the city, and driving the girls of our set out of their wits with envy?"

Sophie laughed at her friend's despairing cry, and turning round said quietly, —

"I wrote to Mr. Hammond last night, and this evening received my reward for being an honest girl. Saul and I are to be married in the spring when Ruth is."

Emily fell prone upon the bed as if the announcement was too much for her, but was up again in an instant to declare with prophetic solemnity, —

"I knew something was going on, but hoped to get you away before you were lost. Sophie, you will repent. Be warned, and forget this sad delusion."

"Too late for that. The pang I suffered yesterday when I thought Saul was dead showed me how well I loved him. To-night he asked me to stay, and no power in the world can part us. Oh! Emily, it is all so sweet, so beautiful, that *everything* is possible, and I know I shall be happy in this dear old home, full of love and peace and honest hearts. I only hope you may find as true and tender a man to live for as my Saul."

Sophie's face was more eloquent than her fervent words, and Emily beautifully illustrated the inconsistency of her sex by suddenly embracing her friend, with the incoherent exclamation, "I think I have, dear! Your brave Saul is worth a dozen old Hammonds, and I do believe you are right."

It is unnecessary to tell how, as if drawn by the irresistible magic of sympathy, Ruth and her mother crept in one by one to join the midnight conference and add their smiles and tears, tender hopes and proud delight to the joys of that memorable hour. Nor how Saul, unable to sleep, mounted guard below, and meeting Randal prowling down to soothe his nerves with a surreptitious cigar found it impossible to help confiding to his attentive ear the happiness that would break bounds and overflow in unusual eloquence.

Peace fell upon the old house at last, and all slept as if some magic herb had touched their eyelids, bringing blissful dreams and a glad awakening.

"Can't we persuade you to come with us, Miss Sophie?" asked Randal next day, as they made their adieux.

"I'm under orders now, and dare not disobey my superior officer," answered Sophie, handing her Major his driving gloves, with a look which plainly showed that she had joined the great army of devoted women who enlist for life and ask no pay but love.

"I shall depend on being invited to your wedding, then, and yours, too, Miss Ruth," added Randal, shaking hands with "the little baggage," as if he had quite forgiven her mockery and forgotten his own brief lapse into sentiment.

Before she could reply Aunt Plumy said, in a tone of calm conviction, that made them all laugh, and some of them look conscious, —

"Spring is a good time for weddin's, and I should n't wonder ef there was quite a number."

"Nor I;" and Saul and Sophie smiled at one another as they saw how carefully Randal arranged Emily's wraps.

Then with kisses, thanks and all the good wishes that happy hearts could imagine, the guests drove away, to remember long and gratefully that pleasant country Christmas.

ON PICKET DUTY

" Better late than never."

"WHAT air you thinkin' of, Phil?"

"My wife, Dick."

"So was I! Ain't it odd how fellers fall to thinkin' of thar little women, when they get a quiet spell like this?"

"Fortunate for us that we do get it, and have such memories to keep us brave and honest through the trials and temptations of a life like ours."

October moonlight shone clearly on the solitary tree, draped with gray moss, scarred by lightning and warped by wind, looking like a venerable warrior, whose long campaign was nearly done; and underneath was posted the guard of four. Behind them twinkled many camp-fires on a distant plain, before them wound a road ploughed by the passage of an army, strewn with the relics of a rout. On the right, a sluggish river glided, like a serpent, stealthy, sinuous, and dark, into a seemingly impervious jungle; on the left, a Southern swamp filled the air with malarial damps, swarms of noisome life,

and discordant sounds that robbed the hour of
its repose. The men were friends as well as
comrades, for though gathered from the four
quarters of the Union, and dissimilar in education, character, and tastes, the same spirit animated all; the routine of camp-life threw them
much together, and mutual esteem soon grew
into a bond of mutual good fellowship.

Thorn was a Massachusetts volunteer; a man
who seemed too early old, too early embittered
by some cross, for, though grim of countenance,
rough of speech, cold of manner, a keen observer
would have soon discovered traces of a deeper,
warmer nature hidden behind the repellent front
he turned upon the world. A true New Englander, thoughtful, acute, reticent, and opin-
ionated; yet earnest withal, intensely patriotic,
and often humorous, despite a touch of Puritan
austerity.

Phil, the " romantic chap," as he was called,
looked his character to the life. Slender,
swarthy, melancholy-eyed, and darkly-bearded;
with feminine features, mellow voice, and alter-
nately languid or vivacious manners. A child
of the South in nature as in aspect, ardent and
proud; fitfully aspiring and despairing; without
the native energy which moulds character and
ennobles life. Months of discipline and devotion
had done much for him, and some deep experience was fast ripening the youth into a man.

Flint, the long-limbed lumberman, from the

wilds of Maine, was a conscript who, when government demanded his money or his life, calculated the cost, and decided that the cash would be a dead loss and the claim might be repeated, whereas the conscript would get both pay and plunder out of government, while taking excellent care that government got very little out of him. A shrewd, slow-spoken, self-reliant specimen, was Flint; yet something of the fresh flavor of the backwoods lingered in him still, as if Nature were loath to give him up, and left the mark of her motherly hand upon him, as she leaves it in a dry, pale lichen, on the bosom of the roughest stone.

Dick " hailed " from Illinois, and was a comely young fellow, full of dash and daring; rough and rowdy, generous and jolly, overflowing with spirits and ready for a free fight with all the world.

Silence followed the last words, while the friendly moon climbed up the sky. Each man's eye followed it, and each man's heart was busy with remembrances of other eyes and hearts that might be watching and wishing as theirs watched and wished. In the silence, each shaped for himself that vision of home that brightens so many camp-fires, haunts so many dreamers under canvas roofs, and keeps so many turbulent natures tender by memories which often are both solace and salvation.

Thorn paced to and fro, his rifle on his shoul-

der, vigilant and soldierly, however soft his heart
might be. Phil leaned against the tree, one hand
in the breast of his blue jacket, on the painted
presentment of the face his fancy was picturing
in the golden circle of the moon. Flint lounged
on the sward, whistling softly as he whittled at
a fallen bough. Dick was flat on his back, heels
in air, cigar in mouth, and some hilarious notion
in his mind, for suddenly he broke into a laugh.

"What is it, lad?" asked Thorn, pausing in
his tramp, as if willing to be drawn from the dis-
turbing thought that made his black brows lower
and his mouth look grim.

"Thinkin' of my wife, and wishin' she was
here, bless her heart! set me rememberin' how
I see her fust, and so I roared, as I always do
when it comes into my head."

"How was it? Come, reel off a yarn, and
let's hear houw yeou hitched teams," said Flint,
always glad to get information concerning his
neighbors, if it could be cheaply done.

"Tellin' how we found our wives wouldn't
be a bad game, would it, Phil?"

"I'm agreeable; but let's have your romance
first."

"Devilish little of that about me or any of
my doin's. I hate sentimental bosh as much as
you hate slang, and should have been a bachelor
to this day if I hadn't seen Kitty jest as I did.
You see, I'd been too busy larkin' round to get
time for marryin', till a couple of years ago,

when I did up the job double-quick, as I 'd like to do this thunderin' slow one, hang it all!' "

"Halt a minute till I give a look, for this picket is n't going to be driven in or taken while I 'm on guard."

Down his beat went Thorn, reconnoitring river, road, and swamp, as thoroughly as one pair of keen eyes could do it, and came back satisfied, but still growling like a faithful mastiff on the watch; performances which he repeated at intervals till his own turn came.

"I did n't have to go out of my own State for a wife, you 'd better believe," began Dick, with a boast, as usual; "for we raise as fine a crop of girls thar as any State in or out of the Union, and don't mind raisin' Cain with any man who denies it. I was out on a gunnin' tramp with Joe Partridge, a cousin of mine, — poor old chap! he fired his last shot at Gettysburg, and died game in a way he did n't dream of the day we popped off the birds together. It ain't right to joke that way; I won't if I can help it; but a feller gets awfully kind of heathenish these times, don't he?"

"Settle up them scores byme-by; fightin' Christians is scurse raound here. Fire away, Dick."

"Well, we got as hungry as hounds half a dozen mile from home, and when a farmhouse hove in sight, Joe said he 'd ask for a bite, and leave some of the plunder for pay. I was visitin'

Joe, did n't know folks round, and backed out
of the beggin' part of the job; so he went ahead
alone. We 'd come out of the woods behind the
house, and while Joe was foragin', I took a rec-
onnoissance. The view was fust-rate, for the
main part of it was a girl airin' beds on the roof
of a stoop. Now, jest about that time, havin'
a leisure spell, I 'd begun to think of marryin',
and took a look at all the girls I met, with an
eye to business. I s'pose every man has some
sort of an idee or pattern of the wife he wants;
pretty and plucky, good and gay was mine, but
I 'd never found it till I see Kitty; and as she
did n't see me, I had the advantage and took an
extra long stare."

"What was her good p'ints, hey?"

"Oh, well, she had a wide-awake pair of eyes,
a bright, jolly sort of a face, lots of curly hair
tumblin' out of her net, a trig little figger, and
a pair of the neatest feet and ankles that ever
stepped. 'Pretty,' thinks I; 'so far so good.'
The way she whacked the pillers, shook the
blankets, and pitched into the beds was a caution;
specially one blunderin' old feather-bed that
would n't do nothin' but sag round in a pig-
headed sort of way, that would have made most
girls get mad and give up. Kitty did n't, but
just wrastled with it like a good one, till she got
it turned, banged, and spread to suit her; then
she plumped down in the middle of it, with a
sarcy little nod and chuckle to herself, that

tickled me mightily. 'Plucky,' thinks I, 'better 'n' better.' Jest then an old woman came flyin' out the back-door, callin', 'Kitty! Kitty! Squire Partridge's son 's here, 'long with a friend; been gunnin', want luncheon, and I 'm all in the suds; do come down and see to 'em.'

"'Where are they?' says Kitty, scrambling up her hair and settlin' her gown in a jiffy, as women have a knack of doin', you know.

"'Mr. Joe 's in the front entry; the other man 's somewheres round, Billy says, waitin' till I send word whether they can stop. I darsn't till I 'd seen you, for I can't do nothin', I 'm in such a mess,' says the old lady.

"'So am I, for I can't get in except by the entry window, and he 'll see me,' says Kitty, gigglin' at the thoughts of Joe.

"'Come down the ladder, there 's a dear. I 'll pull it round and keep it stiddy,' says the mother.

"'Oh, ma, don't ask me!' says Kitty, with a shiver. 'I 'm dreadfully scared of ladders since I broke my arm off this very one. It 's so high, it makes me dizzy jest to think of.'

"'Well, then, I 'll do the best I can; but I wish them boys was to Jericho!' says the old lady, with a groan, for she was fat and hot, had her gown pinned up, and was in a fluster generally. She was goin' off rather huffy, when Kitty called out, —

"'Stop, ma! I 'll come down and help you, only ketch me if I tumble.'

"She looked scared but stiddy, and I'll bet it took as much grit for her to do it as for one of us to face a battery. It don't seem much to tell of, but I wish I may be hit if it wasn't a right down dutiful and clever thing to see done. When the old lady took her off at the bottom, with a good motherly hug, 'Good,' thinks I; 'what more do you want?'"

"A snug little property wouldn't a ben bad, I reckon," said Flint.

"Well, she had it, old skin-flint, though I didn't know or care about it then. What a jolly row she'd make if she knew I was tellin' the ladder part of the story! She always does when I get to it, and makes believe cry, with her head in my breast-pocket, or any such handy place, till I take it out and swear I'll never do so ag'in. Poor little Kit, I wonder what she's doin' now. Thinkin' of me, I'll bet."

Dick paused, pulled his cap lower over his eyes, and smoked a minute with more energy than enjoyment, for his cigar was out and he did not perceive it.

"That's not all, is it?" asked Thorn, taking a fatherly interest in the younger man's love passages.

"Not quite. 'Fore long, Joe whistled, and as I always take short cuts everywhar, I put in at the back-door, jest as Kitty come trottin' out of the pantry with a big berry-pie in her hand. I startled her, she tripped over the sill and down

she come; the dish flew one way, the pie flopped
into her lap, the juice spatterin' my boots and
her clean gown. I thought she 'd cry, scold,
have hysterics, or some confounded thing or
other; but she jest sat still a minute, then looked
up at me with a great blue splash on her face,
and went off into the good-naturedest gale of
laughin' you ever heard in your life. That finished me. 'Gay,' thinks I; 'go in and win.'
So I did; made love hand over hand, while I
stayed with Joe; pupposed a fortnight after,
married her in three months, and there she is,
a tiptop little woman, with a pair of stunnin'
boys in her arms!"

Out came a well-worn case, and Dick proudly
displayed the likeness of a stout, much bejewelled
young woman with two staring infants on her
knee. In his sight, the poor picture was a more
perfect work of art than any of Sir Joshua's
baby-beauties, or Raphael's Madonnas, and the
little story needed no better sequel than the
young father's praises of his twins, the covert
kiss he gave their mother when he turned as if
to get a clearer light upon the face. Ashamed
to show the tenderness that filled his honest
heart, he hummed "Kingdom Coming," relit
his cigar, and presently began to talk again.

"Now, then, Flint, it 's your turn to keep
guard, and Thorn's to tell his romance. Come,
don't try to shirk; it does a man good to talk
of such things, and we 're all mates here."

" In some cases it don't do any good to talk
of such things; better let 'em alone," muttered
Thorn, as he reluctantly sat down, while Flint
as reluctantly departed.

With a glance and gesture of real affection,
Phil laid his hand upon his comrade's knee, saying in his persuasive voice, " Old fellow, it *will*
do you good, because I know you often long to
speak of something that weighs upon you.
You 've kept us steady many a time, and done
us no end of kindnesses; why be too proud to
let us give our sympathy in return, if nothing
more?"

Thorn's big hand closed over the slender one
upon his knee, and the mild expression, so rarely
seen upon his face, passed over it as he replied, —

" I think I could tell you almost anything if
you asked me that way, my boy. It is n't that
I am too proud, — and you 're right about my
sometimes wanting to free my mind, — but it 's
because a man of forty don't just like to open
out to young fellows, if there is any danger of
their laughing at him, though he may deserve
it. I guess there is n't now, and I 'll tell you
how I found my wife."

Dick sat up, and Phil drew nearer, for the
earnestness that was in the man dignified his
plain speech, and inspired an interest in his history, even before it was begun. Looking gravely
at the river and never at his hearers, as if still

a little shy of confidants, yet grateful for the relief of words, Thorn began abruptly : —

" I never hear the number eighty-four without clapping my hand to my left breast and missing my badge. You know I was on the police in New York, before the war, and that 's about all you do know yet. One bitter cold night I was going my rounds for the last time, when, as I turned a corner, I saw there was a trifle of work to be done. It was a bad part of the city, full of dirt and deviltry; one of the streets led to a ferry, and at the corner an old woman had an apple-stall. The poor soul had dropped asleep, worn out with the cold, and there were her goods left with no one to watch 'em. Somebody was watching 'em, however; a girl, with a ragged shawl over her head, stood at the mouth of an alley close by, waiting for a chance to grab something. I 'd seen her there when I went by before, and mistrusted she was up to some mischief; as I turned the corner, she put out her hand and cribbed an apple. She saw me the minute she did it, but neither dropped it nor ran, only stood stock still with the apple in her hand till I came up.

" ' This won't do, my girl,' said I. I never could be harsh with 'em, poor things! She laid it back and looked up at me with a miserable sort of a smile, that made me put my hand in my pocket to fish for a ninepence before she spoke.

" ' I know it won't,' she says. ' I did n't want to do it, it 's so mean, but I 'm awful hungry, sir.'

" ' Better run home and get your supper, then.'

" ' I 've got no home.'

" ' Where do you live? '

" ' In the street.'

" ' Where do you sleep? '

" ' Anywhere; last night in the lock-up, and I thought I 'd get in there again, if I did that when you saw me. I like to go there, it 's warm and safe.'

" ' If I don't take you there, what will you do? '

" ' Don't know. I could go over there and dance again as I used to, but being sick has made me ugly, so they won't have me, and no one else will take me because I have been there once.'

" I looked where she pointed, and thanked the Lord that they would n't take her. It was one of those low theatres that do so much damage to the like of her; there was a gambling place one side of it, an eating saloon the other. I was new to the work then, but though I 'd heard about hunger and homelessness often enough, I 'd never had this sort of thing, nor seen that look on a girl's face. A white, pinched face hers was, with frightened, tired-looking eyes, but so innocent! She was n't more than sixteen, had been pretty once, I saw, looked sick and starved now, and seemed just the most helpless, hopeless little thing that ever was.

" ' You 'd better come to the Station for to-night, and we 'll see to you to-morrow,' says I.

" ' Thank you, sir,' says she, looking as grateful as if I 'd asked her home. I suppose I did speak kind of fatherly. I ain't ashamed to say I felt so, seeing what a child she was; nor to own that when she put her little hand in mine, it hurt me to feel how thin and cold it was. We passed the eating-house where the red lights made her face as rosy as it ought to have been; there was meat and pies in the window, and the poor thing stopped to look. It was too much for her; off came her shawl, and she said in that coaxing way of hers, —

" ' I wish you 'd let me stop at the place close by and sell this; they 'll give a little for it, and I 'll get some supper. I 've had nothing since yesterday morning, and maybe cold is easier to bear than hunger.'

" ' Have you nothing better than that to sell?' I says, not quite sure that she was n't all a humbug, like so many of 'em. She seemed to see that, and looked up at me again with such innocent eyes, I could n't doubt her when she said, shivering with something beside the cold, —

" ' Nothing but myself.' Then the tears came, and she laid her head down on my arm, sobbing, —' Keep me! oh, do keep me safe somewhere!' "

Thorn choked here, steadied his voice with a resolute hem! but could only add one sentence more, —

" That 's how I found my wife."

" Come, don't stop thar. I told the whole
o' mine, you do the same. Whar did you take
her? how 'd it all come round?"

" Please tell us, Thorn."

The gentler request was answered presently,
very steadily, very quietly.

" I was always a soft-hearted fellow, though
you would n't think it now, and when that little
girl asked me to keep her safe, I just did it. I
took her to a good woman whom I knew, for
I had n't any women folks belonging to me, nor
any place but that to put her in. She stayed
there till spring working for her keep, growing
brighter, prettier, every day, and fonder of me,
I thought. If I believed in witchcraft, I
should n't think myself such a fool as I do now,
but I don't believe in it, and to this day I can't
understand how I came to do it. To be sure I
was a lonely man, without kith or kin, had never
had a sweetheart in my life, or been much with
women since my mother died. Maybe that 's
why I was so bewitched with Mary, for she had
little ways with her that took your fancy and
made you love her whether you would or no.
I found her father was an honest fellow enough,
a fiddler in some theatre; that he 'd taken good
care of Mary till he died, leaving precious little
but advice for her to live on. She 'd tried to
get work, failed, spent all she had, got sick, and
was going to the bad, as the poor souls can

hardly help doing with so many ready to give them a shove. It's no use trying to make a bad job better; so the long and short of it was, I thought she loved me; God knows I loved her! and I married her before the year was out."

"Show us her picture; I know you've got one; all the fellows have, though half of 'em won't own up."

"I've only got part of one. I once saved my little girl, and her picture once saved me."

From an inner pocket Thorn produced a woman's housewife, carefully untied it, though all its implements were missing but a little thimble, and from one of its compartments took a flattened bullet and the remnants of a picture.

"I gave her that the first Christmas after I found her. She wasn't as tidy about her clothes as I liked to see, and I thought if I gave her a handy thing like this, she'd be willing to sew. But she only made one shirt for me, and then got tired, so I keep it like an old fool, as I am. Yes, that's the bit of lead that would have done for me, if Mary's likeness hadn't been just where it was."

"You'll like to show her this when you go home, won't you?" said Dick, as he took up the bullet, while Phil examined the marred picture, and Thorn poised the little thimble on his big finger, with a sigh.

"How can I, when I don't know where she is, and camp is all the home I've got!"

The words broke from him like a sudden groan, when some old wound is rudely touched. Both of the young men started, both laid back the relics they had taken up, and turned their eyes from Thorn's face, across which swept a look of shame and sorrow, too significant to be misunderstood. Their silence assured him of their sympathy, and, as if that touch of friendliness unlocked his heavy heart, he eased it by a full confession. When he spoke again, it was with the calmness of repressed emotion, a calmness more touching to his mates than the most passionate outbreak, the most pathetic lamentation; for the coarse camp-phrases seemed to drop from his vocabulary; more than once his softened voice grew tremulous, and to the words "my little girl," there went a tenderness that proved how dear a place she still retained in that deep heart of his.

"Boys, I 've gone so far; I may as well finish; and you 'll see I 'm not without some cause for my stern looks and ways; you 'll pity me, and from you I 'll take the comfort of it. It 's only the old story, — I married her, worked for her, lived for her, and kept my little girl like a lady. I should have known that I was too old and sober for a young thing like that, for the life she led before the pinch came just suited her. She liked to be admired, to dress and dance and make herself pretty for all the world to see; not to keep house for a quiet man like me. Idle-

ness was n't good for her, it bred discontent;
then some of her old friends, who 'd left her in
her trouble, found her out when better times
came round, and tried to get her back again. I
was away all day, I did n't know how things
were going, and she was n't open with me, afraid
she said; I was so grave, and hated theatres so.
She got courage finally to tell me that she was n't
happy; that she wanted to dance again, and
asked me if she might n't. I 'd rather have had
her ask me to put her in a fire, for I *did* hate
theatres, and was bred to; others think they 're
no harm. I do; and knew it was a bad life for
a girl like mine. It pampers vanity, and vanity
is the Devil's help with such; so I said No,
kindly at first, sharp and stern when she kept on
teasing. That roused her spirit. ' I will go!'
she said, one day. ' Not while you are my wife,'
I answered back; and neither said any more, but
she gave me a look I did n't think she could,
and I resolved to take her away from temptation
before worse came of it.

"I did n't tell her my plan; but I resigned
my place, spent a week or more finding and fixing a little home for her out in the wholesome
country, where she 'd be safe from theatres and
disreputable friends, and maybe learn to love
me better when she saw how much she was to
me. It was coming summer, and I made things
look as home-like and as pretty as I could. She
liked flowers, and I fixed a garden for her; she

was fond of pets, and I got her a bird, a kitten,
and a dog to play with her; she fancied gay colors and tasty little matters, so I filled her rooms
with all the handsome things I could afford, and
when it was done, I was as pleased as any boy,
thinking what happy times we 'd have together
and how pleased she 'd be. Boys, when I went
to tell her and to take her to her little home, she
was gone."

" Who with? "

" With those cursed friends of her; a party
of them left the city just then; she was wild to
go; she had money now, and all her good looks
back again. They teased and tempted her; I
was n't there to keep her, and she went, leaving
a line behind to tell me that she loved the old
life more than the new; that my house was a
prison, and she hoped I 'd let her go in peace.
That almost killed me; but I managed to bear
it, for I knew most of the fault was mine; but
it was awful bitter to think I had n't saved her,
after all."

" Oh, Thorn! what did you do? "

" Went straight after her; found her dancing
in Philadelphia, with paint on her cheeks, trin-
kets on her neck and arms, looking prettier than
ever; but the innocent eyes were gone, and I
could n't see my little girl in the bold, handsome
woman twirling there before the footlights.
She saw me, looked scared at first, then smiled,
and danced on with her eyes upon me, as if she
said, —

an' yeou give them up 'cause you only thought abaout their looks an' money. I'm humly, an' I'm poor; but I've loved yeou ever sence we went a-nuttin' years ago, an' yeou shook daown fer me, kerried my bag, and kissed me tew the gate, when all the others shunned me, 'cause my father drank an' I was shabby dressed, ugly, an' shy. Yeou asked me in sport, I answered in airnest; but I don't expect nothin' unless yeou mean as I mean. Like me, Hiram, or leave me, it won't make no odds in my lovin' of yeou, nor helpin' of yeou, ef I kin.'

"'T ain't easy tew say haouw I felt, while she was goin' on that way, but my idees was tumblin' raound inside er me, as ef half a dozen dams was broke loose all tew oncet. One think was ruther stiddier 'n the rest, an' that was that I liked Bewlah more 'n I knew. I begun tew see what kep' me loafin' tew hum so much, sence aunt was took daown; why I wan't in no hurry tew git them other gals, an' haow I come tew pocket my mittens so easy arfter the fust rile was over. Bewlah *was* humly, poor in flesh, dreadful freckled, hed red hair, black eyes, an' a gret mold side of her nose. But I'd got wonted tew her; she knowed my ways, was a fust rate housekeeper, real good-tempered, and pious without flingin' on 't in yer face. She was a lonely creeter, — her folks bein' all dead but one sister, who did n't use her waal, an' somehow I kinder yearned over her, as they say in Scrip-

ter. For all I set **an'** gawped, I was coming
raound fast, though I felt as I used tew, when
I was goin' to shoot the rapids, kinder breathless an' oncertin, whether I 'd come aout right
side up or not. Queer, warn't it?"

"Love, Flint; that was a sure symptom of it."

"Waal, guess 't was; anyway I jumped up all
of a sudden, ketched Bewlah raound the neck,
give her a hearty kiss, and sung aout, ' I 'll dew
it sure 's my name 's Hi Flint!' The words was
scarcely out of my maouth, 'fore daown come
Dr. Parr. He' d ben up tew see aunt, an' said
she would n't last the night threw, prob'ly. That
give me a scare er the wust kind; an' when I
told doctor haow things was, he sez, kinder
jokin', —

"'Better git married right away, then. Par-
son Dill is tew come an' see the old lady, an' he 'll
dew both jobs tew oncet.'

"'Will yeou, Bewlah?' sez I.

"'Yes, Hiram, to 'blige yeou,' sez she.

"With that, I put it fer the license; got it,
an' was back in less 'n half an haour, most tuck-
ered aout with the flurry of the hull concern.
Quick as I 'd been, Beylah hed faound time tew
whip on her best gaoun, fix up her hair, and put
a couple er white chrissanthymums intew her
hand'chif pin. Fer the fust time in her life,
she looked harnsome, — leastways *I* thought so,
— with a pretty color in her cheeks, some-
thin' brighter 'n a larf shinin' in her eyes, and

her lips smilin' an' tremblin', as she come to me an' whispered so 's 't none er the rest could hear, —

" ' Hiram, don't yeou dew it, ef yeou 'd ruther not. I 've stood it a gret while alone, an' I guess I can ag'in.'

" Never yeou mind what I said or done abaout that; but we was merried ten minutes arfter, 'fore the kitchen fire, with Dr. Parr an'. aour hired man, fer witnesses; an' then we all went up tew aunt. She was goan fast, but she understood what I told her, hed strength tew fill up the hole in the will, an' to say, a-kissin' Bewlah, ' Yeou 'll be a good wife, an' naow yeou ain't a poor one.'

" I could n't help givin' a peek tew the will, and there I see not Hiram Flint nor Josiah Flint, but Bewlah Flint, wrote every which way, but as plain as the nose on yer face. ' It won't make no odds, dear,' whispered my wife, peekin' over my shoulder. ' Guess it won't!' sez I, aout laoud; ' I 'm glad on 't, and it ain't a cent more 'n yeou derserve.'

" That pleased aunt. ' Riz me, Hiram,' sez she; an' when I 'd got her easy, she put her old arms raound my neck, an' tried to say, ' God bless you, dear —,' but died a doin' of it; an' I ain't ashamed tew say I boohooed real hearty, when I laid her daown, fer she was dreadf'l good tew me, an' I don't forgit her in a hurry."

" How 's Bewlah ? " asked Dick, after the lit-

tle tribute of respect all paid to Aunt Siloam's
memory, by a momentary silence.

"Fust-rate! that harum-scarum venter er
mine was the best I ever made. She's done
waal by me, hes Bewlah; ben a grand good
haousekeeper, kin kerry on the farm better 'n
me, any time, an' is as dutif'l an' lovin' a wife
as, — waal, as annything that *is* extra dutif'l and
lovin'."

"Got any boys to brag of?"

"We don't think much o' boys daown aour
way; they're 'mazin' resky stock to fetch up,
— alluz breakin' baounds, gittin' intew the
paound, and wurryin' your life aout somehaow
'nother. Gals naow doos waal; I've got six o'
the likeliest the is goin', every one on 'em is the
very moral of Bewlah, — red hair, black eyes,
quiet ways, an' a mold 'side the nose. Baby's
ain't growed yet; but I expect tew see it in a
consid'able state o' forrardness, when I git hum,
an' would n't miss it fer the world."

The droll expression of Flint's face, and the
satisfied twang of his last words, were irresistible. Dick and Phil went off into a shout of
laughter; and even Thorn's grave lips relapsed
into a smile at the vision of six little Flints with
their six little moles. As if the act were an
established ceremony, the "paternal head" produced his pocket-book, selected a worn black-
and-white paper, which he spread in his broad
palm, and displayed with the air of a connoisseur.

" There, thet 's Bewlah! we call it a cuttin';
but the proper name 's a silly-hoot, I b'leeve.
I 've got a harnsome big degarrytype tew hum,
but the heft on 't makes it bad tew kerry raound,
so I took this. I don't tote it abaout inside my
shirt, as some dew, — it ain't my way; but I
keep it in my wallet long with my other valleu'-
bles, and guess I set as much store by it as ef
it was all painted up, and done off to kill."

The " silly-hoot " was examined with interest,
and carefully stowed away again in the old
brown wallet, which was settled in its place with
a satisfied slap; then Flint said briskly, —

" Naouw, Phil, yeou close this interestin' and
instructive meeting; and be spry, fer time 's
most up."

" I have n't much to tell, but must begin with
a confession which I have often longed but never
dared to make before, because I am a coward."

" Sho! who 's goan to b'leeve that o' a man
who fit like a wild-cat, wuz offered permotion
on the field, and reported tew headquarters arfter
his fust scrimmage. Try ag'in, Phil."

" Physical courage is as plentiful as brass buttons, nowadays, but moral courage is a rarer
virtue; and I 'm lacking in it, as I 'll prove.
You think me a Virginian; I 'm an Alabamian
by birth, and was a Rebel three months ago."

This confession startled his hearers, as he
knew it would, for he had kept his secret well.
Thorn laid his hand involuntarily upon his rifle,

Dick drew off a little, and Flint illustrated one of his own expressions, for he " gawped." Phil laughed that musical laugh of his, and looked up at them with his dark face waking into sudden life, as he went on : —

" There 's no treason in the camp, for I 'm as fierce a Federalist as any of you now, and you may thank a woman for it. When Lee made his raid into Pennsylvania, I was a lieutenant in the — well, never mind what regiment, it has n't signalized itself since, and I 'd rather not hit my old neighbors when they are down. In one of the skirmishes during our retreat, I got a wound and was left for dead. A kind old Quaker found and took me home; but though I was too weak to talk, I had my senses by that time, and knew what went on about me. Everything was in confusion, even in that well-ordered place; no surgeon could be got at first, and a flock of frightened women thee'd and thou'd one another over me, but had n't wit enough to see that I was bleeding to death. Among the faces that danced before my dizzy eyes was one that seemed familiar, probably because no cap surrounded it. I was glad to have it bending over me, to hear a steady voice say, ' Give me a bandage, quick! ' and when none was instantly forthcoming to me, the young lady stripped up a little white apron she wore, and stanched the wound in my shoulder. I was not as badly hurt as I supposed, but so worn-out, and faint from loss of blood, they believed me to be dying, and so did I, when the old man took off his hat and said, —

"Friend, if thee has anything to say, thee had better say it, for thee probably has not long to live.'

"I thought of my little sister, far away in Alabama, fancied she came to me, and muttered, 'Amy, kiss me good-by.' The women sobbed at that; but the girl bent her sweet compassionate face to mine, and kissed me on the forehead. That was my wife."

"So you seceded from Secession right away, to pay for that lip-service, hey?"

"No, Thorn, not right away, — to my shame be it spoken. I'll tell you how it came about. Margaret was not old Bent's daughter, but a Massachusetts girl on a visit, and a long one it proved, for she couldn't go till things were quieter. While she waited, she helped take care of me; for the good souls petted me like a baby when they found that a Rebel could be a gentleman. I held my tongue, and behaved my best to prove my gratitude, you know. Of course, I loved Margaret very soon. How could I help it? She was the sweetest woman I had ever seen, tender, frank, and spirited; all I had ever dreamed of and longed for. I did not speak of this, nor hope for a return, because I knew she was a hearty Unionist, and thought she only tended me from pity. But suddenly she decided to go home, and when I ventured to wish she would stay longer, she would not listen, and said, 'I must not stay; I should have gone before.'

"The words were nothing, but as she uttered them the color came up beautifully over all her face, and her eyes filled as they looked away from mine. Then I knew that she loved me, and my secret broke out against my will. Margaret was forced to listen, for I would not let her go, but she seemed to harden herself against me, growing colder, stiller, statelier, as I went on, and when I said in my desperate way, —

"'You should love me, for we are bid to love our enemies,' she flashed an indignant look at me and said, —

"'I will not love what I cannot respect! Come to me a loyal man, and see what answer I shall give you.'

"Then she went away. It was the wisest thing she could have done, for absence did more to change me than an ocean of tears, a year of exhortations. Lying there, I missed her every hour of the day, recalled every gentle act, kind word, and fair example she had given me. I contrasted my own belief with hers, and found a new significance in the words honesty and honor, and, remembering her fidelity to principle, was ashamed of my own treason to God and to herself. Education, prejudice, and interest, are difficult things to overcome, and that was the hottest fight I ever passed through, for as I tell you, I was a coward. But love and loyalty won the day, and, asking no quarter, the Rebel surrendered."

"Phil Beaufort, you're a brick!" cried Dick, with a sounding slap on his comrade's shoulder.

"A brand snatched from the burnin'. Hallelujah!" chanted Flint, seesawing with excitement.

"Then you went to find your wife? How? Where?" asked Thorn, forgetting vigilance in interest.

"Friend Bent hated war so heartily that he would have nothing to do with paroles, exchanges, or any martial process whatever, but bade me go when and where I liked, remembering to do by others as I had been done by. Before I was well enough to go, however, I managed, by means of Copperhead influence and returned prisoners, to send a letter to my father and receive an answer. You can imagine what both contained; and so I found myself penniless, but not poor, an outcast, but not alone. Old Bent treated me like a prodigal son, and put money in my purse; his pretty daughters loved me for Margaret's sake, and gave me a patriotic salute all round when I left them, the humblest, happiest man in Pennsylvania. Margaret once said to me that this was the time for deeds, not words; that no man should stand idle, but serve the good cause with head, heart, and hand, no matter in what rank; for in her eyes a private fighting for liberty was nobler than a dozen gen-

erals defending slavery. I remembered that,
and, not having influential friends to get me a
commission, enlisted in one of her own Massachusetts regiments, knowing that no act of mine
would prove my sincerity like that. You should
have seen her face when I walked in upon her,
as she sat alone, busied with the army work, as
I'd so often seen her sitting by my bed; it
showed me all she had been suffering in silence,
all I should have lost had I chosen darkness instead of light. She hoped and feared so much
she could not speak, neither could I, but dropped
my cloak, and showed her that, through love of
her, I had become a soldier of the Union. How
I love the coarse blue uniform! for when she
saw it, she came to me without a word and kept
her promise in a month."

"Thunder! what a harnsome woman!" exclaimed Flint, as Phil, opening the golden case
that held his talisman, showed them the beautiful,
beloved face of which he spoke.

"Yes! and a right noble woman too. I don't
deserve her, but I will. We parted on our wed-
ding-day, for orders to be off came suddenly,
and she would not let me go until I had given
her my name to keep. We were married in the
morning, and at noon I had to go. Other
women wept as we marched through the city,
but my brave Margaret kept her tears till we
were gone, smiling and waving her hand to me,
— the hand that wore the wedding-ring, — till

I was out of sight. That image of her is before me day and night, and day and night her last words are ringing in my ears, —

"'I give you freely, do your best. Better a true man's widow than a traitor's wife.'

"Boys, I've only stood on the right side for a month; I've only fought one battle, earned one honor; but I believe these poor achievements are an earnest of the long atonement I desire to make for five-and-twenty years of blind transgression. You say I fight well. Have I not cause to dare much? — for in owning many slaves, I too became a slave; in helping to make many freemen, I liberate myself. You wonder why I refused promotion. Have I any right to it yet? Are there not men who never sinned as I have done, and beside whose sacrifices mine look pitifully small? You tell me I have no ambition. I have the highest, for I desire to become God's noblest work, — an honest man, — living, to make Margaret happy in a love that every hour grows worthier of her own, — dying to make death proud to take me."

Phil had risen while he spoke, as if the enthusiasm of his mood lifted him into the truer manhood he aspired to attain. Straight and strong he stood up in the moonlight, his voice deepened by unwonted energy, his eye clear and steadfast, his whole face ennobled by the regenerating power of this late loyalty to country, wife, and self, and bright against the dark blue of his jacket shone the pictured face, the only medal he was proud to wear.

Ah, brave, brief moment, cancelling years of wrong! Ah, fair and fatal decoration, serving as a mark for a hidden foe! The sharp crack of a rifle broke the stillness of the night, and with those hopeful words upon his lips, the young man sealed his purpose with his life.

THE BARON'S GLOVES;

OR,

AMY'S ROMANCE

" All is fair in love and war."

I

HOW THEY WERE FOUND

"WHAT a long sigh! Are you tired, Amy?"

"Yes, and disappointed as well. I never would have undertaken this journey if I had not thought it would be full of novelty, romance, and charming adventures."

"Well, we have had several adventures."

"Bah! losing one's hat in the Rhine, getting left at a dirty little inn, and having our pockets picked, are not what *I* call adventures. I wish there were brigands in Germany — it needs something of that sort to enliven its stupidity."

"How can you call Germany stupid when you have a scene like this before you?" said Helen, with a sigh of pleasure, as she looked from the balcony which overhangs the Rhine at the hotel of the "Three Kings" at Coblentz. Ehrenbreitstein towered opposite, the broad river glittered below, and a midsummer moon lent its enchantment to the landscape.

As she spoke, her companion half rose from

the low chair where she lounged, and showed the pretty, piquant face of a young girl. She seemed in a half melancholy, half petulant mood; and traces of recent illness were visible in the languor of her movements and the pallor of her cheeks.

"Yes, it is lovely; but I want adventures and romance of some sort to make it quite perfect. I don't care what, if something would only happen."

"My dear, you are out of spirits and weary now, to-morrow you'll be yourself again. Do not be ungrateful to uncle or unjust to yourself. Something pleasant will happen, I've no doubt. In fact, something *has* happened that you may make a little romance out of, perhaps, for lack of a more thrilling adventure."

"What do you mean?" and Amy's listless face brightened.

"Speak low; there are balconies all about us, and we may be overheard," said Helen, drawing nearer after an upward glance.

"What is the beginning of a romance?" whispered Amy, eagerly.

"A pair of gloves. Just now, as I stood here, and you lay with your eyes shut, these dropped from the balcony overhead. Now amuse yourself by weaving a romance out of them and their owner."

Amy seized them, and stepping inside the window, examined them by the candle.

"A gentleman's gloves, scented with violets! Here's a little hole fretted by a ring on the third finger. Bless me! here are the initials, 'S. P.,' stamped on the inside, with a coat of arms below. What a fop to get up his gloves in this style! They are exquisite, though. Such a delicate color, so little soiled, and so prettily ornamented! Handsome hands wore these. I'd like to see the man."

Helen laughed at the girl's interest, and was satisfied if any trifle amused her *ennui*.

"I will send them back by the *kellner,* and in that way we may discover their owner," she said.

But Amy arrested her on the way to the door.

"I've a better plan; these waiters are so stupid you'll get nothing out of them. Here's the hotel book sent up for our names; let us look among the day's arrivals and see who 'S. P.' is. He came to-day, I'm sure, for the man said the rooms above were just taken, so we could not have them."

Opening the big book, Amy was soon intently poring over the long list of names, written in many hands and many languages.

"I've got it! Here he is — oh, Nell, he's a baron! Isn't that charming? 'Sigismund von Palsdorf, Dresden.' We *must* see him, for I know he's handsome, if he wears such distracting gloves."

"You'd better take them up yourself, then."

"You know I can't do that; but I shall ask

the man a few questions, just to get an idea what
sort of person the baron is. Then I shall change
my mind and go down to dinner; shall look well
about me, and if the baron is agreeable I shall
make uncle return the gloves. He will thank
us, and I can say I 've known a real baron. That
will be so nice when we go home. Now, don't
be duennaish and say I 'm silly, but let me do as
I like, and come and dress."

Helen submitted, and when the gong pealed
through the house, Major Erskine marched into
the great *salle à manger,* with a comely niece on
each arm. The long tables were crowded, and
they had to run the gauntlet of many eyes as
they made their way to the head of the upper
table. Before she touched her soup, Amy
glanced down the line of faces opposite, and finding none that answered the slight description
elicited from the waiter, she leaned a little forward to examine those on her own side of the
table. Some way down sat several gentlemen,
and as she bent to observe them, one did the
same, and she received an admiring glance from
a pair of fine black eyes. Somewhat abashed,
she busied herself with her soup; but the fancy
had taken possession of her, and presently she
whispered to Helen, —

"Do you see any signs of the baron?"

"On my left; look at the hands."

Amy looked and saw a white, shapely hand
with an antique ring on the third finger. Its

owner's face was averted, but as he conversed
with animation, the hand was in full play, now
emphasizing an opinion, now lifting a glass, or
more frequently pulling at a blond beard which
adorned the face of the unknown. Amy shook
her head decidedly.

"I hate light men, and don't think that is the
baron, for the gloves are a size too small for
those hands. Lean back and look some four or
five seats lower down on the right. See what
sort of person the dark man with the fine eyes
is."

Helen obeyed, but almost instantly bent to her
plate again, smiling in spite of herself.

"That is an Englishman; he stares rudely,
says 'By Jove!' and wears no jewelry or beard."

"Now, I'm disappointed. Well, keep on the
watch, and tell me if you make any discoveries,
for I *will* find the baron."

Being hungry, Amy devoted herself to her
dinner, till dessert was on the table. She was
languidly eating grapes, while Helen talked with
the major, when the word "baron" caught her
ear. The speakers sat at a table behind her, so
that she could not see them without turning
quite round, which was impossible; but she listened eagerly to the following scrap of chat: —

"Is the baron going on to-morrow?" asked
a gay voice in French.

"Yes, he is bound for Baden-Baden. The
season is at its height, and he must make his

game while the ball is rolling, or it is all up with
the open-handed Sigismund," answered a rough
voice.

" Won't his father pardon the last escapade? "
asked a third, with a laugh.

" No, and he is right. The duel was a bad
affair, for the man almost died, and the baron
barely managed to get out of the scrape through
court influence. When is the wedding to be? "

" Never, Palsdorf says. There is everything
but love in the bargain, and he swears he 'll not
agree to it. I like that."

" There is much nobleness in him, spite of his
vagaries. He will sow his wild oats and make
a grand man in time. By the by, if we are going
to the fortress, we must be off. Give Sigismund
the word; he is dining at the other table with
Power," said the gay voice.

" Take a look at the pretty English girl as
you go by; it will do your eyes good, after the
fat Frauleins we have seen of late," added the
rough one.

Three gentlemen rose, and as they passed Amy
stole a glance at them; but seeing several pairs
of eyes fixed on herself, she turned away blushing, with the not unpleasant consciousness that
" the pretty English girl " was herself. Longing
to see which Sigismund was, she ventured to
look after the young men, who paused behind the
man with the blond beard, and also touched the
dark-eyed gentleman on the shoulder. All five

went down the hall and stood talking near the door.

"Uncle, I wish to go," said Amy, whose will was law to the amiable major. Up he rose, and Amy added, as she took his arm, "I'm seized with a longing to go to Baden-Baden and see a little gambling. You are not a wild young man, so you can be trusted there."

"I hope so. Now you are a sensible little woman, and we'll do our best to have a gay time. Wait an instant till I get my hat."

While the major searched for the missing article the girls went on, and coming to the door, Amy tried to open it. The unwieldy foreign lock resisted her efforts, and she was just giving it an impatient little shake, when a voice said behind her, —

"Permit me, mademoiselle;" at the same moment a handsome hand turned the latch, the flash of a diamond shone before her, and the door opened.

"*Merci, monsieur,*" she murmured, turning as she went out; but Helen was close behind her, and no one else to be seen except the massive major in the rear.

"Did you see the baron?" she whispered eagerly, as they went up-stairs.

"No; where was he?"

"He opened the door for me. I knew him by his hand and ring. He was close to you."

"I did not observe him, being busy gathering

up my dress. I thought the person was a waiter, and never looked at him," said Helen, with provoking indifference.

"How unfortunate! Uncle, you are going to see the fortress; we don't care for it; but I want you to take these gloves and inquire for Baron Sigismund Palsdorf. He will be there with a party of gentlemen. You can easily manage it, men are so free and easy. Mind what he is like, and come home in time to tell me all about it."

Away went the major, and the cousins sat on the balcony enjoying the lovely night, admiring the picturesque scene, and indulging in the flights of fancy all girls love, for Helen, in spite of her three-and-twenty years, was as romantic as Amy at eighteen. It was past eleven when the major came, and the only greeting he received was the breathless question, —

"Did you find him?"

"I found something much better than any baron, a courier. I've wanted one ever since we started; for two young ladies and their baggage are more than one man can do his duty by. Karl Hoffman had such excellent testimonials from persons I know, that I did not hesitate to engage him, and he comes to-morrow; so henceforth I've nothing to do but devote myself to you."

"How very provoking! Did you bring the gloves back?" asked Amy, still absorbed in the baron.

The major tossed them to her, and indulged in a hearty laugh at her girlish regrets; then bade them good-night, and went away to give orders for an early start next morning.

Tired of talking, the girls lay down in the two little white beds always found in German hotels, and Amy was soon continuing in sleep the romance she had begun awake. She dreamed that the baron proved to be the owner of the fine eyes; that he wooed and won her, and they were floating down the river to the chime of wedding-bells.

At this rapturous climax she woke to find the air full of music, and to see Helen standing tall and white in the moonlight that streamed in at the open window.

"Hush, hide behind the curtains and listen; it's a serenade," whispered Helen, as Amy stole to her side.

Shrouded in the drapery, they leaned and listened till the song ended, then Amy peeped; a dark group stood below; all were bareheaded, and now seemed whispering together. Presently a single voice rose, singing an exquisite little French canzonet, the refrain of which was a passionate repetition of the word "*Amie.*" She thought she recognized the voice, and the sound of her own name uttered in such ardent tones made her heart beat and her color rise, for it seemed to signify that the serenade was for them. As the last melodious murmur ceased, there came a stifled laugh from below, and something fell into the balcony. Neither dared stir till the sound of departing feet reassured them; then creeping forward Amy drew in a lovely bouquet of myrtle, roses, and great German forget-me-nots, tied with a white ribbon and addressed in a dashing hand to *La belle Helène*.

"Upon my life, the romance has begun in earnest," laughed Helen, as she examined the flowers. "You are serenaded by some unknown nightingale, and I have flowers tossed up to me in the charming old style. Of course it is the baron, Amy."

"I hope so; but whoever it is, they are regular troubadours, and I'm delighted. I know the gloves will bring us fun of some kind. Do you take one and I'll take the other, and see who will find the baron first. Isn't it odd that they knew our names?"

"Amy, the writing on this card is very like that in the big book. I may be bewitched by this mid-summer moonlight, but it really is very like it. Come and see."

The two charming heads bent over the card, looking all the more charming for the dishevelled curls and braids that hung about them as the girls laughed and whispered together in the softly brilliant light that filled the room.

"You are right; it is the same. The men who stared so at dinner are gay students perhaps, and ready for any prank. Don't tell uncle, but let us see what will come of it. I begin to enjoy myself heartily now — don't you?" said Amy, laying her glove carefully away.

"I enjoyed myself before, but I think '*La belle Helène*' gives an added relish to life, *Amie*," laughed Nell, putting her flowers in water; and then both went back to their pillows, to dream delightfully till morning.

II

KARL, THE COURIER

"THREE days, at least, before we reach Baden. How tiresome it is that uncle won't go faster!" said Amy, as she tied on her hat next morning, wondering as she did so if the baron would take the same boat.

"As adventures have begun, I feel assured that they will continue to cheer the way; so resign yourself and be ready for anything," replied Helen, carefully arranging her bouquet in her travelling-basket.

A tap at the door, which stood half open, made both look up. A tall, brown, gentlemanly man, in a gray suit, with a leathern bag slung over his shoulder, stood there, hat in hand, and meeting Helen's eyes, bowed respectfully, saying in good English, but with a strong German accent, —

"Ladies, the major desired me to tell you the carriage waits."

"Why, who — " began Amy, staring with her blue eyes full of wonder at the stranger.

He bowed again, and said, simply, —

" Karl Hoffman, at your service, mademoiselle."

" The courier — oh, yes! I forgot all about it. Please take these things."

Amy began to hand him her miscellaneous collection of bags, books, shawls and cushions.

" I 'd no idea couriers were such decent creatures," whispered Amy, as they followed him along the hall.

" Don't you remember the raptures Mrs. Mortimer used to have over their Italian courier, and her funny description of him? ' Beautiful to behold, with a night of hair, eyes full of an infinite tenderness, and a sumptuous cheek.' "

Both girls laughed, and Amy averred that Karl's eyes danced with merriment as he glanced over his shoulder, as the silvery peal sounded behind him.

" Hush! he understands English; we must be careful," said Helen, and neither spoke again till they reached the carriage.

Everything was ready, and as they drove away, the major, leaning luxuriously back, exclaimed, —

" Now I begin to enjoy travelling, for I 'm no longer worried by the thought of luggage, time-tables, trains, and the everlasting perplexity of thalers, kreutzers, and pfenniges. This man is a treasure; everything is done in the best manner, and his knowledge of matters is really amazing."

"He's a very gentlemanly-looking person," said Amy, eying a decidedly aristocratic foot through the front window of the carriage, for Karl sat up beside the driver.

"He *is* a gentleman, my dear. Many of these couriers are well born and educated, but, being poor, prefer this business to any other, as it gives them variety, and often pleasant society. I've had a long talk with Hoffman, and find him an excellent and accomplished fellow. He has lost his fortune, it seems, through no fault of his own, so being fond of a roving life, turned courier for a time, and we are fortunate to have secured him."

"But one does n't know how to treat him," said Helen. "I don't like to address him as a servant, and yet it's not pleasant to order a gentleman about."

"Oh, it will be easy enough as we go on together. Just call him Hoffman, and behave as if you knew nothing about his past. He begged me not to mention it, but I thought you'd like the romance of the thing. Only don't either of you run away with him, as Ponsonby's daughter did with her courier, who was n't a gentleman, by the way."

"Not handsome enough," said Amy. "I don't like blue eyes and black hair. His manners are nice, but he looks like a gipsy, with his brown face and black beard : does n't he, Nell?"

"Not at all. Gipsies have n't that style of

face; they are thin, sharp, and cunning in feature as in nature. Hoffman has large, well-moulded features, and a mild, manly expression, which gives one confidence in him."

"He has a keen, wicked look in his blue eyes, as you will see, Nell. I mean mischievously, not malignantly wicked. He likes fun, I 'm sure, for he laughed about the 'sumptuous cheek' till his own were red, though he dared not show it, and was as grave as an owl when we met uncle," said Amy, smiling at the recollection.

"We shall go by boat to Biebrich, and then by rail to Heidelberg. We shall get in late to-morrow night, but can rest a day, and then on to Baden. Here we are; now make yourselves easy, as I do, and let Karl take care of everything."

And putting his hands in his pockets, the major strolled about the boat, while the courier made matters comfortable for the day. So easily and well did he do his duty, that both girls enjoyed watching him after he had established them on the shady side of the boat, with camp-stools for their feet, cushions to lean on, books and bags laid commodiously at hand.

As they sailed up the lovely Rhine they grew more and more enthusiastic in their admiration and curiosity, and finding the meagre description of the guide-books very unsatisfactory, Amy begged her uncle to tell her all the legends of picturesque ruin, rock and river, as they passed.

" Bless me, child, I know nothing; but here's
Hoffman, a German born, who will tell you
everything, I dare say. Karl, what's that old
castle up there? The young ladies want to know
about it."

Leaning on the railing, Hoffman told the story
so well that he was kept explaining and describing for an hour, and when he went away to order
lunch, Amy declared it was as pleasant as reading fairy tales to listen to his dramatic histories
and legends.

At lunch the major was charmed to find his
favorite wines and dishes without any need of
consulting dictionary or phrase-book beforehand,
or losing his temper in vain attempts to make
himself understood.

On reaching Biebrich, tired and hungry, at
nightfall, everything was ready for them, and all
went to bed praising Karl, the courier, though
Amy, with unusual prudence, added, —

" He is a new broom now; let us wait a little
before we judge."

All went well next day till nightfall, when a
most untoward accident occurred, and Helen's
adventures began in earnest. The three occupied
a *coupé,* and being weary with long sitting,
Helen got out at one of the stations where the
train paused for ten minutes. A rosy sunset
tempted her to the end of the platform, and there
she found, what nearly all foreign railway stations possess, a charming little garden.

Amy was very tired, rather cross, and passionately fond of flowers, so when an old woman offered to pull a nosegay for "the gracious lady," Helen gladly waited for it, hoping to please the invalid. Twice the whistle warned her, and at last she ran back, but only in time to see the train move away, with her uncle gesticulating wildly to the guard, who shook his stupid German head, and refused to see the dismayed young lady imploring him to wait for her.

Just as the train was vanishing from the station, a man leaped from a second-class carriage at the risk of his neck, and hurried back to find Helen looking pale and bewildered, as well she might, left alone and moneyless at night in a strange town.

"Mademoiselle, it is I; rest easy; we can soon go on; a train passes in two hours, and we can telegraph to Heidelberg that they may not fear for you."

"Oh, Hoffman, how kind of you to stop for me! What should I have done without you, for uncle takes care of all the money, and I have only my watch."

Helen's usual self-possession rather failed her in the flurry of the moment, and she caught Karl's arm with a feminine little gesture of confidence very pleasant to see. Leading her to the waiting-room, he ordered supper, and put her into the care of the woman of the place, while

he went to make inquiries and dispatch the telegram.   In half an hour he returned, finding
Helen refreshed and cheerful, though a trace
of anxiety was still visible in her watchful eyes.

"All goes excellently, mademoiselle. I have
sent word to several posts along the road that
we are coming by the night train, so that Monsieur le Major will rest tranquil till we meet.
It is best that I give you some money, lest such
a mishap should again occur; it is not likely
so soon; nevertheless, here is both gold and
silver.   With this, one can make one's way
everywhere. Now, if mademoiselle will permit
me to advise, she will rest for an hour, as we
must travel till dawn. I will keep guard without and watch for the train."

He left her, and having made herself comfortable on one of the sofas, she lay watching
the tall shadow pass and repass door and window, as Karl marched up and down the platform,
with the tireless tramp of a sentinel on duty. A
pleasant sense of security stole over her, and
with a smile at Amy's enjoyment of the adventure when it was over, Helen fell asleep.

A far-off shriek half woke her, and starting
up, she turned to meet the courier coming in to
wake her. Up thundered the train, every carriage apparently full of sleepy passengers, and the
guard in a state of sullen wrath at some delay,
the consequences of which would fall heaviest
on him.

From carriage to carriage hurried Karl and his charge, to be met with everywhere by the cry, "All full," in many languages, and with every aspect of inhospitality. One carriage only showed two places; the other seats were occupied by six students, who gallantly invited the lady to enter. But Helen shrunk back, saying, —

"Is there no other place?"

"None, mademoiselle; this, or remain till morning," said Karl.

"Where will you go if I take this place?"

"Among the luggage, — anywhere; it is nothing. But we must decide at once."

"Come with me; I'm afraid to be locked in here alone," said Helen, desperately.

"Mademoiselle forgets I am her courier."

"I do not forget that you are a gentleman. Pray come in; my uncle will thank you."

"I will," and with a sudden brightening of the eyes, a grateful glance, and an air of redoubled respect, Hoffman followed her into the carriage.

They were off at once, and the thing was done before Helen had time to feel anything but the relief which the protection of his presence afforded her.

The young gentlemen stared at the veiled lady and her grim escort, joked under their breath, and looked wistfully at the suppressed cigars, but behaved with exemplary politeness till sleep overpowered them, and one after the other dropped off asleep to dream of their respective Gretchens.

Helen could not sleep, and for hours sat studying the unconscious faces before her, the dim landscape flying past the windows, or forgot herself in reveries.

Hoffman remained motionless and silent, except when she addressed him, wakeful also, and assiduous in making the long night as easy as possible.

It was past midnight, and Helen's heavy eyelids were beginning to droop, when suddenly there came an awful crash, a pang of mortal fear, then utter oblivion.

As her senses returned she found herself lying in a painful position under what had been the roof of the car; something heavy weighed down her lower limbs, and her dizzy brain rung with a wild uproar of shrieks and groans, eager voices, the crash of wood and iron, and the shrill whistle of the engine, as it rushed away for help.

Through the darkness she heard the pant as of some one struggling desperately, then a cry close by her, followed by a strong voice exclaiming, in an agony of suspense, —

" My God, will no one come! "

" Hoffman, are you there? " cried Helen, groping in the gloom, with a thrill of joy at the sound of a familiar voice.

" Thank heaven, you are safe. Lie still. I

will save you. Help is coming. Have no fear!"
panted the voice, with an undertone of fervent
gratitude in its breathless accents.

"What has happened? Where are the rest?"

"We have been thrown down an embank-
ment. The lads are gone for help. God only
knows what harm is done."

Karl's voice died in a stifled groan, and Helen
cried out in alarm, —

"Where are you? You are hurt?"

"Not much. I keep the ruins from falling
in to crush us. Be quiet, they are coming."

A shout answered the faint halloo he gave as
if to guide them to the spot, and a moment after,
five of the students were swarming about the
wreck, intent on saving the three whose lives
were still in danger.

A lamp torn from some demolished carriage
was held through an opening, and Helen saw a
sight that made her blood chill in her veins.
Across her feet, crushed and bleeding, lay the
youngest of the students, and kneeling close
beside him was Hoffman, supporting by main
strength a mass of timber, which otherwise
would fall and crush them all. His face was
ghastly pale, his eyes haggard with pain and suspense, and great drops stood upon his forehead.
But as she looked, he smiled with a cheery, —

"Bear up, dear lady, we shall soon be out of
danger. Now, lads, work with a will; my
strength is going fast."

They did work like heroes, and even in her pain and peril, Helen admired the skill, energy, and courage of the young men, who, an hour ago, had seemed to have no ideas above pipes and beer. Soon Hoffman was free, the poor senseless youth lifted out, and then, as tenderly as if she were a child, they raised and set her down, faint but unhurt, in a wide meadow, already strewn with sad tokens of the wreck.

Karl was taken possession of as well as herself, forced to rest a moment, drink a cordial draught from some one's flask, and be praised, embraced, and enthusiastically blessed by the impetuous youths.

"Where is the boy who was hurt? Bring him to me. I am strong now. I want to help. I have salts in my pocket, and I can bind up his wounds," said Helen, soon herself again.

Karl and Helen soon brought back life and sense to the boy, and never had human face looked so lovely as did Helen's to the anxious comrades when she looked up in the moonlight with a joyful smile, and softly whispered, —

"He is alive."

For an hour terrible confusion reigned, then the panic subsided a little, and such of the carriages as were whole were made ready to carry away as many as possible; the rest must wait till a return train could be sent for them.

A struggle of course ensued, for every one wished to go on, and fear made many selfish.

The wounded, the women and children, were taken, as far as possible, and the laden train moved away, leaving many anxious watchers behind.

Helen had refused to go, and had given her place to poor Conrad, thereby overwhelming his brother and comrades with gratitude. Two went on with the wounded lad; the rest remained, and chivalrously devoted themselves to Helen as a body-guard.

The moon shone clearly, the wide field was miles from any hamlet, and a desolate silence succeeded to the late uproar, as the band of waiters roamed about, longing for help and dawn.

"Mademoiselle, you shiver; the dew falls, and it is damp here; we must have a fire;" and Karl was away to a neighboring hedge, intent on warming his delicate charge if he felled a forest to do it.

The students rushed after him, and soon returned in triumph to build a glorious fire, which drew all forlorn wanderers to its hospitable circle. A motley assemblage; but mutual danger and discomfort produced mutual sympathy and good will, and a general atmosphere of friendship pervaded the party.

"Where is the brave Hoffman?" asked Wilhelm, the blond student, who, being in the Werther period of youth, was already madly in love with Helen, and sat at her feet catching cold in the most romantic manner.

" Behold me! The little ones cry for hunger, so I ransack the ruins and bring away my spoils. Eat, Kinder, eat and be patient."

As he spoke Karl appeared with an odd collection of baskets, bags, and bottles, and with a fatherly air that won all the mothers, he gave the children whatever first appeared, making them laugh in spite of weariness and hunger by the merry speeches which accompanied his gifts.

" You too need something. Here is your own basket with the lunch I ordered you. In a sad state of confusion, but still eatable. See, it is not bad," and he deftly spread on a napkin before Helen cold chicken, sandwiches, and fruit.

His care for the little ones as well as for herself touched her and her eyes filled, as she remembered that she owed her life to him, and recalled the sight of his face in the overturned car.

Her voice trembled a little as she thanked him, and the moonlight betrayed her wet eyes. He fancied she was worn out with excitement and fatigue, and anxious to cheer her spirits, he whispered to Wilhelm and his mates, —

" Sing, then, comrades, and while away this tedious night. It is hard for all to wait so long, and the babies need a lullaby."

The young men laughed and sang as only German students can sing, making the night musical with blithe drinking songs, tender love-lays, battle-hymns, and Volkslieder sweeter than any songs across the water.

Every heart was cheered and warmed by the magic of the music, the babies fell asleep, strangers grew friendly, fear changed to courage, and the most forlorn felt the romance of that bivouac under the summer sky.

Dawn was reddening the east when a welcome whistle broke up the camp. Every one hurried to the railway, but Helen paused to gather a handful of blue forget-me-nots, saying to Hoffman, who waited with her wraps on his arm, —

"It has been a happy night, in spite of the danger and discomfort. I shall not soon forget it; and take these as a souvenir."

He smiled, standing bare-headed in the chilly wind, for his hat was lost, his coat torn, hair dishevelled, and one hand carelessly bound up in his handkerchief. Helen saw these marks of the night's labors and perils for the first time, and as soon as they were seated desired to see his hand.

"It is nothing, — a scratch, a mere scratch, I give you my word, mademoiselle," he began, but Wilhelm unceremoniously removed the handkerchief, showing a torn and bleeding hand which must have been exquisitely painful.

Helen turned pale, and with a reproachful glance skilfully bound it up again, saying, as she handed a silken scarf to Wilhelm, —

"Make of that a sling, please, and put the poor hand in it. Care must be taken, or harm will come of it."

Hoffman submitted in bashful silence, as if surprised and touched by the young lady's interest. She saw that, and added gratefully, —

"I do not forget that you saved my life, though you seem to have done so. My uncle will thank you better than I can."

"I already have my reward, mademoiselle," he returned, with a respectful inclination and a look she could neither understand nor forget.

III

AMY'S ADVENTURE

THE excitement and suspense of the major and Amy can be imagined when news of the accident reached them. Their gratitude and relief were intense when Helen appeared next morning, with the faithful Hoffman still at his post, though no longer able to disguise the fact that he was suffering from his wound.

When the story had been told, Karl was put under the surgeon's care, and all remained at Heidelberg for several days to rest and recover.

On the afternoon of the last day the major and young ladies drove off to the castle for a farewell view. Helen began to sketch the great stone lion's head above the grand terrace, the major smoked and chatted with a party of English artists whom he had met, and Amy, with a little lad for a guide, explored the old castle to her heart's content.

The sun set, and twilight began to fall when Helen put up her pencils, and the major set off to find Amy, who had been appearing and disappearing in every nook and cranny of the half-ruined castle.

Nowhere could he find her, and no voice answered when he called. The other visitors were gone, and the place seemed deserted, except by themselves and the old man who showed the ruins.

Becoming alarmed lest the girl had fallen somewhere, or lost her way among the vaults where the famous Tun lies, the major called out old Hans with his lantern, and searched high and low.

Amy's hat, full of flowers and ferns, was found in the Lady's Walk, as the little terrace is called, but no other trace appeared, and Helen hurried to and fro in great distress, fearing all manner of dangers.

Meanwhile Amy, having explored every other part of the castle, went to take another look at the Tun, the dwarf, and the vaults.

Now little Anderl, her guide, had a great fear of ghosts, and legions were said to haunt the ruins after nightfall, so when Amy rambled on deeper and deeper into the gloom the boy's courage ebbed away with every step; yet he was ashamed to own his fear, seeing that she had none.

Amy wanted to see a certain cell, where a nun was said to have pined to death because she would not listen to the Margraf's love. The legend pleased the romantic girl, and forgetful of waning daylight, gathering damps, and Anderl's reluctant service, she ran on, up steps and down, delighted with little arched doors, rusty chains on the walls, glimpses of sky through shattered roofs, and all manner of mysterious nooks and corners. Coming at last to a narrow cell, with a stone table, and heavy bolts on the old door, she felt sure this was poor Elfrida's prison, and called Anderl to come on with his candle, for the boy had lighted one, for his own comfort rather than hers. Her call was unanswered, and glancing back, she saw the candle placed on the ground, but no Anderl.

"Little coward, he has run away," she said, laughing; and having satisfied her curiosity, turned to retrace her steps, — no easy task to one ignorant of the way, for vault after vault opened on both sides, and no path was discernible. In vain she tried to recall some landmark, the gloom had deepened and nothing was clear. On she hurried, but found no opening, and really frightened, stopped at last, calling the boy in a voice that woke a hundred echoes. But Anderl had fled home, thinking the lady would find her way back, and preferring to lose his kreutzers to seeing a ghost.

Poor Amy's bewilderment and alarm increased with every moment's delay, and hoping to come out somewhere, she ran on till a misstep jostled the candle from her hand and extinguished it.

Left in the dark, her courage deserted her, and she screamed desperately, like a lost child, and was fast getting into a state of frantic terror, when the sound of an approaching step reassured her.

Holding her breath, she heard a quick tread drawing nearer, as if guided by her cries, and, straining her eyes, she caught the outline of a man's figure in the gloom.

A sensation of intense joy rushed over her, and she was about to spring forward, when she remembered that as she could speak no German how could she explain her plight to the stranger, if he understood neither French nor English?

Fear took possession of her at the thought of meeting some rough peasant, or some rollicking student, to whom she could make no intelligible appeal or explanation.

Crouching close against the wall, she stood mute till the figure was very near. She was in the shadow of an angle, and the man paused, as if looking for the person who called for help.

"Who is lost here?" said a clear voice, in German.

Amy shrunk closer to the wall, fearing to speak, for the voice was that of a young man, and a low laugh followed the words, as if the speaker found the situation amusing.

"Mortal, ghost or devil, I'll find it," exclaimed the voice, and stepping forward, a hand groped for and found her.

"Lottchen, is it thou? Little rogue, thou shalt pay dearly for leading me such a chase."

As he spoke he drew the girl toward him, but

with a faint cry, a vain effort to escape, Amy's
terror reached its climax, and spent with fatigue
and excitement, she lost consciousness.

"Who the deuce is it, then? Lottchen never
faints on a frolic. Some poor little girl lost in
earnest. I must get her out of this gloomy place
at once, and find her party afterward."

Lifting the slight figure in his arms, the young
man hurried on, and soon came out through a
shattered gateway into the shrubbery which surrounds the base of the castle.

Laying her on the grass, he gently chafed her
hands, eying the pale, pretty face meantime with
the utmost solicitude.

At his first glimpse of it he had started, smiled
and made a gesture of pleasure and surprise,
then gave himself entirely to the task of recov-
ering the poor girl whom he had frightened out
of her senses.

Very soon she looked up with dizzy eyes, and
clasping her hands imploringly, cried, in English,
like a bewildered child, —

"I am lost! Oh, take me to my uncle."

"I will, the moment you can walk. Upon my
soul, I meant to help you when I followed; but
as you did not answer, I fancied it was Lottchen,
the keeper's little girl. Pardon the fright I 've
caused you, and let me take you to your friends."

The true English accent of the words, and the
hearty tone of sincerity in the apology, reassured
Amy at once, and, rising, she said, with a faint
smile and a petulant tone, —

"I was very silly, but my guide ran away, my candle went out, I lost the path, and can speak no German; so I was afraid to answer you at first; and then I lost my wits altogether, for it's rather startling to be clutched in the dark, sir."

"Indeed it is. I was very thoughtless, but now let me atone for it. Where is your uncle, Miss Erskine?" asked the stranger, with respectful earnestness.

"You know my name?" cried Amy in her impulsive way.

"I have that happiness," was the answer, with a smile.

"But I don't know *you,* sir;" and she peered at him, trying to see his face in the darkness, for the copse was thick, and twilight had come on rapidly.

"Not yet; I live in hope. Shall we go? Your uncle will be uneasy."

"Where are we?" asked Amy, glad to move on, for the interview was becoming too personal even for her, and the stranger's manner fluttered her, though she enjoyed the romance of the adventure immensely.

"We are in the park which surrounds the castle. You were near the entrance to it from the vaults when you fainted."

"I wish I had kept on a little longer, and not disgraced myself by such a panic."

"Nay, that is a cruel wish, for then I should have lost the happiness of helping you."

They had been walking side by side, but were forced to pause on reaching a broken flight of steps, for Amy could not see the way before her.

"Let me lead you; it is steep and dark, but better than going a long way round through the dew," he said, offering his hand.

"Must we return by these dreadful vaults?" faltered Amy, shrinking back.

"It is the shortest and safest route, I assure you."

"Are you sure you know the way?"

"Quite sure. I have lived here by the week together. Do you fear to trust me?"

"No; but it is so dark, and everything is so strange to me. Can we get down safely? I see nothing but a black pit."

And Amy still hesitated, with an odd mixture of fear and coquetry.

"I brought you up in safety; shall I take you down again?" asked the stranger, with a smile flickering over his face.

Amy felt rather than saw it, and assuming an air of dignified displeasure, motioned him to proceed, which he did for three steps; then Amy slipped, and gladly caught at the arm extended to save her.

Without a word he took her hand and led her back through the labyrinth she had threaded in her bewilderment. A dim light filled the place, but with unerring steps her guide went on till they emerged into the courtyard.

Major Erskine's voice was audible, giving directions to the keeper, and Helen's figure visible as she groped among the shadows of the ruined chapel for her cousin.

"There are my friends.   Now I am safe. Come and let them thank you," cried Amy, in her frank, childlike warmth of manner.

"I want no thanks — forgive me — adieu," and hastily kissing the little hand that had lain so confidingly in his, the stranger was gone.

Amy rushed at once to Helen, and when the lost lamb had been welcomed, chidden, and exulted over, they drove home, listening to the very brief account which Amy gave of her adventure.

"Naughty little gad-about, how could you go and terrify me so, wandering in vaults with mysterious strangers, like the Countess of Rudolstadt.   You are as wet and dirty as if you had been digging a well, yet you look as if you liked it," said Helen, as she led Amy into their room at the hotel.

"I do," was the decided answer, as the girl pulled a handkerchief off her head, and began to examine the corners of it.   Suddenly she uttered a cry and flew to the light, exclaiming, —

"Nell, Nell, look here!   The same letters, ' S. P.,' the same coat of arms, the same perfume — it was the baron!"

"What? who? are you out of your mind?" said Helen, examining the large, fine cambric handkerchief, with its delicately stamped initials

under the stag's head, and three stars on a heart-
shaped shield. "Where did you get it?" she
added, as she inhaled the soft odor of violets
shaken from its folds.

Amy blushed and answered shyly, "I did n't
tell you all that happened before uncle, but now
I will. My hat was left behind, and when I recovered my wits after my fright, I found this tied
over my head. Oh, Nell, it was very charming
there in that romantic old park, and going
through the vaults with him, and having my
hand kissed at parting. No one ever did that
before, and I like it."

Amy glanced at her hand as she spoke, and
stood staring as if struck dumb, for there on her
forefinger shone a ring she had never seen before.

"Look! look! mine is gone, and this in its
place! Oh, Nell, what shall I do?" she said,
looking half frightened, half pleased.

Helen examined the ring and shook her head,
for it was far more valuable than the little pearl
one which it replaced. Two tiny hands of finest
gold were linked together about a diamond of
great brilliancy; and on the inside appeared
again the initials, "S. P."

"How did it happen?" she asked, rather
sternly.

"Upon my word, I don't know, unless he put
it on while I was stupidly fainting. Rude man,
to take advantage of me so. But, Nell, it is
splendid, and what *shall* I do about it?"

"Tell uncle, find out the man and send back his things. It really is absurd, the manner in which German boys behave;" and Helen frowned, though she was strongly tempted to laugh at the whole thing.

"He was neither a German nor a boy, but an English gentleman, I'm sure," began Amy, rather offended.

"But 'S. P.' is a baron, you know, unless there are two Richmonds in the field," broke in Helen.

"I forgot that; never mind, it deepens the mystery; and after this performance, I'm prepared for any enormity. It's my fate; I submit," said Amy, tragically, as she waved her hand to and fro, pleased with the flash of the ring.

"Amy, I think on the whole I won't speak to uncle. He is quick to take offence, especially where we are concerned. He does n't understand foreign ways, and may get into trouble. We will manage it quietly ourselves."

"How, Nell?"

"Karl is discreet; we will merely say we found these things and wish to discover the owner. He may know this 'S. P.' and, having learned his address, we can send them back. The man will understand; and as we leave to-morrow, we shall be out of the way before he can play any new prank."

"Have in Karl at once, for if I wear this lovely thing long I shall not be able to let it go at all.

How dared the creature take such a liberty!" and Amy pulled off the ring with an expression of great scorn.

"Come into the *salon* and see what Karl says to the matter. Let me speak, or you will say too much. One must be prudent before —"

She was going to say " servants," but checked herself, and substituted " strangers," remembering gratefully how much she owed this man.

Hoffman came, looking pale, and with his hand in a sling, but was as gravely devoted as ever, and listened to Helen's brief story with serious attention.

"I will inquire, mademoiselle, and let you know at once. It is easy to find persons if one has a clue. May I see the handkerchief?"

Helen showed it. He glanced at the initials, and laid it down with a slight smile.

"The coat-of-arms is English, mademoiselle."

"Are you sure?"

"Quite so; I understand heraldry."

"But the initials stand for Sigismund Palsdorf, and we know he is a German baron," broke in Amy, forgetting prudence in eagerness.

"If mademoiselle knows the name and title of this gentleman it will not be hard to find him."

"We only fancy it is the same because of the initials. I dare say it is a mistake, and the man is English. Inquire quietly, Hoffman, if you please, as this ring is of value, and I wish to restore it to its owner," said Helen, rather sharply.

"I shall do so, mademoiselle," and with his gentlemanly bow, the courier left the room.

"Bless me, what's that?" cried Amy, a moment afterward, as a ringing laugh echoed through the corridor, — a laugh so full of hearty and infectious merriment that both girls smiled involuntarily, and Amy peeped out to see who the blithe personage might be.

An old gentleman was entering his room near by, and Karl was just about to descend the stairs. Both looked back at the girlish face peeping at them, but both were quite grave, and the peal of laughter remained a mystery, like all the rest of it.

Late in the evening Hoffman returned to report that a party of young Englishmen had visited the castle that afternoon, and had left by the evening train. One of them had been named Samuel Peters, and he, doubtless, was the owner of the ring.

A humorous expression lurked in the courier's eye as he made his report, and heard Amy exclaim, in a tone of disgust and comical despair, —

"Samuel Peters! That spoils all the romance and dims the beauty of the diamond. To think that a Peters should be the hero to whom I owe my safety, and a Samuel should leave me this token of regard!"

"Hush, Amy," whispered Helen. "Thanks, Hoffman; we must wait now for chance to help us."

IV

"ROOM for one here, sir," said the guard, as the train stopped at Carlsruhe next day, on its way from Heidelberg to Baden.

The major put down his guide-book, Amy opened her eyes, and Helen removed her shawl from the opposite seat, as a young man, wrapped in a cloak, with a green shade over his eyes, and a general air of feebleness, got in and sank back with a sigh of weariness or pain. Evidently an invalid, for his face was thin and pale, his dark hair cropped short, and the ungloved hand attenuated and delicate as a woman's. A sidelong glance from under the deep shade seemed to satisfy him regarding his neighbors, and drawing his cloak about him with a slight shiver, he leaned into the corner and seemed to forget that he was not alone.

Helen and Amy exchanged glances of compassionate interest, for women always pity invalids, especially if young, comely and of the opposite sex. The major took one look, shrugged his shoulders, and returned to his book.

Presently a hollow cough gave Helen a pretext for discovering the nationality of the newcomer.

"Do the open windows inconvenience you, sir?" she asked, in English.

No answer; the question evidently unintelligible.

She repeated it in French, lightly touching his cloak to arrest his attention.

Instantly a smile broke over the handsome mouth, and in the purest French he assured her that the fresh air was most agreeable, and begged pardon for annoying them with his troublesome cough.

"Not an invalid, I hope, sir?" said the major, in his bluff yet kindly voice.

"They tell me I can have no other fate; that my malady is fatal; but I still hope and fight for my life; it is all I have to give my country now."

A stifled sigh and a sad emphasis on the last word roused the sympathy of the girls, the interest of the major.

He took another survey, and said, with a tone of satisfaction, as he marked the martial carriage of the young man, and caught a fiery glance of the half-hidden eyes, —

"You are a soldier, sir?"

"I was; I am nothing now but an exile, for Poland is in chains."

The words "Poland" and "exile" brought up all the pathetic stories of that unhappy coun-

try which the three listeners had ever heard, and
won their interest at once.

"You were in the late revolution, perhaps?"
asked the major, giving the unhappy outbreak
the most respectful name he could use.

"From beginning to end."

"Oh, tell us about it; we felt much sympathy
for you, and longed to have you win," cried Amy,
with such genuine interest and pity in her tone,
it was impossible to resist.

Pressing both hands upon his breast, the young
man bent low, with a flush of feeling on his pale
cheek, and answered eagerly, —

"Ah, you are kind; it is balm to my sore heart
to hear words like these. I thank you, and tell
you what you will. It is but little that I do, yet
I give my life, and die a long death, instead of
a quick, brave one with my comrades."

"You are young to have borne a part in a
revolution, sir," said the major, who pricked up
his ears like an old war-horse at the sound of
battle.

"My friends and myself left the University
at Varsovie, as volunteers; we did our part, and
now all lie in their graves but three."

"You were wounded, it seems?"

"Many times. Exposure, privation, and sorrow will finish what the Russian bullets began.
But it is well. I have no wish to see my country
enslaved, and I can no longer help her."

"Let us hope that a happier future waits for

you both. Poland loves liberty too well, and has suffered too much for it, to be kept long in captivity."

Helen spoke warmly, and the young man listened with a brightening face.

"It is a kind prophecy; I accept it, and take courage. God knows I need it," he added, low to himself.

"Are you bound for Italy?" said the major, in a most un-English fit of curiosity.

"For Geneva first, Italy later, unless Montreaux is mild enough for me to winter in. I go to satisfy my friends, but doubt if it avails."

"Where is Montreaux?" asked Amy.

"Near Clarens, where Rousseau wrote his Heloise, and Vevay, where so many English go to enjoy Chillon. The climate is divine for unfortunates like myself, and life more cheap there than in Italy."

Here the train stopped again, and Hoffman came to ask if the ladies desired anything.

At the sound of his voice the young Pole started, looked up, and exclaimed, with the vivacity of a foreigner, in German, —

"By my life, it is Karl! Behold me, old friend, and satisfy me that it is thyself by a handshake."

"Casimer! What wind blows thee hither, my boy, in such sad plight?" replied Hoffman, grasping the slender hand outstretched to him.

"I fly from an enemy for the first time in my

life, and, like all cowards, shall be conquered in
the end. I wrote thee I was better, but the wound
in the breast reopened, and nothing but a miracle
will save me. I go to Switzerland; and thou?"

"Where my master commands. I serve this
gentleman, now."

"Hard changes for both, but with health thou
art king of circumstances, while I?— Ah well,
the good God knows best. Karl, go thou and
buy me two of those pretty baskets of grapes;
I will please myself by giving them to these pity-
ing angels. Speak they German?"

"One, the elder; but they understand not this
rattle of ours."

Karl disappeared, and Helen, who *had* understood the rapid dialogue, tried to seem as unconscious as Amy.

"Say a friendly word to me at times; I am
so homesick and faint-hearted, my Hoffman.
Thanks; they are almost worthy the lips that
shall taste them."

Taking the two little osier baskets, laden with
yellow and purple clusters, Casimer offered them,
with a charming mixture of timidity and grace,
to the girls, saying, like a grateful boy, —

"You give me kind words and good hopes;
permit that I thank you in this poor way."

"I drink success to Poland," cried Helen, lifting a great, juicy grape to her lips, like a little
purple goblet, hoping to hide her confusion under
a playful air.

The grapes went round, and healths were drunk
with much merriment, for in travelling on the
Continent it is impossible for the gruffest, primmest person to long resist the frank courtesy and
vivacious chat of foreigners.

The major was unusually social and inquisi-
tive, and while the soldiers fought their battles
over again the girls listened and took notes, with
feminine wits on the alert to catch any personal
revelations which might fall from the interesting
stranger. The wrongs and sufferings of Poland
were discussed so eloquently that both young
ladies were moved to declare the most undying
hatred of Russia, Prussia, and Austria, the most
intense sympathy for "poor Pologne." All day
they travelled together, and as Baden-Baden approached, they naturally fell to talking of the
gay place.

"Uncle, I must try my fortune once. I 've
set my heart upon it, and so has Nell. We want
to know how gamblers feel, and to taste the fas-
cination of the game which draws people here
from all parts of Europe," said Amy, in her half-
pleading, half-imperious way.

"You may risk one napoleon each, as I fool-
ishly promised you should, when I little thought
you would ever have an opportunity to remind
me of my promise. It 's not an amusement for
respectable Englishwomen, or men either. You
will agree with me there, monsieur?" and the
major glanced at the Pole, who replied, with his
peculiar smile: —

" Surely, yes. It is great folly and waste of time and money; yet I have known one man who found some good in it, or, rather, brought good out of it. I have a friend who has a mania for giving. His own fortune was spent in helping needy students at the University, and poor professors. This displeased his father, and he refused supplies, except enough for his simple personal wants. Sigismund chafed at this, and being skilful at all games, as a gentleman may be in the way of amusement, he resolved to play with those whose money was wasted on frivolities, and give his winnings to his band of paupers."

" How did it succeed, this odd fancy? " asked Helen, with an interested face, while Amy pinched her arm at the word " Sigismund."

" Excellently. My friend won often, and as his purpose became known it caused no unkind feeling, this unusual success, for fortune seemed to favor his kind object."

" Wrong, nevertheless, to do evil that good may come of it," said the major, morally.

" It may be so; but it is not for me to censure my benefactor. He has done much for my countrymen and myself, and is so truly noble I can see no fault in him."

" What an odd name! Sigismund is German, is it not? " asked Amy, in the most artless tone of interest.

" Yes, mademoiselle, and Palsdorf is a true German; much courage, strength and intellect, with the gayety and simplicity of a boy. He hates slavery of all kinds, and will be free at all costs. He is a good son, but his father is tyrannical, and asks too much. Sigismund will not submit to sell himself, and so is in disgrace for a time."

"Palsdorf! — was not that the name of the count or baron we heard them talking of at Coblentz?" said Helen to Amy, with a well-feigned air of uncertainty.

"Yes; I heard something of a duel and a broken betrothal, I think. The people seemed to consider the baron a wild young man, so it could not have been your friend, sir," was Amy's demure reply, glancing at Helen with mirthful eyes, as if to say, "How our baron haunts us!"

"It is the same, doubtless. Many consider him wild, because he is original, and dares act for himself. As it is well known, I may tell you the truth of the duel and the betrothal, if you care to hear a little romance."

Casimer looked eager to defend his friend, and as the girls were longing to hear the romance, permission was given.

"In Germany, you know, the young people are often betrothed in childhood by the parents, and sometimes never meet till they are grown. Usually all goes well; but not always, for love cannot come at command. Sigismund was plighted, when a boy of fifteen, to his young cousin, and then sent away to the University till of age. On returning, he was to travel a year or two, and then marry. He gladly went away, and with increasing disquiet saw the time draw near when he must keep his troth-plight."

" Hum! loved some one else. Very unfortunate to be sure," said the major with a sigh.

" Not so; he only loved his liberty, and pretty Minna was less dear than a life of perfect freedom. He went back at the appointed time, saw his cousin, tried to do his duty and love her; found it impossible, and, discovering that Minna loved another, vowed he would never make her unhappiness as well as his own. The old baron stormed, but the young one was firm, and would not listen to a marriage without love; but pleaded for Minna, wished his rival success, and set out again on his travels."

" And the duel?" asked the major, who took less interest in love than war.

" That was as characteristic as the other act. A son of one high in office at Berlin circulated false reports of the cause of Palsdorf's refusal of the alliance — reports injurious to Minna. Sigismund settled the matter in the most effectual manner, by challenging and wounding the man. But for court influence it would have gone hardly with my friend. The storm, however, has blown over; Minna will be happy with her lover, and Sigismund with his liberty, till he tires of it."

" Is he handsome, this hero of yours?" said Amy, feeling the ring under her glove, for in spite of Helen's advice, she insisted on wearing it, that it might be at hand to return at any moment, should chance again bring the baron in their way.

"A true German of the old type; blond and blue-eyed, tall and strong. My hero in good truth — brave and loyal, tender and true," was the enthusiastic answer.

"I hate fair men," pouted Amy, under her breath, as the major asked some question about hotels.

"Take a new hero, then; nothing can be more romantic than that," whispered Helen, glancing at the pale, dark-haired figure wrapped in the military cloak opposite.

"I will, and leave the baron to you;" said Amy, with a stifled laugh.

"Hush! Here are Baden and Karl," replied Helen, thankful for the interruption.

All was bustle in a moment, and taking leave of them with an air of reluctance, the Pole walked away, leaving Amy looking after him wistfully, quite unconscious that she stood in everybody's way, and that her uncle was beckoning impatiently from the carriage door.

"Poor boy! I wish he had some one to take care of him," she sighed, half aloud.

"Mademoiselle, the major waits;" and Karl came up, hat in hand, just in time to hear her and glance after Casimer, with an odd expression.

V

LUDMILLA

" **I** WONDER what that young man's name was. Did he mention it, Helen?" said the major, pausing in his march up and down the room, as if the question was suggested by the sight of the little baskets, which the girls had kept.

" No, uncle; but you can easily ask Hoffman," replied Helen.

" By the way, Karl, who was the Polish gentleman who came on with us?" asked the major a moment afterward, as the courier came in with newspapers.

" Casimer Teblinski, sir."

" A baron?" asked Amy, who was decidedly a young lady of one idea just then.

" No, mademoiselle, but of a noble family, as the ' ski ' denotes, for that is to Polish and Russian names what ' von ' is to German and ' de ' to French."

" I was rather interested in him. Where did you pick him up, Hoffman?" said the major.

" In Paris, where he was with fellow-exiles."

" He is what he seems, is he? — no impostor, or anything of that sort? One is often deceived, you know."

"On my honor, sir, he is a gentleman, and as brave as he is accomplished and excellent."

"Will he die?" asked Amy, pathetically.

"With care he would recover, I think; but there is no one to nurse him, so the poor lad must take his chance and trust in heaven for help."

"How sad! I wish we were going his way, so that we might do something for him — at least give him the society of his friend."

Helen glanced at Hoffman, feeling that if he were not already engaged by them, he would devote himself to the invalid without any thought of payment.

"Perhaps we are. You want to see the Lake of Geneva, Chillon, and that neighborhood. Why not go now, instead of later?"

"Will you, uncle? That's capital! We need say nothing, but go on and help the poor boy, if we can."

Helen spoke like a matron of forty, and looked as full of maternal kindness as if the Pole were not out of his teens.

The courier bowed, the major laughed behind his paper, and Amy gave a sentimental sigh to the memory of the baron, in whom her interest was failing.

They only caught a glimpse of the Pole that evening at the Kursaal, but next morning they met, and he was invited to join their party for a little expedition.

The major was in fine spirits, and Helen assumed her maternal air toward both invalids, for the sound of that hollow cough always brought a shadow over her face, recalling the brother she had lost.

Amy was particularly merry and charming, and kept the whole party laughing at her comical efforts to learn Polish and teach English as they drove up the mountainside to the old Schloss.

"I'm not equal to mounting all those steps for a view I've seen a dozen times; but pray take care of the child, Nell, or she'll get lost again, as at Heidelberg," said the major, when they had roamed about the lower part of the place; for a cool seat in the courtyard and a glass of beer were more tempting than turrets and prospects to the stout gentleman.

"She shall not be lost; I am her body-guard. It is steep — permit that I lead you, mademoiselle;" Casimer offered his hand to Amy, and they began their winding way. As she took the hand, the girl blushed and half smiled, remembering the vaults and the baron.

"I like this better," she said to herself, as they climbed step by step, often pausing to rest in the embrasures of the loopholes, where the sun glanced in, the balmy wind blew, and vines peeped from without, making a pretty picture of the girl, as she sat with rosy color on her usually pale cheeks, brown curls fluttering about her forehead, laughing lips, and bright eyes full of pleasant changes. Leaning opposite in the narrow stairway, Casimer had time to study the little tableau in many lights, and in spite of the dark glasses, to convey warm glances of admiration, of which, however, the young coquette seemed utterly unconscious.

Helen came leisurely after, and Hoffman followed with a telescope, wishing, as he went, that his countrywomen possessed such dainty feet as those going on before him, for which masculine iniquity he will be pardoned by all who have seen the foot of a German Fraulein.

It was worth the long ascent, that wide-spread landscape basking in the August glow.

Sitting on a fallen block of stone, while Casimer held a sun-umbrella over her, Amy had raptures at her ease; while Helen sketched and asked questions of Hoffman, who stood beside her, watching her progress with interest. Once when, after repeated efforts to catch a curious effect of light and shade, she uttered an impatient little exclamation, Karl made a gesture as if to take the pencil and show her, but seemed to recollect himself and drew back with a hasty " Pardon, mademoiselle." Helen glanced up and saw the expression of his face, which plainly betrayed that for a moment the gentleman had forgotten he was a courier. She was glad of it, for it was a daily trial to her to order this man about; and following the womanly impulse, she smiled and offered the pencil, saying simply, —

"I felt sure you understood it; please show me."

He did so, and a few masterly strokes gave the sketch what it needed. As he bent near her to do this, Helen stole a glance at the grave, dark face, and suddenly a disturbed look dawned in the eyes fixed on the glossy black locks pushed off the courier's forehead, for he had removed his hat when she spoke to him. He seemed to feel that something was amiss, shot a quick glance at her, returned the pencil and rose erect, with an almost defiant air, yet something of shame in his eye, as his lips moved as if to speak impetuously. But not a word did he utter, for Helen touched her forehead significantly, and said in a low tone, —

"I am an artist; let me recommend Vandyke brown, which is *not* affected by heat."

Hoffman looked over his shoulder at the other pair, but Amy was making an ivy wreath for her hat, and the Pole pulling sprays for the absorbing work. Speaking rapidly, Karl said, with a peculiar blending of merriment, humility, and anxiety in his tone, —

"Mademoiselle, you are quick to discover my disguise; will you also be kind in concealing? I have enemies as well as friends, whom I desire to escape; I would earn my bread unknown; Monsieur le Major keeps my foolish secret; may I hope for equal goodness from yourself?"

"You may, I do not forget that I owe my life

to you, nor that you are a gentleman. Trust me,
I never will betray you."

"Thanks, thanks! there will come a time
when I may confess the truth and be myself, but
not yet," and his regretful tone was emphasized
by an impatient gesture, as if concealment was
irksome.

"Nell, come down to lunch; uncle is signal-
ling as if he'd gone mad. No, monsieur, it is
quite impossible; you cannot reach the harebells
without risking too much; come away and forget that I wanted them."

Amy led the way, and all went down more
quietly than they came up, especially Helen and
Hoffman. An excellent lunch waited on one of
the tables in front of the old gateway, and having done justice to it, the major made himself
comfortable with a cigar, bidding the girls keep
near, for they must be off in half an hour. Hoffman went to see to the horses, Casimer strolled
away with him, and the young ladies went to
gather wild flowers at the foot of the tower.

"Not a harebell here; isn't it provoking,
when they grow in tufts up there, where one
can't reach them. Mercy, what's that? Run,
Nell, the old wall is coming down!"

Both had been grubbing in a damp nook, where
ferns and mosses grew luxuriantly; the fall of
a bit of stone and a rending sound above made
them fly back to the path and look up.

Amy covered her eyes, and Helen grew pale,

for part way down the crumbling tower, clinging like a bird to the thick ivy stems, hung Casimer, coolly gathering harebells from the clefts
of the wall.

"Hush; don't cry out or speak; it may startle
him. Crazy boy! Let us see what he will do,"
whispered Helen.

"He can't go back, the vines are so torn and
weak; and how will he get down the lower wall?
for you see the ivy grows up from that ledge,
and there is nothing below. How could he do
it? I was only joking when I lamented that
there were no knights now, ready to leap into
a lion's den for a lady's glove," returned Amy,
half angry.

In breathless silence they watched the climber
till his cap was full of flowers, and taking it
between his teeth, he rapidly swung down to the
wide ledge, from which there appeared to be no
way of escape but a reckless leap of many feet on
to the turf below.

The girls stood in the shadow of an old gateway, unperceived, and waited anxiously what
should follow.

Lightly folding and fastening the cap together,
he dropped it down, and, leaning forward, tried
to catch the top of a young birch rustling close
by the wall. Twice he missed it; the first time
he frowned, but the second he uttered an em-
phatic, "Deuce take it!"

Helen and Amy looked at each other with a
mutual smile and exclamation, —

"He knows some English, then!"

There was time for no more — a violent rustle, a boyish laugh, and down swung the slender tree, with the young man clinging to the top.

As he landed safely, Helen cried, "Bravo!" and Amy rushed out, exclaiming reproachfully, yet admiringly, —

"How could you do it and frighten us so? I shall never express a wish before you again, for if I wanted the moon you'd rashly try to get it, I know."

"*Certainement,* mademoiselle," was the smiling reply. Casimer presented the flowers, as if the exploit was a mere trifle.

"Now I shall go and press them at once in uncle's guide-book. Come and help me, else you will be in mischief again." And Amy led the way to the major with her flowers and their giver.

Helen roamed into one of the ruined courts for a last look at a fountain which pleased her eye. A sort of cloister ran round the court, open on both sides, and standing in one of these arched nooks, she saw Hoffman and a young girl talking animatedly. The girl was pretty, well dressed, and seemed refusing something for which the other pleaded eagerly. His arm was about her, and she leaned affectionately upon him, with a white hand now and then caressing his face, which was full of sparkle and vivacity now. They seemed about to part as Helen looked, for the maiden standing on tiptoe, laughingly offered her blooming cheek, and as Karl kissed it warmly, he said in German, so audibly Helen heard every word, —

" Farewell, my Ludmilla. Keep silent and I shall soon be with you. Embrace the little one, and do not let him forget me."

Both left the place as they spoke, each going a different way, and Helen slowly returned to her party, saying to herself in a troubled tone, —

" ' Ludmilla ' and ' the little one ' are his wife and child, doubtless. I wonder if uncle knows that."

When Hoffman next appeared she could not resist looking at him; but the accustomed gravity was resumed, and nothing remained of the glow and brightness he had worn when with Ludmilla in the cloister.

VI

CHATEAU DE LA TOUR

HELEN looked serious and Amy indignant when their uncle joined them, ready to set out by the afternoon train, all having dined and rested after the morning's excursion.

"Well, little girls, what's the matter now?" he asked, paternally, for the excellent man adored his nieces.

"Helen says it's not best to go on with the Pole, and is perfectly nonsensical, uncle," began Amy, petulantly, and not very coherently.

"Better be silly now than sorry by and by. I only suggested that, being interesting, and Amy romantic, she might find this young man too charming, if we see too much of him," said Helen.

"Bless my soul, what an idea!" cried the major. "Why, Nell, he's an invalid, a Catholic, and a foreigner, any one of which objections are enough to settle that matter. Little Amy isn't so foolish as to be in danger of losing her heart to a person so entirely out of the question as this poor lad, is she?"

" Of course not. *You* do me justice, uncle.
Nell thinks she may pity and pet any one she likes
because she is five years older than I, and entirely forgets that she is a great deal more attractive than a feeble thing like me. I should
as soon think of losing my heart to Hoffman as
to the Pole, even if he was n't what he is. One
may surely be kind to a dying man, without being
accused of coquetry;" and Amy sobbed in the
most heart-rending manner.

Helen comforted her by withdrawing all objections, and promising to leave the matter in
the major's hands. But she shook her head privately when she saw the ill-disguised eagerness
with which her cousin glanced up and down the
platform after they were in the train, and she
whispered to her uncle, unobserved, —

" Leave future meetings to chance, and don't
ask the Pole in, if you can help it."

" Nonsense, my dear. You are as particular
as your aunt. The lad amuses me, and you can't
deny you like to nurse sick heroes," was all the
answer she got, as the major, with true masculine
perversity, put his head out of the window and
hailed Casimer as he was passing with a bow.

" Here, Teblinski, my good fellow, don't
desert us. We 've always a spare seat for you,
if you have n't pleasanter quarters."

With a flush of pleasure the young man came
up, but hesitated to accept the invitation till
Helen seconded it with a smile of welcome.

Amy was in an injured mood, and, shrouded in a great blue veil, pensively reclined in her corner as if indifferent to everything about her. But soon the cloud passed, and she emerged in a radiant state of good humor, which lasted unbroken until the journey ended.

For two days they went on together, a very happy party, for the major called in Hoffman to see his friend and describe the places through which they passed. An arrangement very agreeable to all, as Karl was a favorite, and every one missed him when away.

At Lausanne they waited while he crossed the lake to secure rooms at Vevay. On his return he reported that all the hotels and *pensions* were full, but that at La Tour he had secured rooms for a few weeks in a quaint old chateau on the banks of the lake.

"Count Severin is absent in Egypt, and the housekeeper has permission to let the apartments to transient visitors. The suite of rooms I speak of were engaged to a party who are detained by sickness — they are cheap, pleasant, and comfortable. A *salon* and four bed-rooms. I engaged them all, thinking that Teblinski might like a room there till he finds lodgings at Montreaux. We can enter at once, and I am sure the ladies will approve of the picturesque place."

"Well done, Hoffman; off we go without delay, for I really long to rest my old bones in something like a home, after this long trip," said

the major, who always kept his little troop in
light marching order.

The sail across that loveliest of lakes prepared
the new-comers to be charmed with all they saw;
and when, entering by the old stone gate, they
were led into a large saloon, quaintly furnished
and opening into a terrace-garden overhanging
the water, with Chillon and the Alps in sight,
Amy declared nothing could be more perfect,
and Helen's face proved her satisfaction.

An English widow and two quiet old German
professors on a vacation were the only inmates
besides themselves and the buxom Swiss housekeeper and her maids.

It was late when our party arrived, and there
was only time for a hasty survey of their rooms
and a stroll in the garden before dinner.

The great chamber, with its shadowy bed,
dark mirrors, ghostly wainscot-doors and narrow
windows, had not been brightened for a long
time by such a charming little apparition as Amy
when she shook out her airy muslins, smoothed
her curls, and assumed all manner of distracting
devices for the captivation of mankind. Even
Helen, though not much given to personal vanity, found herself putting flowers in her hair, and
studying the effect of bracelets on her handsome
arms, as if there was some especial need of looking her best on this occasion.

Both were certainly great ornaments to the
drawing-room that evening, as the old professors

agreed while they sat blinking at them, like a
pair of benign owls. Casimer surprised them by
his skill in music, for, though forbidden to sing
on account of his weak lungs, he played as if
inspired. Amy hovered about him like a moth;
the major cultivated the acquaintance of the
plump widow; and Helen stood at the window,
enjoying the lovely night and music, till something happened which destroyed her pleasure in
both.

The window was open, and, leaning from it,
she was watching the lake, when the sound of a
heavy sigh caught her ear. There was no moon,
but through the starlight she saw a man's figure
among the shrubs below, sitting with bent head
and hidden face in the forlorn attitude of one
shut out from the music, light, and gayety that
reigned within.

" It is Karl," she thought, and was about to
speak, when, as if startled by some sound she
did not hear, he rose and vanished in the gloom
of the garden.

" Poor man! he thought of his wife and child,
perhaps, sitting here alone while all the rest make
merry, with no care for him. Uncle must see to
this; " and Helen fell into a reverie till Amy
came to propose retiring.

" I meant to have seen where all these doors
led, but was so busy dressing I had no time, so
must leave it for my amusement to-morrow.
Uncle says it 's a very Radcliffian place. How

like an angel that man did play!" chattered
Amy, and lulled herself to sleep by humming the
last air Casimer had given them.

Helen could not sleep, for the lonely figure
in the garden haunted her, and she wearied herself with conjectures about Hoffman and his
mystery. Hour after hour rung from the
cuckoo-clock in the hall, but still she lay awake,
watching the curious shadows in the room, and
exciting herself with recalling the tales of German goblins with which the courier had amused
them the day before.

"It is close and musty here, with all this old
tapestry and stuff about; I'll open the other
window," she thought; and, noiselessly slipping
from Amy's side, she threw on wrapper and slippers, lighted her candle and tried to unbolt the
tall, diamond-paned lattice. It was rusty and
would not yield, and, giving it up, she glanced
about to see whence air could be admitted. There
were four doors in the room, all low and arched,
with clumsy locks and heavy handles. One
opened into a closet, one into the passage; the
third was locked, but the fourth opened easily,
and, lifting her light, she peeped into a small
octagon room, full of all manner of curiosities.
What they were she had no time to see, for her
startled eyes were riveted on an object that turned
her faint and cold with terror.

A heavy table stood in the middle of the room,
and seated at it, with some kind of weapon before

him, was a man who looked over his shoulder, with a ghastly face half hidden by hair and beard, and fierce black eyes as full of malignant menace as was the clinched hand holding the pistol. One instant Helen looked, the next flung to the door, bolted it and dropped into a chair, trembling in every limb. The noise did not wake Amy, and a moment's thought showed Helen the wisdom of keeping her in ignorance of this affair. She knew the major was close by, and possessing much courage, she resolved to wait a little before rousing the house.

Hardly had she collected herself, when steps were heard moving softly in the octagon room. Her light had gone out as she closed the door, and sitting close by in the dark, she heard the sound of some one breathing as he listened at the key-hole. Then a careful hand tried the door, so noiselessly that no sleeper would have been awakened; and as if to guard against a second surprise, the unknown person drew two bolts across the door and stole away.

"Safe for a time; but I'll not pass another night under this roof, unless this is satisfactorily cleared up," thought Helen, now feeling more angry than frightened.

The last hour that struck was three, and soon the summer dawn reddened the sky. Dressing herself, Helen sat by Amy, a sleepless guard, till she woke, smiling and rosy as a child. Saying nothing of her last night's alarm, Helen went down to breakfast a little paler than usual, but otherwise unchanged. The major never liked to be disturbed till he had broken his fast, and the moment they rose from the table he exclaimed, —

" Now, girls, come and see the mysteries of Udolpho."

" I 'll say nothing, yet," thought Helen, feeling braver by daylight, yet troubled by her secret, for Hoffman might be a traitor, and this charming chateau a den of thieves. Such things had been, and she was in a mood to believe anything.

The upper story was a perfect museum of antique relics, very entertaining to examine. Having finished these, Hoffman, who acted as guide, led them into a little gloomy room containing a straw pallet, a stone table with a loaf and pitcher on it, and, kneeling before a crucifix, where the light from a single slit in the wall fell on him, was the figure of a monk. The waxen mask was life-like, the attitude effective, and the cell excellently arranged. Amy cried out when she first saw it, but a second glance reassured her, and she patted the bald head approvingly, as Karl explained, —

" Count Severin is an antiquarian, and amuses himself with things of this sort. In old times there really was a hermit here, and this is his effigy. Come down these narrow stairs, if you please, and see the rest of the mummery."

Down they went, and the instant Helen looked about her, she burst into a hysterical laugh, for there sat her ruffian, exactly as she saw him, glaring over his shoulder with threatening eyes, and one hand on the pistol. They all looked at her, for she was pale, and her merriment unnatural; so, feeling she had excited curiosity, she gratified it by narrating her night's adventure. Hoffman looked much concerned.

" Pardon, mademoiselle, the door should have been bolted on this side. It usually is, but that room being unused, it was forgotten. I remembered it, and having risen early, crept up to make sure that you did not come upon this ugly thing unexpectedly. But I was too late, it seems; you have suffered, to my sorrow."

" Dear Nell, and that was why I found you so pale and cold and quiet, sitting by me when I woke, guarding me faithfully as you promised you would. How brave and kind you were! "

" Villain! I should much like to fire your own pistols at you for this prank of yours."

And Casimer laughingly filliped the image on its absurdly aquiline nose.

" What in the name of common sense is this goblin here for? " demanded the major, testily.

" There is a legend that once the owner of the chateau amused himself by decoying travellers here, putting them to sleep in that room, and by various devices alluring them thither. Here, one step beyond the threshold of the door, was a trap, down which the unfortunates were precipitated to the dungeon at the bottom of the tower, there to die and be cast into the lake through a water-gate, still to be seen. Severin keeps this flattering likeness of the rascal, as he does the monk above, to amuse visitors by daylight, not at night, mademoiselle."

And Hoffman looked wrathfully at the image, as if he would much enjoy sending it down the trap.

"How ridiculous! I shall not go about this place alone, for fear of lighting upon some horror of this sort. I've had enough; come away into the garden; it's full of roses, and we may have as many as we like."

As she spoke Amy involuntarily put out her hand for Casimer to lead her down the steep stone steps, and he pressed the little hand with a tender look which caused it to be hastily withdrawn.

"Here are your roses. Pretty flower; I know its meaning in English, for it is the same with us. To give a bud to a lady is to confess the beginning of love, a half open one tells of its growth, and a full-blown one is to declare one's passion. Do you have that custom in your land, mademoiselle?"

He had gathered the three as he spoke, and held the bud separately while looking at his companion wistfully.

"No, we are not poetical, like your people, but it is a pretty fancy," and Amy settled her bouquet with an absorbed expression, though inwardly wondering what he would do with his flowers.

He stood silent a moment, with a sudden flush sweeping across his face, then flung all three into the lake with a gesture that made the girl start, and muttered between his teeth:

"No, no; for me it is too late."

She affected not to hear, but making up a second bouquet, she gave it to him, with no touch of coquetry in compassionate eyes or gentle voice.

"Make your room bright with these. When one is ill nothing is so cheering as the sight of flowers."

Meantime the others had descended and gone their separate ways.

As Karl crossed the courtyard a little child ran to meet him with outstretched arms and a shout of satisfaction. He caught it up and carried it away on his shoulder, like one used to caress and be caressed by children.

Helen, waiting at the door of the tower while the major dusted his coat, saw this, and said, suddenly, directing his attention to man and child, —

"He seems fond of little people. I wonder if he has any of his own."

"Hoffman? No, my dear; he's not married; I asked him that when I engaged him."

"And he said he was not?"

"Yes; he's not more than five or six-and-twenty, and fond of a wandering life, so what

should he want of a wife and a flock of bant-
lings? "

" He seems sad and sober sometimes, and I
fancied he might have some domestic trouble to
harass him. Don't you think there is something
peculiar about him? " asked Helen, remembering Hoffman's hint that her uncle knew his wish
to travel incognito, and wondering if he would
throw any light upon the matter. But the major's face was impenetrable and his answer unsatisfactory.

" Well, I don't know. Every one has some
worry or other, and as for being peculiar, all
foreigners seem more or less so to us, they are
so unreserved and demonstrative. I like Hoffman more and more every day, and shall be sorry
when I part with him."

" Ludmilla is his sister, then, or he did n't tell
uncle the truth. It is no concern of mine; but
I wish I knew," thought Helen anxiously, and
then wondered why she should care.

A feeling of distrust had taken possession of
her and she determined to be on the watch, for
the unsuspicious major would be easily duped,
and Helen trusted more to her own quick and
keen eye than to his experience. She tried to
show nothing of the change in her manner; but
Hoffman perceived it, and bore it with a proud
patience which often touched her heart, but never
altered her purpose.

VII

AT FAULT

FOUR weeks went by so rapidly that every one refused to believe it when the major stated the fact at the breakfast-table, for all had enjoyed themselves so heartily that they had been unconscious of the lapse of time.

"You are not going away, uncle?" cried Amy, with a panic-stricken look.

"Next week, my dear; we must be off, for we 've much to do yet, and I promised mamma to bring you back by the end of October."

"Never mind Paris and the rest of it; this is pleasanter. I 'd rather stay here — "

There Amy checked herself and tried to hide her face behind her coffee-cup, for Casimer looked up in a way that made her heart flutter and her cheeks burn.

"Sorry for it, Amy; but go we must, so enjoy your last week with all your might, and come again next year."

"It will never be again what it is now," sighed Amy; and Casimer echoed the words "next

year," as if sadly wondering if the present year
would not be his last.

Helen rose silently and went into the garden,
for of late she had fallen into the way of reading
and working in the little pavilion which stood in
an angle of the wall, overlooking lake and mountains.

A seat at the opposite end of the walk was
Amy's haunt, for she liked the sun, and within
a week or two something like constraint had ex-
isted between the cousins. Each seemed happier
apart, and each was intent on her own affairs.
Helen watched over Amy's health, but no longer
offered advice or asked confidence. She often
looked anxious, and once or twice urged the
major to go, as if conscious of some danger.

But the worthy man seemed to have been bewitched as well as the young folks, and was quite
happy sitting by the plump, placid widow, or
leisurely walking with her to the chapel on the
hillside.

All seemed waiting for something to break up
the party, and no one had the courage to do it.
The major's decision took every one by surprise,
and Amy and Casimer looked as if they had
fallen from the clouds.

The persistency with which the English lessons had gone on was amazing, for Amy usually
tired of everything in a day or two. Now, however, she was a devoted teacher, and her pupil
did her great credit by the rapidity with which

he caught the language. It looked like pleasant play, sitting among the roses day after day, Amy affecting to embroider while she taught, Casimer marching to and fro on the wide, low wall, below which lay the lake, while he learned his lesson; then standing before her to recite, or lounging on the turf in frequent fits of idleness, both talking and laughing a great deal, and generally forgetting everything but the pleasure of being together. They wrote little notes as exercises — Amy in French, Casimer in English, and each corrected the other's.

All very well for a time; but as the notes increased the corrections decreased, and at last nothing was said of ungrammatical French or comical English and the little notes were exchanged in silence.

As Amy took her place that day she looked forlorn, and when her pupil came her only welcome was a reproachful —

" You are very late, sir."

" It is fifteen of minutes yet to ten clocks," was Casimer's reply, in his best English.

" Ten o'clock, and leave out ' of ' before minutes. How many times must I tell you that? " said Amy, severely, to cover her first mistake.

" Ah, not many times; soon all goes to finish, and I have none person to make this charming English go in my so stupide head."

" What will you do then? "

" I *jeter* myself into the lake."

"Don't be foolish; I'm dull to-day, and want to be cheered up; suicide isn't a pleasant subject."

"Good! See here, then — a little *plaisanterie* — what you call joke. Can you will to see it?" and he laid a little pink cocked-hat note on her lap, looking like a mischievous boy as he did so.

"'Mon Casimer Teblinski;' I see no joke;" and Amy was about to tear it up, when he caught it from destruction, and holding it out of reach, said, laughing wickedly, —

"The 'mon' is one abbreviation of 'monsieur,' but you put no little — how do you say? — period at the end of him; it goes now in English — '*My* Casimer Teblinski,' and that is of the most charming address."

Amy colored, but had her return shot ready.

"Don't exult; that was only an oversight, not a deliberate deception like that you put upon me. It was very wrong and rude, and I shall not forgive it."

"*Mon Dieu!* where have I gone in sinning! I am a *polisson*, as I say each day, but not a villain, I swear to you. Say to me that which I have made of wrong, and I will do penance."

"You told me '*Ma drogha*' was the Polish for 'My pupil,' and let me call you so a long time; I am wiser now," replied Amy, with great dignity.

"Who has said stupidities to you, that you doubt me?" and Casimer assumed an injured look, though his eyes danced with merriment.

"I heard Hoffman singing a Polish song to little Roserl, the burden of which was, '*Ma drogha, Ma drogha,*' and when I asked him to translate it, those two words meant, 'My darling.' How dare you, ungrateful creature that you are!"

As Amy spoke, half-confusedly, half-angrily, Casimer went down upon his knees, with folded hands and penitent face, exclaiming, in good English, —

"Be merciful to me a sinner. I was tempted, and I could not resist."

"Get up this instant, and stop laughing. Say your lesson, for this will be your last," was the stern reply, though Amy's face dimpled all over with suppressed merriment.

He rose meekly, but made such sad work with the verb "To love," that his teacher was glad to put an end to it, by proposing to read her French to him. It was "Thaddeus of Warsaw," a musty little translation which she had found in the house, and begun for her own amusement. Casimer read a little, seemed interested, and suggested that they read it together, so that he might correct her accent. Amy agreed, and they were in the heart of the sentimental romance, finding it more interesting than most modern readers, for the girl had an improved Thaddeus before her, and the Pole a fairer, kinder Mary Beaufort.

Dangerous times for both, but therein lay the charm; for, though Amy said to herself each

night, " Sick, Catholic, and a foreigner, — it can
never be," yet each morning she felt, with increasing force, how blank her day would be without
him. And Casimer, honorably restraining every
word of love, yet looked volumes, and in spite
of the glasses, the girl felt the eloquence of the
fine eyes they could not entirely conceal.

To-day, as she read, he listened with his head
leaning on his hand, and though she never had
read worse, he made no correction, but sat so
motionless, she fancied at last that he had actually fallen asleep. Thinking to rouse him, she
said, in French, —

" Poor Thaddeus! don't you pity him? —
alone, poor, sick, and afraid to own his love."

" No, I hate him, the absurd imbecile, with
his fine boots and plumes, and tragedy airs. He
was not to be pitied, for he recovered health, he
found a fortune, he won his Marie. His sufferings were nothing; there was no fatal blight on
him, and he had time and power to conquer his
misfortunes, while I — "

Casimer spoke with sudden passion, and pausing abruptly, turned his face away, as if to hide
some emotion he was too proud to show.

Amy's heart ached, and her eyes filled, but her
voice was sweet and steady, as she said, putting
by the book, like one weary of it, —

" Are you suffering to-day? Can we do anything for you? Please let us, if we may."

" You give me all I can receive; no one can

help my pain yet; but a time will come when
something may be done for me; then I will
speak." And, to her great surprise, he rose and
left her, without another word.

She saw him no more till evening; then he
looked excited, played stormily, and would sing
in defiance of danger. The trouble in Amy's face
seemed reflected in Helen's, though not a word
had passed between them. She kept her eye on
Casimer, with an intentness that worried Amy,
and even when he was at the instrument Helen
stood near him, as if fascinated, watching the
slender hands chase one another up and down
the keys with untiring strength and skill.

Suddenly she left the room and did not return. Amy was so nervous by that time, she
could restrain herself no longer, and slipping out,
found her cousin in their chamber, poring over
a glove.

"Oh, Nell, what is it? You are so odd to-
night I can't understand you. The music ex-
cites me, and I 'm miserable, and I want to know
what has happened," she said, tearfully.

" I 've found him! " whispered Helen, eagerly,
holding up the glove with a gesture of triumph.

" Who? " asked Amy, blinded by her tears.

" The baron."

" Where? — when? " cried the girl, amazed.

" Here, and now."

" Don't take my breath away; tell me quick,
or I shall get hysterical."

"Casimer is Sigismund Palsdorf, and no more a Pole than I am," was Helen's answer.

Amy dropped in a heap on the floor, not fainting, but so amazed she had neither strength nor breath left. Sitting by her, Helen rapidly went on, —

"I had a feeling as if something was wrong, and began to watch. The feeling grew, but I discovered nothing till to-day. It will make you laugh, it was so unromantic. As I looked over uncle's things when the laundress brought them this afternoon, I found a collar that was not his. It was marked 'S. P.,' and I at once felt a great desire to know who owned it. The woman was waiting for her money, and I asked her. 'Monsieur Pologne,' she said, for his name is too much for her. She took it into his room, and that was the end of it."

"But it may be another name; the initials only a coincidence," faltered Amy, looking frightened.

"No, dear, it isn't; there is more to come. Little Roserl came crying through the hall an hour ago, and I asked what the trouble was. She showed me a prettily-bound prayer-book which she had taken from the Pole's room to play with, and had been ordered by her mother to carry back. I looked into it; no name, but the same coat-of-arms as the glove and the handkerchief. To-night as he played I examined his hands; they are peculiar, and some of the pecu-

liarities have left traces on the glove. I am sure
it is he, for on looking back many things confirm
the idea. He says he is a *polisson,* a rogue, fond
of jokes, and clever at playing them. The Germans are famous for masquerading and practical
jokes; this is one, I am sure, and uncle will be
terribly angry if he discovers it."

"But why all this concealment?" cried Amy.
"Why play jokes on us? You look so worried
I know you have not told me all you know or
fear."

"I confess I do fear that these men are political plotters as well as exiles. There are many
such, and they make tools of rich and ignorant
foreigners to further their ends. Uncle is rich,
generous, and unsuspicious; and I fear that
while apparently serving and enjoying us they
are using him."

"Heavens, it may be! and that would account
for the change we see in him. I thought he was
in love with the widow, but that may be only
a cloak to hide darker designs. Karl brought
us here, and I dare say it is a den of conspira-
tors!" cried Amy, feeling as if she were getting
more of an adventure than she had bargained for.

"Don't be alarmed! I am on the watch, and
mean to demand an explanation from uncle, or
take you away on my own responsibility, if I
can."

Here a maid tapped to say that tea was served.

"We must go down, or some one will suspect

trouble. Plead headache to excuse your paleness, and I 'll keep people away. We will manage the affair and be off as soon as possible," said Helen, as Amy followed her, too bewildered to answer.

Casimer was not in the room, the major and Mrs. Cumberland were sipping tea side by side, and the professors roaming vaguely about. To leave Amy in peace, Helen engaged them both in a lively chat, and her cousin sat by the window trying to collect her thoughts. Some one was pacing up and down the garden, hatless, in the dew.

Amy forgot everything but the danger of such exposure to her reckless friend. His cloak and hat lay on a chair; she caught them up and glided unperceived from the long window.

" You are so imprudent I fear for you, and bring your things," said a timid voice, as the little white figure approached the tall black one, striding down the path tempestuously.

" You to think of me, forgetful of yourself! Little angel of kindness, why do you take such care of me? " cried Casimer, eagerly taking not only the cloak, but the hands that held it.

" I pitied you because you were ill and lonely. You do not deserve my pity, but I forgive that, and would not see you suffer," was the reproachful answer, as Amy turned away.

But he held her fast, saying earnestly, —

" What have I done? You are angry. Tell me my fault and I will amend."

" You have deceived me."

" How? "

" Will you own the truth? " and in her eagerness to set her fears at rest, Amy forgot Helen.

" I will."

She could not see his face, but his voice was
steady and his manner earnest.

" Tell me, then, is not your true name Sigismund Palsdorf? "

He started, but answered instantly, —

" It is not."

" You are not the baron? " cried Amy.

" No; I will swear it if you wish."

" Who, then, are you? "

" Shall I confess? "

" Yes, I entreat you."

" Remember, you command me to speak."

" I do. Who are you? "

" Your lover."

The words were breathed into her ear as softly
as ardently, but they startled her so much she
could find no reply, and, throwing himself down
before her, Casimer poured out his passion with
an impetuosity that held her breathless.

" Yes, I love you, and I tell it, vain and dishonorable as it is in one like me. I try to hide
it. I say ' it cannot be.' I plan to go away. But
you keep me; you are angel-good to me; you
take my heart, you care for me, teach me, pity
me, and I can only love and die. I know it is
folly; I ask nothing; I pray to God to bless you

always, and I say, Go, go, before it is too late for you, as now for me!"

"Yes, I must go — it is all wrong. Forgive me. I have been very selfish. Oh, forget me and be happy," faltered Amy, feeling that her only safety was in flight.

"Go! go!" he cried, in a heart-broken tone, yet still kissed and clung to her hands till she tore them away and fled into the house.

Helen missed her soon after she went, but could not follow for several minutes; then went to their chamber and there found Amy drowned in tears, and terribly agitated.

Soon the story was told with sobs and moans, and despairing lamentations fit to touch a heart of stone.

"I do love him — oh, I do; but I did n't know it till he was so unhappy, and now I 've done this dreadful harm. He 'll die, and I can't help him, see him, or be anything to him. Oh, I 've been a wicked, wicked girl, and never can be happy any more."

Angry, perplexed, and conscience-stricken, for what now seemed blind and unwise submission to the major, Helen devoted herself to calming Amy, and when at last the poor, broken-hearted little soul fell asleep in her arms, she pondered half the night upon the still unsolved enigma of the Baron Sigismund.

VIII

MORE MYSTERY

"UNCLE, can I speak to you a moment?" said Helen, very gravely, as they left the breakfast-room next morning.

"Not now, my dear, I 'm busy," was the hasty reply, as the major shawled Mrs. Cumberland for an early promenade.

Helen knit her brows irefully, for this answer had been given her half a dozen times lately when she asked for an interview. It was evident he wished to avoid all lectures, remonstrances, and explanations; and it was also evident that he was in love with the widow.

"Lovers are worse than lunatics to manage, so it is vain to try to get any help from him," sighed Helen, adding, as her uncle was gallantly leading his stout divinity away into the garden: "Amy has a bad headache, and I shall stay to take care of her, so we can't join your party to Chillon, sir. We have been there once, so you need n't postpone it for us."

"Very well, my dear," and the major walked away, looking much relieved.

As Helen was about to leave the *salon* Casimer appeared. A single glance at her face assured him that she knew all, and instantly assuming a confiding, persuasive air that was irresistible, he said, meekly, —

" Mademoiselle, I do not deserve a word from you, but it desolates me to know that I have grieved the little angel who is too dear to me. For her sake, pardon that I spoke my heart in spite of prudence, and permit me to send her this."

Helen glanced from the flowers he held to his beseeching face, and her own softened. He looked so penitent and anxious, she had not the heart to reproach him.

" I will forgive you and carry your gift to Amy on one condition," she said, gravely.

" Ah, you are kind! Name, then, the condition, I implore you, and I will agree."

" Tell me, then, on your honor as a gentleman, are you not Baron Palsdorf? "

" On my honor as a gentleman, I swear to you I am not."

" Are you, in truth, what you profess to be? "

" I am, in truth, Amy's lover, your devoted servant, and a most unhappy man, with but a little while to live. Believe this and pity me, dearest Mademoiselle Helène."

She did pity him, her eyes betrayed that, and her voice was very kind, as she said, —

" Pardon my doubts. I trust you now, and

wish with all my heart that it was possible to make you happy. You know it is not, therefore I am sure you will be wise and generous, and spare Amy further grief by avoiding her for the little time we stay. Promise me this, Casimer."

" I may see her if I am dumb? Do not deny me this. I will not speak, but I must look at my little and dear angel when she is near."

He pleaded so ardently with lips and hands, and eager eyes, that Helen could not deny him, and when he had poured out his thanks she left him, feeling very tender toward the unhappy young lover, whose passion was so hopeless, yet so warm.

Amy was at breakfast in her room, sobbing and sipping, moaning and munching, for, though her grief was great, her appetite was good, and she was in no mood to see anything comical in cracking eggshells while she bewailed her broken heart, or in eating honey in the act of lamenting the bitterness of her fate.

Casimer would have become desperate had he seen her in the little blue wrapper, with her bright hair loose on her shoulders, and her pretty face wet with tears, as she dropped her spoon to seize his flowers, — three dewy roses, one a bud, one half and the other fully blown, making a fragrant record and avowal of the love which she must renounce.

" Oh, my dear boy! how can I give him up, when he is so fond, and I am all he has? Helen, uncle must let me write or go to mamma. She shall decide; I can't; and no one else has a right to part us," sobbed Amy, over her roses.

"Casimer will not marry, dear; he is too generous to ask such a sacrifice," began Helen, but Amy cried indignantly, —

"It is no sacrifice; I'm rich. What do I care for his poverty?"

"His religion!" hinted Helen, anxiously.

"It need not part us; we can believe what we will. He is good; why mind whether he is Catholic or Protestant?"

"But a Pole, Amy, so different in tastes, habits, character, and beliefs. It is a great risk to marry a foreigner: races are so unlike."

"I don't care if he is a Tartar, a Calmuck, or any of the other wild tribes; I love him, he loves me, and no one need object if I don't."

"But, dear, the great and sad objection still remains —his health. He just said he had but a little while to live."

Amy's angry eyes grew dim, but she answered, with soft earnestness, —

"So much the more need of me to make that little while happy. Think how much he has suffered and done for others; surely I may do something for him. Oh, Nell, can I let him die alone and in exile, when I have both heart and home to give him?"

Helen could say no more; she kissed and comforted the faithful little soul, feeling all the while such sympathy and tenderness that she wondered at herself, for with this interest in the love of another came a sad sense of loneliness, as if she was denied the sweet experience that every woman longs to know.

Amy never could remain long under a cloud, and seeing Helen's tears, began to cheer both her cousin and herself.

" Hoffman said he might live with care, don't you remember? and Hoffman knows the case better than we. Let us ask him if Casimer is worse. You do it; I can't without betraying myself."

" I will," and Helen felt grateful for any pretext to address a friendly word to Karl, who had looked sad of late, and had been less with them since the major became absorbed in Mrs. Cumberland.

Leaving Amy to compose herself, Helen went away to find Hoffman. It was never difficult, for he seemed to divine her wishes and appear uncalled the moment he was wanted. Hardly had she reached her favorite nook in the garden when he approached with letters, and asked with respectful anxiety, as she glanced at and threw them by with an impatient sigh, —

" Has mademoiselle any orders? Will the ladies drive, sail, or make a little expedition? It is fine, and mademoiselle looks as if the air would refresh her. Pardon that I make the suggestion."

" No, Hoffman, I don't like the air of this place, and intend to leave as soon as possible." And Helen knit her delicate dark brows with an expression of great determination. " Switzerland is the refuge of political exiles, and I hate plots and disguises; I feel oppressed by some mystery, and mean to solve or break away from it at once."

She stopped abruptly, longing to ask his help, yet withheld by a sudden sense of shyness in approaching the subject, though she had decided to speak to Karl of the Pole.

" Can I serve you, mademoiselle? If so, pray command me," he said, eagerly, coming a step nearer.

" You can, and I intend to ask your advice, for there can be nothing amiss in doing so, since you are a friend of Casimer's."

" I am both friend and confidant, mademoiselle," he answered, as if anxious to let her understand that he knew all, without the embarrassment of words. She looked up quickly, relieved, yet troubled.

" He has told you, then? "

" Everything, mademoiselle. Pardon me if this afflicts you; I am his only friend here, and the poor lad sorely needed comfort."

" He did. I am not annoyed; I am glad, for I know you will sustain him. Now I may speak freely, and be equally frank. Please tell me if he is indeed fatally ill? "

"It was thought so some months ago; now I hope. Happiness cures many ills, and since he has loved, he has improved. I always thought care would save him; he is worth it."

Hoffman paused, as if fearful of venturing too far; but Helen seemed to confide freely in him, and said, softly, —

"Ah, if it were only wise to let him be happy. It is so bitter to deny love."

"God knows it is!"

The exclamation broke from Hoffman as if an irrepressible impulse wrung it from him.

Helen started, and for a moment neither spoke. She collected herself soonest, and without turning, said, quietly, —

"I have been troubled by a strong impression that Casimer is not what he seems. Till he denied it on his honor I believed him to be Baron Palsdorf. Did he speak the truth when he said he was not?"

"Yes, mademoiselle."

"Then, Casimer Teblinski is his real name?"

No answer.

She turned sharply, and added, —

"For my cousin's sake, I must know the truth. Several curious coincidences make me strongly suspect that he is passing under an assumed name."

Not a word said Hoffman, but looked on the ground, as motionless and expressionless as a statue.

Helen lost patience, and in order to show how much she had discovered, rapidly told the story of the gloves, ring, handkerchief, prayer-book and collar, omitting all hint of the girlish romance they had woven about these things.

As she ended, Hoffman looked up with a curious expression, in which confusion, amusement, admiration and annoyance seemed to contend.

" Mademoiselle," he said, gravely, " I am about to prove to you that I feel honored by the confidence you place in me. I cannot break my word, but I will confess to you that Casimer does *not* bear his own name."

" I knew it! " said Helen, with a flash of triumph in her eyes. " He *is* the baron, and no Pole. You Germans love masquerades and jokes. This is one, but I must spoil it before it is played out."

" Pardon; mademoiselle is keen, but in this she is mistaken. Casimer is *not* the baron; he did fight for Poland, and his name is known and honored there. Of this I solemnly assure you."

She stood up and looked him straight in the face. He met her eye to eye, and never wavered till her own fell.

She mused a few minutes, entirely forgetful of herself in her eagerness to solve the mystery.

Hoffman stood so near that her dress touched him, and the wind blew her scarf against his hand; and as she thought he watched her while his eyes kindled, his color rose, and once he opened his lips to speak, but she moved at the instant, and exclaimed, —

" I have it! "

" Now for it," he muttered, as if preparing for some new surprise or attack.

" When uncle used to talk about the Polish revolution, there was, I remember a gallant young Pole who did something brave. The name just flashed on me, and it clears up my doubts. Stanislas Prakora — ' S. P.' — and Casimer is the man."

Helen spoke with an eager, bright face, as if sure of the truth now; but, to her surprise, Hoffman laughed, a short, irrepressible laugh, full of hearty but brief merriment. He sobered in a breath, and with an entire change of countenance said, in an embarrassed tone, —

" Pardon my rudeness; mademoiselle's acuteness threw me off my guard. I can say nothing till released from my promise; but mademoiselle may rest assured that Casimer Teblinski is as good and brave a man as Stanislas Prakora."

Helen's eyes sparkled, for in this reluctant reply she read confirmation of her suspicion, and thought that Amy would rejoice to learn that her lover was a hero.

" You *are* exiles, but still hope and plot, and never relinquish your hearts' desire? "

" Never, mademoiselle! "

" You are in danger? "

"In daily peril of losing all we most love and long for," answered Karl, with such passion that Helen found patriotism a lovely and inspiring thing.

"You have enemies?" she asked, unable to control her interest, and feeling the charm of these confidences.

"Alas! yes," was the mournful reply, as Karl dropped his eyes to hide the curious expression of mirth which he could not banish from them.

"Can you not conquer them, or escape the danger they place you in?"

"We hope to conquer, we cannot escape."

"This accounts for your disguise and Casimer's false name?"

"Yes. We beg that mademoiselle will pardon us the anxiety and perplexity we have caused her, and hope that a time will soon arrive when we may be ourselves. I fear the romantic interest with which the ladies have honored us will be much lessened, but we shall still remain their most humble and devoted servants."

Something in his tone nettled Helen, and she said sharply, —

"All this may be amusing to you, but it spoils my confidence in others to know they wear masks. Is your name also false?"

"I am Karl Hoffman, as surely as the sun shines, mademoiselle. Do not wound me by a doubt," he said, eagerly.

"And nothing more?"

She smiled as she spoke, and glanced at his darkened skin with a shake of the head.

" I dare not answer that."

" No matter; I hate titles, and value people for their own worth, not for their rank."

Helen spoke impulsively, and, as if carried away by her words and manner, Hoffman caught her hand and pressed his lips to it ardently, dropped it, and was gone, as if fearing to trust himself a moment longer.

Helen stood where he left her, thinking, with a shy glance from her hand to the spot where he had stood, —

" It *is* pleasant to have one's hand kissed, as Amy said. Poor Karl, his fate is almost as hard as Casimer's."

Some subtile power seemed to make the four young people shun one another carefully, though all longed to be together. The major appeared to share the secret disquiet that made the rest roam listlessly about, till little Roserl came to invite them to a *fête* in honor of the vintage. All were glad to go, hoping in the novelty and excitement to recover their composure.

The vineyard sloped up from the chateau, and on the hillside was a small plateau of level sward, shadowed by a venerable oak now hung with garlands, while underneath danced the chateau servants with their families, to the music of a pipe played by little Friedel. As the gentlefolk approached, the revel stopped, but the major, who was in an antic mood and disposed to be gracious, bade Friedel play on, and as Mrs. Cumberland refused his hand with a glance at her weeds, the major turned to the Count's buxom housekeeper, and besought her to waltz with him. She assented, and away they went as nimbly as the best. Amy laughed, but stopped to blush, as Casimer came up with an imploring glance, and whispered, —

"Is it possible that I may enjoy one divine waltz with you before I go?"

Amy gave him her hand with a glad assent, and Helen was left alone. Every one was dancing but herself and Hoffman, who stood near by, apparently unconscious of the fact. He glanced covertly at her, and saw that she was beating time with foot and hand, that her eyes shone, her lips smiled. He seemed to take courage at this, for, walking straight up to her, he said, as coolly as if a crown-prince, —

"Mademoiselle, may I have the honor?"

A flash of surprise passed over her face, but there was no anger, pride, or hesitation in her manner, as she leaned toward him with a quiet "Thanks, monsieur."

A look of triumph was in his eyes as he swept her away to dance, as she had never danced before, for a German waltz is full of life and spirit, wonderfully captivating to English girls, and German gentlemen make it a memorable experience when they please. As they circled round the rustic ball-room, Hoffman never took his eyes off Helen's, and, as if fascinated, she looked up at him, half conscious that he was reading her heart as she read his. He said not a word, but his face grew very tender, very beautiful in her sight, as she forgot everything except that he had saved her life and she loved him. When they paused, she was breathless and pale; he also; and seating her he went away to bring her a glass of wine. As her dizzy eyes grew clear, she saw a little case at her feet, and taking it up, opened it. A worn paper, containing some faded forget-me-nots and these words, fell out, —

"Gathered where Helen sat on the night of August 10th."

There was just time to restore its contents to the case, when Hoffman returned, saw it, and looked intensely annoyed as he asked, quickly, —

"Did you read the name on it?"

"I saw only the flowers;" and Helen colored beautifully as she spoke.

"And read *them?*" he asked, with a look she could not meet.

She was spared an answer, for just then a lad came up, saying, as he offered a note, —

"Monsieur Hoffman, madame, at the hotel, sends you this, and begs you to come at once."

As he impatiently opened it, the wind blew the paper into Helen's lap. She restored it, and in the act, her quick eye caught the signature, "Thine ever, Ludmilla."

A slight shadow passed over her face, leaving it very cold and quiet. Hoffman saw the change, and smiled, as if well pleased, but assuming suddenly his usual manner, said deferentially, —

"Will mademoiselle permit me to visit my friend for an hour? — she is expecting me."

"Go, then, we do not need you," was the brief reply, in a careless tone, as if his absence was a thing of no interest to any one.

"Thanks; I shall not be long away;" and giving her a glance that made her turn scarlet with anger at its undisguised admiration, he walked away, humming gayly to himself Goethe's lines, —

> " Maiden's heart and city's wall
> Were made to yield, were made to fall;
> When we've held them each their day,
> Soldier-like we march away."

IX

" S. P." AND THE BARON

DINNER was over, and the *salon* deserted by all but the two young ladies, who sat apart, apparently absorbed in novels, while each was privately longing for somebody to come, and with the charming inconsistency of the fair sex, planning to fly if certain somebodies *did* appear.

Steps approached; both buried themselves in their books; both held their breath and felt their hearts flutter as they never had done before at the step of mortal man. The door opened; neither looked up, yet each was conscious of mingled disappointment and relief when the major said, in a grave tone, " Girls, I 've something to tell you."

" We know what it is, sir," returned Helen, coolly.

" I beg your pardon, but you don't, my dear, as I will prove in five minutes, if you will give me your attention."

The major looked as if braced up to some momentous undertaking; and planting himself be-

fore the two young ladies, dashed bravely into
the subject.

"Girls, I 've played a bold game, but I 've won
it, and will take the consequences."

"They will fall heaviest on you, uncle," said
Helen, thinking he was about to declare his love
for the widow.

The major laughed, shrugged his shoulders,
and answered, stoutly, —

"I 'll bear them; but you are quite wrong, my
dear, in your surmises, as you will soon see.
Helen is my ward, and accountable to me alone.
Amy's mother gave her into my charge, and
won't reproach me for anything that has passed
when I explain matters. As to the lads they
must take care of themselves."

Suddenly both girls colored, fluttered, and became intensely interested. The major's eyes
twinkled as he assumed a perfectly impassive expression, and rapidly delivered himself of the following thunderbolt, —

"Girls, you have been deceived, and the young
men you love are impostors."

"I thought so," muttered Helen, grimly.

"Oh, uncle, don't, don't say that!" cried Amy,
despairingly.

"It 's true, my dears; and the worst of it is,
I knew the truth all the time. Now, don't have
hysterics, but listen and enjoy the joke as I do.
At Coblentz, when you sat in the balcony, two
young men overheard Amy sigh for adventures,

and Helen advise making a romance out of the
gloves one of the lads had dropped. They had
seen you by day; both admired you, and being
idle, gay young fellows, they resolved to devote
their vacation to gratifying your wishes and enjoying themselves. We met at the Fortress; I
knew one of them, and liked the other immensely;
so when they confided their scheme to me I
agreed to help them carry it out, as I had perfect confidence in both, and thought a little adventure or two would do you good."

" Uncle, you were mad," said Helen; and Amy
added, tragically, —

" You don't know what trouble has come of
it."

" Perhaps I was; that remains to be proved.
I do know everything, and fail to see any trouble,
so don't cry, little girl," briskly replied the inex-
plicable major. " Well, we had a merry time
planning our prank. One of the lads insisted
on playing courier, though I objected. He 'd
done it before, liked the part, and would have his
way. The other could n't decide, being younger
and more in love; so we left him to come into
the comedy when he was ready. Karl did cap-
itally, as you will allow; and I am much attached to him, for in all respects he has been
true to his word. He began at Coblentz; the
other, after doing the mysterious at Heidelberg,
appeared as an exile, and made quick work with
the prejudices of my well-beloved nieces — hey,
Amy ? "

"Go on; who are they?" cried both girls, breathlessly.

"Wait a bit; I'm not bound to expose the poor fellows to your scorn and anger. No; if you are going to be high and haughty, to forget their love, refuse to forgive their frolic, and rend their hearts with reproaches, better let them remain unknown."

"No, no; we will forget and forgive, only speak!" was the command of both.

"You promise to be lenient and mild, to let them confess their motives, and to award a gentle penance for their sins?"

"Yes, we promise!"

"Then, come in, my lads, and plead for your lives."

As he spoke the major threw open the door, and two gentlemen entered the room — one, slight and dark, with brilliant black eyes; the other tall and large, with blond hair and beard. Angry, bewildered, and shame-stricken as they were, feminine curiosity overpowered all other feelings for the moment, and the girls sat looking at the culprits with eager eyes, full of instant recognition; for though the disguise was off, and neither had seen them in their true characters but once, they felt no doubt, and involuntarily exclaimed, —

"Karl!"

"Casimer."

"No, young ladies; the courier and exile are

defunct, and from their ashes rise Baron Sigismund Palsdorf, my friend, and Sidney Power, my nephew. I give you one hour to settle the matter; then I shall return to bestow my blessing or to banish these scapegraces forever."

And, having fired his last shot, the major prudently retreated, without waiting to see its effect.

It was tremendous, for it carried confusion into the fair enemy's camp; and gave the besiegers a momentary advantage of which they were not slow to avail themselves.

For a moment the four remained mute and motionless: then Amy, like all timid things, took refuge in flight, and Sidney followed her into the garden, glad to see the allies separated. Helen, with the courage of her nature, tried to face and repulse the foe; but love was stronger than pride, maiden shame overcame anger, and, finding it vain to meet and bear down the steady, tender glance of the blue eyes fixed upon her, she dropped her head into her hands and sat before him, like one conquered but too proud to cry "Quarter." Her lover watched her till she hid her face, then drew near, knelt down before her, and said, with an undertone of deep feeling below the mirthful malice of his words, —

"Mademoiselle, pardon me that I am a foolish baron, and dare to offer you the title that you hate. I have served you faithfully for a month, and, presumptuous as it is, I ask to be allowed to serve you all my life. Helen, say you forgive the deceit for love's sake."

" No; you are false and forsworn. How can
I believe that anything is true? "

And Helen drew away the hand of which he
had taken possession.

" Heart's dearest, you trusted me in spite of
my disguise; trust me still, and I will prove that
I am neither false nor forsworn. Catechise me,
and see if I was not true in spite of all my seeming deception."

" You said your name was Karl Hoffman,"
began Helen, glad to gain a little time to calm
herself before the momentous question came.

" It is; I have many, and my family choose to
call me Sigismund," was the laughing answer.

" I 'll never call you so; you shall be Karl,
the courier, all your life to me," cried Helen, still
unable to meet the ardent eyes before her.

" Good; I like that well; for it assures me
that all my life I shall be something to you, my
heart. What next? "

" When I asked if you were the baron, you
denied it."

" Pardon! I simply said my name was Hoffman. You did not ask me point blank if I was
the baron; had you done so, I think I should
have confessed all, for it was very hard to restrain myself this morning."

" No, not yet; I have more questions; " and
Helen warned him away, as it became evident
that he no longer considered restraint necessary.

" Who is Ludmilla? " she said, sharply.

"My faith, that is superb!" exclaimed the baron, with a triumphant smile at her betrayal of jealousy. "How if she is a former love?" he asked, with a sly look at her changing face.

"It would cause me no surprise; I am prepared for anything."

"How if she is my dearest sister, for whom I sent, that she might welcome you and bring the greetings of my parents to their new daughter?"

"Is it, indeed, so?"

And Helen's eyes dimmed as the thought of parents, home and love filled her heart with tenderest gratitude, for she had long been an orphan.

"*Leibchen,* it is true; to-morrow you shall see how dear you already are to them, for I write often and they wait eagerly to receive you."

Helen felt herself going very fast, and made an effort to harden her heart, lest too easy victory should reward this audacious lover.

"I may not go; I also have friends, and in England we are not won in this wild way. I will yet prove you false; it will console me for being so duped if I can call you traitor. You said Casimer had fought in Poland."

"Cruelest of women, he did, but under his own name, Sidney Power."

"Then, he was not the brave Stanislas?— and there is no charming Casimer?"

"Yes, there are both,—his and my friends, in Paris; true Poles, and when we go there you shall see them."

" But his illness was a ruse ? "

" No; he was wounded in the war and has been ill since. Not of a fatal malady, I own; his cough misled you, and *he* has no scruples in fabling to any extent. I am not to bear the burden of his sins."

" Then, the romances he told us about your charity, your virtues, and — your love of liberty were false ? " said Helen, with a keen glance, for these tales had done much to interest her in the unknown baron.

Sudden color rose to his forehead, and for the first time his eyes fell before hers, — not in shame, but with a modest man's annoyance at hearing himself praised.

" Sidney is enthusiastic in his friendship, and speaks too well for me. The facts are true, but he doubtless glorified the simplest by his way of telling it. Will you forgive my follies, and believe me when I promise to play and duel no more ? "

" Yes."

She yielded her hand now, and her eyes were full of happiness, yet she added, wistfully, —

" And the betrothed, your cousin, Minna, — is she, in truth, not dear to you ? "

" Very dear, but less so than another; for I could not learn of her in years what I learned in a day when I met you. Helen, this was begun in jest, — it ends in solemn earnest, for I love my liberty, and I have lost it, utterly and forever.

Yet I am glad; look in my face and tell me you
believe it."

He spoke now as seriously as fervently, and
with no shadow on her own, Helen brushed back
the blond hair and looked into her lover's face.
Truth, tenderness, power, and candor were written there in characters that could not lie; and
with her heart upon her lips, she answered, as
he drew her close, —

" I do believe, do love you, Sigismund! "

Meanwhile another scene was passing in the
garden. Sidney, presuming upon his cousinship,
took possession of Amy, bidding her " strike but
hear him." Of course she listened with the usual
accompaniment of tears and smiles, reproaches
and exclamations, varied by cruel exultations and
coquettish commands to go away and never dare
approach her again.

" *Ma drogha,* listen and be appeased. Years
ago you and I played together as babies, and our
fond mammas vowed we should one day mate.
When I was a youth of fourteen and you a mite
of seven I went away to India with my father,
and at our parting promised to come back and
marry you. Being in a fret because you could n't
go also, you haughtily declined the honor, and
when I offered a farewell kiss, struck me with
this very little hand. Do you remember it? "

" Not I. Too young for such nonsense."

" I do, and I also remember that in my boyish
way I resolved to keep my word sooner or later,
and I 've done it."

"We shall see, sir," cried Amy, strongly tempted to repeat her part of the childish scene as well as her cousin, but her hand was not free, and he got the kiss without the blow.

"For eleven years we never met. You forgot me, and 'Cousin Sidney' remained an empty name. I was in India till four years ago; since then I 've been flying about Germany and fighting in Poland, where I nearly got my quietus."

"My dear boy, were you wounded?"

"Bless you, yes; and very proud of it I am. I 'll show you my scars some day; but never mind that now. A while ago I went to England, seized with a sudden desire to find my wife."

"I admire your patience in waiting; so flattering to me, you know," was the sharp answer.

"It looks like neglect, I confess; but I 'd heard reports of your flirtations, and twice of your being engaged, so I kept away till my work was done. Was it true?"

"I never flirt, Sidney, and I was only engaged a little bit once or twice. I did n't like it, and never mean to do so any more."

"I shall see that you don't flirt; but you are very much engaged now, so put on your ring and make no romances about any 'S. P.' but myself."

"I shall wait till you clear your character; I 'm not going to care for a deceitful impostor. What made you think of this prank?"

"You did."

" I? How?"

" When in England I saw your picture, though
you were many a mile away, and fell in love with
it.   Your mother told me much about you, and
I saw she would not frown upon my suit.   I
begged her not to tell you I had come, but let
me find you and make myself known when I
liked.   You were in Switzerland, and I went
after you.   At Coblentz I met Sigismund, and
told him my case; he is full of romance, and
when we overheard you in the balcony we were
glad of the hint.   Sigismund was with me when
you came, and admired Helen immensely, so he
was wild to have a part in the frolic.   I let him
begin, and followed you unseen to Heidelberg,
meaning to personate an artist.   Meeting you
at the castle, I made a good beginning with the
vaults and the ring, and meant to follow it up
by acting the baron, you were so bent on finding
him, but Sigismund forbade it.   Turning over
a trunk of things left there the year before, I
came upon my old Polish uniform, and decided
to be a Thaddeus."

" How well you did it! Wasn't it hard to act
all the time?" asked Amy, wonderingly.

" Very hard with Helen, she is so keen, but
not a bit so with you, for you are such a confiding soul any one could cheat you.   I 've betrayed
myself a dozen times, and you never saw it.   Ah,
it was capital fun to play the forlorn exile, study
English, and flirt with my cousin."

"It was very base. I should think you'd be devoured with remorse. Are n't you sorry?"

"For one thing. I cropped my head lest you should know me. I was proud of my curls, but I sacrificed them all to you."

"Peacock! Did you think that one glimpse of your black eyes and fine hair would make such an impression that I should recognize you again?"

"I did, and for that reason disfigured my head, put on a mustache, and assumed hideous spectacles. Did you never suspect my disguise, Amy?"

"No. Helen used to say that she felt something was wrong, but I never did till the other night."

"Did n't I do that well? I give you my word it was all done on the spur of the minute. I meant to speak soon, but had not decided how, when you came out so sweetly with that confounded old cloak, of which I'd no more need than an African has of a blanket. Then a scene I'd read in a novel came into my head, and I just repeated it *con amore*. Was I very pathetic and tragical, Amy?"

"I thought so then. It strikes me as ridiculous now, and I can't help feeling sorry that I wasted so much pity on a man who —"

"Loves you with all his heart and soul. Did you cry and grieve over me, dear little tender thing? and do you think now that I am a heartless fellow, bent only on amusing myself at the expense of others? It 's not so; and you shall see how true and good and steady I can be when I have any one to love and care for me. I 've been alone so long it 's new and beautiful to be petted, confided in, and looked up to by an angel like you."

He was in earnest now; she felt it, and her anger melted away like dew before the sun.

" Poor boy! You will go home with us now, and let us take care of you in quiet England. You 'll play no more pranks, but go soberly to work and do something that shall make me proud to be your cousin, won't you? "

" If you 'll change ' cousin ' to ' wife ' I 'll be and do whatever you please. Amy, when I was a poor, dying, Catholic foreigner you loved me and would have married me in spite of everything. Now that I 'm your well, rich, Protestant cousin, who adores you as that Pole never could, you turn cold and cruel. Is it because the romance is gone, or because your love was only a girl's fancy, after all? "

" You deceived me and I can't forget it; but I 'll try," was the soft answer to his reproaches.

" Are you disappointed that I 'm not a baron? "

" A little bit."

" Shall I be a count? They gave me a title in Poland, a barren honor, but all they had to offer, poor souls, in return for a little blood.

a face full of smiles and tears, a second rush
was made, and congratulations, salutes, exclamations and embraces were indulged in to every
one's satisfaction.

As the excitement subsided the major said,
simply, —

"We were married yesterday at Montreaux.
Let me hope that you will prove as faithful as I
have been, as happy as I am, as blest as I shall
be. I loved this lady in my youth, have waited
many years, and am rewarded at last, for love
never comes too late."

The falter in his cheery voice, the dimness of
his eyes, the smile on his lips, and the gesture
with which he returned the pressure of the hand
upon his arm, told the little romance of the good
major's life more eloquently than pages of fine
writing, and touched the hearts of those who
loved him.

"I have been faithful for eleven years. Give
me my reward soon, won't you, dear?" whispered Sidney.

"Don't marry me to-morrow, and if mamma
is willing I'll think about it by and by," answered Amy.

"It is beautiful! let us go and do likewise,"
said Sigismund to his betrothed.

But Helen, anxious to turn the thoughts of
all from emotions too deep for words, drew from
her pocket a small pearl-colored object, which
she gave to Amy with mock solemnity, as she

said, turning to lay her hand again in her lover's, —

"Amy, our search is over. *You* may keep the
gloves; *I* have the baron."

MY RED CAP

" He who serves well need not fear to ask his wages."

I

IT was under a blue cap that I first saw the
honest face of Joe Collins. In the third
year of the late war a Maine regiment was
passing through Boston, on its way to Washington. The Common was all alive with troops and
the spectators who clustered round them to say
God-speed, as the brave fellows marched away
to meet danger and death for our sakes.

Every one was eager to do something; and,
as the men stood at ease, the people mingled
freely with them, offering gifts, hearty grips of
the hand, and hopeful prophecies of victory in
the end. Irresistibly attracted, my boy Tom and
I drew near, and soon, becoming excited by the
scene, ravaged the fruit-stands in our neighborhood for tokens of our regard, mingling candy
and congratulations, peanuts and prayers, apples
and applause, in one enthusiastic jumble.

While Tom was off on his third raid, my attention was attracted by a man who stood a little
apart, looking as if his thoughts were far away.
All the men were fine, stalwart fellows, as Maine
men usually are; but this one over-topped his

comrades, standing straight and tall as a Norway pine, with a face full of the mingled shrewdness, sobriety, and self-possession of the typical New Englander. I liked the look of him; and, seeing that he seemed solitary, even in a crowd, I offered him my last apple with a word of interest. The keen blue eyes met mine gratefully, and the apple began to vanish in vigorous bites as we talked; for no one thought of ceremony at such a time.

"Where are you from?"

"Woolidge, ma'am."

"Are you glad to go?"

"Wal, there's two sides to that question. I calk'late to do my duty, and do it hearty; but it *is* rough on a feller leavin' his folks, for good, maybe."

There was a sudden huskiness in the man's voice that was not apple-skins, though he tried to make believe that it was. I knew a word about home would comfort him, so I went on with my questions.

"It is very hard. Do you leave a family?"

"My old mother, a sick brother, — and Lucindy."

The last word was uttered in a tone of intense regret, and his brown cheek reddened as he added hastily, to hide some embarrassment, —

"You see, Jim went last year, and got pretty well used up; so I felt as if I'd ought to take my turn now. Mother was a regular old hero about it and I dropped everything, and come off. Lucindy did n't think it was my duty; and that made it awful hard, I tell you."

"Wives are less patriotic than mothers," I began; but he would not hear Lucindy blamed, and said quickly, —

"She ain't my wife yet, but we calk'lated to be married in a month or so; and it was wus for her than for me, women lot so on not being disappointed. I *could n't* shirk, and here I be. When I git to work, I shall be all right: the first wrench is the tryin' part."

Here he straightened his broad shoulders, and turned his face toward the flags fluttering far in front, as if no backward look should betray the longing of his heart for mother, home, and wife. I liked that little glimpse of character; and when Tom returned with empty hands, reporting that every stall was exhausted, I told him to find out what the man would like best, then run across the street and get it.

"I know without asking. Give us your purse, and I 'll make him as happy as a king," said the boy, laughing, as he looked up admiringly at our tall friend, who looked down on him with an elder-brotherly air pleasant to see. While Tom was gone, I found out Joe's name and business, promised to write and tell his mother how finely the regiment went off, and was just expressing a hope that we might meet again, for I too was going to the war as nurse, when the order to

" Fall in! " came rolling down the ranks, and the
talk was over. Fearing Tom would miss our
man in the confusion, I kept my eye on him till
the boy came rushing up with a packet of to-
bacco in one hand and a good supply of cigars in
the other. Not a romantic offering, certainly,
but a very acceptable one, as Joe's face proved,
as we scrambled these treasures into his pockets,
all laughing at the flurry, while less fortunate
comrades helped us, with an eye to a share of
these fragrant luxuries by and by. There was
just time for this, a hearty shake of the big hand,
and a grateful " Good-by, ma'am; " then the
word was given, and they were off. Bent on
seeing the last of them, Tom and I took a short
cut, and came out on the wide street down which
so many troops marched that year; and, mounting some high steps, we watched for our man, as
we already called him.

As the inspiring music, the grand tramp, drew
near, the old thrill went through the crowd, the
old cheer broke out. But it was a different scene
now than in the first enthusiastic, hopeful days.
Young men and ardent boys filled the ranks then,
brave by instinct, burning with loyal zeal, and
blissfully unconscious of all that lay before them.
Now the blue coats were worn by mature men,
some gray, all grave and resolute: husbands and
fathers, with the memory of wives and children
tugging at their heart-strings; homes left desolate behind them, and before them the grim cer-

said Joe, trying to make light of one of the greatest misfortunes a man can suffer.

" That is bad, but it might have been worse.
Keep up your spirits, Joe; and we will soon have
you fitted out with a new arm almost as good
as new."

" I guess it won't do much lumberin', so that
trade is done for. I s'pose there 's things left-
handed fellers can do, and I must learn 'em as
soon as possible, since my fightin' days are over,"
and Joe looked at his one arm with a sigh that
was almost a groan, helplessness is such a trial
to a manly man, — and he was eminently so.

" What can I do to comfort you most, Joe?
I 'll send my good Ben to help you to bed, and
will be here myself when the surgeon goes his
rounds. Is there anything else that would make
you more easy? "

" If you could just drop a line to mother to
let her know I 'm alive, it would be a sight of
comfort to both of us. I guess I 'm in for a long
spell of hospital, and I 'd lay easier if I knew
mother and Lucindy warn't frettin' about me."

He must have been suffering terribly, but he
thought of the women who loved him before
himself, and, busy as I was, I snatched a moment to send a few words of hope to the old
mother. Then I left him " layin' easy," though
the prospect of some months of wearing pain
would have daunted most men. If I had needed
anything to increase my regard for Joe, it would

have been the courage with which he bore a very bad quarter of an hour with the surgeons; for his arm was in a dangerous state, the wound in the head feverish for want of care; and a heavy cold on the lungs suggested pneumonia as an added trial to his list of ills.

" He will have a hard time of it, but I think he will pull through, as he is a temperate fellow, with a splendid constitution," was the doctor's verdict, as he left us for the next man, who was past help, with a bullet through his lungs.

" I don'no as I hanker to live, and be a burden. If Jim was able to do for mother, I feel as if I would n't mind steppin' out now I 'm so fur along. As he ain't, I s'pose I must brace up, and do the best I can," said Joe, as I wiped the drops from his forehead, and tried to look as if his prospect was a bright one.

" You will have Lucindy to help you, you know; and that will make things easier for all."

" Think so? 'Pears to me I could n't ask her to take care of three invalids for my sake. She ain't no folks of her own, nor much means, and ought to marry a man who can make things easy for her. Guess I 'll have to wait a spell longer before I say anything to Lucindy about marryin' now; " and a look of resolute resignation settled on Joe's haggard face as he gave up his dearest hope.

" I think Lucindy will have something to say, if she is like most women, and you will find the burdens much lighter, for sharing them between you. Don't worry about that, but get well, and go home as soon as you can."

"All right, ma'am;" and Joe proved himself a good soldier by obeying orders, and falling asleep like a tired child, as the first step toward recovery.

For two months I saw Joe daily, and learned to like him very much, he was so honest, genuine, and kind-hearted. So did his mates, for he made friends with them all by sharing such small luxuries as came to him, for he was a favorite; and, better still, he made sunshine in that sad place by the brave patience with which he bore his own troubles, the cheerful consolation he always gave to others. A droll fellow was Joe at times, for under his sobriety lay much humor; and I soon discovered that a visit from him was more efficacious than other cordials in cases of despondency and discontent. Roars of laughter sometimes greeted me as I went into his ward, and Joe's jokes were passed round as eagerly as the water-pitcher.

Yet he had much to try him, not only in the ills that vexed his flesh, but the cares that tried his spirit, and the future that lay before him, full of anxieties and responsibilities which seemed so heavy now when the strong right arm, that had cleared all obstacles away before, was gone. The letters I wrote for him, and those he received, told the little story very plainly; for he read them to me, and found much comfort in talking over his affairs, as most men do when illness makes them dependent on a woman. Jim was evidently sick and selfish. Lucindy, to judge from the photograph cherished so tenderly under Joe's pillow, was a pretty, weak sort of a girl, with little character or courage to help poor Joe with his burdens. The old mother was very like her son, and stood by him "like a hero," as he said, but was evidently failing, and begged him to come home as soon as he was able, that she might see him comfortably settled before she must leave him. Her courage sustained his, and the longing to see her hastened his departure as soon as it was safe to let him go; for Lucindy's letters were always of a dismal sort, and made him anxious to put his shoulder to the wheel.

"She always set consider'ble by me, mother did, bein' the oldest; and I would n't miss makin' her last days happy, not if it cost me all the arms and legs I 've got," said Joe, as he awkwardly struggled into the big boots an hour after leave to go home was given him.

It was pleasant to see his comrades gather round him with such hearty adieus that his one hand must have tingled; to hear the good wishes and the thanks called after him by pale creatures in their beds; and to find tears in many eyes beside my own when he was gone, and nothing was left of him but the empty cot, the old gray wrapper, and the name upon the wall.

I kept that card among my other relics, and
hoped to meet Joe again somewhere in the world.
He sent me one or two letters, then I went home;
the war ended soon after, time passed, and the
little story of my Maine lumberman was laid
away with many other experiences which made
that part of my life a very memorable one.

III

SOME years later, as I looked out of my window one dull November day, the only cheerful thing I saw was the red cap of a messenger who was examining the slate that hung on a wall opposite my hotel. A tall man with gray hair and beard, one arm, and a blue army-coat. I always salute, figuratively at least, when I see that familiar blue, especially if one sleeve of the coat is empty; so I watched the messenger with interest as he trudged away on some new errand, wishing he had a better day and a thicker pair of boots. He was an unusually large, well-made man, and reminded me of a fine building going to ruin before its time; for the broad shoulders were bent, there was a stiffness about the long legs suggestive of wounds or rheumatism, and the curly hair looked as if snow had fallen on it too soon. Sitting at work in my window, I fell into the way of watching my Red Cap, as I called him, with more interest than I did the fat doves on the roof opposite, or the pert sparrows hopping in the mud below. I liked the steady way in which he plodded on through fair weather or foul, as if intent on doing well the one small

service he had found to do. I liked his cheerful
whistle as he stood waiting for a job under the
porch of the public building where his slate hung,
watching the luxurious carriages roll by, and the
well-to-do gentlemen who daily passed him to
their comfortable homes, with a steady, patient
sort of face, as if wondering at the inequalities
of fortune, yet neither melancholy nor morose
over the small share of prosperity which had
fallen to his lot.

I often planned to give him a job, that I might
see him nearer; but I had few errands, and little
Bob, the hall-boy, depended on doing those: so
the winter was nearly over before I found out
that my Red Cap was an old friend.

A parcel came for me one day, and bidding
the man wait for an answer, I sat down to write
it, while the messenger stood just inside the door
like a sentinel on duty. When I looked up to
give my note and directions, I found the man
staring at me with a beaming yet bashful face,
as he nodded, saying heartily, —

"I mistrusted it was you, ma'am, soon's I
see the name on the bundle, and I guess I ain't
wrong. It's a number of years sence we met,
and you don't remember Joe Collins as well as
he does you, I reckon?"

"Why, how you have changed! I've been seeing you every day all winter, and never knew
you," I said, shaking hands with my old patient,
and very glad to see him.

" Nigh on to twenty years makes consid'able
of a change in folks, 'specially if they have a
pretty hard row to hoe."

" Sit down and warm yourself while you tell
me all about it; there is no hurry for this answer, and I 'll pay for your time."

Joe laughed as if that was a good joke, and
sat down as if the fire was quite as welcome as
the friend.

" How are they all at home?" I asked, as he
sat turning his cap round, not quite knowing
where to begin.

" I have n't got any home nor any folks
neither; " and the melancholy words banished the
brightness from his rough face like a cloud.
" Mother died soon after I got back.   Suddin',
but she was ready, and I was there, so she was
happy.   Jim lived a number of years, and was
a sight of care, poor feller; but we managed to
rub along, though we had to sell the farm: for
I could n't do much with one arm, and doctor's
bills right along stiddy take a heap of money.
He was as comfortable as he could be; and, when
he was gone, it was n't no great matter, for there
was only me, and I don't mind roughin' it."

" But Lucindy, where was she?" I asked very
naturally.

" Oh! she married another man long ago.
Could n't expect her to take me and my misfor-
tins.   She 's doin' well, I hear, and that 's a comfort anyway."

There was a look on Joe's face, a tone in Joe's voice as he spoke, that plainly showed how much he had needed comfort when left to bear his misfortunes all alone. But he made no complaint, uttered no reproach, and loyally excused Lucindy's desertion with a simple sort of dignity that made it impossible to express pity or condemnation.

"How came you here, Joe?" I asked, making a sudden leap from past to present.

"I had to scratch for a livin', and can't do much; so, after tryin' a number of things, I found this. My old wounds pester me a good deal, and rheumatism is bad winters; but, while my legs hold out, I can git on. A man can't set down and starve; so I keep waggin' as long as I can. When I can't do no more, I s'pose there's almshouse and hospital ready for me."

"That is a dismal prospect, Joe. There ought to be a comfortable place for such as you to spend your last days in. I am sure you have earned it."

"Wal, it does seem ruther hard on us when we've give all we had, and give it free and hearty, to be left to knock about in our old age. But there's so many poor folks to be took care of, we don't get much of a chance, for *we* ain't the beggin' sort," said Joe, with a wistful look at the wintry world outside, as if it would be better to lie quiet under the snow, than to drag out his last painful years, friendless and forgotten, in some refuge of the poor.

" Some kind people have been talking of a home for soldiers, and I hope the plan will be carried out. It will take time; but, if it comes to pass, you shall be one of the first men to enter that home, Joe, if I can get you there."

" That sounds mighty cheerin' and comfortable, thanky, ma'am. Idleness is dreadful tryin' to me, and I 'd ruther wear out than rust out; so I guess I can weather it a spell longer. But it will be pleasant to look forrard to a snug harbor bymeby. I feel a sight better just hearin' tell about it." He certainly looked so, faint as the hope was; for the melancholy eyes brightened as if they already saw a happier refuge in the future than almshouse, hospital, or grave, and, when he trudged away upon my errand, he went as briskly as if every step took him nearer to the promised home.

After that day it was all up with Bob, for I told my neighbors Joe's story, and we kept him trotting busily, adding little gifts, and taking the sort of interest in him that comforted the lonely fellow, and made him feel that he had not outlived his usefulness. I never looked out when he was at his post that he did not smile back at me; I never passed him in the street that the red cap was not touched with a military flourish; and, when any of us beckoned to him, no twinge of rheumatism was too sharp to keep him from hurrying to do our errands, as if he had Mercury's winged feet.

Now and then he came in for a chat, and
always asked how the Soldiers' Home was pros-
pering; expressing his opinion that " Boston was
the charitablest city under the sun, and he was
sure he and his mates would be took care of
somehow."

When we parted in the spring, I told him
things looked hopeful, bade him be ready for a
good long rest as soon as the hospitable doors
were open, and left him nodding cheerfully.

IV

BUT in the autumn I looked in vain for Joe.
The slate was in its old place, and a messenger came and went on his beat; but a
strange face was under the red cap, and this man
had two arms and one eye. I asked for Collins,
but the new-comer had only a vague idea that he
was dead; and the same answer was given me
at headquarters, though none of the busy people
seemed to know when or where he died. So I
mourned for Joe, and felt that it was very hard
he could not have lived to enjoy the promised
refuge; for, relying upon the charity that never
fails, the Home was an actual fact now, just
beginning its beneficent career. People were
waking up to this duty, money was coming in,
meetings were being held, and already a few
poor fellows were in the refuge, feeling themselves no longer paupers, but invalid soldiers
honorably supported by the State they had served.
Talking it over one day with a friend, who spent
her life working for the Associated Charities,
she said, —

"By the way, there is a man boarding with

one of my poor women, who ought to be got
into the Home, if he will go. I don't know much
about him, except that he was in the army, has
been very ill with rheumatic fever, and is friendless. I asked Mrs. Flanagin how she managed
to keep him, and she said she had help while he
was sick, and now he is able to hobble about, he
takes care of the children, so she is able to go
out to work. He won't go to his own town,
because there is nothing for him there but the
almshouse, and he dreads a hospital; so strug-
gles along, trying to earn his bread tending
babies with his one arm. A sad case, and in your
line; I wish you'd look into it."

"That sounds like my Joe, one arm and all.
I'll go and see him; I've a weakness for soldiers, sick or well."

I went, and never shall forget the pathetic
little tableau I saw as I opened Mrs. Flanagin's
dingy door; for she was out, and no one heard
my tap. The room was redolent of suds, and
in a grove of damp clothes hung on lines sat a
man with a crying baby laid across his lap, while
he fed three small children standing at his knee
with bread and molasses. How he managed
with one arm to keep the baby from squirming
on to the floor, the plate from upsetting, and
to feed the hungry urchins who stood in a row
with open mouths, like young birds, was past
my comprehension. But he did, trotting baby
gently, dealing out sweet morsels patiently, and

whistling to himself, as if to beguile his labors cheerfully.

The broad back, the long legs, the faded coat, the low whistle were all familiar; and, dodging a wet sheet, I faced the man to find it was indeed my Joe! A mere shadow of his former self, after months of suffering that had crippled him for life, but brave and patient still; trying to help himself, and not ask aid though brought so low.

For an instant I could not speak to him, and, encumbered with baby, dish, spoon, and children, he could only stare at me with a sudden brightening of the altered face that made it full of welcome before a word was uttered.

"They told me you were dead, and I only heard of you by accident, not knowing I should find my old friend alive, but not well, I'm afraid?"

"There ain't much left of me but bones and pain, ma'am. I'm powerful glad to see you all the same. Dust off a chair, Patsey, and let the lady set down. You go in the corner, and take turns lickin' the dish, while I see company," said Joe, disbanding his small troop, and shouldering the baby as if presenting arms in honor of his guest.

"Why did n't you let me know how sick you were? And how came they to think you dead?" I asked, as he festooned the wet linen out of the way, and prepared to enjoy himself as best he could.

"I did send once, when things was at the
wust; but you had n't got back, and then somehow I thought I was goin' to be mustered out
for good, and so would n't trouble nobody. But
my orders ain't come yet, and I am doing the
fust thing that come along. It ain't much, but
the good soul stood by me, and I ain't ashamed
to pay my debts this way, sence I can't do it in
no other;" and Joe cradled the chubby baby in
his one arm as tenderly as if it had been his own,
though little Biddy was not an inviting infant.

"That is very beautiful and right, Joe, and I
honor you for it; but you were not meant to
tend babies, so sing your last lullabies, and be
ready to go to the Home as soon as I can get
you there."

"Really, ma'am? I used to lay and kind of
dream about it when I could n't stir without
yellin' out; but I never thought it would ever
come to happen. I see a piece in the paper
describing it, and it sounded dreadful nice.
Should n't wonder if I found some of my mates
there. They were a good lot, and deservin' of
all that could be done for 'em," said Joe, trotting
the baby briskly, as if the prospect excited him,
as well it might, for the change from that damp
nursery to the comfortable quarters prepared for
him would be like going from Purgatory to Paradise.

"I don't wonder you don't get well living in
such a place, Joe. You should have gone home to

Woolwich, and let your friends help you," I said, feeling provoked with him for hiding himself.

" No, ma'am! " he answered, with a look I never shall forget, it was so full of mingled patience, pride, and pain. " I have n't a relation in the world but a couple of poor old aunts, and they could n't do anything for me. As for asking help of folks I used to know, I could n't do it; and if you think I 'd go to Lucindy, though she is wal off, you don't know Joe Collins. I 'd die fust! If she was poor and I rich, I 'd do for her like a brother; but I could n't ask no favors of her, not if I begged my vittles in the street, or starved. I forgive, but I don't forgit in a hurry; and the woman that stood by me when I was down is the woman I believe in, and can take my bread from without shame. Hooray for Biddy Flanagin! God bless her! " and, as if to find a vent for the emotion that filled his eyes with grateful tears, Joe led off the cheer, which the children shrilly echoed, and I joined heartily.

" I shall come for you in a few days; so cuddle the baby and make much of the children before you part. It won't take you long to pack up, will it? " I asked, as we subsided with a general laugh.

" I reckon not as I don't own any clothes but what I set in, except a couple of old shirts and them socks. My hat 's stoppin' up the winder, and my old coat is my bed-cover. I 'm awful shabby, ma'am, and that 's one reason I don't go out more. I can hobble some, but I ain't got used to bein' a scarecrow yet," and Joe glanced from the hose without heels that hung on the line to the ragged suit he wore, with a resigned expression that made me long to rush out and buy up half the contents of Oak Hall on the spot.

Curbing this wild impulse I presently departed with promises of speedy transportation for Joe, and unlimited oranges to assuage the pangs of parting for the young Flanagins, who escorted me to the door, while Joe waved the baby like a triumphal banner till I got round the corner.

There was such a beautiful absence of red tape about the new institution that it only needed a word in the right ear to set things going; and then, with a long pull, a strong pull, and a pull all together, Joe Collins was taken up and safely landed in the Home he so much needed and so well deserved.

A happier man or a more grateful one it would be hard to find, and if a visitor wants an enthusiastic guide about the place, Joe is the one to take, for all is comfort, sunshine, and good-will to him; and he unconsciously shows how great the need of this refuge is, as he hobbles about on his lame feet, pointing out its beauties, conveniences, and delights with his one arm, while his face shines, and his voice quavers a little as he says gratefully, —

" The State don't forget us, you see, and this is a Home wuth havin'. Long life to it! "

WHAT THE BELLS SAW AND SAID

[Written in 1867.]

"Bells ring others to church, but go not in themselves."

NO one saw the spirits of the bells up there in the old steeple at midnight on Christmas Eve. Six quaint figures, each wrapped in a shadowy cloak and wearing a bell-shaped cap. All were gray-headed, for they were among the oldest bell-spirits of the city, and "the light of other days" shone in their thoughtful eyes. Silently they sat, looking down on the snow-covered roofs glittering in the moonlight, and the quiet streets deserted by all but the watchmen on their chilly rounds, and such poor souls as wandered shelterless in the winter night. Presently one of the spirits said, in a tone, which, low as it was, filled the belfry with reverberating echoes, —

"Well, brothers, are your reports ready of the year that now lies dying?"

All bowed their heads, and one of the oldest answered in a sonorous voice: —

"My report is n't all I could wish. You know I look down on the commercial part of our city and have fine opportunities for seeing what goes

on there. It 's my business to watch the business
men, and upon my word I 'm heartily ashamed
of them sometimes. During the war they did
nobly, giving their time and money, their sons
and selves to the good cause, and I was proud
of them. But now too many of them have fallen
back into the old ways, and their motto seems to
be, ' Every one for himself, and the devil take
the hindmost.' Cheating, lying and stealing are
hard words, and I don't mean to apply them to
all who swarm about below there like ants on
an ant-hill — *they* have other names for these
things, but I 'm old-fashioned and use plain
words. There 's a deal too much dishonesty in
the world, and business seems to have become
a game of hazard in which luck, not labor, wins
the prize. When I was young, men were years
making moderate fortunes, and were satisfied
with them. They built them on sure founda-
tions, knew how to enjoy them while they lived,
and to leave a good name behind them when
they died.

" Now it 's anything for money; health, happiness, honor, life itself, are flung down on that
great gaming-table, and they forget everything
else in the excitement of success or the desperation of defeat. Nobody seems satisfied either,
for those who win have little time or taste to
enjoy their prosperity, and those who lose have
little courage or patience to support them in ad-
versity. They don't even fail as they used to.

In my day when a merchant found himself embarrassed he did n't ruin others in order to save himself, but honestly confessed the truth, gave up everything, and began again. But now-a-days after all manner of dishonorable shifts there comes a grand crash; many suffer, but by some hocus-pocus the merchant saves enough to retire upon and live comfortably here or abroad. It 's very evident that honor and honesty don't mean now what they used to mean in the days of old May, Higginson and Lawrence.

"They preach below here, and very well too sometimes, for I often slide down the rope to peep and listen during service. But, bless you! they don't seem to lay either sermon, psalm or prayer to heart, for while the minister is doing his best, the congregation, tired with the breathless hurry of the week, sleep peacefully, calculate their chances for the morrow, or wonder which of their neighbors will lose or win in the great game. Don't tell me! I 've seen them do it, and if I dared I 'd have startled every soul of them with a rousing peal. Ah, they don't dream whose eye is on them, they never guess what secrets the telegraph wires tell as the messages fly by, and little know what a report I give to the winds of heaven as I ring out above them morning, noon, and night." And the old spirit shook his head till the tassel on his cap jangled like a little bell.

"There are some, however, whom I love and

honor," he said, in a benignant tone, " who honestly earn their bread, who deserve all the success
that comes to them, and always keep a warm
corner in their noble hearts for those less blest
than they. These are the men who serve the city
in times of peace, save it in times of war, deserve
the highest honors in its gift, and leave behind
them a record that keeps their memories green.
For such an one we lately tolled a knell, my
brothers; and as our united voices pealed over
the city, in all grateful hearts, sweeter and more
solemn than any chime, rung the words that made
him so beloved, —

" ' Treat our dead boys tenderly, and send
them home to me.' "

He ceased, and all the spirits reverently un-
covered their gray heads as a strain of music
floated up from the sleeping city and died among
the stars.

" Like yours, my report is not satisfactory in
all respects," began the second spirit, who wore
a very pointed cap and a finely ornamented cloak.
But, though his dress was fresh and youthful,
his face was old, and he had nodded several times
during his brother's speech. " My greatest afflic-
tion during the past year has been the terrible
extravagance which prevails. My post, as you
know, is at the court end of the city, and I see all
the fashionable vices and follies. It is a marvel
to me how so many of these immortal creatures,
with such opportunities for usefulness, self-im-

provement and genuine happiness can be content
to go round and round in one narrow circle of
unprofitable and unsatisfactory pursuits. I do
my best to warn them; Sunday after Sunday I
chime in their ears the beautiful old hymns that
sweetly chide or cheer the hearts that truly listen
and believe; Sunday after Sunday I look down
on them as they pass in, hoping to see that my
words have not fallen upon deaf ears; and Sunday after Sunday they listen to words that should
teach them much, yet seem to go by them like
the wind. They are told to love their neighbor,
yet too many hate him because he possesses more
of this world's goods or honors than they; they
are told that a rich man cannot enter the kingdom of heaven, yet they go on laying up perish-
able wealth, and though often warned that moth
and rust will corrupt, they fail to believe it till
the worm that destroys enters and mars their
own chapel of ease. Being a spirit, I see below
external splendor and find much poverty of heart
and soul under the velvet and the ermine which
should cover rich and royal natures. Our city
saints walk abroad in threadbare suits, and under
quiet bonnets shine the eyes that make sunshine
in the shady places. Often as I watch the glittering procession passing to and fro below me, I
wonder if, with all our progress, there is to-day
as much real piety as in the times when our
fathers, poorly clad, with weapon in one hand
and Bible in the other, came weary distances to

worship in the wilderness with fervent faith unquenched by danger, suffering and solitude.

"Yet in spite of my fault-finding I love my children, as I call them, for all are not butterflies. Many find wealth no temptation to forgetfulness of duty or hardness of heart. Many give freely of their abundance, pity the poor, comfort the afflicted, and make our city loved and honored in other lands as in our own. They have their cares, losses, and heartaches as well as the poor; it is n't all sunshine with them, and they learn, poor souls, that

> ' Into each life some rain must fall,
> Some days must be dark and dreary.'

"But I 've hopes of them, and lately they have had a teacher so genial, so gifted, so well-beloved that all who listen to him must be better for the lessons of charity, good-will and cheerfulness which he brings home to them by the magic of tears and smiles. We know him, we love him, we always remember him as the year comes round, and the blithest song our brazen tongues utter is a Christmas carol to the Father of ' The Chimes!' "

As the spirit spoke his voice grew cheery, his old face shone, and in a burst of hearty enthusiasm he flung up his cap and cheered like a boy. So did the others, and as the fairy shout echoed through the belfry a troop of shadowy figures, with faces lovely or grotesque, tragical or gay, sailed by on the wings of the wintry wind and waved their hands to the spirits of the bells.

As the excitement subsided and the spirits re-seated themselves, looking ten years younger for that burst, another spoke. A venerable brother in a dingy mantle, with a tuneful voice, and eyes that seemed to have grown sad with looking on much misery.

"He loves the poor, the man we 've just hurrahed for, and he makes others love and remember them, bless him!" said the spirit. "I hope he 'll touch the hearts of those who listen to him here and beguile them to open their hands to my unhappy children over yonder. If I could set some of the forlorn souls in my parish beside the happier creatures who weep over imaginary woes as they are painted by his eloquent lips, that brilliant scene would be better than any sermon. Day and night I look down on lives as full of sin, self-sacrifice and suffering as any in those famous books. Day and night I try to comfort the poor by my cheery voice, and to make their wants known by proclaiming them with all my might. But people seem to be so intent on business, pleasure or home duties that they have no time to hear and answer my appeal. There 's a deal of charity in this good city, and when the people do wake up they work with a will; but I can't help thinking that if some of the money lavished on luxuries was spent on necessaries for the poor, there would be fewer

tragedies like that which ended yesterday. It's
a short story, easy to tell, though long and hard
to live; listen to it.

"Down yonder in the garret of one of the
squalid houses at the foot of my tower, a little
girl has lived for a year, fighting silently and
single-handed a good fight against poverty and
sin. I saw her when she first came, a hopeful,
cheerful, brave-hearted little soul, alone, yet not
afraid. She used to sit all day sewing at her
window, and her lamp burnt far into the night,
for she was very poor, and all she earned would
barely give her food and shelter. I watched her
feed the doves, who seemed to be her only
friends; she never forgot them, and daily gave
them the few crumbs that fell from her meagre
table. But there was no kind hand to feed and
foster the little human dove, and so she starved.

" For a while she worked bravely, but the poor
three dollars a week would not clothe and feed
and warm her, though the things her busy fingers
made sold for enough to keep her comfortably
if she had received it. I saw the pretty color
fade from her cheeks; her eyes grew hollow, her
voice lost its cheery ring, her step its elasticity,
and her face began to wear the haggard, anxious
look that made its youth doubly pathetic. Her
poor little gowns grew shabby, her shawl so thin
she shivered when the pitiless wind smote her,
and her feet were almost bare. Rain and snow
beat on the patient little figure going to and fro,

each morning with hope and courage faintly
shining, each evening with the shadow of despair gathering darker round her. It was a hard
time for all, desperately hard for her, and in her
poverty, sin and pleasure tempted her. She resisted, but as another bitter winter came she
feared that in her misery she might yield, for
body and soul were weakened now by the long
struggle. She knew not where to turn for help;
there seemed to be no place for her at any safe
and happy fireside; life's hard aspect daunted
her, and she turned to death, saying confidingly,
'Take me while I'm innocent and not afraid
to go.'

"I saw it all! I saw how she sold everything that would bring money and paid her little
debts to the utmost penny; how she set her poor
room in order for the last time; how she tenderly bade the doves good-by, and lay down on
her bed to die. At nine o'clock last night as my
bell rang over the city, I tried to tell what was
going on in the garret where the light was dying
out so fast. I cried to them with all my
strength, —

"'Kind souls, below there! a fellow-creature
is perishing for lack of charity! Oh, help her
before it is too late! Mothers, with little daughters on your knees, stretch out your hands and
take her in! Happy women, in the safe shelter
of home, think of her desolation! Rich men,
who grind the faces of the poor, remember that

this soul will one day be required of you! Dear Lord, let not this little sparrow fall to the ground! Help, Christian men and women, in the name of Him whose birthday blessed the world!'

"Ah me! I rang, and clashed, and cried in vain. The passers-by only said, as they hurried home, laden with Christmas cheer: 'The old bell is merry to-night, as it should be at this blithe season, bless it!'

"As the clocks struck ten, the poor child lay down, saying, as she drank the last bitter draught life could give her, 'It's very cold, but soon I shall not feel it;' and with her quiet eyes fixed on the cross that glimmered in the moonlight above me, she lay waiting for the sleep that needs no lullaby.

"As the clock struck eleven, pain and poverty for her were over. It was bitter cold, but she no longer felt it. She lay serenely sleeping, with tired heart and hands, at rest forever. As the clocks struck twelve, the dear Lord remembered her, and with fatherly hand led her into the home where there is room for all. To-day I rung her knell, and though my heart was heavy, yet my soul was glad; for in spite of all her human woe and weakness, I am sure that little girl will keep a joyful Christmas up in heaven."

In the silence which the spirits for a moment kept, a breath of softer air than any from the snowy world below swept through the steeple and seemed to whisper, "Yes!"

"Avast there! fond as I am of salt water, I
don't like this kind," cried the breezy voice of
the fourth spirit, who had a tiny ship instead
of a tassel on his cap, and who wiped his wet
eyes with the sleeve of his rough blue cloak.
"It won't take me long to spin my yarn; for
things are pretty taut and ship-shape aboard our
craft. Captain Taylor is an experienced sailor,
and has brought many a ship safely into port in
spite of wind and tide, and the devil's own whirl-
pools and hurricanes. If you want to see earnestness come aboard some Sunday when the Captain's on the quarter-deck, and take an observa-
tion. No danger of falling asleep there, no more
than there is up aloft, 'when the stormy winds
do blow.' Consciences get raked fore and aft,
sins are blown clean out of the water, false colors
are hauled down and true ones run up to the
masthead, and many an immortal soul is warned
to steer off in time from the pirates, rocks and
quicksands of temptation. He's a regular re-
volving light, is the Captain, — a beacon always
burning and saying plainly, 'Here are life-boats,
ready to put off in all weathers and bring the
shipwrecked into quiet waters.' He comes but
seldom now, being laid up in the home dock,
tranquilly waiting till his turn comes to go out
with the tide and safely ride at anchor in the
great harbor of the Lord. Our crew varies a
good deal. Some of 'em have rather rough voy-
ages, and come into port pretty well battered;

land-sharks fall foul of a good many, and do
a deal of damage; but most of 'em carry brave
and tender hearts under the blue jackets, for
their rough nurse, the sea, manages to keep
something of the child alive in the grayest old
tar that makes the world his picture-book. We
try to supply 'em with life-preservers while at
sea, and make 'em feel sure of a hearty welcome
when ashore, and I believe the year '67 will sail
away into eternity with a satisfactory cargo.
Brother North-End made me pipe my eye; so
I 'll make him laugh to pay for it, by telling a
clerical joke I heard the other day. Bell-ows
did n't make it, though he might have done so,
as he 's a connection of ours, and knows how to
use his tongue as well as any of us. Speaking
of the bells of a certain town, a reverend gentleman affirmed that each bell uttered an appropriate remark so plainly, that the words were
audible to all. The Baptist bell cried, briskly,
' Come up and be dipped! come up and be
dipped!' The Episcopal bell slowly said, ' Apos-
tol-ic suc-cess-ion! apos-tol-ic suc-cess-ion!' The
Orthodox bell solemnly pronounced, ' Eternal
damnation! eternal damnation!' and the Metho-
dist shouted, invitingly, ' Room for all! room
for all!'"

As the spirit imitated the various calls, as only
a jovial bell-sprite could, the others gave him a
chime of laughter, and vowed they would each
adopt some tuneful summons, which should

reach human ears and draw human feet more willingly to church.

"Faith, brother, you 've kept your word and got the laugh out of us," cried a stout, sleek spirit, with a kindly face, and a row of little saints round his cap and a rosary at his side. "It 's very well we are doing this year; the cathedral is full, the flock increasing, and the true faith holding its own entirely. Ye may shake your heads if you will and fear there 'll be trouble, but I doubt it. We 've warm hearts of our own, and the best of us don't forget that when we were starving, America — the saints bless the jewel! — sent us bread; when we were dying for lack of work, America opened her arms and took us in, and now helps us to build churches, homes and schools by giving us a share of the riches all men work for and win. It 's a generous nation ye are, and a brave one, and we showed our gratitude by fighting for ye in the day of trouble and giving ye our Phil, and many another broth of a boy. The land is wide enough for us both, and while we work and fight and grow together, each may learn something from the other. I 'm free to confess that your religion looks a bit cold and hard to me, even here in the good city where each man may ride his own hobby to death, and hoot at his neighbors as much as he will. You seem to keep your piety shut up all the week in your bare, white churches, and only let it out on Sundays, just a trifle musty

with disuse. You set your rich, warm and soft
to the fore, and leave the poor shivering at the
door. You give your people bare walls to look
upon, common-place music to listen to, dull sermons to put them asleep, and then wonder why
they stay away, or take no interest when they
come.

"We leave our doors open day and night;
our lamps are always burning, and we may come
into our Father's house at any hour. We let
rich and poor kneel together, all being equal
there. With us abroad you 'll see prince and
peasant side by side, school-boy and bishop, mar-
ket-woman and noble lady, saint and sinner,
praying to the Holy Mary, whose motherly arms
are open to high and low. We make our
churches inviting with immortal music, pictures
by the world's great masters, and rites that are
splendid symbols of the faith we hold. Call it
mummery if ye like, but let me ask you why
so many of your sheep stray into our fold? It 's
because they miss the warmth, the hearty, the
maternal tenderness which all souls love and long
for, and fail to find in your stern, Puritanical
belief. By Saint Peter! I 've seen many a luke-
warm worshipper, who for years has nodded in
your cushioned pews, wake and glow with something akin to genuine piety while kneeling on
the stone pavement of one of our cathedrals, with
Raphael's angels before his eyes, with strains of
magnificent music in his ears, and all about him,

in shapes of power or beauty, the saints and
martyrs who have saved the world, and whose
presence inspires him to follow their divine example. It's not complaining of ye I am, but
just reminding ye that men are but children after
all, and need more tempting to virtue than they
do to vice, which last comes easy to 'em since
the Fall. Do your best in your own ways to get
the poor souls into bliss, and good luck to ye.
But remember, there's room in the Holy Mother
Church for all, and when your own priests send
ye to the divil, come straight to us and we'll
take ye in."

"A truly Catholic welcome, bull and all," said
the sixth spirit, who, in spite of his old-fashioned
garments, had a youthful face, earnest, fearless
eyes, and an energetic voice that woke the echoes
with its vigorous tones. "I've a hopeful report,
brothers, for the reforms of the day are wheel-
ing into rank and marching on. The war isn't
over nor rebeldom conquered yet, but the Old
Guard has been 'up and at 'em' through the
year. There has been some hard fighting, rivers
of ink have flowed, and the Washington dawdlers
have signalized themselves by a 'masterly in-
activity.' The political campaign has been an
anxious one; some of the leaders have deserted;
some been mustered out; some have fallen gallantly, and as yet have received no monuments.
But at the Grand Review the Cross of the
Legion of Honor will surely shine on many a

brave breast that won no decoration but its virtue here; for the world's fanatics make heaven's heroes, poets say.

"The flock of Nightingales that flew South during the 'winter of our discontent' are all at home again, some here and some in Heaven. But the music of their womanly heroism still lingers in the nation's memory, and makes a tender minor-chord in the battle-hymn of freedom.

"The reform in literature is n't as vigorous as I could wish; but a sharp attack of mental and moral dyspepsia will soon teach our people that French confectionery and the bad pastry of Wood, Braddon, Yates & Co. is not the best diet for the rising generation.

"Speaking of the rising generation reminds me of the schools. They are doing well; they always are, and we are justly proud of them. There may be a slight tendency toward placing too much value upon book-learning; too little upon home culture. Our girls are acknowledged to be uncommonly pretty, witty and wise, but some of us wish they had more health and less excitement, more domestic accomplishments and fewer ologies and isms, and were contented with simple pleasures and the old-fashioned virtues, and not quite so fond of the fast, frivolous life that makes them old so soon. I am fond of our girls and boys. I love to ring for their christenings and marriages, to toll proudly for the brave lads in blue, and tenderly for the innocent creatures whose seats are empty under my old roof. I want to see them anxious to make Young America a model of virtue, strength and beauty, and I believe they will in time.

"There have been some important revivals in religion; for the world won't stand still, and we must keep pace or be left behind to fossilize. A free nation must have a religion broad enough to embrace all mankind, deep enough to fathom and fill the human soul, high enough to reach the source of all love and wisdom, and pure enough to satisfy the wisest and the best. Alarm bells have been rung, anathemas pronounced, and Christians, forgetful of their creed, have abused one another heartily. But the truth always triumphs in the end, and whoever sincerely believes, works and waits for it, by whatever name he calls it, will surely find his own faith blessed to him in proportion to his charity for the faith of others.

"But look! — the first red streaks of dawn are in the East. Our vigil is over, and we must fly home to welcome in the holidays. Before we part, join with me, brothers, in resolving that through the coming year we will with all our hearts and tongues, —

> 'Ring out the old, ring in the new,
> Ring out the false, ring in the true;
> Ring in the valiant man and free,
> Ring in the Christ that is to be.'"

Then hand in hand the spirits of the bells floated away, singing in the hush of dawn the sweet song the stars sung over Bethlehem, — " Peace on earth, good will to men."

THE END.

BON
HOMME

Leonard Hutchins

2 - 12 - 14

By Leonard Hutchins

DEDICATION

This book is dedicated to Phyllis, my wife since August 31, 1950.

CONTENTS

FOREWORD

I recall the first time I met Leonard Hutchins back in 2001; at the time he was writing an "On Aging" column on behalf of the Aroostook Area Agency on Aging. Unlike many freelance writers who I only knew from the distance of an e-mail or occasional phone call, Leonard liked to drop by the printing plant in person to see me, discuss his article and sometimes just say "Hello" and ask me how I was doing.

It was during these brief but memorable visits that I got to know the man and, much later, his mission.

My first impression of the man was one that could not have come from a phone call or electronic message. His face, more precisely his expression, spoke volumes. His dry sense of humor, also, could easily have been missed or misunderstood if delivered digitally. I am glad that Leonard prefers to do business, and develop lasting friendships, in person. It is becoming a forgotten art I am afraid.

Over the years I grew to appreciate and admire Leonard's quick wit and wealth of wisdom collected through years and experience. I especially like the way he worked it into his writing, whether it was a monthly column, letter to the editor, or, more lately, a chapter book.

Leonard has a knack for knowing how to make learning fun. Although I was not fortunate enough to have had him as a teacher, I know he never misses a chance to "sneak" a little physics or history into his stories. He recognizes a "teaching moment' when it comes along and always works it into his lesson plan.

His original plan for "Bon Homme" was to run it one chapter at a time in the weekly newspaper under the guise of Newspapers in Education, an ongoing effort by publishers to get younger readers interested in current events and the democratic process. However Leonard's timing was bad as the deep economic recession was making finding available space for the ongoing project all but impossible.

I am sorry to say Leonard's manuscript sat in a box on my desk for nearly five years. I had read and offered my edits but had nowhere to publish it in-house. I knew it was good — real good — and wanted others to read it … it haunted me during that time. Also, I knew it would be appreciated on many levels, not only a young audience.

Finally last fall, after reading a self-published book by a man from Houlton who had connections to our newspaper, I knew there was a home for "Bon Homme" and a way to help Leonard's story see the light of day and get the full appreciation it deserved. I pitched the ebook solution to his daughter Dottie and the rest, as they say, is history.

And, how fitting it is that "Bon Homme" will be available to the reading public in time for the 2014 World Acadian Congress and Junior World biathlon championships — two events that this book pays homage to in Leonard's own "sneaky" kind of way. Enjoy!

Mark Putnam, managing editor
Northeast Publishing Company
December 31, 2013
Presque Isle, Maine

ACKNOWLEDGMENTS

I thank the many people who helped with this effort. My Ashland Community High School students, 1962-1980, their parents, and older local friends who lived Eddie's experience, told me the setting, and gave me pictures. Sister Mary Denis Schwartz, RSM, Sisters of Mercy, and Eileen Carey, vice president, Maine Winter Sports Center, gave much needed help. Mark Putnam, managing editor of four local newspapers, encouraged and guided this project to publication, and Aroostook County Artist Judy Sherman once again created the perfect illustrations to help bring my words to life. With great patience, friends at the Mark and Emily Turner Library in Presque Isle found and provided me with books I needed. I also appreciate Michael Gudreau of Northeast Publishing who helped digitally scan and prepare Judy's full-color paintings for proper reproduction in book format. Finally, many thanks goes to family friends Rita Sherman, Sharon Craig, and Susan Beaulier, for their proofreading assistance; and, to my daughter Dottie for understanding my computer.

This book is a tribute to the efforts of the Maine Winter Sports Center and their several facilities. More kids ski now.

1. GRADUATION DAY

This is it. Graduation. The end. Done. No more school. No more student. Grow up and get a job. Get a great job so Mom won't make me quit and go to high school.

This goes through my mind during our West End School eighth grade graduation. I sit at my back row seat near the back door to the woodshed and boys' privy. Mom sits in the seat beside me. My coat covers my desk because I don't want Mom to see my initials in my desk.

I go up front and give the salutatorian's welcoming address. In some schools being salutatorian, second in the class, is a big deal. However, Janice Chase and I are the only students in our class, so it's fair to say I'm the class dummy.

Janice goes up front and gives the valedictory address. Her black shoes lace up just above her ankles. Her brown dress, which Mom helped her make, hangs to her shoe tops. The dress has ruffles on the shoulders which are angel wings on Janice. She has a big pin on the dress just under her chin, and her brown hair is pinned up some way. She looks twenty years old, she is beautiful, and I haven't got a clue what she says.

There are four windows on each side of our school room and eighteen seats and desks are screwed to the floor around a wood-burning stove. There is another back door to the girls' privy and a front door to outdoors beside the teacher's desk. All I see is Janice in her new dress.

I sense movement and glance at Mom. She reaches across to the seat beyond her and touches Mr. Chase's arm. Mr. Chase is wiping his eyes with a handkerchief. My seventh-grade brother, Jason, is sitting in the seat beyond Mr. Chase.

I look up front again. Our teacher, Miss Rogers, is sitting in a student seat beside the stove. My first-grade sisters, Martha and Mary, Dingie and

Dongie when Mom isn't around, are sitting in small seats right in front of Janice. Their black hair hangs to their waists and their blue dresses spread at their ankles so they look like two kites. They would stand up with Janice if Miss Rogers would let them.

The rest of my eight schoolmates are home starting summer vacation, but my school room seems full to me. The people here are big in my life.

Janice finishes her valedictory address, and we clap. She deserves it even if I don't know what she said. She walks back with Dingie and Dongie following her like they are on a short kite string. She sits in the seat in front of her father, and the girls try to squeeze onto the seat beside her. They have to take the seats on either side.

Miss Rogers has some certificates for us, and Dingie and Dongie go back up front with her. They have some deal cooked up which I don't know about.

Dingie reads a certificate. "*West End School, June, 1925. This is to thank Janice Chase for helping me teach Mary and Martha Clark to read. Signed, Miss Agnes Rogers.*"

Janice looks surprised. Apparently she doesn't know about this deal either. She goes up front and accepts her certificate—with thanks and hugs.

Dongie reads, "*West End School, June, 1925. This is to thank Edward Clark for being the best janitor I ever had. When I arrive in the morning our school is always, without exception, neat, clean, and warm. Signed, Miss Agnes Rogers.*"

Wow. I sit there, and my mouth is most likely dropped open. Mom pokes my shoulder so I go up front to accept my certificate. I don't know if they hug me or I hug them.

Miss Rogers says, "Our school Board of Directors voted to give you a bonus, Ed." She gives me an envelope. "You can open it now," she says. I open it, and it's a five dollar bill. This is a month's janitor's pay.

After a while my brain works, and I tell Miss Rogers, "Thank you very much."

I give the five dollars to Mom, and she is crying. I haven't seen Mom cry since Dad's funeral two years ago. Dad died in a logging accident.

"Mom," I say, "are you sick?"

She wipes her eyes with the five dollar bill and says, "Oh. Look what I'm doing."

She puts the money in her pocketbook and wipes her eyes with a handkerchief. "No, Eddie, I'm not sick. This is one of the happiest days of my life. Your father and I wanted our children to have the education we missed. You are taking a big step forward today, and I am happy. Also Eddie, I am going to do something today I have never done before."

Mom goes up front. She has on a red dress she rebuilt from something or other. She is always doing that, and it really looks good. When Miss Rogers gives her a certificate it crosses my mind that Mom is also in on this deal I don't know about.

Mom says, "I am proud today. This is the first time I have read in public." She reads, "*West End School. June, 1925. This is to thank Janice Chase for a special class project teaching Mrs. Edna Clark to read. Signed, Miss Agnes Rogers.*"

I look at Janice. Now she is staring, and her mouth is hanging open. She doesn't look that dumb very often.

Mom says, "Janice, because of you I can read 'Cinderella' with my girls. We now have glass slippers and pumpkin coaches in our lives."

Janice's brain kicks in quicker than mine. She closes her mouth, goes up and hugs Mom, and she gets another certificate.

It comes as a surprise to me that Mom is as pretty as Janice.

Now about that "Cinderella" thing. Janice spent a lot of time last winter at our place. She read "Cinderella"—many times— with Mom and the girls. She read at first. Pretty soon Mom and the girls started to read. They read "Cinderella"—out loud of course—about a million times each. I'll tell you what. I've had about enough of "Cinderella".

But look, that isn't all bad because I got to walk Janice home. "Cinderella" is a story, but Janice is real.

There is more. Janice and I go up on the platform, and Miss Rogers has graduation certificates for us. That is the end of the program.

But there is still more. Mom says, "Eddie, Mr. Chase wants to talk to you." Janice and I go up back to Mr. Chase's seat, and Mom takes my coat from my desk and gives it to me. "Don't forget your coat," she says.

Janice hops up and sits on my initials carved in my desk. I owe her one.

"Ed," Mr. Chase says, "we're building a dam at 30-Mile Depot. Our cookee was a farmer from Quebec. He had to leave two weeks ago to plant his crop, and it's hard to find men to work in the woods during summer. Our cook really needs a cookee. Pay is ninety cents a day, and that is seven days a week." Mr. Chase smiles. "We have to eat every day, you know. Do you want the job?"

Wow. A cookee is a cook's helper. He splits wood, washes pots and pans, carries water, and keeps the cook room more or less cleaned up.

Like I was saying—Wow. Can I believe this? I need a good job, and here it is.

"What's ninety times seven?" I say out loud, but I'm talking to myself.

Janice and Jason say together, "Six dollars and thirty cents."

"Wow," I say out loud. "Of course I'll take it. When do I start?"

Mr. Chase says, "The tote wagon leaves Ashland Depot Monday morning. It stops at 10-Mile Depot Monday night, 20-Mile Depot Tuesday night, and it gets to 30-Mile Depot Wednesday afternoon. You can start Thursday morning. I'll guarantee you there will be wood to split and dishes to wash."

All my life I heard about logging from Dad and our neighbors. I waited a long time to be part of it, but Mom kept me in school—of course. But here it is. Here is the chance I've been waiting for.

Tote wagons carry supplies to logging depots which store food, tools, and hay and grain for nearby logging camps. Horses can pull loaded wagons and sleds ten or so miles a day.

Ashland is the local headquarters for the Great Northern Paper Company. Logging camps and depots are located along the Machias River in the woods west of Ashland. In winter, logs are cut into four-foot lengths and hauled to the river on sleds. Wood is driven down the river to Ashland in spring time when snow melts and water is high. There the wood is pulled from the river, loaded onto railroad cars, and hauled down state to the Great Northern Paper Company mill.

"Hey, Mr. Chase," I say. "You need a cookee now, you say. How about if I walk in tomorrow and start work Sunday? That would give me four more days' work. Mom can use another—let's see—three dollars and sixty cents."

"Edward," Mom says, "you can't do that. Nobody can walk thirty miles in a day."

"Look, Mom," I say. I show Mom my good janitor certificate. I have to talk fast. When Mom calls me Edward, she isn't happy. "I build the school fire every morning at five o'clock. I run across the bridge to Ashland and run my paper delivery route. I run back to school, and I'm not late. And the last three weeks I've been planting potatoes after school. That's about like thirty-five miles a day."

Mom says, "Edward, you could get lost in the muddy mess of logging roads in the woods. We would never find you."

"Look, Mom," I say, "I've been hunting and fishing for quite a ways along that road. It's a good hard road now that the spring mud has dried up. It goes pretty much straight west, and you can't mistake it for a little side road."

Mr. Chase says to Mom, "He's got that right. And you know, Edna, Fred Jorgensen, the game warden, walks and skis further than that in a day. Fred shows up unexpectedly to check logging camps for illegal use of game. Besides, Peter and Ruth LeBlanc are camp sitting at 10-Mile Depot this summer. Ed could stop there for a night. Or there is a Quebec couple camp sitting at 20-Mile Depot. They would put Ed up for a night." He says to me, "Those ladies can really cook." He says to Mom, "I could call them on the Maine Forest Service telephone."

"Roy," Mom says, "whose side are you on?"

My brain takes a fraction of a second timeout. This is the first time I hear Mom and Mr. Chase use each other's first names. I can't sweat that now. Time in again. How can I convince Mom I can do thirty miles?

"He can do it, Mom," Jason says. I owe Jason one.

"Yes, he can, Mrs. Clark," Janice says. I owe her another one.

Mom looks from one of us to the other. She is in the middle, and her eyes look like a mouse watching four cats. "Thirty miles," she says. "Peter and Ruth are at 10-Mile," she says.

I think I've won—with some help.

Tears come to Mom's eyes. Here comes her handkerchief again. This time I'm not going to ask if she's sick. I don't think she's happy either, and now I'm not sure I've won.

"Eddie," Mom says, "sit down."

I sit, and Mom's tears are gone. She is a small lady, and standing up she looks straight into my eyes. What is this? I wonder.

"Eddie," Mom says, "I lost your father to a logging accident. I do not want to lose my children, but this is a splendid opportunity for you and for us. I know you have to find your own way. It is time for you to go, but promise me two things. First, you will take no dangerous chances. Second, you will be back this fall to go to high school."

I win. Well, sort of, but now I feel like the mouse watching four cats. She doesn't cut me much slack on school, but look I think, I've got a super job for the summer. I'll do one thing at a time and talk about high school later.

"OK, Mom. You got it," I say. I stand up so I don't feel like the mouse any more. "Mr. Chase," I say, "can you fix it so Mom gets my pay?"

"No problem, Ed," he says. "Payday is every two weeks. The check will be made out to Edna so she can endorse it."

"Oh," Mom says. "Is it OK if I just print my name?"

"You'll be able to sign those checks. Guaranteed," Janice says to Mom.

"That doesn't seem possible," Mom says. "But with you, Janice, everything is possible. I can read now—except for hard words, and my boys help me with them."

"Yeah, Jason," I say, "and something else you need to do is my paper route.

You've been over it plenty of times. Saturday is payday, so you collect twenty-five cents from each customer tomorrow. You keep one dollar forty and give the rest to the people at the store. Give Mom the dollar, and you get the forty cents. Got it? And keep wood split ahead for Mom's stove. Do you think you can do that?"

"Well, let's see," Jason says. "I've been splitting quite a lot of Mom's wood for a couple years now. I'm finally going to get paid the full forty cents for delivering your papers, and I also get our room all to myself. I can handle that. Guaranteed."

I know I shouldn't ask Jason that kind of question.

"Hey," Dingie says, "How come you're going somewhere? You won't be here to play with us."

"I got a job in the woods, Dingie," I say. "You and Dongie play with Jason."

I loused up, and I know it's coming.

"Edward, that is not their names," Mom says.

"You can't do that," Dongie says. She begins to sniffle.

"I need someone to play with," Janice says. "I've got a new book, too. It's called 'Alice's Adventures In Wonderland.' We can read it together. OK?"

The girls don't have to think about that at all. They both say, "OK."

I owe Janice another one, and I'm on my way.

2. HEADING TO 30-MILE DEPOT

It's five o'clock the next morning. The sun isn't up, but there's enough light to travel. Jason and I stop where the West End Road forks.

Jason says, "I know I've got to take care of Mom and the girls, but I'd like to go with you. I'm old enough to do something."

I say, "There'll be plenty of haying jobs pretty soon. Talk to Janice, too. She said she gets lonesome when Mr. Chase goes in the woods."

"OK. Look, when you get to 5-Mile Brook, look under the bridge for trout. Remember the fish we caught there last summer?"

"Can't forget them. I'll send letters out on the tote wagon. Write and tell me how everyone is doing. OK?"

Jason nods OK. We shake hands, and he walks east past the paper company office and stable, toward the bridge, Ashland, and the paper route. I walk west into the woods.

My mind checks my pack sack. Matches. Compass. Hunting knife. Coal tar insect repellent. Four pairs of socks. Four bandanna handkerchiefs. Two changes of clothes. A jacket. Some paper and pencils for letters. A bag of peanuts and raisins. I wear a hat with a broad brim all around to shade my neck and shed rain.

Leaving home wasn't bad this morning. Dingie and Dongie weren't up, and Mom didn't cry.

I remember Janice didn't visit to read with Mom and the girls last night, and I wonder if she is upset with me. Maybe I ought to go back and talk to her, but I won't get to 30-Mile if I go back. I hope she's not upset with me. I'll write to her.

The road is wagon wheel ruts in the bottom of a giant brown groove cut through the green forest. It is mostly dry and packed hard by horse hooves, the tracks all pointing east out of the woods. The crews bring horses out when the snow melts and logging stops for the summer.

The Great Northern Paper Company and the Maine Forest Service share a telephone wire which stretches from tree to tree. It goes through white glass things which are wired to trees. It goes up over hills and down in low places. As I walk I wonder how much a mile of wire weighs. How about thirty five miles?

The sun rises above the trees, and it's warm on my back. I keep a long, steady stride.

In a low spot, water runs over the road where beaver plugged a log culvert. I hop over it as best I can, but I get the bottom of my blue jean pant legs wet. I pick up an ash stick with no bark. Beaver ate the bark. I whittle off little branches as I walk, and I have a walking stick.

This is a great day. I remember other times I walked this road to hunt and fish, and I recognize this odd-shaped rock or that super big tree. A shiny black raven croaks like a frog at me as it glides over the trees. Those things can make about any sound you can imagine.

I'm walking down a long slope, and there is a log bridge at the bottom. This is 5-Mile Brook already. I've walked five miles. Hey, I think, thirty miles is going to be a piece of cake.

I take off my pack and hat, lie on the bridge logs, and look into the deep pool under the bridge. Wow. The trout in there would drive Jason nuts. I know one of those fish is fingertip to elbow long.

I remember. I didn't bring any fish hooks. That's numb.

Hey wait, I think, I'm going to work. I've got to move.

I put my pack and hat on, pick up my walking stick, and walk. All the same, if I have to come out for school this fall I might get back to catch those trout.

I walk past a patch of ashes and charcoal. I remember Dad telling me about the loggers always stopping to boil the kettle here at 5-Mile Brook.

A gray Canada jay flies out of the woods, lights on a bush, and chirps at me. We call them gorbeys, and they are my favorite birds. They always show up to beg for food, but I don't have anything for them this morning. Beyond 5-Mile Brook is new country to me, but it is no different. Up hills, down dips, telephone wire all the way.

Grass grows along the sunny roadsides but not in the shady woods, so there are rabbits chomping here and there. They are changing from winter white to summer brown, and they look pretty scruffy. I walk almost up to them before they hop into the shadows.

There are more deer than I expected. Does scoot their little spotted fawns into the woods long before I get to them.

I walk watching rabbits and deer, trees and blue sky, and I'm surprised once in a while. A big black spot a long ways down the road is a bear. It shuffles into the woods before I get to the place, but I see bear claw marks

Illustration 2-1: *Heading to 30-Mile Depot* by Judy Sherman

in the dirt road. Once I think someone is walking a dark brown horse out of the woods, but it's a moose. Long before we meet, old big and homely saunters off into the woods.

I see a lot of partridges, some with a bunch of little, brown, fuzzy chicks. I think they are supposed to be called grouse. They peck around in the road and eat buds and new leaves in poplar trees.

The sun is up quite high, and my back is getting sweaty under my pack sack. I look up from watching a rabbit, and I can't believe it. There, down the road is a set of log buildings and a bridge. It's 10-Mile Depot and the Machias River.

Even at a distance, I recognize Mr. LeBlanc. He sees me, and soon Mrs. LeBlanc steps out onto the road.

"Eddie," Mr. LeBlanc says as I approach. "It's only ten o'clock. We got a call from Mr. Chase, but we didn't expect you until this afternoon."

"It's a good day for a walk," I say as Mr. LeBlanc lifts my pack off my shoulders. That feels good, and the air feels cold on my sweaty back. He sets my load on the dingle platform, and I drop my walking stick and hat beside it. I smell doughnuts.

It seems like I've been here before. I remember Dad talking about logging camps, and they're all alike. There is a log cook room with stoves, a walled-off corner for cooks and cookees, cooking space, and dining tables. There is a log bunk room with a heating stove in the middle and two-tier bunks for the crew along three walls. There is a table down one side for wash pans, and maybe a little window here or there.

The dingle is a supply room between the cook room and bunk room. It has back and front log walls and a roof that extends out over an open front porch. All of the floors are logs cut flat on top with an adze.

The filer and blacksmith have separate cabins for shops. The filer keeps logging tools in good working condition, and the blacksmith keeps the horses' shoes fixed up.

The horses' stable is a log building with sheds for hay and grain built on.

"Come in, Eddie, come in," Mrs. LeBlanc says. "I have new doughnuts for you, and some cold milk from the spring."

The hot cook room smells like the biggest doughnut in the world. A baking sheet piled with fresh doughnuts covers one end of a 10-man kitchen table. Mrs. LeBlanc is the only other woman in the world who can cook like my mother. That cold milk really does it, and in fifteen minutes I feel ashamed of how much I'm eating. Mrs. LeBlanc sits beside me smiling and maybe grinning.

"Eddie," Mr. LeBlanc says when he comes in, "Mr. Chase said on the telephone that he is surprised you are here so soon. You can sleep in the bunk room tonight."

"After those doughnuts, I can make it to 30-Mile. And I thank you very much for them," I say to Mrs. LeBlanc.

Their clock says ten thirty. I'm doing OK.

They follow me out to the dingle and say nothing as I put on my pack and pick up my walking stick and hat.

"Eddie," Mr. LeBlanc says as I step off the dingle platform, "are you sure you want to go?"

"For ninety cents a day I can do it, Mr. LeBlanc. Only twenty more miles to go," I say. "Thanks again for the doughnuts."

"Wait, Eddie," Mrs. LeBlanc says. She rushes back into the cook room, comes back and gives me a bag of doughnuts. "There. Now you have a good walk."

I cross the log bridge over the Machias River and walk maybe a quarter mile to the top of a small hill. When I look back, they are still in the road in front of the dingle. We wave, and I walk west over the hill.

Mile after mile is the same. Well, sort of. My pack pulls on my shoulders more, and I'm glad the beaver cut me a walking stick. It helps.

The telephone wire just keeps going. I wonder if words take longer to go farther on a telephone wire. I wonder if the road and the wire continue beyond 30-Mile Depot. I'll find out before long.

The sun is high and hot.

A small run of clear, cold water trickles beside the road. I stop, set my pack on the road, drink cold water, and dig out my doughnuts. Here comes a gorbey to beg. It finds me at the right time, and we share the goodies.

I go on, but I catch myself slowing up to watch partridge, deer, rabbits, anything. I concentrate on keeping a long, steady stride—uphill, downhill, around curves, and along straight stretches.

I think about stopping again to rest but I wonder if I'm doing OK. I walk around a curve in the road, and I see a bridge and a set of log buildings like those at 10-Mile Depot. It's 20-Mile Depot. I'm hot and my legs really need a rest, but I'm happy—and I'm doing OK.

Wow. The smell of beef stew almost changes the color of the fresh air. Maybe I run that quarter mile.

I drop my pack, hat, and walking stick on the dingle platform. Someone shouts from the cook room, and a couple rushes out onto the dingle. They talk. They smile. They shake my hand. They talk more. Of their French I understand only "Eddie" and "Monsieur Chassee." The man holds one fist in front of his mouth and the other to his ear like he is talking on a telephone. I understand that Mr. Chase called them about me. I soon know their names are Madam Evangeline and Monsieur Honre Cote.

Also, I soon know that Madam Evangeline Cote makes a beef stew that tastes as good as it smells. As I concentrate on the stew, I notice it's 2 o'clock. My legs are feeling the twenty miles, but the beef stew has carrots, potatoes, turnip, and stuff that must be magic. It perks up my legs. I can walk ten more miles.

I'm full, but Madam Cote isn't done. She sets a mug of steaming tea in front of me—and a frosted chocolate cake. Full or not, that chocolate cake is too good to pass up. I eat chocolate cake and drink tea until I'm ashamed of myself. The more I eat, the brighter is Madam Cote's smile.

I can't eat any more. I just can't eat any more. I tell them several times, "Thank you."

They smile and take me to the bunk room. In one corner a bunk is made up.

"Coushay. Eddie," they say.

I know they mean that is my bunk. I shake my head, point down the road, and tell them, "Ten miles. 30-Mile Depot."

They understand, but they look sad. Monsieur Cote lifts the pack, and I slide my arms under the shoulder straps. He gives me my hat and walking stick, and Madam Cote gives me the leftover cake in a box.

I thank them again, and I walk over 20-Mile Brook bridge to a curve in the road. I look back, and as at 10-Mile Depot my new friends are still watching. We wave, and I walk west.

I concentrate on my stride, and I'm OK for a half mile or so. Then things get heavier, the pack, my head, my legs, my boots. My walking stick keeps my stride going.

I'm surprised to notice the sun has moved ahead of me. It's moving faster than I am, and I drop my head so my visor shades my eyes.

I tell myself to keep up my stride. I'm tired. I wonder if I should have stopped at 20-Mile Depot. Maybe, I think, I should go back.

I remember that both Janice and Jason said I could do thirty miles. I said I could do it. OK, I say to myself, cut the pity. Make your feet keep up with your big mouth. I concentrate on my stride.

I have to push myself, but I do OK for quite a ways. I have room in my stomach for the cake Madam Cote gave me, so I push my walking stick under a pack basket strap. I use one hand to hold the cake box, and I eat with the other hand. Sure enough, gorbeys come for their share, and we eat the whole thing in a mile or so.

I'm in trouble. Cake sticks in my throat, and there is no water close. I walk, and my eyes blur with tears. I really concentrate on my stride. I have to get water.

There are holes in the road and along the sides of the road. As I hurry I look for water in every hole. A big hole has water in the bottom. I slip out of my pack, lay on my stomach, and by stretching my neck I reach the water with my mouth.

I sit up. With a mouth full of water I swallow and push the cake down, but my mouth tastes like mud.

I'm losing time. I turn my pack shoulder straps up then lay back and slide my arms under the shoulder straps. I roll over onto my hands and knees, push myself up with my walking stick, and walk on.

I wonder why there are holes all over the place, and it dawns on me that people are gathering rocks. Why, I wonder, would people do that? I see stumps and tree limbs where trees have been cut. Again it dawns on me that this must be part of the dam project. I must be close to 30-Mile Depot.

Around a curve, rock carts and steel horse-drawn dirt scoops are in the road. I walk to the rock carts, rest my pack on a wheel, and look down into a deep gorge. A huge ditch is ripped open across the bottom, a rock-filled log crib nearly fills the hole, and a brook filters through the rocks. It's easy to see that the dam will be the crib built to the top of the gorge.

Wow, I think to myself, I'd sure like to help build that dam.

I hear men shout and laugh. The sun is low so I can't see ahead, but I walk a quarter mile or so to 30-Mile Depot. About two dozen men sit along the dingle platform watching two guys pitch a game of horseshoes.

They stand up and stare at me.

Leonard Hutchins

3. COOKEE

These guys stand up and stare at me like I'm a ghost or something, and they're a scruffy looking bunch. They all wear suspenders over plaid shirts holding up dark colored pants cut off above ankle high calked boots. They have a week's worth of whiskers, mostly gray, and their mostly gray hair points everywhere, except three or four are bald.

"Hello," I say. "My name is Ed Clark. Mr. Chase hired me to be your cookee."

One of the men says, "Parlee vou Fransay?" or something like that. It sounds like a question.

I say, "I'm sorry. I don't understand you. Do you speak English?"

"I do little English," another man says. "You are really Eddie like Monsieur Chassee say on telephone?" He holds one fist in front of his mouth and the other against his ear.

"Yes."

"We don't think you can come this far today. You walk from Ashland?"

"Yes."

They talk about me. It must be me they're talking about because they all look at me once in a while. They repeat a word that sounds like "bonum." I wonder if they are going to kick me out or something.

"Eddie," the fellow who speaks English says, "my name Andre Cyr." He sticks his hand out and we shake. That means the same in any language. As tired as I am, I feel better. "We," Mr. Cyr says to me as he waves his hand to include all of the men, "think you are good man."

"Bonum. Bonum," they say. Every one of them shakes my hand, and I feel strength and sincerity in the handshakes. I feel like a moving picture star or something, but I don't know what I did to deserve the fuss.

15

Illustration 3-1: *Lumber Camp at 30-Mile Depot* by Judy Sherman

The last handshake is with a man wearing thick, thick glasses. His 'Bonum' sounds like he talks from the bottom of a lake. "Emile Pelletier," he gurgles as he points to his chest. He lifts my pack from my shoulders with one hand and points to the cook room. "Arrive," he says. I guess I'm supposed to arrive in the cook room.

Inside the really big cook room two huge cook stoves overheat the place. I mean it's really hot. The clock shows 7 o'clock in the orange glow of a dozen kerosene lamps hanging from roof logs.

The cook is a big man with a short, black beard. He wears pants and a jacket that might have been white at one time. His hat looks like a white but rusty stove pipe, and it makes him look seven feet tall. He is washing black iron cooking pots in a black iron sink.

Mr. Cyr and Mr. Pelletier talk French with the cook. I only understand Eddie, Ashland, and Monsieur Chassee.

With no change in expression the cook glances at me, points at the sink, and says "Lavey," or something.

"Nun. Nun," Mr. Cyr and Mr. Pelletier say. There is a lot of French and none of it sounds good. Downright ugly, in fact. The cook says Fransay and Anglay a lot. Every time he says Anglay he points at me. I think I'm going to get fired before I go to work.

Mr. Pelletier tosses my pack on a bunk in a walled-off corner. "Eddie. Coushay." He says to me. I know that is my bunk so I toss my walking stick and hat underneath.

Mr. Cyr pours me a cup of coffee from the biggest coffee pot I ever saw. He takes a half dozen molasses cookies from a bucket, puts them on a tin plate, and gives me my supper.

I sit on the edge of my bunk, balance my plate on my knees, and eat my supper. I'm surprised the coffee doesn't dissolve the cup, but I can hardly believe the cookies. I can't span one with my outstretched thumb and fingers, and they're as good as they're big.

I feel so tired I don't want to get up from my bunk.

"Eddie," Mr. Cyr says, "You sleep. Will be something for you do in morning."

At least I didn't get fired. I pull a couple of shirts from my pack and roll them up for a pillow. I toss my pack under my bunk and lay down, and I'm going to sleep. I remember that I didn't take my boots off, but I don't care. Shouts sound ugly and mean and soon far away.

There is a tight grip on my arm, and I feel like a doll being worked over by a big dog. I look into the cook's eyes, he lets go of my arm, and I stand up.

"Boy," the cook says.

A glance at the clock shows 4 o'clock. "Boy?" I say.

"Anglay," he says. It sounds like a grumble, and he shakes his head like he is disgusted. He sticks his chin and lower lip out at me, then goes to a stove, lifts a cover, and points at the fire. He points at an empty woodbox beside the stoves then at the back door. "Boy," he says again. I open the back door and learn some French. There is a wood pile out there. Boy must be wood.

These stoves are a lot bigger than any I've seen before. The fire boxes hold two-foot sticks of wood, so I saw two-foot blocks from the tree trunks piled there. The buck saw is as dull as a piece of rope, and I split the blocks into stove wood with a cracked-handled axe. After a while I get the woodbox filled.

"Lavay," the cook tells me as he points to black iron pots and griddles in the sink. That is the word he used last night. It must mean wash. "Lav," the cook says. He gives me a bucket and points at tubs of hot water on one of the stoves. I guess lav is water.

I dip a bucket of hot water from a tub, pour it over the pots and griddles, and scrub them with a brush in the sink.

"Savon. Savon," the cook yells at me.

Just when I need it I have some good luck. All with only undershirts on or no shirts at all, Mr. Cyr comes in for breakfast with several other men. The cook gives him a lot of French.

Illustration 3-2: *The Cook at 30-Mile Depot* by Judy Sherman

Mr. Cyr shows me slabs of yellow soap and a kitchen knife. "Cut soap in water," he says.

More French from the cook. Mr. Cyr says, "Be sure rinse soap from dishes."

"OK," I say. "Look, is there an axe handle around here I can put in my axe?"

Mr. Cyr says, "I am filer. I have axe for you."

While I'm scrubbing pots and griddles I watch the cook work. He keeps eggs, bacon, and pancakes cooking on three griddles then slides them off onto three trays before anything burns. He's good.

I stop washing pots long enough to carry the trays to the tables. There are pots of coffee and trays of bread and doughnuts already on the tables, and I wonder if I was supposed to do that. I wonder if I overslept.

The men eat like there is no tomorrow, but there is no conversation at the tables. When they leave several say, "Mercy, Eddie. Bonum."

Mr. Cyr says, "Thank you, Eddie. You are good man."

I guess mercy means thank you. Does bonum mean good man? Why would they call me a good man? I remember that Mr. Chase is bilingual, and I decide to ask him.

I get ten minutes to eat, and that is time enough. Everything is so first-class good. I'd kill myself eating if I had more time. My boss is crabby, but he can really cook. In the morning the coffee isn't bad either.

The cook says, "Lav," and he points to a shoulder yoke and two buckets behind a stove. He goes to the back door and points to a path into the woods beyond the wood pile. I carry the yoke and buckets into the woods and learn more French. There is a good-sized spring, so Lav means water. Now, I think, I've got to concentrate and remember all of this French. It takes me an hour or so to fill the water tubs on one of the stoves.

Time for more French. The cook says, "Plat," and he points at the tin plates on the tables. He points to the sink and says, "Lavay." Plat must be plate. He's telling me to wash the dishes I guess.

Hey, I say to myself, I'm getting this French thing. I try to remember how long it's been since I really worked at learning something. I guess it's been a while.

I'm doing OK washing the breakfast dishes when Mr. Cyr opens the woodshed door and beckons for me to come out.

"I have saw for you," he says. Wow, he certainly does. It's a crosscut saw with handles on only one end. It has no rust at all, and the big teeth are filed to perfection. I saw a block of wood from a log in just a shade over no time at all.

"Mercy," I say.

Mr. Cyr smiles. I guess my French pronunciation isn't too great. "I have axe for you," he says.

This axe is a piece of art. The steel head is polished and sharp enough to shave mosquitoes. The handle is white ash. It would be as beautiful in a museum as it is in that woodshed. I set on end the block of wood I sawed and split it with one swing.

"Mercy very much," I say. "Did you make this handle?"

"Wee," he says. "I use donker and fro to split wood like cedar shake on roof." He points to the roof shakes sticking out beyond side logs. "I have draw shave and spoke shave to make shape. You come to shop someday. I show you."

The cook comes to the woodshed door, points a finger at me, and jerks a thumb at the sink. I return to the sink, and my boss points to soap suds on a washed plate.

"Rinsay, rinsay, rinsay," he growls. He dumps plenty of water over the plates.

I just learned more. First, rinsay means rinse, and second, I'd better rinse the cooking stuff better. Come to think of it, I remember Mom telling Jason and me that soap left on dishes will make you sick.

As I work at the sink, I keep an eye on the cook. There is an oven on each side of the fire box in both stoves. Four ovens. I watch him take a dozen loaves of bread from one oven and slide in four baking sheets of ginger bread. He sets the baked bread on a shelf under the roof shakes. From another oven he takes out six baked pies, slides in six pies, then sets the baked pies up on the shelf. He checks four dozen potatoes baking in another oven, then checks with a big kitchen fork three huge chunks of salted meat cooking in the fourth oven.

I hear laughter, shouts, and clanking steel. A game of horseshoes is going on outside in front of the dingle. Men come into the cook room two or three at a time and dip hot water in wash basins from a tub, but they don't talk. I go after more wood and see men carrying fresh evergreen branches into the bunk room to freshen up their mattresses. Men with fresh shaves and combed hair hang washed clothes on bushes, and they talk and laugh outdoors. I guess Sunday is cleanup day.

I guess Sunday is also extra pie day. The cook room has a great cooking setup. There is a long cooking table made of smooth lumber like the dining tables and benches. Above the cooking table is a smooth slanted shelf, and above the shelf is another shelf for several barrels of flour. The cook reaches up, tips a barrel, and shakes flour onto the slanted board. When he needs flour in a bowl or on the cooking table he just pulls some down from the slanted shelf.

He starts with flour, tubs of pie filling, lard, water, and salt. Before I get a batch of dishes washed, the cooking table is covered with pies ready to bake. The floor is a lot cruddier than when he started, but that is no big deal I guess. He doesn't tell me to clean it up.

Next, more lessons. The cook lifts empty flour barrels from the top shelf and sets them on the floor. "Farina," he says as he points to the dingle so I roll the empty barrels into the dingle storeroom.

On big shelves there are barrels and boxes of food, tools, pots and pans, new work clothes and boots, and more. A lot of snowshoes are hanging from roof rafter logs. I can't see everything because not much light gets through only one door. A small room in a corner is partitioned off with split boards, and I guess that's Mr. Chase's office.

I roll full barrels of flour into the kitchen, and the cook sets them up onto the shelf as easily as if they're empty. I learn farina is flour and my boss is a very strong man.

I set the table for dinner—plates, cups, knives, forks, spoons. I set on the food—beef, potatoes, bread, gingerbread, and pies. Soon the men come into the cook room, most of them stripped to the waist, and I can't believe how much these guys eat.

However, there are more leftovers than I can eat. But I try. Then I clear the tables, wash dishes, split wood, and carry water.

My boss points at my bunk and says, "Couchay," or something. This is the middle of the afternoon. Why, I wonder does he want me to sleep now?

I take my boots and socks off. My socks smell like thirty miles so I put them in the bottom of my pack sack. Clean socks feel great, and I don't even remember lying down.

Mr. Cyr shakes me awake. "Eddie," he says, "cook say you do wood, water, dishes, and keep fire going for hot water. Wake him 3 o'clock."

"Yup. Yup." I say as I put on my boots. Mr. Cyr leaves. The cook is snoring in the next bunk, and it is 8 o'clock.

As I carry water from the spring, with a kerosene lantern to see by, I think about my first day. I guess it went OK—sort of.

As I work in the cook room I think about my family and Janice—many miles away. I wash cooking pots and pans, and I wonder how Mom is doing. I guess Jason is watching out for her. While I'm sawing and splitting wood I have crazy ideas. Wouldn't it be fun to have Dingie and Dongie playing around the cook room? Wouldn't it be great to have Janice to talk to as I split wood?

After that, days and nights mix one into another—until the tote wagon arrives on Wednesday afternoon with Mr. Chase.

Leonard Hutchins

4.   FROM COOKEE TO COOK

Wednesday afternoon the cook room is as hot as ever, and I'm bare to the waist, sweating, and washing dishes. Rock carts clatter and horse hooves clomp on the road out front, so I don't notice when the tote wagon arrives.

When Mr. Chase walks in, the cook speaks to him in French. Mr. Chase answers and shakes his head, no. The cook speaks louder, and Mr. Chase speaks softer and shakes his head again. The cook yells, shakes his fist at the boss, pulls his pack sack from under his bunk, and stomps out. Mr. Chase follows the cook and talks to him out front on the dingle, then I hear the boss go into his office room. I glance out the door and see Mr. Chase give the cook some money, and the cook leaves walking west.

Mr. Chase comes back in the cook room, nods his head in greeting to me, and sits on a dining bench. He hangs his head and rubs his forehead.

I say, "It's none of my business, but what was all that about?"

Mr. Chase says, "It's your business, Eddie. Prohibition is the law of the land, and the company doesn't allow whiskey anyway. It's nothing but trouble in logging camps. I didn't bring what he ordered so he left for Quebec."

"He's a mean guy."

"Don't judge him too harshly, Eddie. He's a sick man, an alcoholic. Be that as it may, we need a cook—bad—right now."

"Look," I say, "How about if I catch up to him and try to get him to come back?"

"Thanks, but that won't work. He's made up his mind."

Mr. Chase walks to the stoves and opens one oven at a time. In one are a dozen loaves of bread. In another are two humongous beef roasts. Maybe four dozen potatoes are baking in another, and four big pans of ginger bread look about done in the fourth. He closes the doors and looks

23

at me.

"Look, Mr. Chase," I say, "I'll try cooking until you can find someone."

"I'll consider that a favor, Ed. I'll get a cookee for you. I've got to check on how the dam is coming along, but I'll get on the telephone after a cook." Mr. Chase starts to leave.

He turns back, reaches up to the flour barrel shelf, and lifts a book down. "This is the company cook book. Start on page one, and read the instructions. Cooks get a dollar ten a day." He grins and turns to leave again.

Again he turns back, takes some paper and a pencil from his shirt pocket, and gives it to me. "Almost forgot. Here's a letter from Janice. She sent you some paper and a pencil." He leaves.

Just like that. There I stand—thinking I'm the cook, the crew depends on me, and I don't know how to cook. I have a letter from Janice. We used to sneak notes to each other at school so nobody would know we cared for each other. Her father gives me her letter, so he knew all along that we care. I've got a girlfriend and everyone knows it. Does that mean I'm grown up—at least some?

Well, now I've got to prove it. Got to get my act together. Got to watch the stuff cooking so it won't burn. Got to finish washing the dishes. Got to get more water. Got to split more wood and keep the fires going. Got to check the dingle for groceries for next week. Got to read the cook book. Got to read Janice's letter. Got to get the stuff out of the oven before it burns.

Read Janice's letter first. No, check the ginger bread. I stick a knife in the middle of a loaf like the cook did. No raw dough sticks to the knife so it's done. I move the pans from the oven to the cooking table. Now, read Janice's letter.

Dear Eddie,

Congratulations for your thirty-mile walk. Jason and I knew you could do it.

Dad and I went to his office Saturday afternoon to check with the telephone on your progress. You were at 20-Mile.

There were two hostlers in the company stables looking after about sixty big, beautiful horses. When Dad told the men what you were doing, they made a dollar bet. The hostlers live in the company boarding house, and the man who won the bet must have told everyone.

After Mass Sunday, Dad felt like a celebrity. Everyone talked to him about you. Father Belanger, our assistant priest, acted like a kid. He is a nice man, and he was on the running team at his seminary.

Dad is pleased to have you for cookee. He says it is hard to find people to work in the woods during summer in the heat and flies.

I'm having fun reading "Alice's Adventures in Wonderland" with Martha and Mary. I wish I had brothers and sisters. I wish my Mom hadn't died when I was born. But I'm lucky. I have Jimmie and Cora for almost grandparents and your family for an almost Mom and almost brothers and sisters.

It is strange. You get a good job in the woods, and I feel grown up. In school, we sneaked notes to each other, and at supper time Dad asked me if I would like for him to take a letter to you. Just like that. He knew that I cared. I like writing letters now, but the notes were fun.

It is going to be a long summer. As usual, I'm living with Cora and Jimmie while Dad is in the woods. I'm glad to have your family to visit.

I'll get a letter on the tote wagon for you every week.

Janice.

Getting my first real letter from Janice is great. I feel like a man. Getting a job I don't know how to do is not great. I'm worried. I don't want to ruin the cooking and let Mr. Chase down. I've got to read the cookbook like Mr. Chase said.

I read. There aren't any instructions—just recipes and cooking times and temperatures. Well, that's instructions I guess.

Emile Pelletier, the blacksmith, walks in. "Bonjoor, Eddie. Cookee," he says, and he points his finger at his chest. Hey, great. Mr. Chase found some help for me already.

"Wee," I say. I smile and grin.

"Eddie, lira?" Emile asks something. He points to the cookbook then to my eyes.

Lira. I wonder what the word means.

Emile points to a word then to my eyes again. Then he points to the next word and back to my eyes. He places his hand on the page then taps my head with a finger. "Lira?" he asks.

I think he's asking if I'm reading. Lira must mean read. "Wee," I tell him.

He smiles. He whacks me on my back. "Bonum. Bonum," he says. "Tarzan. Tarzan," he shouts at me like he's a happy kid.

I can't imagine what is going on, and I still don't know what bonum means. I remember reading "Tarzan of the Apes." Tarzan has a famous yell, but I wonder what Tarzan has to do with me. I guess the word must mean something else in French.

Emile runs out front on the dingle and yells in French at a teamster going toward the dam. The teamster yells, "Tarzan," and lets out a yell that would make the ape man proud.

I guess Tarzan means the same in French and English and he is big with these guys. I don't have a clue what I have to do with this.

So anyway, Emile is a great cookee. He finishes washing the dishes and works on the woodpile.

I have to get something cooking for tomorrow. The recipes for pea soup and baked beans look foolproof. I put a pot, about ten gallons, of dry beans, salt pork, and water in the oven and a pot of dry peas in water on the stove. I'm cutting up a ham to put in the peas when Andre Cyr comes in carrying a book. He's got a smile so wide it hooks around his ears like Emile's glasses.

"Eddie," he says, "you lira? You read?"

I guessed right. Lira means read. "Wee," I say.

Emile comes in from the woodpile with a smile like Andre's, and the two trade some French.

"Eddie," Andre says. He shows me a Tarzan book. "You read us 'Tarzan' after supper. We all do cookee. Emile must shoe horse. Cannot cookee all time. OK?"

It takes me a while to sort that out, then it seems too good to be true. I get all my cookee work done, and all I have to do is read. That's OK. Then I remember what Mom said at graduation. *"Janice, because of you I can read 'Cinderella' with my girls. We now have glass slippers and pumpkin coaches in our lives."*

Beyond the horizon of my dim brain, the sun begins to rise. I can read. I can read the cookbook. I can read "Tarzan" to my friends. I wish Miss Rogers were here. I would say, *"Miss Rogers, because of you I can read the cookbook. I can read 'Tarzan' to my friends. We will have vines to swing on, victory yells, and jungle animals in our lives."*

"OK, look," I say to Andre. "This sounds good to me. I guess I should ask Mr. Chase."

Andre says, "I ask Monsieur Chassee before I come. He say, 'OK. Good idea.' He grin."

"OK," I say, "'Tarzan' is on tonight."

Emile does some French with Andre. Something about melass.

Andre says, "Eddie, when cook have no cookee he say he have no time to do molasses. Emile will do molasses—OK?"

I figure if they did something with molasses before it must be OK, so I tell him, "Wee."

Andre leaves with the Tarzan book, and he is smiling wide.

Emile is the cookee that every cook wants. He does wood, water, and dishes. He sets the tables. He goes to the dingle and comes back with six two-quart canning jars of molasses for the tables. He sets a plate on each jar to keep flies out, and he smiles all the time.

I take the stuff out of the ovens before it burns, but I have to keep something cooking or there won't be anything for tomorrow. The baking powder biscuit recipe looks easy. I mix up a batch, and it turns out to be about five gallons of dough. I roll it out on the cooking table and look for a biscuit cutter. No biscuit cutter. I pull Emile to the cooking table and make circles with my fingers over the dough. Emile reaches up to the flour barrel shelf, pulls down a section of six-inch stove pipe, and cuts biscuits. Soon I have ovens full of six-inch biscuits.

I am among friends. We don't have to speak the same language.

Supper goes OK, but Emile saves my neck. I forgot to make tea, and Emile has a tub boiling on a stove. There is much French and laughter. Molasses covers every plate on the table, and six-inch biscuits sop it up like floor mops. The old cook is gone, and these guys are a different bunch.

Mr. Chase eats with the men, and a stranger wouldn't know he's the boss.

Every man knows about the "Tarzan" deal, so after supper I have two dozen cookees. Before it's dark outside there is more wood and water than I need. The dishes are washed and the cook room is cleaned up. Well, maybe not the floor.

Mr. Chase goes into his office in the dingle, and I hear the telephone bell jingling.

I guess he is looking for a cook, and I sure wish him good luck.

With no fire in the bunk room stove, the place is cool and comfortable. There are a bunch of kerosene lamps hanging from the rafters, and one sitting on the cold stove beside the Tarzan book. There is a seat-height block of wood beside the stove—for me.

The men sit on the bottom tier of bunks along three sides of the room, all facing the reader—me.

I feel as uncomfortable as if I were sitting in Miss Rogers' seat up front with my whole school looking at me. I've got more men looking at me now than there were kids in school, but I have to read because I promised.

I read a sentence at a time in English, and Andre translates into French. The mutineers maroon baby Tarzan's family in the jungle. Time out for discussion, and there is a decision.

Andre says, "We wish mutineers work in our crew. We bury them in dam."

I read more. Baby Tarzan's parents die, an ape mother loses her baby, and adopts Tarzan. Time out for more discussion.

The decision is, "We think Tarzan do OK drink animal milk. We drink cow milk. Also, some boy and girl drink goat milk."

I don't get much of the book read that evening, but I'm not uncomfortable any more. How can I be uncomfortable among friends?

I go back to the hot cook room, put water in the pea soup and beans, and write Janice a letter.

Dear Janice,

My life has gone crazy. I just learned the cookee trade, more or less. You don't have to be a mental giant to split wood, carry water, and wash dishes.

Then the cook quit. Mr. Chase wants me to cook because I can read the cookbook. He's trying to find an experienced cook. I got a temporary raise from ninety cents to a dollar ten a day. So that's how my life is going.

It's strange. You wrote that you feel grown up because Mr. Chase offered to carry your letter to me. I felt the same way when he gave me your letter. I remembered that we used to sneak notes at school. A crazy life isn't all bad.

You know what? We have evening entertainment almost like radio. I'm reading "Tarzan of the Apes" in English, one sentence at a time, to the French-speaking crew. The bilingual filer translates. They stop the reading when they want to discuss something. I didn't think reading a book could be so much fun.

I listened to you and Mom and the girls read "Cinderella" all last winter. That was OK for a while. "Tarzan" is a good change. Have you read "Tarzan"?

Supper went OK tonight, but I served the old cook's food. Tomorrow I'm on my own. If I don't die from my cooking, I'll write you next week.

Eddie

5.   MOM SAVES THE DAY

After reading "Tarzan" for my friends and writing my first real letter to Janice I feel great. I add water to the beans and pea soup so they won't burn, and I'm sure I'll make it as a cook.

At 11 o'clock I lie down for a short nap.

Emile shakes me awake at 5 o'clock. I jump up, and the crew is coming in for breakfast. Both the beans and the pea soup are boiled dry, scorched on the bottom, and hardened to a crust on top. I'm sure I blew it as a cook.

Emile breaks up the crust on the pea soup and beans into hand-sized pieces. He loads the pieces onto serving platters, and puts them on the tables.

I pour pea soup into serving pots for each table, and I've got sense enough not to mix the burned stuff on the bottom with the stuff that pours. The stuff that pours tastes pretty good, but I have no idea how I'm going to get the burned stuff off the bottom.

The beans are something else. They taste sort of like baked beans, but they are hard as buckshot. I have to concentrate to chew them. I have no idea how I messed them up, but if I find a way to get the burned stuff off the bottom of the pea soup pot, I'll do the bean pot the same way.

Uncombed, unshaven, and shirtless, but all smiling, the crew comes by twos and threes into the hot cook room. "Bonjoor, Eddie," they say. "Lira 'Tarzan'. Bonum. Bonum." They pat my back. These guys don't know their strength, and I move out of the way so they can't reach me.

Mr. Chase comes in, and I ask, "Mr. Chase, what does 'bonum' mean in French?"

He thinks for a while.

"These guys say 'bonum' to me," I explain.

"Oh. That is 'bon homme.' As they use the expression, it means 'good man.' You know by now that these men are hard workers and they pride themselves on being good men. You amazed them when you walked thirty miles to start work four days early. It's your nickname, Eddie. You are 'Bon Homme' Clark."

Wow. This is great. Bon Homme. This is almost as great as getting a letter from Janice.

I guess it won't be so great when they try to eat their breakfast. I watch them, and they put on a pretty good front, laughing and talking. However, some of their glances give their thoughts away. I messed up breakfast, and everyone knows it. Be that as it may, they use extra molasses and eat the whole works.

Leaving the cook room they say, "Lira 'Tarzan'. Bon Homme. Bon Homme, Eddie." I never would guess that reading would cover for bad cooking.

After breakfast Andre stays to do the dishes. He shaves soap into hot water and sets the pots on the stove to boil. That is some kind of good soap because the pots come out like new. Everyone but me knows what to do in the kitchen.

I check the dingle storeroom for groceries for next week. I make sure I give Janice's letter and my grocery list, including an extra barrel of molasses, to the tote teamster.

From day to day I gain experience cooking. A tub of salted beef steaks makes a pretty good meal. There are a bunch of tubs of pie filling, and I do quite well with pies—I think. There is a pile of dried salted cod fish in a corner. I find a recipe for potato fish cakes, and I think that is a good meal. These guys eat all of everything, and it's hard to tell if a meal is good or not unless I really pay attention to body language at the tables.

While reading the cookbook one day, I find out how I messed up the baked beans. There are instructions after all—on the back of the recipe page. You have to soak dry beans overnight before you bake them. Also you put onions, salt pork, and molasses in them. I make another batch, keep them from boiling dry, and they are OK.

The crew keeps their end of the bargain. The cookee work is done early every evening—well, except the floor, and nobody sweats that.

"Tarzan" time. Tarzan finds and learns to use a knife. Discussion time, and Andre interprets. If Tarzan worked in our crew, he would learn to use a felling axe, broad axe, adze, and crosscut saw. He might become Bon Homme Tarzan.

"Tarzan" time again. Tarzan learns to make rope and use it for snares to catch big jungle cats. Discussion time. The crew would teach him to harness horses to pull logs and rock carts.

More "Tarzan" time. He eats the big jungle cats raw. A very short discussion. Tarzan is not going to cook at 30-Mile.

Another "Tarzan" time. Tarzan studies children's books left long ago by his parents, and he learns to read. Discussion. Tarzan would have no time to learn to read if he worked at 30-Mile. All the same, it is very good to read. Do Tarzan books come in French?

On Tuesday, Andre moves his tools to Emile's blacksmith shop and he moves from his filer's cabin into the bunk room. I wonder about that, but I guess it's none of my business.

All day Wednesday I think about getting a letter from Janice when the tote team arrives, but the tote team is late.

It's as hot as ever in the cook room, and I'm stripped to the waist taking pies from an oven. Someone says in English, "Hey, do you need a cookee?" It's Jason carrying a pack sack. My eyeballs must have popped out.

"What in the world are you doing here? Who is taking care of Mom and the girls? Who is doing the paper route? Does Mom know…."

Mom walks in. She is smiling, and I can't even get my mouth to work.

"Hello, Eddie," she says. She looks around the cook room, and she stops smiling. "Oh my soul," she says as she looks at the two stoves. She looks at the cooking table. "Oh my soul." She looks at the floor. "What did I get myself into?" She closes her eyes.

I grab Mom's shoulders. "Mom, are you OK? Mom, what are you doing here? Mom, are Dingie and Dongie here?"

Mom opens her eyes looking up into mine. I think I'm going to catch it for the Dingie and Dongie thing, but that's not it. She smiles again. She says, "Martha and Mary are living with Janice at Cora and Jimmie's. I came to eat your cooking tonight just to see how to cook for a crew, because I am the cook starting tomorrow. Jason and I will be your cookees tonight. Here is a letter from Janice." She gives me the letter.

Mr. Chase comes in and smiles at me. Or maybe he's grinning. He says, "Ed, if you don't take those pies out of the oven, they're going to burn."

As I rescue the pies I say to Mom, "Maybe you ought to rest tonight and start tomorrow."

"I'll do no such thing. I have my things all moved into Mr. Cyr's cabin. Now, what's to be done?"

Well, that explains why Andre moved into the bunk room.

Mr. Chase points a bunk out to Jason, and he tosses his pack onto his bunk then stands with Mom awaiting orders.

They are soon good cookees. Jason sheds his shirt, and his T-shirt is sweaty already. Mom puts on a white apron over her blue shoe-length dress. She has a big pin at the neck of her red and white checked blouse. Supper is on the tables in no time.

Hey, talk about a lifestyle change. It's not just mine. I just put a T-shirt on. When the men come in they aren't after supper. They fill wash pans with water and go back to the bunk room. When they come back for supper they are washed, shaved, combed, and they all wear shirts. Every one of them says, "Bonjoor Madam Clark. Benvenu" before he sits to eat.

Mom replies, "Bonjoor Monsieur. Mercy."

"What was all that about?" I ask Mom.

"They said, 'Good day, Mrs. Clark. Welcome.' I said, 'Good day, Sir. Thank you.' Eddie, I wish now that I had taught you children the French I learned from my neighbors."

"I'm learning. Still, I'm the only one in camp that didn't know you were coming."

Mom just smiles. "Eddie," she says, "I'm in trouble. I know it has to be hot because the stoves are going, but those stoves and that cooking table are so big I can't work on them. Is there something I can stand on? And is there a mop here? I've got to clean that floor."

There is no way a mop can help that floor, and I think about it. Before Dad's accident, he used to build camps, and he told me about floors. When they made a place, they cut the floor logs flat with an adze then they laid up the wall logs on the floor. I guess it wouldn't hurt to adze the dirt and another quarter inch of wood off the floor. It's good for a try.

The men say as they leave, "Mercy, Madam Clark."

When Andre comes by he also says, "No 'Tarzan' tonight, Eddie. Talk mear."

"OK," I say. I guess "mear" means Mom. "Say, can I use an adze for a while?"

In a few minutes, back comes Andre with an adze. An adze is like an axe with the blade on cross ways. You stand with your feet apart and swing the adze between your feet like a pendulum. You have to put some beef into an axe to split wood or chop trees down, but you swing an adze with a soft touch. You just cut a little bit for a chip.

I take Mom to the dingle storeroom and show her what we have for groceries. She decides we are going to have bacon, eggs, and pancakes for breakfast. I can't imagine Mom cooking bacon, eggs, and pancakes fast enough to feed a couple dozen men, but I think I'm going to see tomorrow if she can do it.

Jason and I go to Mom's cool cabin and talk for a while, and I'm still hardly believing they are here.

It occurs to me that I have a letter from Janice.

Dear Eddie,

You wrote that your life has gone crazy. Guess what. My life is following yours.

First, you leave for the woods and I'm sad. I miss you. Next, your Mom and Jason go to the woods. I'm sad again. I miss them.

But I'm happy because you all want good jobs for the summer. Also, I'm happy because Martha and Mary are living with me at Cora and Jimmie's.

Your Mom didn't want to leave the girls, and she wouldn't have gone to work if the girls hadn't spent so much time with me. Besides, the girls and Cora and Jimmie are delighted with the setup.

Eddie, for the first time in my life I'm earning a lot of money. I will earn a dollar forty a week delivering papers, and your Mom pays me two dollars a week for babysitting. I didn't want to take it because the girls are my friends, but your Mom said I earn it because babysitting is important and responsible work.

Your Mom and I went to the company office to talk to Dad on the telephone. Dad told me he really needed your Mom and Jason. He said that by babysitting the girls I am part of the project. I'm proud, and I'm getting rich.

The girls and I spend a lot of time with the company horses. The horses are so big and beautiful and gentle. They come to the fence, and we rub their noses. The hostlers say the horses are better behaved when we are at the fence, but I think they are kidding us.

"Alice's Adventures in Wonderland" is a great and crazy story. Maybe I'll try "Tarzan" some time. Hey, maybe your crew would like "Alice".

I am very happy, but I miss you all.

Love,

Janice

I stare at the floor.

"Janice is a nice girl," Mom says.

"You noticed."

Jason and I can't stay with Mom for long, because we have to get the cook room ready for breakfast.

It's good to work with Jason. We prop the door to the wood pile open so we can talk. He saws and splits wood and I adze the crud off the floor. He's a strong kid, and he splits wood as well as I do. He carries water and washes dishes, and I carry armloads of cruddy floor shavings to the wood pile.

The clean floor is amazing. It's almost white, and the whole room is brighter.

But the room is still hot. Somehow, I think to myself, there must be a way to cool the place off for Mom.

But at least we can get Mom up where she can cook. We saw four wood cookies about eight inches thick from a big cedar log. We lay one in front of each stove and two side by side in front of the long cooking table. Mom can step up on the wood cookies and do her thing.

Jason sacks out, and I write a letter to Janice.

Dear Janice,

What can happen next? Mom is cook and Jason is cookee with me.

Nothing ever, ever surprised me as much as Mom and Jason coming to 30-Mile. They are going to be a lot of help, and they wouldn't be here if you didn't have the girls.

The men really respect Mom. They combed their hair and wore shirts for supper tonight. She made a big hit when she spoke some French to them. I didn't know Mom knew any French, and I'm learning a few words.

Reading "Tarzan" with the men is better all the time. The story says Tarzan eats raw animals he kills. The men said Tarzan would be a good man in the crew, but they don't want him for cook.

I'm glad you found sixty big friends in the horse pasture. When I had my summer haying jobs, the horses were usually the best ones in the crew to get along with.

Aside from the cook that quit, the men here are great to work with, but it sure would be nice to go out to visit you on Sundays. Remember the stories Miss Rogers read us about the flying horse? It would be a cold ride in winter, but if I could catch a flying horse I'd be out to visit. Come to think of it, I'll watch for a flying moose. They are faster than work horses.

Love,

Eddie

It's 12 o'clock. I sack out, and I wonder how I can cool the cook room off for Mom.

I must have slept, because I wake up. It's 3 o'clock, and I know how to cool the cook room.

6. FROM THE KITCHEN TO THE DAM

Next morning Jason is stuffing wood into the stoves, and I'm slicing bacon on the cooking table. Mom comes into the cook room and lights right up with a big smile. She claps her hands. She bends down and slides her fingers over the clean, white floor logs.

"I can't believe that clean floor," she says.

"Ed borrowed a broom," Jason says. He grins and shows Mom the adze behind the stove.

"I like that broom," Mom says. She steps up onto a wood cookie in front of a stove. "There," she says. "Now I'm big enough to be a camp cook."

The men, all as neat as they were for supper last night, come in for breakfast.

Until that time, I hadn't paid much attention to Mom cooking. She is fast. She says, "Oh my soul." when she first sees each big camp cooking utensil. Then she puts it to use. She soon has six dozen eggs scrambled and cooking in two frying pans and a dozen pancakes at a time cooking on a griddle. I think I'm doing OK keeping one griddle of bacon from burning. Jason has to run to put it all on the tables.

When Mr. Chase comes into the cook room, he is carrying a chair. He stops in the middle of the floor and stares down at the white logs. He sets the chair beside the cooking table. Mom nods her head in thanks.

"Did you adze the floor?" he asks me.

"I hope you don't mind," I say.

"Not at all. Good work," he says.

"Mr. Chase," I say while I'm tending the cooking bacon, "how about if I raise the bottom ends of the roof shakes above the stoves? The heat can go out, but the roof will still shed water."

Mr. Chase looks up at the roof shakes. He closes his eyes and his mouth drops open. He closes his fingers in a fist and taps his forehead with his knuckles. He looks at me and gets control of his mouth.

"Why didn't I think of that?" he says. "Do it. I'll ask Andre to give you a hand after breakfast."

"Look," I say, "There are some first aid supplies in the dingle. If I could have some of the gauze bandage material, I'd try to make screen doors to keep flies from the stable out and let cool air in."

"You're thinking all the time, Eddie. I'll give some gauze to Andre, and I'll order more for our first aid supplies. I would like to have Andre make the screen doors so you can help Edna and Jason get settled in the cook room. After that, how would you like to work on the dam? Every crib log needs flats adzed on the ends so they fit together."

"I'd like to start last week."

"Pay is a dollar a day."

"I'll take that reduction in pay just to work where I can do something right."

The deal is made. We both grin.

Soon after breakfast Andre is back with a hammer and some nails. We tell Mom what we are going to do. We shinny up onto the roof and pry up the shakes. Hot air streams up through the vent. A few extra nails secure the shakes where we want them.

"Hey," Jason yells up through the vent, "that's great. It's cooler already."

Andre and I slide off the roof and go back into the cook room to feel the change.

Mom says to me, "Eddie, thank you." She pats my arm, and I am proud.

"Madame Clark," Andre says. He points to the chair which Mr. Chase left. "Chaise a bascule? Aaah—chair bascule? Aaah—rocking chair? You like rocking chair?"

"Yes," Mom says. "I would like a rocking chair."

"OK. I bend some rocker soon. Monsieur Chassee say I make screen door. You will have some day."

Mom says, "Merci."

Andre smiles and heads toward the blacksmith shop and his tools. Jason shaves soap into chips and washes the breakfast dishes. Mom wants to make pies, so I go to the dingle after tubs of pie filling.

When I come back to the cook room with pie filling Mom is working pretty fast through the early stages of an ugly. The flour barrel is too high for her to reach even when she stands on a wood cookie. Jason wants to stand on the cooking table to get the flour Mom needs. Mom isn't about to allow Jason to clomp all over her clean cooking table in his dirty boots.

I roll another barrel of flour from the dingle to beside the cooking table, and I pry the top off. Mom can dip out what flour she needs for now. There has to be some way for her to dump flour onto the slanted board where she can reach what she needs. I think about the flour problem while I'm splitting wood.

Later when I'm carrying water, Andre comes in with two sticks of wood about three feet long.

"Madame Clark," Andre says, "OK I put rocker in hot water? Will bend soon." He points to a tub of water on a stove. "All clean," he adds and he shows Mom the wood.

"Oui, Monsieur," Mom says.

While the rocker sticks are soaking on the stove, I rinse and wipe the pots and pans Jason washes. I keep looking at the slanted flour board. Soon I see in my mind a flour barrel in a cradle with rockers. I imagine Mom tipping the cradle and dumping the flour she needs onto the slanted board. I think that would work.

As I work, I watch Mom preparing dinner. In four ovens she has a roast, potatoes, pies, and bread. She mixes and rolls out biscuits. At first, she didn't believe the stove pipe biscuit cutter any more than I did. She said, "Oh, my soul," each time she cut each of the first dozen biscuits. She slid the biscuits into the oven when the bread came out. What really impressed me was the few minutes now and again she had to sit, relax, and read.

What is she reading? You guessed it. "Cinderella".

Leonard Hutchins

7. JASON'S TARZAN YELL

This is hard for me to believe. My crew, two dozen old, tough, experienced loggers, are all washed and combed and listening to my mother read "Cinderella". They don't understand her words, but they say nothing. If they want salt, molasses, or whatever, they point.

Just like when I read "Tarzan", Mom reads a while in English and Andre repeats in French. The men discuss that part of the story, and Andre translates for Mom, Jason and me. Jason is washing dishes, but he's listening.

"Sour, jealous half-sisters not lucky," Andre says. "Could be happy. Will not be happy. Also, fairy godmother not so good for young girl as real grandmother. We know. Some are grandfathers." He points to Jacques and several other older guys.

Mom's smile flashes.

She reads on, and there is more discussion. Andre says, "Fairy godmother make good dress. Real grandmother do better. Mademoiselle Cinderella carriage not too great. Pretty girl should have better than pumpkin. If she go to ball from 30-Mile, she ride in new painted and decorated rock cart with real horses—for sure, not mice. We grandfathers will be teamster—for sure, not rats."

Mom wiggles in her chair, bends forward, and reads on.

There is a long discussion. Andre says, "We grandfathers will tie up horses and go to ball too. Prince better be good with our little girl. We let Mademoiselle Cinderella stay more than midnight. She not have to run away. She not lose shoe. Dance is big time for young girl."

Mom giggles but she has to get back to her cooking job. She closes her book and keeps her smile as she checks whatever is cooking for tomorrow.

I'm confused. This isn't how I understand "Cinderella", and I wonder, is everything I read going to change as I grow older?

At the same time, I'm not confused. I know for sure if I don't find Mom something else to read I'm going to hear "Cinderella" all summer.

"How about listening to some 'Tarzan', Jason," I say after supper.

"Can't. Got to get ready for tomorrow," Jason says, but I help him with the dishes, Jacques splits wood, and Alcide carries water.

"Hey, Mom," I say, "come in the bunk room with us and listen to 'Tarzan'."

"Edward," Mom says, "I will not for any reason go into that bunk room when the men are there. You can be sure of that. I will sit in Roy's office and listen to you."

So Jason and I go in for a "Tarzan" session, and we get to a part of the story about a jungle ceremony. Tarzan jumps up onto a high place, thumps his chest with his fist, and screams his yell of triumph and defiance.

Andre tells the story, but before a discussion can start Alcide jumps up onto the cold stove. He does a Tarzan yell that nearly lifts the shakes off the roof. We have a good laugh, and we hear Mom and Mr. Chase laughing in the dingle office.

When Alcide jumps down Jason jumps up and does a yell. Well, sort of. My voice is pretty well changed, but Jason's isn't. His yell turns into a scream that would scare a den of bears.

We don't have time to start laughing again when the bunk room door bangs open against the log wall. Mom zips in. I never saw her eyes so big.

"Jason—Jason—Jason," she yells.

Mom sees Jason, and he's looking pretty sheepish standing up there above her on the stove. I guess she thinks Jason is safe, because she closes her eyes and shakes her head.

None of us dare to laugh.

Mom looks around the room at the crew sitting on their bunks. Her face rosies up, she smiles, shrugs her shoulders, turns her hands palms up, and says, "Pardon. Pardon. Pardon."

Mr. Chase is holding the door, and I can tell he is trying hard not to grin. Mom walks to the door, turns, nods her head to the men, then leaves. She is still red faced, but she's smiling.

We all want to laugh, but we don't, and that is the end of "Tarzan" for that night.

As far as I know, that's the first mistake Mom ever made. At least, she thinks it's a mistake. I think this is a fun part of growing up. When the time comes right I will kid Mom about going into the bunk room. Right now I just want to give her a hug, but I guess she might not be in the mood.

Next morning, Mom's face is a little rosier than usual, but she is too busy with breakfast to be very embarrassed for long. Breakfast is good. What else would it be?

Illustration 7-1: *Jason Doing the Tarzan Yell* by Judy Sherman

Wearing my new calked boots, I walk to the dam project and Mr. Chase is already there. As the men arrive, he talks to them about their part of the work.

Alcide motions for me to sit on a log, and he pulls one of my pant legs down and catches it on a boot calk. He points to his pant legs cut off at his boot tops, then he makes a motion with his finger like he's cutting my pant legs off. Hey, short pant legs don't catch on boot calks and trip a person up.

I jack knife my pant legs off and tell Alcide, "Mercy."

Jacques points for me to walk on the dam logs, and he and Alcide watch as I walk across the gorge. I don't slip at all. I guess my smile tells my partners how I feel about my new boots.

Today I adze logs on the road, and I also help roll them to their places in the dam log basket. We're building the basket faster than the rock carts can fill it.

Near the middle of the dam the men are building something into the log basket.

On one of my log rolling trips Mr. Chase comes by so I stop for a minute.

"Mr. Chase," I say, "What are they building here?"

"Two sluiceways, Ed. One will be higher than the other, and they will have wood gates. When we close the gates the dam fills with water, and we dump in logs. When we lift the top gate, the wood and water go that way." Mr. Chase points downstream. "Fast," he adds and he grins. "We'll dump in more wood and lift the lower gate. There goes more logs and water. Fast. In spring when winter snow melts, dams fill with water in just about no time. I'll tell you what Ed, driving logs on fast water is something great to see." Mr. Chase is smiling and all excited as he tells me about the dam.

I think a minute and say, "You know something, Mr. Chase? Dad told me the same thing. 'Driving logs on fast water is something great to see.'"

Mr. Chase's face changes to serious. "Ed," he says, "your dad was a very good man. He would be proud that you have already earned your nickname, 'Bon Homme'."

"Thanks." I say. "Hey look, I'd better get going before Alcide or Jacques comes after me."

"You'll be setting up today to broadaxe some logs so they fit together for the sluiceways," Mr. Chase says.

"OK," I say, and I go back to our log pile.

I feel guilty because I talked to Mr. Chase so long. Jacques is carrying a chopping axe, a broadaxe, two log dogs, and a sledge hammer from the blacksmith shop. I should have come back to help him.

Dad told me about using these tools, and it seems like he is here working with me. A chopping axe has a sharp cutting bit on both ends of the axe head. A broadaxe is well named. The single cutting bit is about a foot long with a bevel only on one side. Dad said that a skilled axe man can snap straight chalk lines on a log and hew smooth, straight surfaces the entire length of a log. Log dogs have two prongs like really big chicken wire staples. Sledge hammering one prong into the log you're cutting and the other into a bed log holds the log in place while you're working.

I help Alcide place two short logs on the road for bed logs, and with peaveys we lift a long log onto the bed logs.

Hewing smooth, straight surfaces starts with straight lines. Our chalk line is a strong cord about thirty feet long. Alcide rubs blue chalk on the line from a fist-sized chalk ball, and Alcide and Jacques pull the chalked line tight and straight against the log. When I pick the line up in the middle and release it against the log, the chalk snaps off the line onto the log. We have a straight blue chalk line on our log, and we snap three more lines to mark the log in quarters. Then we fasten the log to the bed with log dogs.

Jacques stands on the lined log and chops a notch to two of the lines about every yard. Alcide follows with the broadaxe hewing to the lines from notch to notch. It is hard for me to believe that what was a round log now has a flat side as smooth as if it were sawed in a mill.

With peaveys we loosen the log dogs, turn the log a quarter turn, and reset the log dogs. I point to the chopping axe and to myself, and Jacques gives me the axe.

Illustration 7-2: *Hewing Logs* by Judy Sherman

It's learning time again. Listening to Dad tell about this was fun and easy, but chopping a notch in a log just deep enough to touch two lines is something else. My teachers give me time to learn, but my notches don't look good. Alcide hews to the line between my notches, and the second flat looks almost as good as the first one. The thing about great teachers is they make their pupils look good. Miss Rogers is also good at that.

After I cut a few logs my notches look better, and I feel I've learned something today.

Once again supper time that night is "Cinderella" time.

Once again my crew, hard working men one and two generations older than me, understand the story different from me.

After a crew discussion Andre explains, "Cinderella is best catch. She learn to work—cook, clean house, sew. Prince learn nothing. Well, maybe he dance good, but that's all. Prince is lucky one to get Mademoiselle Cinderella."

Hey, I think, maybe I'm learning something. Janice is as great as Cinderella.

Saturday morning I have no idea I have a hard lesson coming. My partners give me the broadaxe which Alcide swings like a hatchet. The thing feels like a guillotine blade. I read a story about a guillotine, and stories like that aren't hard to remember. Come to think of it, if the French had broadaxes maybe they wouldn't need guillotines. Anyway, Jacques notches a log, and I try to swing the broadaxe like a chopping axe. Everyone but me knows that's not going to work.

Alcide stands beside me where I can see his hand out of the corner of my eye. He makes a pendulum motion. I swing the broadaxe about like an adze, and it cuts better. He turns and tips his hand to show me how to adjust my stroke. My heavy tool cuts better with each adjustment.

Log after log, my cuts look better, but my back and arms feel like my legs did on the day I walked in. I am slowing down fast when dinner time comes. The noon break and a good dinner spruce me up, but I'm not feeling great about the middle of the afternoon.

The men on the dam whoop and yell and look down the road. I turn around and here comes Father Belanger, the young priest in Janice's church, riding a saddle horse. Everyone but me takes a break and gathers around Father Belanger. I take a break and sit on the log I'm axing.

I have no idea this guy, Father Belanger, visits logging camps. I remember seeing him in Ashland. When I ran my paper route early in the morning, I sometimes saw him running too—just for the fun of it I guess. I remember Janice wrote that he was on a running team at his school.

I don't understand the French, but the body language near Father Belanger is all good. Smiles and handshakes go around. He is about my size, and like me he steps aside to avoid pats on the back from guys like Alcide.

I hear my name and 'Bon Homme' in the French talk. The whole crew including Mr. Chase comes with Father Belanger and his horse to where I'm sitting. Sitting on that log really feels good, but I stand and shake hands with a new friend in my crew.

"Eddie," Father Belanger says, "Congratulations for walking thirty miles in a day. You deserve to be called 'Bon Homme'."

As he speaks, he lifts a book from a saddle bag hanging on his horse.

"Thank you very much," I say.

"Janice asked me to give you this book," Father Belanger says. "She said there is a letter inside for you. She also sent letters to your mother and Jason."

"Thanks again," I say.

Hey, I can't believe I'm so lucky. The book is "Alice's Adventures in Wonderland". This is exactly the book Mom needs to read to the crew at supper time.

I'm not going to hear "Cinderella" all summer after all.

"Janice is a fine young lady," Father Belanger says to me.

Wow. My crew is standing around. I'm glad they don't all speak English. Janice's father is right beside me. Her priest, of all people, is talking to me about my girlfriend. I feel like I'm in the newspaper or something, but I don't know if I'm in the court news or on the social events page.

"Yes, she is," I say. What else would I say?

"Ed," Father Belanger says, "we have church field days. One of the events this fall is a three-mile cross country run. Would you run for my parish?"

"But…Well…Aaah. Look, I don't go to your church. Hey, look, let me think about this, OK?"

"OK. When you come out for school this fall, I'll coach you. Right now I'm starved. Do you think your mother would feed me?"

I take out Janice's letter and give the book to Father Belanger. I tell him, "In Mom's kitchen, you're more apt to eat yourself to death than starve. Would you give this book to Mom?"

Mr. Chase and the priest, leading his horse, walk to the camp. I go back to work, and I force my stiff back and arms to bend.

Every tired aching part of me is happy when quitting time comes. When I get to the cook room, I walk toward my bunk room corner fishing Janice's letter out of my pocket. Jason is out after wood or water. I glance at Mom, and something doesn't look right. I look again.

Mom is crying.

Leonard Hutchins

8.   MOM AND MR. CHASE?!

"Mom" I say, "what's wrong?"

She takes a handkerchief from her apron pocket and wipes tears from her cheeks.

"Nothing, Eddie. The girls sent Jason and me some drawings. See?" There on the cooking table beside "Alice's Adventures in Wonderland" are pictures Dingie and Dongie sent. She turns a picture over.

"Would you read this for me? I think Janice wrote it. I can read printed things, but the way people bend letters together when they write makes it hard for me."

Dear Mrs. Clark and Jason, The girls and I are having a great time. We finished our book, and we want you to read it. We visit the horses at the company pasture. Father Belanger is ready to go, so I don't have time for a letter now. I'll send you a letter on the tote wagon. Janice

"Isn't that nice?" Mom says. "How did your day go on the dam?"

There is something wrong. When Mom cries because she's happy, she also smiles. Mom isn't smiling.

"Things couldn't be better, Mom. I feel great," I say.

I know I lied to Mom, but I don't want her to worry about me. I'm sure Mom lied to me, but I don't know why. I don't remember ever doubting Mom's word, and I wonder if this is another part of growing up.

Instead of sacking out on my bunk, I sit in Mom's rocking chair. I make believe I'm not hurting as I read Janice's note on the back of another drawing.

47

Dear Eddie, Father Belanger stopped by on his way to 30-Mile. We sent your Mom a book. How about you and Jason helping her with new words? I'll send a letter on the tote wagon. Love, Janice

There are a few pots to be washed in the sink so I work on them just to keep my arms and back from cramping up.

When Andre comes in for supper he has a barrel cradle with rockers. We set it up on the flour shelf with a barrel of flour. It tips easy, and Mom can tip the flour she needs down on the cooking table.

"Mercy," she says, and she is back to flashing a smile.

Supper goes OK. Mom shows the men her new book, and Andre says they will listen another night because of a church service in the bunk room. Mom shows Dingie's and Dongie's drawings. The men pass them around and discuss them.

Hey, do I ever learn something or what. Some of these guys, as tough as loggers come, wiped tears from their eyes. They miss their kids, and I never even suspected this. Maybe, I guess, Jason and I get along OK because they sort of adopted us as their kids.

After supper, church goes OK I guess. I carry water while Jason is doing the dishes, and we hear singing from the bunk room.

I'm confused. Usually Mr. Chase comes to the cook room and walks to Mom's cabin with her after she is done for the day. Tonight he stays in his office in the dingle, and I walk with Mom. She doesn't act like there is anything wrong, but I just don't know. I'm too tired to think about it.

I sack out, but I don't remember taking my boots off. I don't even remember hitting the bunk.

Breakfast is pancakes, molasses, bacon, pies, doughnuts, the usual great stuff. Father Belanger keeps several conversations going, and he does OK with his breakfast, too. However, when he leaves the cook room, Mom and Mr. Chase hardly nod a goodbye. It just doesn't seem right.

I go out on the dingle porch with my crew and the priest. Someone has Father Belanger's horse saddled and waiting out front, and he mounts up and waves.

"Hey, wait," I say. I go back, dig some paper and a pencil from under my bunk, and write Janice a note.

Dear Janice, Thanks a bunch for the book. Mom liked reading "Cinderella" to the crew as much as they liked the story, but they think it should be changed. Father Belanger is as good as you said. He's waiting to leave. I'll have a letter for you on the next tote wagon. Love, Eddie.

"For Janice," I say as I give the note to Father Belanger.

"She'll be proud to see you run for our team," he says as he sticks the note in his saddle bag.

"I'll think about that."

His horse kicks up clumps of dirt as it saunters toward Ashland. It seems to me that some special event is over. The camp returns to the way it was, and I feel the sore muscles I had when Father Belanger came.

"Eddie," Andre says, "We put on screen door. OK?"

I go to the blacksmith shop with Andre, and he gives me the froe, donker, carpenters wood plane, and hammer to carry. He puts some nails in his pocket, and carries two screen doors. "Madame Clark need place for picture," he says on our way back to the cook room. I don't know what that's about.

We use pieces of leather horse harness for hinges when we hang the doors in place. Mom pushes the wood door open and stands in the cool stream of air coming in through the screen door. When she smiles and says, "Mercy," she looks like she did before the priest came. We hang the other screen in the wood pile door, and Mom gets cool air from both sides of the stoves. She smiles again.

"OK. We make place for picture," Andre says as he takes the froe, donker, and carpenter's wood plane to the wood pile.

He saws an about six-foot section from the big cedar log which we used for Mom's wood cookies. He places one end against the side of the camp and holds the froe against the other end. He glances at me, nods his head, and I swing the donker. Soon we have two half logs, and soon after that we have two cedar planks, each about two feet wide and six feet long. He smoothes rough places with the wood plane.

Mom gives us a strange look as we nail the two planks to the camp wall next to the dining tables. Then Andre moves a kerosene lamp so it lights the planks.

"Madame Clark have little one picture for us?" Andre says to Mom. He gives Mom the hammer and some nails.

Mom looks at the boards, then at the nails. She looks again. Then she squeals, smiles, and runs out of the cook room. Soon she is back with Dingie's and Dongie's drawings, and she nails them to her new bulletin board. She looks at them so long that a batch of bread is a little dark.

"Mercy. Mercy. Mercy," she says to us as she pulls the overcooked bread from the oven.

Andre nods and smiles.

I'm happy I don't have to work on the dam Sundays. I'm still hurting, so to keep my sore arms and back loosened up I split some wood for Jason.

Dinner is great. Mr. Chase talks and jokes with everyone. Mom brags about the girls' drawings on the bulletin board. She uses all the French she knows and maybe some she doesn't. She has some gingerbread to go with our pies.

Mom says she isn't going to read "Alice's Adventures in Wonderland" to the men until she learns the new words. I listen to her read for a while Sunday afternoon, and she doesn't need all that much help.

Mom reads for the crew during supper.

My friends and I think with different languages, but we agree that this is a strange story. Alice wanders away from her big sister and we say the sister should be punished for being so careless. With Andre interpreting, I tell the crew that I don't let my little sisters get away from me. Mom smiles.

Alice follows a big white rabbit into its hole. The crew says rabbits don't come big enough to dig a kid-sized hole, so this has to be a white bear. Our bears are black, but Alcide says some places in Quebec have white bears. Alice falls a long, long ways down the hole. The men say this is a mine shaft. No animal could dig that far.

I'm glad the men say they have done enough "Tarzan" for now. I guess that either "Alice's Adventures in Wonderland" is more interesting than "Tarzan" or Mom reads better than I do. Anyway, I'm glad to get another good night's sleep.

I do better Monday than I guessed I would. When I use the chopping axe and broadax, my muscles loosen up.

The guys building the sluiceways need several lengths of logs so Jacques brings a two-man crosscut saw from the blacksmith shop. Our saw is a blade about as wide as your hand, five feet long, and it has a handle sticking up on each end. The teeth are shaped and filed to cut a log when we pull it back and forth. We cut logs to the needed length in a couple of minutes.

For me, Tuesday and Wednesday morning are even better than Monday. Alcide, Jacques, and I trade jobs, and we each use all of the tools. Different tools require different muscles, so no part of me gets too tired. I like that.

Wednesday afternoon is something else. I lay our adze down, and a rock cart runs over the handle. I run down to the dingle after another handle, take a couple steps across the dingle porch, and push the door open.

Wow. Whoa. Holy smoke. Mom and Mr. Chase are kissing.

"Mom. Mom," I say, "What are you doing?"

Mom and Mr. Chase look at me like two kids caught stealing cookies. I know I asked a dumb question. I know I've got to control my brain.

"Mom, should you do that?"

There is another dumb question. I've got to control my brain—some way.

Mom says, "Oh, my soul," but she still has control of her brain. She takes my hand. "Come sit down," she says as she leads me into the cook room. "Jason, we need to talk," she says. Jason leaves the dishes, and we sit on a dining bench. Mr. Chase brings Mom her rocking chair, and he sits on a bench with Jason and me.

"Roy and I should have talked to you boys before," Mom says. "We want to marry, and we hope that all of our children will also want that. Eddie, we should have talked to all of you together the night before you left for 30-Mile. Right now, we just don't know what to do. The girls are in town. You are here. Father Belanger will not marry us until he has time to teach me about the church. Roy is responsible for building the dam, and he needs us all here. I can't go back in town now to learn about the church. As I said, we don't know what to do."

My brain is sort of functioning again, and I decide not to ask Mom if old people like her and Mr. Chase should get married.

"Look, Mr. Chase," I say, "you're the boss here at 30-Mile. Can't you tell Father Belanger to marry you and Mom when he is here?"

Mr. Chase shakes his head. "But I really tried to convince him that he should do that," he says.

"Well, I think he should have done it," I say.

Mom smiles.

"I'm with Ed," Jason says. Mom smiles again.

"Look," I say, "so Janice and the girls don't know you want to be married?"

"They don't," Mr. Chase says. "I'll ask Janice what she thinks about it when I send her a letter on the tote team tomorrow morning."

"You know what?" I say. "I came down here to get an adze handle. I better get back to the dam."

I shake Mr. Chase's hand and tell him, "Congratulations."

I hug Mom and tell her, "Congratulations." She is crying, but that is OK. She is also smiling.

I think my job at 30-Mile is changing me fast. This is the first time I hug Mom, and feel as grown up as she is—well, more or less.

So while I get the adze handle I tell myself that now I know why Mom and Mr. Chase weren't too happy with Father Belanger. I walk toward the dam, and here comes the tote wagon. The teamster gives me Janice's letter. I know I should get back to the job, but I read the letter anyway.

Dear Eddie,

Father Belanger gave me your note. I can't quite imagine a bunch of loggers listening to "Cinderella". They must be a fun bunch. I bet they'll like "Alice's Adventures in Wonderland".

I'm not surprised that the men like your Mom as cook and story reader. I think she does everything right, and the girls and I miss her.

Dad thinks your Mom does everything right, too. They have been doing more and more things together during the last year when Dad has been out of the woods. He told me on the telephone that she would be the best cook he could find. I know they are in love, and I'm happy they are together. I really hope they get married.

Hey, I'd like to be your sister. You have two great sisters. Do you need another one?

Mary and Martha were happy with my idea of sending drawings to their Mom. They are great kids. I still feel guilty when I think of being paid for babysitting. They are my friends.

Almost every day we go to see the horses. The hostlers let us ride so I made myself and the twins split skirts. The horses are fun.

Eddie, I miss you very much. I'm having fun with the girls, but I'll be glad when you come out of the woods this fall.

Love, Janice

I stand in the road leaning on the adze handle, and two thoughts come to my mind. First, if I had read Janice's letter on my way to get the adze handle, I wouldn't have been so surprised and acted so dumb. Second, if I were as smart as Janice, I would have known what was coming. Then another thought comes to mind. There is no way I will ever be anywhere near as smart as Janice.

I fold Janice's letter, slide it into my pocket, and walk toward the dam. Yet another thought comes to mind. If Janice becomes my sister, it won't be right for me to take her to a dance. Guys just don't take their sisters to dances. Hey, that can't happen.

And still another thought. How much crazier can my life get?

9. LEARNING TO MEASURE IN FRENCH

With my new adze handle, I get back to work. As I'm cutting flats on my log, I think that life on the dam is a lot less complicated than life in the cook room. I try to think how it will be if Mom marries Mr. Chase, and all of my thoughts start and end with "if." If this. If that. Mr. Chase knows his business and he's fair, so I guess it would be good for Mom. She's all for it.

While I'm working, Mr. Chase walks by and says, "This is a great day, Ed." He smiles, and heads out on the dam.

"Yeah, it is."

Soon Mr. Chase walks back with a broken measuring tape. Measuring tapes never last very long. He talks to Jacques and Alcide in French then goes to Emile's blacksmith shop.

At quitting time, Mr. Chase and Emile look at two ten-foot sections of chain stretched on the dingle porch. I get a basin of water in the cook room and wash my face and hands in the bunk room. The men are shaving—for Mom, of course. I think it will be great to grow a beard, but now it's convenient not to shave.

When I go back on the dingle porch, Mr. Chase and Emile are still looking at the chain.

"Ed," Mr. Chase says, "I'm sick and tired of broken measuring tapes. This chain won't break, but we need to mark it so we can measure with it. The best idea we have is to tie something to it to mark every foot. Have you got a better idea?"

Hey. Can I believe this? Mr. Chase is asking for my opinion. I'm busy patting myself on my back, and it takes a while for me to think about the chain.

"Well," I say, "we could paint each foot a different color, but the paint would soon wear off."

"That's what we thought. I guess tying something to it is the way to go."

He says something to Emile, and we go in for supper. I'm proud. Mr. Chase asks for my idea. I'm part of this outfit.

Mom is proud, too. Dingie's and Dongie's drawings are up on the bulletin board, and some of the men have their kids' and grandkid's pictures there. Everyone looks at the bulletin board before supper, and the guys who have kids' pictures there make sure everyone knows.

During supper, Mom rocks in her chair and reads about Alice eating and drinking things that make her bigger and smaller. The men discuss this for quite a while. There is a lot of laughter with the French.

Andre says, "We need this girl. We need stuff that make her little and big. If we are little, we crawl in logs and do things better. If we are big we move logs like little sticks. For sure, we need Alice to build dam."

After supper Mom goes for a walk with Mr. Chase, and I sit under the picture board lamp and write Janice a letter.

Dear Janice,

You are really right about Mom and Mr. Chase. They told Jason and me they want to get married. Mom asked if it was OK with us, and we said it was. Mr. Chase said he is going to ask you about it. There is no need for that. I know you have already made up your mind. Also, I'm sure Dingie and Dongie want you for a sister.

Father Belanger wouldn't marry them when he was here. It seems that Mom has to learn about your church first. Mom says that she is going to learn whatever it is right when we come out of the woods this fall.

This deal is more confusing than Mom showing up to be cook. Hey, do you know something? Old people kiss just like we do. I saw Mom and Mr. Chase kissing.

This sure changes things, but I don't know how much. You're going to be my sister, and as far as I know brothers only kiss little sisters. Hey, that's not going to work. Maybe we'll just have to be sure nobody is around.

Brothers don't take their sisters to dances either. That's not fair for us. There must be a way around that. We'll check on it, OK?

Thanks for sending the book about Alice. I really had enough 'Cinderella'. Mom checked out the new words, and it didn't take her very long.

She reads during supper. Nothing makes sense in that book, but the men want Alice to help them build the dam. They want her to give them some of the stuff that makes her bigger and smaller. When they are smaller they can get inside the log framework and fix things. When they are bigger they can handle logs like little sticks.

It's good that you and the girls ride the horses in the pasture. Hey, maybe you can get a few horses to pasture around the house next summer.

Love from your brother almost. I can hardly believe I'm writing this.
Eddie

"Hey, Jason," I say as I help him with the dishes, "Janice wrote that she knew Mom and Mr. Chase wanted to get married. Did you know about that?"

"I didn't have a clue. It seems OK to me, but I wonder what Dad would think about it."

"It wouldn't be happening if Dad were alive. I guess we all have to deal with what happens."

"Do you think Dingie and Dongie will go along with it?"

"They'll think living with Janice is the way to go. In fact, Janice won't have any time to herself."

"Looks like you and Janice will have permanent chaperones."

"We'll see about that," I say.

It doesn't take long for me to split enough wood for tomorrow and Jason to carry water. We lift a full barrel up into the flour barrel cradle then sack out.

Jason turns over and snores.

I try to think. I've been the man in our house since Dad died, and now Mr. Chase is moving in. Maybe Mom won't need me anymore so I feel left out. Janice has always been the woman in her house, and now Mom is moving in. But Janice is happy about the whole thing, so I guess she doesn't feel left out. Maybe I shouldn't feel that way.

My brain freezes up like January. I can't decide anything because everything is "if" or "maybe."

My brain thaws out—sort of. One of the "maybes" turns into a great idea. Maybe Mom will have so much to think about she'll forget I'm supposed to go back to school. Maybe I'll stay in the woods and work this winter. That is a good idea to sleep on.

Breakfast is better than OK. Mom tops off bacon, ham, and pancakes with raisin gingerbread and some kind of really good whipped canned-milk topping. We finish breakfast when someone gets the last of the gingerbread.

At our log-cutting setup beside the dam Mr. Chase talks French to a couple of the men who are building the sluiceway. He gives them one of the measuring chains.

"Ed," he says as he gives me the other chain, "these fellows, Lionel and Joel, will measure on the dam for each log they need. They will tell you the measurements, and you use your chain to mark a log. You guys," he points to Alcide, Jacques, and me, "can cut the log to fit. You need to learn to measure in French," he says to me.

He walks away to talk to others. Just like that. I look at the chain in my hand. I look at Lionel with the other chain. Probably my mouth drops open, and the four guys with me begin to grin.

Jacques and Alcide always tell me with a little body language what to do, but now they just keep grinning. Body language doesn't do numbers all that great.

I know these guys don't understand English, but I tell them anyway. "You know, I went to school eight years, and I thought I learned enough. Now I've got to learn more, and I'm not even in school." The four guys still grin.

I wonder if they use ten numbers in French like they do in English. I stretch my chain out on a log and count the spaces marked with twine tied into links. There are ten spaces. Hey, things are looking up, so now I've got to learn what they call each space.

I point at the first space, hold up one finger, and look at my teachers for an answer. They get the idea.

Lionel says, "Oon."

I repeat, "Oon."

I point at the second space and hold up two fingers. Lionel says, "Doo."

I repeat, "Doo," then I count, "Oon. Doo."

Three is tra. Four is quart. Five, sink. Six, six. Seven, sep. Eight, heet. Nine, noof. Ten, dix.

With Lionel coaching I count back and forth along the chain a half dozen times, and I've pretty well gotten French numbers.

I know from looking at the spillways that the base logs will be more than twenty feet long. I think if I try to remember more than ten numbers I can get the project into trouble. For instance, if we hew three or four flats on a log cut too short, both the log and the time is wasted. So, I wonder to myself, how do I measure more than ten feet?

I think, hey, Miss Rogers talked about that. Not about building spillways, but she talked about repeating ten numbers like from one to ten, eleven to twenty, and twenty one to thirty. I can use the ten foot chain more than once.

A twenty-odd foot long log is lying on our bed logs. I mark it at the first ten feet and say to Lionel, "Dix."

"Wee," he says.

I lay the chain on the second ten feet, mark the log again, and say, "Dix. Dix."

Lionel nods his head to agree.

I lay the chain on the rest of the log, and the end is between three and four feet. I point to the third foot on the chain and say, "Dix. Dix. Tra."

Lionel nods again.

The end mark is five links more than twenty three feet. I move my finger from link to link and count "Oon, doo, tra, quart, and sink." I point to a link and look at Lionel for a word.

He says, "Chain."

I walk the measured length of the log, point to each measurement and say, "Dix, dix, tra, sink chain."

Lionel smiles and says, "Wee."

Alcide yells, "Bon Homme." I get a pat on my back which nearly knocks me over the measured log.

Lionel and Joel leave for the spillways. There are rock carts and teamsters there. Also, maybe a dozen men are working here and there. Pretty soon Lionel yells to me, "Eddie. Dix, dix, quart, tra chain." Every man on the dam laughs like that is the best joke he ever heard. They all wave to me.

I feel silly, but I measure and mark a log and wonder what I did wrong. It happens again. Lionel yells a measurement, and everyone laughs.

The next time Mr. Chase walks by I ask, "Why is everyone laughing at me?"

Mr. Chase smiles. "Eddie," he says, "they are not laughing at you. They are laughing with you. You figured out a way to communicate, and even if it isn't your usual French, it still works. Because you're trying, we're all with you."

"Hey," I say, "Thanks a bunch."

In a day or so my French is an old joke, and nobody laughs any more. We measure and cut so many logs that it is just part of the project. There doesn't seem to be any end to logs they need for the sluiceways. Some long, some short, some with three flat sides, some cut square.

But the rock supply is something else. The teamsters with rock carts take longer and longer to find loads of smaller and smaller rocks. This is not good. The rocks have to be big enough so they don't fall out of the crib between the logs.

We need more rocks, but we have too many chips. When we chop notches to chalked lines we get a bunch of small chips. When we hew to the lines from notch to notch we get a bunch of big chips. Pretty soon we're up to our knees in chips. I carry away armloads of big chips, I kick the little chips away, but I can't keep up with the problem.

One day my brain works. Usually logging is a winter job, and I remember there are snow shovels in the dingle. Next morning I take a snow shovel to the project and shovel chips away. That is OK for a few days then I have a mound of chips all around our chopping bunk.

This is a serious nuisance, and it takes something serious to prime my brain. I remember I saw horse scoops the day I walked in. They were used on this project to scoop mud from bedrock under the dam. I ask Mr. Chase, and he has one of the teamsters get a scoop to move our chips.

Jacques, Alcide and I stand out of the way across the road while the chips get scooped away. While we are waiting, up the road comes a load of hay for our horses. I think that if I didn't have my job on the dam I would likely have pitched that hay onto that wagon. The teamster stops and gives me a letter.

"From Janice," he says. "She is a good girl. She and the little ones ride horses in the pasture."

"Thanks," I tell him, and I read the letter.

Dear Eddie,

Just a note. Didn't know until just now a load is going to 30-Mile. Girls and I are Happy. Happy. Knew they were in love. Making dresses for the fall wedding for me and girls. Hope your Mom will let me make her wedding dress.

Janice

So that's it. Mom and Mr. Chase will be married this fall. My only question is, will I come back and finish the dam with my crew?

Anyway, our chips are gone, and quitting time comes. Supper is as great as ever, and Mom reads more of the crazy "Alice" story. The men sit longer than usual to laugh and change the story several times.

Usually, Mom and Mr. Chase go for a walk after supper, but they stay in the cook room tonight. I'm helping Jason do pots and plates.

Mom says, "Boys, come sit down. We need to talk."

10. STAYING AT 30-MILE DEPOT

Jason and I sit on a cook room bench, and Mr. Chase moves the rocking chair close for Mom. I wonder what is going to happen next in the cook room.

Mom says, "Would you boys like to work here at 30-Mile this winter?"

Jason says what I'm thinking, "Huh?"

"We'll have your school books sent in, and you'll have to do your lessons," Mom says.

Hey, I think, Mom isn't kidding.

"Boys," Mr. Chase says, "you are each doing a very good job. On her first camp cook job, Edna is a professional. The Clark family is an important part of the dam project, and I hope we can work it out with Janice and Cora so you can all stay."

I'm so happy my brain turns cart wheels. "Yeah. Yeah." I say. "This is a great idea. Let's go for it, Jason."

"Well, yeah," Jason says. "But look, if I do the eighth grade here, do I go into high school next year?"

"As I recall, Jason," Mr. Chase says, "you earned top grades last year. If you keep up that good work, you'll be in high school on time. Guaranteed"

I don't need my grades hashed over so I say, "You'll get married when we're home for Christmas. Right?"

"Well....." Mr. Chase says. "Father Belanger said he needs more time to do what needs to be done."

I see tears in Mom's eyes.

"Hey," I say, "that's not fair. Besides, Janice is making dresses for a fall wedding."

"Boys," Mom says, "look at our picture board."

Jason and I turn to look. There is more of Dingie's and Dongies art, and quite a few more kid's pictures, including Janice's.

"Every one of us whose children's pictures are there would rather be home with them. However, their needs are our responsibility. We can best meet our responsibility here. Our wants, including a wedding, will have to wait."

When I turn back around Mom's tears are gone.

"And there is something else," Mom says, "I want all three of my girls to know that women, in this day and age, can be both mothers and professionals. I will not be a good example for them if I quit on my first job."

My brain isn't turning cartwheels any more. "Your three girls?" I ask.

Mom smiles. She says, "Janice is my daughter now. The wedding ceremony will come in due time."

My brain might even be limping. For the first time, a job means more than just growing up for me. It means growing up for Mom too. An adult growing up is a new idea to me. And Janice is already my sister. And Dingie and Dongie are young women. They are Martha and Mary.

Mr. Chase says, "Tomorrow, I'll get the telephone operator at the office to have Janice call us before she and the girls ride the horses. If everyone agrees with this, we'll do it."

"They'll do it," I say.

"Yup," Jason says, "they'll do it."

Later when Jason and I sack out, I try to think. I look at the picture board. I can't keep any idea in my head long enough to make sense of it, and Jason snores like a thunderstorm.

Next morning when we go to work on the dam Mr. Chase stays in his dingle office. Alcide, Jacques, and I measure, mark, and hew flats on a couple of logs, but I'm thinking about a telephone call. Every once in a while I look up at the telephone wire going by the dam.

Pretty soon, here comes Mr. Chase. "Ed," he says as he walks by, "Father Belanger will bring in school books for you and Jason." He also says something in French to Alcide and Jacques.

Wow. Hey. Just like that my life changes. I'm going to finish the dam, and I'm so happy that even my ears are smiling. I'm happy for Mom too. She is going to finish her first professional job. All three of her daughters, Janice, Martha, and Mary, had better grow up and become professional somethings or other. At least one of them is going to get married, too.

I don't expect it, so I'm not watching for it. Alcide steps up behind me and whacks me on the back. I almost fall over the log we're hewing.

"Bon Homme," he yells.

As I try to get over the whack, Jacques and Alcide jabber about something or other. They are all happy and excited, but the only word I can make out is *racket,* and I hear it quite often. I wonder if these guys play tennis, but I don't think so.

Word gets around the crew, and dinner time is pretty noisy. Every guy who comes into the cook room stops to chat with Mom. She is all lit up, and she gives them a lot of French. It occurs to me that these guys remember my cooking, and they are glad Mom is staying.

Supper would be as noisy as dinner, but Mom reads about the croquet game in the "Alice" story. The men decide they want no part of the queen of hearts, but they would put the executioner to work squaring logs with a broadaxe.

I have a dismal thought. It is just about a sure bet that Mom is going to read either "Alice" or "Cinderella" over and over all winter. I might read "Tarzan" again, but that won't improve things all that much. What we need is a library in the dingle.

After supper I help Jason with the dishes. There is a book I haven't seen before on the cooking table, and every once in a while he stops to read a little.

"What's the book?" I ask.

"It's the 'Great Northern Paper Company Scaling Manual'." We're going to stay here for the winter, and Jimmie is going to be boss at the McNally Pond Camp further down the road. Mr. Chase wants me to measure the wood they cut."

"Hey, that sounds complicated. Do you think you can do it?"

"It's a piece of cake," Jason says. He pats the book.

I ought to know enough not to ask Jason a question like that. He learns math like a starving cat eats mice.

Anyway, things go OK with the log work at the dam. Every day we get a few more logs squared for the sluiceways, and every day more leaves turn to fall colors. But I feel bad for the rock cart teamsters because they work harder and find fewer rocks.

Loads of hay and grain for winter arrive almost every day, and the hay sheds beside the stable fill up. When I see strange horses, I wonder if my sisters rode them.

One afternoon about quitting time, here comes Father Belanger on his riding horse, and his saddle bags are bulging. Every guy on the project gathers to trade handshakes, laughs, and French with the young priest. Again, I hear the word, *racket,* several times and the men look at me. I wonder what I have to do with tennis.

When it's my turn to greet the priest, he says, "Eddie, we're going to have a fall field day the weekend before school starts. I'm sorry you won't be out to run for my parish, but that's OK. We're going to have a winter field day when you're out for Christmas. You can win for us on snowshoes."

This guy doesn't give up. "Now look, Father Belanger," I say as I shake his hand, "I don't think I can be on your team. I don't belong to your church."

"Hey, Eddie," he says, "Janice is going to snowshoe for us in the girl's races. You want to be on her team, don't you?" He is talking to me through both a grin and a smile, and he really knows how to twist a guy's arm.

"Now look," I say, "I'll talk to Janice about this. But changing the subject, will you help me out with a little French? My friends use the word, *racket*, quite often and they seem to be talking about me. Do they want me to play tennis or something?"

"We're not changing the subject, Eddie," Father Belanger says. "In French, *racquette* is snowshoe." He talks French with the crew and Mr. Chase for a while then switches to English for me. "Your crew wants you to represent this camp in a snowshoe race. Every year the Madawaska Company camp west of here has a race before they leave the woods for Christmas. No Great Northern Paper Company camp has ever entered a competitor. You know how to snowshoe, don't you?"

"Well, yeah, but why me?"

"Eddie, you walked thirty miles in a day. Your nickname is 'Bon Homme'."

Mr. Chase says, "The only other person I know about who has walked that far in a day is the game warden, Mr. Jorgensen. And incidentally, he skis even farther."

"What if I don't win," I ask.

"Just being the first to compete for our company will be a win, Ed," Mr. Chase says.

"Well, OK. I ought to be able to at least finish a race. I'll do it." I say to Mr. Chase. "But I'm not saying I can be on your parish team," I say to Father Belanger.

"This is great," Father Belanger says. "After I say Mass this evening, we'll talk to you about training for the race."

Father Belanger says something in French to the men. Everyone yells, "Bon Homme." I remember in time, and I step aside so Alcide doesn't give me one of his pats on my back.

"By the way," Father Belanger says as he mounts his horse, "I have schoolbooks for you and Jason." He pats his saddle bags. "Also," he fishes letters from his jacket pocket and gives one to me. "Here's a letter from Janice." He gives a letter to Mr. Chase, too.

It's so close to quitting time that we follow Father Belanger to camp. Before supper I sit on my bunk and read Janice's letter.

62

Dear Eddie,

I'm sad and mad and ugly and disappointed. I hid from Martha and Mary so I could cry. You're not coming out of the woods until Christmas and Father Belanger won't marry your Mom and my Dad until next summer. It's not fair. I tried to get Father Belanger to marry them now at 30-Mile, but he won't do it.

I talked to Father Belanger about us too. It is just as I thought. Even when we are brother and sister we can still be boyfriend and girlfriend. Now we know for sure. You better not dump me. Ha. Ha.

I talked to Miss Rogers. She says she is going to miss us next year. She says Jason might as well study your high school books because he can do the work OK.

Mr. Andersen at the high school gave me books for you and Jason. You are supposed to send your work in to me on the tote wagon, and I will give it to our teachers.

Hey, Father Belanger wants me to run for our parish in the Fall Field Day races and to snowshoe in the Christmas Field Day races. He gave me a pair of knee-length running pants so I can practice. I wouldn't dare to wear those pants in public if the priest hadn't given them to me. They are also better than a split skirt for riding horses.

Do you know what? I'm just beginning to know how great your Mom is. She doesn't quit. She really wants to finish the dam job at 30-Mile. She says I am making it happen by keeping the girls. She can't fool me. She is the one who is making it happen.

Cora showed me how to use her sewing machine. It has a treadle I pump with my feet to make the needle go really fast. I'm working on pink dresses for Mary and Martha and a blue dress for me. I was hurrying so they would be done for a fall wedding, but I don't have to hurry anymore. Mom said on the telephone that I can make her wedding suit, too. She wants navy blue. That will be hard, but I've got time to do a good job.

A lot of the horses are hauling hay and grain to logging camps. Soon most of them will be in the woods working this winter. I'm making Mary and Martha a pair of running pants like mine. Dresses are not too great for riding horses.

All my love,
Janice

I feel guilty. Janice is all upset about our working at 30-Mile this winter, and I'm all happy. But I'm with Janice about the wedding. Father Belanger should do that now.

Mom holds a letter and shows Mr. Chase pieces of cloth, some pink and some blue. She's smiling, so she's OK.

Jason picks over a pile of schoolbooks on the cooking table. There is a library there, and Jason and I are supposed to read them all in one winter— and work too.

There has to be a way around this. I think if I read half and Jason reads half we can give each other short rundowns. If you know a little, you can fake a lot.

Supper doesn't take long, and the crew goes to the bunk room for Father Belanger's church service. Jason has the algebra book open, and he reads a little, washes dishes for a while, then reads some more.

I look at the rest of the books. I lay General Science and United States History aside for Jason to go with Algebra. Wow. Here are three books that are going to save me from "Cinderella" and "Alice's Adventures in Wonderland". Here are "The Adventures of Tom Sawyer", "Robinson Crusoe", and " Treasure Island". Jason and I each have three books. I can read to the crew and do my homework all at once. I can live with this.

After the church service Mr. Chase comes back to the cook room. "Eddie," he says, "how about coming in to talk about training for the snowshoe race."

In I go. I'll tell you what, this deal is an experience. Two dozen guys stand up yelling at each other. Body language says everyone knows what he is talking about, and everyone else ought to believe him. If volume taught French, I'd be an instant Frenchman.

However, when Emile talks with his gurgley voice, everyone shuts up and listens.

After Emile speaks the bunk room is quiet, and Andre says, "You run in boots heavy like snowshoe."

There is more uproar, and Emile talks again.

Andre says, "Run maybe ten miles Sundays you have time."

Uproar, then Emile again.

Andre says, "Run sprints to dam work days."

Emile speaks to Andre.

Andre says, "Emile and me make you racing racquette. We win bet on you."

"Wait," I say. "I don't want you to lose your money."

They don't listen, and I can't quit. That night my brain runs snowshoe races all night, and I finish last every time.

11. LEARNING TO RUN SPRINTS

Father Belanger's horse is saddled, and after breakfast he is mounted ready to go. The crew is standing around in front of the dingle to see me run my first sprint, and Mom and Jason come out from the cook room. The air is a little nippy, so I'm wearing a wool jacket and knit wool hat. Away I go full tilt toward the dam, everyone cheers, and Father Belanger's horse gallops beside me. Hey, this is great. I'm the hero.

I run with all I've got. The horse's hooves clop, clop, clop and my calked boots clomp, clomp, clomp on the dirt road. I hear my crew yelling, "Bon Homme. Bon Homme." Hey, this really is great.

It's three or four hundred yards to the dam, and at about one hundred yards I'm in trouble. I can't breathe fast enough, salty sweat stings my eyes, I see red flashes, and the road looks like it's weaving around. This is not great. I know I'm showing off, and I'm paying for it.

Father Belanger yells, "You're running too fast, Ed."

I know that.

He says, "Pace yourself so you will have wind enough to make it to the dam."

He is first-class right. I slow down so I breathe better, and the road stops weaving around. The red flashes fade, and when I wipe sweat out of my eyes I see better. I do OK—sort of.

At the dam I slump down onto the log we were hewing when we quit yesterday. I shed my hat and jacket and drop my head nearly to my knees. Sweat drips off my nose, and my throat tastes like a tin can.

Father Belanger slides down from his horse and sits beside me. "Ed," he says, "you just taught yourself one of the most important rules in distance running. Running too fast loses as many distance races as running too slow. Congratulations." We shake hands, and he wipes my sweat from his hand onto his pants.

I nod my head to tell him thanks. I'm not about to tell him I was dumb enough to show off so I'll let him think I was just dumb enough to run too fast.

Father Belanger says as he sits on the log beside me, "Emile won the Madawaska Company snowshoe race five years in a row before the Great War. He was the best, and he knows how to train for a race. He said he wants to coach you."

"Hey, thanks," I say. "That will be great."

By the time the crew walks to the dam I feel more or less OK. There is a lot of French, I get a lot of handshakes, and Emile keeps his arm around my shoulder. When he talks to everyone he sounds like the brook tumbling over rocks through the dam crib. I don't let Alcide get behind me where he can give me one of his pats on my back.

Father Belanger mounts his horse to ride back to Ashland, "I'll be back for the snowshoe race before Christmas," he says. One of my old friends will be there, and I really need to win a couple of bucks from him. I'm going to bet on our man."

I say, "If you bet your horse, you might have to walk home."

As we laugh, I remember that I didn't write to Janice. Dumb. Dumb.

"Father Belanger," I say, "look, I forgot to write Janice a letter. Have you got some paper and a pencil? Can you wait a minute?"

From his saddle bag he gives me a pad of paper and a pencil. As I write, my hand shakes a little from my dumb showing off.

Dear Janice,

My life went crazy again. I'm going to compete for my camp in a snowshoe race. My crew is going to bet on me.

I'm so mixed up that I forgot to write you a letter. Sorry. Father Belanger is waiting to leave. I'll get a letter on the next tote wagon. Promise.

I'm looking forward to Christmas. Let's go on a snowshoe hike.

Love, Eddie.

As Father Belanger rides away I get on with hewing the log.

At noontime I run back to the cook room. I push myself but I don't show off, and I'm sure I make better time than this morning. My afternoon sprints to and from the dam are even better. Over the next couple of days I'm pleased with my progress. Andre and Mr. Chase say Emile thinks I'm doing OK, and he, for sure, is going to bet on me.

When I run, I have a minute or two to look around, and every day more leaves change to fall colors.

One afternoon up the road comes a team of horses pulling a wagon followed by four horses and a dozen or so men walking. They stop at the dam and I recognize my Ashland neighbors.

"Hey, Bon Homme," they say as we shake hands, "you did OK to walk to 30-Mile. You showed these Quebecers we are all good men in Ashland." There is a lot of laughing and French talk among my crew and my neighbors as they look at the dam. I don't understand all of the words, but body language says my neighbors are impressed with our dam and my crew is proud of our work.

Jimmie Roberts stands beside me. Jimmie and Cora live near our home and just beyond the West End School. Janice, and this year the girls too, live with Cora when Mr. Chase and Jimmie are working in the woods.

"Eddie," Jimmie says, "We haven't heard anything but good about you since you came to 30-Mile. You're a good logger like the rest of us. Your father would be proud of you."

"Thanks, Jimmie," I say. "Mr. Chase told me that, and I appreciate it from both of you."

I feel good. All my life I looked up to my Dad, Mr. Chase, and Jimmie. They are respected as good men, and now I have earned a place among them.

Working in the woods is the place for me.

Jimmie says, "I'm camp boss this winter, and we're going to cut from McNally Pond Camp. We'll get our tools and groceries from your depot dingle, but right now we have some fresh beef. The weather is cool, the meat is covered with grain bags, and we poured cold water on it from every brook. I'm sure it's not spoiled. I wonder if we could trade some fresh beef with Edna for supper tonight."

"Wow," I say. "We haven't had fresh meat for three months. Mom will feed you for a week for fresh meat."

The McNally Pond crew and their horses wander down the road toward the cook room. That's quite a ways, but I hear my neighbors yelling to Mom and Jason.

At quitting time I run a faster than usual sprint. I smell steaks cooking a hundred yards from the camp, and the cook room sounds and smells like a neighborhood cookout. The McNally Pond Camp cook is helping Mom, and she's smiling like Alice's Cheshire cat.

It sounds strange to hear a bunch of people speaking English, but as soon as the Quebec men arrive everyone switches to French. I know enough French to know what they are talking about, but not enough to know what they are saying. I think that I won't be a real logger until I learn French, and I'm trying.

After a noisy supper of fresh steak and potatoes, pie, and gingerbread, the crew, except Jimmie, goes to the bunk room. Jason has to talk scaling with Mr. Chase and Jimmie. I do the dishes, but I'm close enough to hear the conversation.

"Look, Jason," Jimmie says, "You're a smart, honest boy, but I'm nervous because you don't have any scaling experience. The right scale is the difference between us losing our shirts and making a fair profit."

"OK, Mr. Roberts," Jason says. "You're cutting four foot length wood and piling it four feet high, right?"

Jimmie nods.

"You get paid by the cord which is 128 cubic feet, right?"

Jimmie nods again.

"Every eight feet of a pile is a cord. Four feet wide times four feet high times eight feet long is 128 cubic feet, OK?"

Jimmie glances at Mr. Chase. Then he nods again.

"Now I know there will be humps and hollows in the ground, and I'll be fair if I have to add or subtract cubic feet. But I don't want someone piling wood over a stump or rock or something to make it look like there are more cubic feet than there really are."

Jimmie's jaw drops a little, and he looks at Mr. Chase.

Mr. Chase grins. He says, "He read the book."

I'm feeling pretty proud of my little brother right about now. Also, I'm happy that he's doing our algebra.

Jimmie says, "OK, Jason. Let's try this. Roy will come with you for your first scale. Roy and I will also scale each man's wood. If our three figures are within five percent, you're our scaler."

"OK," Jason says.

Mr. Chase and Jimmie sit and discuss tools and equipment to be issued to McNally Pond Camp from the dingle. Jason helps me with the dishes, and he lays the algebra book and some paper on the cooking table. As we work he looks at the book once in a while, wipes his hand on his pants, and writes some crazy-looking marks on the paper. He's already doing page thirty-something.

Next morning I have my Ashland neighbors as well as my crew to see me off for the morning sprint. I wave and I smile, but I don't show off. I just run to the dam.

After maybe two hours Mr. Chase gets the stuff issued to Jimmie and his crew. He walks to the dam, talks to Alcide and Jacques, and he looks worried.

"Eddie," he says to me, "we're going to stop the rock carts today because there aren't enough rocks left for them to haul. Somewhere, sometime, somehow before next spring we've got to find rocks. But now I want you three to set up three more log-hewing beds. The rock cart teamsters haven't had experience with a broadaxe, so I want you three to teach them how to square logs. Next spring we'll need dozens of squared logs to face the upstream side of the dam. OK?"

"OK," I say.

As Mr. Chase talks to a rock cart teamster, it dawns on me that I'm supposed to teach experienced loggers, old enough to be my father, something about logging. And I don't even speak their language. I wonder if they will put up with me.

I make a few trips to the blacksmith shop. We need broadaxes, chopping axes, log dogs, sledge hammers, chalk lines, and chalk. Six teamsters leave their rock carts off the road and take their horses to the stable. On their way back to the dam they stop at the blacksmith shop to help me carry tools. By dinner time we have three new log-hewing bunks set up.

After dinner, Alcide and Jacques explain to the teamsters what we're doing as we chalk line a log, set log dogs, chop notches, and hew to the line with a broadaxe. The teamsters don't have trouble chalk lining their logs or notching with chopping axes. But just as I did, they try to use a broadaxe like a chopping axe.

For once it doesn't matter that I can't speak French. Teaching how to use a broadaxe is something words don't do well. Just as Alcide taught me to use the tool, we stand where the new axe men can see our hands. With swinging motions, twisting wrists, and twitching fingers we teach the skill. The older loggers accept me, and I feel as important as Miss Rogers at the West End School.

I don't feel so important any more when I run my sprints. My crew doesn't even yell at me, but Emile always watches me. I can tell the sprints are paying off. I'm sure I'm faster, and after a run it takes less time to get my wind back.

It's more fun to run slower over a longer distance on Sundays. One Sunday morning when the leaves are about gone I rest on my bunk after a run. Mr. Chase is helping Mom and Jason in the cook room.

I say mostly to myself, "I wish I knew how far I run."

"Well," Mr. Chase says, "You could measure your pace and pace off a mile or two."

"You could measure the circumference of a rock cart wheel and figure how many revolutions it takes for a mile. I think that would be pretty accurate," Jason says.

"Edna," Mr. Chase says, "that boy is bright."

Mom smiles.

Jason grins. He says, "Look Ed, you pull the rock cart, and I'll count the revolutions."

"Not hardly, Smartie," I say. "I'll borrow a horse to pull the rock cart, but you can count the revolutions."

That works great. I carry my chopping axe from the dam site. At each half mile for five miles toward Ashland I cut a blaze spot on a tree.

"There, Jason," I say, "I want to practice running the ten-mile race distance, and five miles each way will do it. The half-mile markers will show me how far I have left to run."

Jason says as we bump along going back to camp, "I wish I could run like you."

"Try it," I say.

"Oh, everyone would think I'm just showing off if I ran with you," Jason says. "But I'll tell you what. I'm going to run on the road to McNally Pond Camp when I scale. That's three miles, and no one will see me and make fun of me."

"Hey," I say, "maybe they'd put you in the race."

"Oh, I don't think so."

The rock cart rattles and bumps so bad that we get off and walk. We are a half mile or so from the dam site when I look at a hill near the road. Not many trees grow on it, only bushes. It's mostly a big rock outcrop.

I guess everyone gets an odd idea once in a while, and I get one right then. Most of my odd ideas are pretty dumb, so I decide I better think this one over before I let anyone know what goes on in my head.

Jason yells at me. He is sixty yards or so down the road with the rock cart, and I'm standing there looking at the hill.

"Yeah. Yeah," I yell back, and I run to catch up with him.

"What'd you see?" Jason asks.

"Nothing. Just looking."

Jason gives me a funny look. So what? He doesn't tell me everything he's thinking.

We leave the rock cart beside the road where we found it, and I put my chopping axe where it belongs. I'm still thinking as we walk the horse back to the stable, and I think my idea might work. We meet Mom and Mr. Chase out for a walk.

"Mr. Chase," I say, "Maybe I found the rocks we need for the dam."

12. DISCOVERING THE OUTCROP

Mentioning rocks gets Mr. Chase's full attention.

"Where?" he asks.

"About a half mile back a hillside is a rock ledge, but it doesn't look very solid. Bushes grow from cracks. I've watched farmers dynamite big rocks into smaller pieces they could move. Maybe if we put dynamite in the cracks in that ledge…"

Mr. Chase's mouth drops open. He stares at me for maybe a minute, but he isn't looking at me. His face shows things happening in his brain.

"You know, Ed, you might have just solved our rock problem. But we might need a rock drill so we can place the charge deep in the ledge. Let's go look."

"Roy," Mom says. It's the voice she uses when she says, "Edward" to get my attention. She has Mr. Chase's attention. "Eddie does not know how to use dynamite."

"OK, right Edna, right. The company has men who do that. Let's go look."

"You and Eddie go. I should get back to the cook room."

Mom, Jason, and the horse walk toward 30-Mile Depot, and I go back to the ledge with Mr. Chase.

He stands in the road for maybe five minutes staring at the ledge. I have no idea it's coming, but he gives me a whack on my back just like Alcide does.

"Bon Homme," he says, "the men gave you the right nickname. You're a good man. You found all the rocks we need. It's too late to get a rock drill in here before snow time this fall, but we'll be ready next spring."

He walks back toward camp, but he's almost running and he's smiling. I keep up, but my eyes are watering from the whack.

71

Illustration 12-1: *Discovering the Outcrop* by Judy Sherman

That afternoon I jog down the road past the ledge then back toward camp, maybe four or five miles. It feels good. The air is cool, leaves are gone, and evergreens are dark, dark green.

This is Sunday and we have the day off, but smoke is coming from the blacksmith forge chimney. Emile and Andre are there so I stop in. Lying on the forge fire is a steel pipe maybe eight feet long and as big as your head.

Steam is rising from an open end.

Andre says, "We make fish snowshoe for you. You do good with long snowshoe. Weigh not much. Go fast. We win money." He smiles.

"But look," I say, "maybe I won't win. Maybe…."

They don't listen. Emile pulls a thin piece of steaming wood from the pipe. They bend it to fit a fish-shaped form about four feet long. The form is shaped to bend the front end of the fish shape up. It is easy to imagine a narrow, four-foot long, lightweight snowshoe with turned up front. It is a racing snowshoe frame for sure. My friends pull two more steaming pieces of wood from the pipe and bend them onto forms.

Andre says as he points to the third snowshoe frame, "We do one more. Snowshoe break sometime in race."

I think that my friends cut no corners. They do their part, and if I don't win the race, it will be my fault.

Every day things go pretty well for me except the idea nags me that my crew might lose money on me. At the dam project, the teamsters haul logs from the woods to us, and we hew them square. We keep a horse busy scooping away chips from the four log hewing beds and hauling squared logs to a pile near the dam crib.

One day I'm cookee for Mom, and Jason goes to McNally Pond Camp with Mr. Chase to scale wood. Jason's figures are within a percent of Jimmie's and Mr. Chase's so Jason is scaler. He earns a dollar fifteen for his scaling days. I get a dollar a day, period. Maybe I ought to learn math.

We get our first snow flurry, and Mom gets upset because snow blows in the roof vents and falls on her cooking. I help Andre close the vents and store the cheese cloth screen doors in the dingle.

As usual, I get a letter from Janice on the tote wagon. She's happy as a colt let loose for the first time. She tells me again that her running pants are much better than a split skirt. She runs every night and does better all the time, and the twins run themselves ragged trying to keep up. She is really looking forward to running two races at the Fall Field Day next Saturday.

She says she's doing OK in school. That means she gets A on every assignment. She complains that Father Belanger should marry Mom and Mr. Chase at Christmas time no matter what. She says she has a little time now and again to sew on wedding dresses. She misses the horses which are now in the woods working for the winter, but there are a few left to haul tote wagons. She's doing great.

I write to her about me training for the snowshoe race and about Emile and Andre making racing snowshoes. I tell her Mom is doing great, and Jason is scaling wood for our neighbors at McNally Pond Camp. Mr. Chase is happy to know we can blow up a few tons of rocks next spring. We're doing great.

Every day I think of Janice running at West End School and laughing all the way. I think she'll do OK in her races. Every day I sprint faster to and from the dam. Now I'm running as fast as I did showing off on my first day, but I'm in a lot better shape so it's easy. The trouble is I don't know how good I have to be to win the snowshoe race. I still worry about losing my friends' bet money.

Can you believe this? Can I believe this? The only time I forget about the snowshoe race is when I'm reading a high school literature book.

One night after supper in the bunk room, I start reading *"Treasure Island"*. The men watch Andre and Emile weave leather thongs into the snowshoe frames as I read and Andre translates. But nothing happens. There is no discussion like there was with "Tarzan", "Cinderella", and "Alice's Adventures in Wonderland". I like the story, but I guess nobody else does so I read two chapters and stop.

Next day I find I'm wrong. Everyone is discussing "Treasure Island". I don't know what they are saying, but the names are the same in French and English. They talk about Jim, Squire Trelawney, Dr. Livesey, Bill, and Black Dog. By their body language I know they are not happy, and I think they decide to forget "Treasure Island".

That night in the bunk room I find I'm wrong again. Andre catches me up on what the crew thinks. They guess that a bunch of thieves are going to fight over stolen property, and the Admiral Benbow isn't a safe place for Jim and his parents. The crew watches Andre and Emile weave thongs into snowshoe frames and listens to more "Treasure Island". Still, there is no discussion.

The next day is Fall Field Day Saturday. All I can think about is Janice running two races. She is quite little, and I'm afraid she might get hurt.

That Sunday Jason has to scale wood at McNally Pond Camp. I fish Dad's packsack out from under my bunk and I give it to Jason to carry his scaling papers.

"The Clark family pride goes with this packsack," I tell Jason.

"I'm not going thirty miles, but I'll make good time. Promise," Jason says.

I'm cookee for Mom that day. I wish I could use the telephone to call out to see how Janice did in the races, but the telephone is only for business.

Just as he says, Jason makes good time. He leaves at about six in the morning and goes three miles to McNally Pond Camp. He scales a dozen or so piles of logs scattered here and there in the woods, has dinner with our neighbors, and comes back to 30-Mile Depot early in the afternoon. He is wet with sweat.

I remember that Jason said he wished he could run like me, and I guess he did today. This is a new thing with him. He wouldn't run in the races we ran around the West End School.

Next morning Jason is cookee again, so he gets up first. When he comes back from the outhouse he says, "Hey, we've got a foot of snow. Get up and walk a path to Mom's cabin."

I think he's pulling my leg, but he isn't. I look out the door, and snow is even with the dingle porch floor. There are snowshoe prints in the snow. I don't have to walk a path to Mom's cabin because Mr. Chase is carrying Mom, and he stands her on the dingle.

Mom says, "Thank you," and she hurries into the cook room.

Illustration 12-2: *Larrigans* by Judy Sherman

"Snowshoes today, Ed." Mr. Chase says as he loosens his snowshoe bindings and leans the snowshoes against the dingle wall. "I'll get you a pair of larrigans when you pick up your snowshoes after breakfast."

"OK," I say, and I smile, but I don't feel all good because an old feeling comes back. I know that Mr. Chase is the guy for Mom, but I'm not the man of our house anymore. It's Mr. Chase who helped Mom over the snow. Then I think of Janice, and I feel OK again.

I wish I knew how Janice did in the Fall Field Day races. I hope she didn't get hurt.

After breakfast Mr. Chase issues snow shovels, snowshoes, and to me a pair of larrigans which the rest of the crew already has. Larrigans are knee-high, lace-up moccasins. They are used with snowshoes because boots with hard soles and calks ruin snowshoes. Also snow doesn't fall into larrigans.

Illustration 12-3: *Calked Boots* by Judy Sherman

Our company snowshoes are oval like bear paws and, sure enough, they are called bear paw snowshoes. They have heavy frames and thick, tough, leather webbing. They are good for working in the woods among trees and bushes, but they are heavy and clumsy. You have to pick up your knee every step to lift the snowshoe out of the snow for the next step.

Sometimes the front catches in the snow and trips you. Since the things are almost as wide as they are long, you have to walk spread-legged like you wet your pants. About the only good you can say about the things is that they are better than wading in deep snow. The company buys the things by the wagonload so they're cheap. Just about everyone buys a pair to keep in the woodshed.

I'm not running a sprint because of the snow this morning so I snowshoe to the dam first to pack a path for the rest of the crew. This is the hardest I've worked since I showed off on my first sprint. I should have let horses go first. Their weight and hard hooves really pack snow.

It takes us a couple hours to shovel enough snow at the dam so we can start, then we trade our snowshoes and larrigans for calked boots. Calked boots don't slip on hard-packed snow and snow-covered logs.

Things in my head don't go on as usual. All day I wonder how Janice did in the races. At night I dream about those races. They turn out different every time, but win or lose, Janice is always laughing.

Wednesday is tote wagon day, so I watch the road and hope for a letter from Janice. Because of the snow, the tote wagon is a tote sled, and of course it's late. But I get my letter.

Dear Eddie,

I had a bad time at the Fall Field Day. A lot of kids came on the train from other towns, and every girl but me wore split skirts.

In the church girls' room a girl said, "Come on girls. We can't stay here with someone wearing boys' pants." Her friends laughed and they hurried out. I felt terrible, but I didn't have my split skirt to wear. I had to run in my running pants.

My first race was only one hundred yards so I started fast, and I was ahead. I looked back to see how the other girls were doing, and I could hardly believe what I saw. Every girl was holding up her split skirt so she could run faster. There were a lot of people watching, and everyone could see their bare legs and sometimes even their knees. I was so amazed that I forgot to watch where I was running, and when I stepped in a hole in the field, I fell. Martha and Mary screamed at me to get up and run faster, but I finished last.

"Hey," one girl said to me after the race, "you'd look better running in the boys' races."

"Only girls wearing girls' clothes win girls' races," another girl said.

"You ought to be ashamed of yourself," other girls said.

I told Father Belanger that I didn't want to run in the girls' quarter-mile race, and did I get a surprise. He held my shoulders until I had to look up into his eyes. He never did that before.

He said, "Janice, I know what the girls are saying, and I know why they are saying those things. They know you could have won at one hundred yards. They don't want you to think you can win the quarter mile. It's not your running pants they care about. It's your head. Janice, don't let your competition win in your head."

At first I was mad at the girls for doing that to me. Then I was mad at myself for letting them do that to me.

By the time the quarter-mile race started I was really steamed up, and I started too fast. At about half way I couldn't breathe fast enough, everything looked flashing red and blurry, and my legs wobbled. I didn't look back, and I won before I fell. Martha and Mary walked with me for a half hour before I could walk by myself. My mouth tasted like eating soup with an iron spoon.

Then I got mad all over again. The girl who made fun of me in the girls' room said, "OK Missy, you're not going to have it easy again. We're going to have running pants for the Christmas Field Day snowshoe races. And you've been practicing. We're going to practice too, and we're going to get you."

Eddie, I'll tell you what. Dad has a pair of almost round company snowshoes in the woodshed, and I'm going to learn to use them. Those girls are not going to get me.

Hey, after I beat them on snowshoes let's go snowshoeing for the fun of it. Maybe there will be a full moon.

Love, Janice

Wow, I think this doesn't sound like Janice. Janice always laughs when she runs. I start to read the letter again, and a red mitten slides in front of the paper.

13. LEARNING TO SNOWSHOE

I look up from Janice's letter and the red mitten. It's Alcide's mitten, and he is standing there grinning at me. He points to a horse and teamster with another log for us so I fold the letter and get back to work.

After work I go to the cook room, and Mom is all lit up and smiling. She has letters from Janice and the girls. On the bulletin board is a drawing by Martha and Mary showing Janice winning her race.

I read Janice's letter again, and it is just as I thought. It doesn't sound like Janice. I remember my girl laughing as she runs races around the West End School. From the letter it is plain that she didn't laugh during the Fall Field Day races. She runs to win. Janice Chase is a competitor. She won a race, and she is only a freshman.

I think about my snowshoe race. My competition will be grown men experienced on snowshoes, and my crew will bet on me. I think that I have no chance to win.

Then I remember that Father Belanger told Janice, "Don't let your competition win in your head." I feel ashamed of myself, and I decide to stop thinking like a dog with its tail between its legs. I'll train harder. My competition might be grown and experienced, but they'll know that I'm in the race.

Emile and Andre bring my new racing snowshoes when they came to the cook room for supper. I know I should say "Thank you," but my mouth and brain don't work when I hold my snowshoes. Even spiders couldn't do better weaving webs of fine leather thongs into the graceful, varnished, fish-shaped frames. They have sturdy bindings with small brass buckles to hold them on my larrigans.

When everyone comes in for supper I pass the snowshoes around. There is a lot of French, smiles all around, and pats on the back for Andre and Emile. My brain and mouth work again, and I tell them, "Mercy."

Andre says, "You welcome. You pay us in race. We win bet on you. Emile teach you snowshoe after supper."

In front of the dingle after supper, in as much light as a half-moon offers, I strap my new snowshoes on over my larrigans. I walk a few steps for all my friends watching from the dingle. Wow, bear paw snowshoes are heavy, slow, and awkward like a log sled, but racing snowshoes are light, fast, and sleek like a sleigh. They feel like they are part of my feet when I jog a few steps toward the dam.

"Eddie," Andre says, and I stop. My crew looks like a circle of shadows as they gather around me.

Emile stands beside me, his thick glasses reflecting the moonlight. He talks to me, his voice a gurgle, and Andre translates.

"You see railroad train engine?"

"Wee."

"You see big rod push train wheel?"

"Wee."

"Rod go up and straight ahead." Emile moves his foot in a forward arc.

"Wee."

"Rod go down and straight back under wheel." Emile places his foot down and steps forward.

"Wee."

"You snowshoe like rod. Up—only straight ahead. Down—only straight back.
Up—down—up—down—only straight." Emile holds my arm as we jog out of the circle of loggers on the hard snow, and Andre runs beside us.

Emile coughs, staggers, and drops to his knees. His cough sounds like a woodpecker pounding on a hollow tree. Andre and I kneel beside him, and Andre pats him on the back with both hands.

The crew gathers around us and Emile gets better. When he stops coughing, Andre and I help him stand up.

Andre talks to Emile and points toward the bunk room. Emile shakes his head, and his glasses flash moonlight. He talks to me again, and Andre interprets.

"Eddie, you see big ball on clock swing straight?" With elbows bent so his forearms are parallel with the snow, Emile swings his arms back and forth like a clock pendulum. "Arm move like ball on clock. Always straight. Not flap like bird wing. OK, Eddie?"

"OK," I say.

"Eddie, you see horse head go up and down when horse walk?"

"Wee," I say.

"Not for you, Eddie. You keep head straight. Not side to side. Not up and down. Only straight, Eddie. OK?" His arm extended, Emile points his finger straight ahead.

"OK," I say.

"One more thing, Eddie. Keep shoulder up. Chest big like train boiler. Lot of air. OK?"

Emile coughs again. It sounds like a raven croaking far away in a thick swamp. The crew walks to the bunk room with him, and when they close the bunk room door I don't hear the raven any more.

Through black tree shadows I jog toward the dam on packed snow, and my new snowshoes feel as natural as four-foot feet. In my mind I see train wheels and push rods. My snowshoes move up, straight ahead, down, straight back—over and over and over. My stride feels great.

I see a clock pendulum in my mind, and my arms swing straight ahead, straight back, straight ahead, straight back with my stride. My arms feel right.

I think of bobbing horses' heads. I think that bobbing my head would waste energy. I hold my head straight like Emile said and my shoulders up. My chest feels like a train boiler, and I feel like I am drifting over my snowshoes.

When I jog past the dam and onto soft, unpacked snow I learn how really good my new snowshoes are. If I had bear paw snowshoes I would have to lift my knees every step to lift the snowshoes above the snow. My fish-shaped snowshoes are balanced so the train wheel push rod motion lifts the turned up fronts above the snow. The pointed backs drag along.

I feel like I could go forever, but I turn at the rock ledge and jog back toward 30-Mile Depot. I think I am a lucky guy to have perfect snowshoes and a great coach. Then I remember that I have to do my part. I have to win. I can't let my friends lose money they bet on me. The push rods in my mind turn faster, my stride lengthens, and I feel cold air rushing into my lungs and over my face.

While I take off my snowshoes in front of the dingle I decide to ask Mom if she thinks running races will hurt Janice. After all, Janice is a pretty small girl. When I go in the cook room there is Emile having a cup of tea, and Mom is showing him the girls' drawing of Janice winning a race. I don't understand the French conversation, but it is for sure that they think Janice should be running races. I decide not to ask Mom about it.

Dear Janice, I write.

Hey, you really did great at the Fall Field Day. Congratulations. I hope I can do OK in my race. I have to because my friends are betting on me. I'm worried, and I'm going to train harder.

Janice, two of my friends here made me a pair of racing snowshoes. I did a couple miles on them tonight, and you will have to try them to see how great they are.

I worked on company snowshoes like the pair you have. If you learn to snowshoe on those things, you'll fly on my snowshoes. How about we both use my snowshoes for the Christmas Field Day? I thought about it a lot, and I just don't feel right about competing for your church because I don't belong. I won't be on your team, but I want you to win anyway.

It's only a few weeks until Christmas. Doing the Christmas Field Day will be OK, but I really want to snowshoe with you for the fun of it. You can use my new snowshoes.

I started reading "Treasure Island". My friends think the bunch of thieves coming to the Admiral Benbow Inn is nothing but bad news.

Love, Eddie

Hey, maybe we can snowshoe together more than one night.

Thursday morning I give Janice's letter to Mom to put with her letters. I put larrigans and my snowshoes on so I can snowshoe sprint to the dam. I need my calked boots for work so I tie the laces together and hang the boots over my shoulders.

"Eddie," Andre says, "I take boots to blacksmith shop. You leave snowshoe there and take boot."

"OK," I say. "I can snowshoe better without my boots hanging to me."

"Go, Eddie," Andre says. "Race come soon."

When I step off the beaten path and sprint in soft snow I feel like I'm drifting along with blowing, swirling snow. I want to take the day off and drift to Ashland to see Janice. I stop at the blacksmith shop, put on my cold boots, and go to work.

The morning goes about as usual. At our log hewing bed we square two logs. At noon I go to the blacksmith shop for my snowshoes and Andre and Emile have the steam pipe on the forge fire. They are bending snowshoe frames smaller than my snowshoes.

"Madam Clark need snowshoe," Andre says. Emile grins.

Well imagine that, I think. Mom is going to snowshoe. As I sprint to the cook room, I imagine Mom snowshoeing. Her dress drags in deep snow. Then I try to imagine Mom snowshoeing in running pants, and that warps my brain. I just cannot imagine my mother wearing running pants. I decide that I won't mention Mom's snowshoes.

Every day I sprint harder. On Sunday Jason goes on bear paw snowshoes to scale wood at McNally Pond Camp. I get the cookee work caught up and snowshoe to the two and a half-mile marker and back. It feels great. I am more and more amazed at how good my racing snowshoes feel.

That afternoon it gets a little dark and Jason hasn't returned. Mom is upset and jittery so I snowshoe down the road under the telephone wire to find Jason. My brother and a moose or two are the only traffic on the road so he had to break a trail in foot-deep snow for three miles on bear paw snowshoes. I think about that. That is a very tough piece of work, and I wonder if he made it. I jog faster.

No need to worry. Around a curve in the road, here comes Jason.

"Did you make it to McNally Pond Camp?" I ask.

"Had to. That's where the job is."

"Did you get the wood scaled?"

"Of course I did. That's what I went for."

"How are you feeling?"

"Ugly. Whoever invented bear paw snowshoes ought to have to wear them forever—even to bed."

I turn around, and to pack the trail a little more and make it easier for Jason I snowshoe ahead. I wonder to myself if I could do what my little brother did. I'm proud of him. He is tough as a bag of hammers—and smart, too.

Mom settles down when we get back to the cook room. While I put supper on the tables, Jason makes out his scale reports.

When he gives the reports to Mr. Chase, Jason says, "Do you suppose that Andre and Emile would make me a pair of snowshoes like Eddie's?"

"I'm sure they would," Mr. Chase says. "I'll talk to them."

"You know something, Jason," I say, "If you want to really go faster, you ought to have a pair of skis and a pole like the game warden, Mr. Jorgensen. You've seen him ski. Nobody on snowshoes can go anywhere near as fast."

Jason thinks for a minute. "Wow," he says, "that would be something. He can really go. I'd sure like to have a pair of skis, but Mr. Jorgensen's skis came from Sweden. Nobody around here knows how to make skis."

"Jason," I say, "Andre and Emile can make a clock if they want to." I ask Mr. Chase, "Would it be OK if we ask them to make Jason a pair of skis and a pole?"

Mr. Chase says, "You know, that might make Jason's scaling job a lot easier. I'll talk to them about it."

During supper, Mr. Chase talks to Emile and Andre in French, and I watch the body language. At first they listen while they eat. Soon they stop eating and begin to grin.

They talk to the other men at the table, and everyone but Mr. Chase laughs.

"Eddie," Andre says as he points a thumb at Mr. Chase, "Our boss make joke with us. He say Jason need seven-foot-long snowshoe."

"They don't believe that people use skis," Mr. Chase says. He turns his hands palms up and raises his eyebrows. He is sort of half grinning, half smiling, and the rest confused.

"Hey, Andre," I say, "Mr. Chase isn't joking, but it's skis and not snowshoes that he's talking about."

"Ski?" Andre says. "That is what Mr. Chassee say. Tell me what is ski."

"Look," I say, "snowshoes go like a train wheel push rod, right?" I make circle motions with my hands.

"OK," Andre says.

"Skis are all wood, and they stay flat on the snow. You skid them along like you walk." I put my hands flat on the table and push first one ahead then the other. "They hold you up in the snow, and you use a long pole to push you along faster—you know, like you pole a canoe." I hold my hand over my head to show the length of the pole, and I make a motion like I am pushing with the long pole.

Andre stares at the table, and his face shows that his mind is working on a strange new idea.

He glances at me and says, "Mr. Chassee say they make snow skid in Sweden."

"Yes."

Andre says, "Someone in Sweden have good idea. We make many snow skid and put together for toboggan. In Sweden they put one skid on each foot. I have to see snow skid work that way. We have spare skid in blacksmith shop for fix toboggan. We put snowshoe harness on two skids for Jason."

14. SKIS FOR JASON

After supper I read more of "Treasure Island" in the bunk room. My friends are more sure all the time that nothing good will come of pirates and stolen money. They agree that Jim should burn the treasure map.

When I've read enough, Andre says, "Emile and me go to blacksmith shop. Put snowshoe harness on snow skid for Jason."

"Hey," I say, "would it be OK if I go to help you?"

Andre smiles at me. "That is why I tell you," he says.

I take the book back to the cook room and tell Jason, "I'm going to the blacksmith shop with Emile and Andre to make you a pair of skis."

Jason glances up from his algebra book. "Yeah. Right," he says. I knew he wouldn't believe me. He's reading close to the end of the book.

In the shop I trim the wicks, clean the globes, and light half a dozen lamps. We can see OK, and Emile builds a wood fire on the forge which gives us more light and some heat.

I hadn't noticed them before, but lying in a rack are a few toboggan repair boards which had been split from an ash log. They are about as wide as your hand and bent up on one end like the front of a toboggan. Emile selects two, brushes off dust, and lays them on a workbench.

"For snow skid OK?" Andre asks.

"They are shorter and turned up on the front more than Mr. Jorgensen's skis." I say. "I think they'll be OK for Jason if we trim the fronts."

"Where to cut you show," Andre says.

With a sharp-pointed leather awl I scratch curves on the turned-up ends to outline ski fronts.

From a tool chest Emile selects a small saw with a narrow blade while Andre clamps one of the boards in a vise. So Emile can see the scratches better, Andre and I hold lamps close. Orange lamp light flashes from Emile's thick glasses and the bright saw blade as he cuts the ski nose curve.

He cuts the nose curve on the second board, and I lay them side by side on the bench. They are a pair of skis—just like Mr. Jorgensen's, but short enough for Jason. At first I feel like I've seen a miracle. Then I remember how good my craftsmen friends are.

"Need snowshoe harness," Andre says to me. He and Emile talk French as he picks a pair of snowshoe harnesses from a box under the bench.

From scraps of board he picks out from under the bench Andre cuts two pieces about a foot long. He chisels in each piece a slot big enough for a snowshoe harness strap.

As my friends work together, their shadows, cast from six lanterns and the forge fire, flick and flit on the log walls and shake roof. They drill holes in the short boards, screw them to the middle of the skis, and attach harness straps through the chiseled slots.

Jason has a pair of skis.

Andre pulls a steel-pointed pick pole, perhaps nine feet long, from a pile on another rack. The poles are used by loggers during a log drive to push logs stuck in bushes back into the stream.

"Jason need pole for push snow skid. OK?" he asks.

"OK," I agree. "But look, the push pole I saw had a round cone near the point. That keeps the pole from sinking too far into the snow when you push. Can you do that?"

"Can do that."

They saw a wood cookie from a six-inch post, drill a pole-sized hole in the center, and nail it onto the pole near the point.

Jason has a ski set.

There is a little moonlight and it is only midnight or so, so we go to the cook room. As usual, the lamp by the bulletin board is burning, but it's still pretty dark.

Jason is sleeping and I shake him. "We've got your skis," I say.

Jason grunts. "Ed," he says, "I snowshoed all day. I did the dishes. I've got to get up early. I'm tired, I don't feel like joking, now go to bed."

Andre says, "Jason, we have snow skid for you."

Bug-eyed, Jason sits up. "Whoa," he says when he sees Andre holding his skis.

"Wow," he says, and he hops out of bed in his longies.

"Boot we fit to snow skid," Andre says. "You dress. We see snow skid work." While Jason dresses, Andre and Emile adjust the ski bindings to fit Jason's boots.

Jason slides his feet into his boots right on his skis. He clatters across the cook room, and I hold the door open for him. When Jason clatters through the cook room door, Mr. Chase, barefooted and in his longies, opens the dingle door to see what is going on.

Jason steps his skis onto the snow and stumbles a couple of awkward strides. He makes the first ski tracks at 30-Mile Depot. Andre gives him the pole, and Jason becomes a different kid. Pushing hand over hand with the long pole, his awkward strides become long smooth slides. He soon disappears into dim moonlight.

We hear, "Whoopie Deeeeee," from the dark.

Pretty soon, back he comes. The first thing that appears in the dim moonlight is his smile bobbing up and down as he pumps with his pole.

"Thank you very much," Jason says to Andre and Emile.

Next morning, Mr. Chase comes into the cook room early. Soon, here comes Mom.

"Oh my soul," Mom says, "Mr. Jorgensen is here. There are ski tracks on the road. He must have come last night to see if we are cooking game animals." Mom sees Jason's skis leaning against his bunk. "He must be in the bunk room. When he comes for breakfast, I'll show him that I am running a legal cook room."

Pretty soon, in comes the crew for breakfast. They talk and look the skis over like they are inspecting a miracle. Several of the men pat Jason on the back, and he grins.

I glance at Mom. Her mouth is hanging open, and there are tears on her face. What, I wonder, is wrong.

Andre says to Mr. Chase and Mom, "Maybe late breakfast? We see Jason push snow skid now?"

"Yes," Mom says. She hugs Andre, reaches up, and pats his cheek. "Thank you," she says. Then she hugs Emile, pats his cheek, and tells him, "Mercy. Mercy."

What in the world, I wonder, is going on with Mom. I've never seen her do such a thing. And Mr. Chase is standing there smiling. He doesn't mind at all.

The whole crew goes out front, Jason puts on his skis, and he really looks good pushing with his pole and skiing up and down the road. Every guy in the crew shakes his head like he can't believe what he's seeing.

Someone yells, "Bon Homme, Jason." I join the crew yelling, "Bon Homme, Jason."

I look at Mom standing on the dingle platform with Mr. Chase, and she is still crying. Hard. My brain ticks. I think that until Jason got his skis it was me out there being cheered on, and I was proud. I remember that Jason said he wished he could run like me. Now he is out there being cheered on, and Jason is proud. Jason is Mom's boy just like me, and now Mom is happy for him just like she's happy for me. I wish it didn't take me so long to understand women.

So anyway, the next week is just like all the rest—only different. I snowshoe sprint to and from the dam and nobody pays any attention. I'm old stuff. Jason skis past the dam a couple times a day, and everyone stops work to cheer him on.

I think this isn't fair. The crew is going to bet on me and they don't pay any attention to me anymore. Then I think that I ought to be ashamed of myself for being jealous. I decide to train harder, and maybe I won't be ashamed of myself in the race.

Wednesday is tote sled day, and I get a letter from Janice.

Dear Eddie,

I made ankle-length running pants, but snowshoeing is terrible. Because I'm not used to pulling the things along, the muscles in my shins are so sore I can hardly walk. I try not to limp at school. Some of the girls still tease me about wearing knee-length running pants, and I don't want them to know I'm practicing with snowshoes. I'm not going to stop practicing, and the girls who teased me at the races aren't going to get me.

But Christmas is coming soon, and my woods family is coming out to town for a while. That is going to be very good, and I am happy. I miss you all, but having the twins with me helps me every day.

I am still disappointed that the wedding won't happen at Christmas. We'll just have to wait until next summer.

I love you,
Janice

When I get a letter from Janice now I think of the flying moose I wish I had to ride out to visit her on Sundays. I'd even go to church with her. After supper I write to her.

Dear Janice,

I had no idea that so many new things could happen in a logging camp. Bear paw snowshoes were too slow for Jason on the days he scales logs. We told my friends Emile and Andre about Mr. Jorgensens, the game warden's, skis. They made Jason a pair from toboggan boards, and Jason is learning to use them and a push pole. He is fast. I wish there were ski races for him to enter.

Your sore shins won't last long. When I first used a broadaxe I was so sore I almost wanted to quit. With Mom here, I knew better than to even mention that. I'm sure you'll feel OK in a few days. Hang in there. I think you'll like my snowshoes when you use them.

I'll tell you what. I keep telling myself I'm not going to worry about my friends losing their money betting on me in the snowshoe race. I can't help worrying. I dream about it every night. I'm training as hard as I can, and I'll be glad when the race is over.

There is another reason too. After the race we're going out to spend Christmas with you.

I'm with you. I wish Mom and Mr. Chase could get married at Christmas, but next summer isn't that far away.

Love,
Eddie

On my way to work Thursday morning I give Janice's letter to the tote sled driver.

Jason's skiing adds some spice to my work day. Just like with my snowshoeing the crew pays less attention, but I can see Jason getting better and faster. I wonder how much faster he will make it to McNally Pond Camp on skis.

Saturday afternoon when Jason returns from skiing down the road, Andre yells and beckons for him to stop. I'm too far away to hear what they say, but Jason leaves his skis at the blacksmith shop and walks to the cook room.

At suppertime I ask Jason, "What are they doing to your skis?"

"They painted them," Jason says.

"How come?" I ask.

"They say they paint toboggans to make them pull easier, so they painted my skis."

That doesn't make sense to me, but I don't say anything because Andre and Emile know more about toboggans than I do.

"Eddie," Mom says, "I want you to go with Jason tomorrow and take a pair of snowshoes for him. I don't know if he can manage on his new skis that far, and I don't want him to be alone in the woods."

"I'll cookee," Mr. Chase says.

"OK," I say, and I thank my lucky star. I get a day off, and I'm going to see just what Jason and his skis can do.

Next morning at the blacksmith shop we find that the skis are painted only on the bottoms. Neither of us can figure that out until Jason fastens on the skis and gives himself a push with his pole.

"Wow," he says as he slides away. I don't catch up to him before he pushes again. With every stride he gets further ahead of me.

Jason stops at the dingle to wait for me. Mr. Chase is there with a pair of bear paw snowshoes for me to take in case Jason needs them. I catch up, and I take the snowshoes to make Mom feel better. I don't think Jason is going to need snowshoes.

"What is the stuff they painted on the skis?" I ask.

Mr. Chase says, "It's a mixture of leather oil we use to keep horse harnesses pliable and shellac to stick the oil to wood. It works great on toboggans. Is it good on skis?"

"Slipperier than a snotty eel," Jason says. He grins, pushes with his pole, and away he goes.

I soon find out what Jason and his skis can do. Just beyond 30-Mile Depot I sort of keep up with him going up a little hill. Then he's gone, and I really snowshoe hard. By the time I get to McNally Pond Camp, Jason is nearly done his scaling job.

As I sit on the dingle to rest I look at the telephone wire going west out of sight beside the woods road. Jimmie comes out of the cook room to talk.

"Hey, Eddie," he says, "Your little brother is faster than you, huh?"

"Those skis are something else," I say. "The only time I can make him work is going up a hill. Other than that, he's gone."

"Too bad we couldn't sneak Jason into the snowshoe race. We'd know the winner."

I think about that. That would be fun, but I guess the race officials wouldn't allow it.

While I'm thinking about Jason skiing in a snowshoe race, I hear a sound that doesn't belong in the woods. But I listen, and I hear it again. A raven makes almost every sound there is, but a raven can't make that sound. Guaranteed. It's a train whistle. It's a long ways away, but it really is a train whistle. At least it sounds like it.

"Jimmie," I say, "am I going crazy? Is that a train whistle I hear?"

15. TWO POLES ARE BETTER THAN ONE

"No," Jimmie says, and he grins. "You aren't going crazy. That's a train whistle, but it's on a log hauler."

"Wait a minute," I say. "Do you mean that there's a set of railroad tracks over there in the woods?"

"No. A log hauler has a train engine, but it doesn't run on wheels and rails. On the back it has two steel treads made in sections that hinge and go around like long snowshoes. It has snow skids on the front like Jason's skis but a lot bigger."

"Hey, I'd like to see that," I say.

"You will. We got a telephone call from our company boss in Ashland this morning. He said the Madawaska Company called him. They built a bridge three miles west of here over Musquacook Stream. Their crews will have a road snow-packed to here for the snowshoe race next Saturday. It will be a six-mile race—three miles to Musquacook Stream Bridge and three miles back. All of their competitors and the Madawaska Company owner, Mr. Lacroix himself, are coming here. This is the first year the Great Northern Paper Company has a competitor in the race, you know. That's you, Ed. And by the way, the log hauler is going to haul the wood we're cutting here at McNally Pond Camp. They can get it to the mill cheaper that way."

My mouth is hanging open—I think. And maybe my brain too. The race is next Saturday, a week sooner than I thought, and a lot of other stuff will happen. I don't know about the other stuff, but if I don't win here my crew will lose the money they bet on me. What is worse, if I come in last here in front of Jimmie and the rest of my neighbors, I won't ever dare to show my face in Ashland. There is nothing to say, so I close my mouth—I think.

"Oh yeah," Jimmie says. "The boss said to tell you that Father Belanger will be here for the race—for sure."

Jason returns from his job, slides into the camp yard, and the crew comes out of the bunk room to talk to him about his new skis.

It's about the middle of the morning, so Jason and I decide to go back to 30-Depot rather than wait for dinner. Again, I really work on my snowshoes while Jason slips along on his skis not even breaking a sweat.

We come to the hill where, on the way in, I could sort of keep up to Jason going uphill. Going downhill is something else. Jason speeds up and he isn't even poling. Down the hill far ahead of me he bends forward, holds his pole crossways like outstretched arms, and yells, "Whoopie deeeeee." He really speeds up as he gets to the bottom of the hill and a turn in the road. I hear him yell, "Nooooooo," as he zips out of sight straight into trees and puckerbrush.

I'm scared. If Jason hit a tree going that fast he could be hurt bad. I snowshoe downhill as fast as I can.

Hey, I'll tell you what. If Mom were here she would be some upset. Here comes Jason wading out of the woods through knee-deep snow. He's carrying his skis which are OK, but his pole is broken in two about equal pieces. That wouldn't kink Mom too much. It's what he's saying that would split her seam. Usually Jason is a pretty quiet kid.

"Look," I say, "why didn't you turn the corner?"

"So how do I turn a corner with long, straight skis?"

"You do it the same as I do it with long, straight snowshoes," I tell him. "To turn left you lift your left ski and set it down at a little angle to the left, then lift your right ski and set it down parallel with your left ski. You do that often enough and fast enough to make the corner." I know I never skied, but this works with snowshoes.

"I should'a thought'a that," Jason says. He straps on his skis and starts back up the hill pushing with a half pole in each hand.

"Hey," I say, "we've got to get to 30-Mile for dinner. Why are you going back up the hill?"

"I'm going to make that corner if it takes me all day," he yells back to me.

He goes part way up the hill poling with a half pole in each hand. He turns his long skis around a few degrees per step, and here he comes. Our going and coming has the snow packed pretty well, so when he gets to the bottom of the hill he is coming like a rabbit ahead of a bobcat.

I don't think he can make the curve, but I should know better. He lifts his skis one after the other and slide-steps around the corner and out of sight. Just like that. I plug along as fast as I can to catch up with him.

"You know, Ed," Jason says as he steps his skis around toward the hill again, "I think two short poles are better than one long one."

"Hey, c'mon," I say, "You can't play on that hill all day. We got to get back for dinner."

"Go ahead. I'll catch up with you. I'm going to make that curve from the top of the hill."

Yeah. Right. Not hardly. I remember I'm carrying snowshoes for Jason in case he can't manage his skis. If I go home to dinner and Jason breaks his leg, I have no idea what Mom would do. And I'm not going to find out.

By the time I get back around the corner, Jason is at the top of the hill. Here he comes down the packed trail again picking up speed like a rock dropped into a deep well.

Leaning forward, knees bent, and ski poles trailing behind like the tail of an airplane, he zips past me. Nothing else in the woods goes that fast. Not moose or deer, not rabbits or bobcats. Birds might fly that fast, but Jason is the fastest thing on the ground. I'm scared. I'm sure he can't make the turn, and I've got to pick him out of the woods.

"Woopeeee deeee," he yells to me, and his hat blows off. He side steps around the turn so fast his skis look like trout fins flicking against fast water. He doesn't even come close to the woods.

I pick up his hat and run to catch up with him. I'm hungry, and I don't want him to go back and ski that hill again.

"Jason," I say as I really work on my snowshoes to keep up with him, "when we finish the dam and go home next summer, let's set up a shop in the woodshed and make skis for Janice and me. I've got to get this snowshoe race over with, but I'll tell you what. I'm tired of working my butt off on snowshoes while you goof off on skis."

Jason grins. He thinks for a few strides. "Hey," he says, "good idea." After a few more strides he says, "We've got to find out exactly what kind of leather oil and shellac is in toboggan paint. The stuff is almost magic."

"Yeah," I say. "And if anyone will buy our skis, we could give them a bottle of 'Jason's Almost Magic.' After that, maybe we could sell some for a dime a bottle."

"That would be better than delivering newspapers," Jason says as he sticks out his hand. We shake hands on our deal.

My little brother skis away from me and out of sight. When I get to 30-Mile he's finishing his dinner.

I hang the bear paw snowshoes in the dingle and lean my snowshoes against the wall beside my bed. "Look Mom," I say, "Stop worrying about Jason and his skis. OK?"

Mom pats my cheek. She's lit right up, all smiles and excited. "I'm going with the crew Saturday to see the race," she tells me.

The place is in an uproar. Everybody talks about the race. My crew pats me on the back and rubs their fingers and thumbs like they are counting money. My stomach cramps up like a wet wool mitten dried too fast over a stove. Not even Mom's pork, beans, and biscuits taste good.

"Ed," Mr. Chase says, "Did you see a log hauler today?"

"No," I tell him as I pick at my dinner, "but I heard a whistle off in the woods." I tell him what Jimmie told me about the race and the log hauler. While I'm talking Mr. Chase just stares at the table in front of him.

"That fellow, Mr. Lacroix, is the sharpest businessman in the Maine woods. He has dozens of logging camps and several thousand men working for him. I hope you have a chance to meet him."

"Wow. Really?"

"Really. And he's as fair and honest as the day is long."

"I hope I meet him."

Monday Jason talks to Andre about his broken push pole. I work and snowshoe. Tuesday Jason skis past the dam with two short, slim ski poles, each with push cones. I work and snowshoe. Wednesday I work, snowshoe, and Janice's letter comes on the tote sled.

Dear Eddie,

Father Belanger told me he is going to the woods to see you race. I want to go, but I must stay with the twins. I didn't tell them I want to go. I don't want them to think I don't love them. I cried, but I made sure they were asleep before I cried.

You are coming home. That is what is most important. It's been six months since you left. It seems like six lifetimes. High school is such a big world, and I am living it without you. It doesn't seem fair.

I've got to stop complaining. I have Martha and Mary, and Mom is so proud that she is a professional cook. Dad writes in every letter that Mom is doing great. He always thanks me for keeping the twins. I really do have to stop complaining.

I'm going to complain again. I finished making wedding dresses for Mom, the twins, and me. The twins look sweet, but they want to wear their new long pink dresses to school. That is not going to happen. I love my dress, and Mom's is best of all. But there will be no wedding until next summer. I wish this were June.

OK. No more complaining. I know you will do your best in the race. I don't care if you place first or last. Just come home for Christmas.

Love,

Janice

P.S. I'm doing OK with my snowshoes, and my shins don't hurt any more. The older girls are not going to get me in the Christmas Field Day races. And I'll see you race, too. I wish you were snowshoeing for our church team.

I snowshoe hard an extra three miles between work and supper, and I feel good. I'm as ready as I can be. I don't write Janice a letter because the tote teamster says he is going to wait until after the race to take us and Jimmie's crew out for Christmas.

After supper I read more "Treasure Island" to the crew. It's the part about what Jim hears when he's in the apple barrel. The men talk only a few minutes.

Andre says, "See? There. We know all time this is bunch of thieves. Jim is lucky they don't eat the apple."

Emile says some French to Andre, and Andre says to me, "No more snowshoe. You ready. You rest."

After I help Jason wash the pots and pans I climb into my bunk, but I don't rest. I wish Janice could come in with Father Belanger to see the race. I hope I don't look too silly in the race. I remember that Janice wrote that high school is a big world. I like my little world at 30-Mile—well, maybe except for the snowshoe race. I wish Janice were here to cook. That's crazy. I think crazy things, but sooner or later I go to sleep.

Thursday is fun because I don't have to snowshoe. The snow is packed, and I walk between the cook room and the dam with my crew.

Thursday night I really wish I knew French. I read the part of "Treasure Island" where Jim leaves the *Hispaniola* and goes ashore on Treasure Island. Andre translates, and the crew argues for a half hour or so.

Andre says, "We don't know if Jim do good to leave boat. He hide on land, but they might sail boat away, but they might get lost on ocean. Get lost on ocean worse than get lost in woods. In woods is good water. We find out later."

Friday afternoon we're putting our tools in Emile's shop so they won't get snowed over during our Christmas break. Father Belanger arrives in his sleigh, and I look to see if Janice is with him. She isn't.

Father Belanger is leading his horse and walking to the bunk room with us when Jason skis past.

"Skis," he says. "Did Mr. Jorgensen give Jason those skis?"

"No. Emile and Andre made them from toboggan boards for Jason when he scales wood at McNally Pond Camp. If I could snowshoe as fast as Jason can ski, I would guarantee you a win tomorrow."

"You're kidding of course."

"Look. It's going to be a six-mile race. I would guarantee you a win and bet you a dollar that I would win by a half mile. Skis are a different world."

"Wow. You're not kidding."

In the cook room Mom is humming as she checks bread baking in the oven. She smiles, gives me a hug, and says, "I'm going to be so proud of you tomorrow."

Pretty soon Jason comes in and leans his skis against the wall. Mom is on her way to give Jason a hug when Father Belanger comes in. Wow. Mom stops, and her face changes from blue-sky sunny to howling-blizzard icy.

"Good afternoon, Mrs. Clark," Father Belanger says.

Mom nods—I think. She goes back to the stove and checks the bread she just checked.

"Jason," Father Belanger says, "Would you like to ski in the race tomorrow if I can arrange it?"

"Wow," Jason says, "I sure would. Do you think you can do it?"

"One moment," Mom says. "I will talk to Jimmie about where the race will be run before I decide."

"Yes, Ma'am," Father Belanger says as he leaves.

"Hey," Jason says to me, "I got a chance."

After supper I help Jason with the cookee stuff, and we put a thick coat of toboggan paint on his skis.

He's as happy as the twins with new dolls.

16. THE RACE

I wake up at 4:30 and Mom, Jason, and Mr. Chase are cooking breakfast. With all the yelling and laughing, breakfast sounds like a Saturday night dance without the music.

After breakfast out in front of the dingle the men load their packsacks onto the tote sled as we wash the breakfast dishes in the cook room.

Father Belanger offers to take Mom and Mr. Chase in his sleigh, but Mom chooses to ride on the tote sled with the crew. Jason and I ride in the sleigh holding our snowshoes, skis, and ski poles. In dim morning twilight, the sleigh runners squeak and crunch on the snow. We are well ahead of the tote wagon when the sun is up enough to filter through trees and glimmer from the telephone wires.

The sun is above the trees when we ride out of the woods in front of McNally Pond Camp. I can believe what I see only because it's there. It is a big, black railroad engine with skids under the front like big skis. Just like Jimmie said, it has treads under the back made in hinged steel sections. Smoke is rising straight up from the smokestack. Like on a regular train engine, there is a place on back with a window for the engineer. Unlike a train, there is also a seat and a steering wheel like in a truck, but it's out front above the front skids.

A man appears in the engineer's window, white steam spurts from something like a big teakettle spout, and two short train-whistle toots sound. Father Belanger's horse snorts and shakes its head. I know my mouth is hanging open, but I can't help it.

Jason can handle his mouth OK. When Jimmie and a whole bunch of men come out of the camp, Jason jumps down from the sleigh and runs over to Jimmie. There is too much yelling and laughing for me to hear the conversation, but I know Jason is fixing Jimmie's story to Mom. I like my little brother. He just sees one of the most astonishing things in his life, and he is trying to get into a race.

Two more men step from the cook room out onto the dingle porch. One is dressed like Father Belanger, and the other is a big man wearing a black hat with a brim all around, a black overcoat, and black knee-length boots. Beside priests, he is the only man in the woods who dresses like he's in town. It has to be Mr. Lacroix.

"Eddie," Father Belanger says, "that man is Edouard Lacroix, an old friend. The priest is also an old friend who won a bet from me when we were going to school. If Jason skis in the race, I'm going to win that money back—with interest." I take the reins, and Father Belanger runs over to greet his friends.

I lead the horse a ways to get away from the hubbub, but that doesn't work. Soon Father Belanger brings his friends to me. They are laughing and speaking French.

Mr Lacroix switches to English. "Edward, I am pleased to meet you, and I thank you for joining us for our race." We shake hands.

Mr. Lacroix's grip is as powerful as Alcide's, and he speaks English with no accent. Soon Jimmie's crew and some men I don't know gather around, and Mr. Lacroix introduces other competitors to me and tells what camps they represent. He switches languages as needed. His manner is man-to-man friendly with everyone. I like the man.

Our tote wagon arrives, and my friends stare at the log hauler just like I did—but not for long. The crowd around me moves to the tote wagon to meet old friends. Sometimes it's more fun to watch conversations than to hear them. Mom talks to Jimmie and Jason. Pretty soon Jason jumps, does a crazy dance, and hugs Mom. He is in the race—if Father Belanger can pull it off. Father Belanger beckons Jason over to meet his Priest friend and Mr. Lacroix. After handshakes, Jason leads the dignitaries to the sleigh beside me and shows them his skis.

"Skis work great," Jason says as he fastens his ski bindings to his boots. He pushes with his poles, slides across packed snow, steps around a half circle, and slides back. "I can do my scaling job faster on skis," he explains.

"You scale wood faster on skis," Mr. Lacroix says, sort of to himself. "Young man," he says to Jason, "I would like very much to see you ski in the race."

"Ya," Jason yells. "Thank you very much, sir."

Father Belanger winks at me and walks away talking French to his priest friend.

I look back at the noisy crowd beside our tote wagon. Mom and Mr. Chase walk from the crowd and around the log hauler. They look and look and shake their heads. The machine is impressive, and that is for sure.

I sort of forget about the race until Mr. Lacroix walks to the log hauler and says something to the engineer. Two spurts of steam make two toots. Some of the men lift racing snowshoes from the log sleds, our tote teamster holds Father Belanger's horse reins, and I take my snowshoes.

Jason and I join eleven other competitors around Mr. Lacroix. He stands beside Jason and talks French. The competitors stare at the skis, glance at each other, shrug their shoulders, and tell Mr. Lacroix, "Wee."

While this is going on I have a chance to look over my competition. Hey, every one of these guys is as old and maybe older than Jacques. They have gray beards, and they might even be bald under their knit hats. I guess I'm going to win this race easy, but I'm not going to embarrass them. I'll back off so it will be a close race.

"OK, Jason," Mr. Lacroix says, "Everyone agrees that you can race."

"Thank you," Jason says, and some of the older men pat him on his shoulder like he's their grandson.

We competitors line up on the road facing west. Mom and Mr. Chase are given their choice of seats with Mr. Lacroix and the two priests when the crowd climbs onto the sleds behind the log hauler.

Jason digs in his ski poles and crouches ready to push off. When the whistle shrieks he's gone like a barnyard dog after a fox in the chicken pen.

Just like when I'm training I see train push rods circling always forward in my mind, and my snowshoes crunch, crunch, crunch forward on hard-packed snow. My forearms swing straight like piston rods, and I feel great.

I hear yelling behind me, so I look back. The rest of the competitors are standing in the road yelling and watching Jason. Everyone on the log sleds is standing up watching Jason. All but Father Belanger. He is sitting on a seat laughing. I look ahead, keep going, and watch Jason step his skis around a turn in the road far, far ahead.

Louder than my snowshoe crunch, crunch I hear whoosh, whoosh, whoosh, like trees falling through still air. I look back again, and the log hauler treads are turning. Smoke is whoosh, whooshing up from the smokestack, and the guy in the seat out front is steering the front skids with his steering wheel. Everyone on the log sleds is standing up yelling. Mom is leaning over the board railing, her arms waving and her mouth going, and Mr. Chase is holding her coat so she won't fall off.

From the corner of my eye I see the pack, their snowshoes circling forward like eleven sets of push rods and their arms pumping piston rod straight. I wonder if Emile taught them to snowshoe. I decide to get a good lead to sort of discourage my competition, and I can slow down at the end to make it a close race.

The road goes up a hill, the loghauler whoosh, whooshing speeds up, and the machine rumbles beside me. Everyone yells, mostly French, but I hear Mom screaming that I'm doing good. I can hear Emile's high-pitched gurgle, and Father Belanger is still laughing. I glance at the thing, and I can hardly believe my eyes. It is pulling four sleds with our crew, Jimmie's crew, and others—maybe fifty people. It rolls ahead of me like I'm not moving, and goes around a turn after Jason. Smoke drifts above the trees.

Illustration 16-1: *The Race* by Judy Sherman

I think my stride is a little too fast for a six-mile race so I glance back. Wow, the pack is gaining on me. Hey, I feel like the fox trying to stay ahead of a whole bunch of barnyard dogs, so I lengthen my stride a little.

I guess we've been going for a half hour or so when I can hear snowshoes crunching right behind me. Pretty soon here comes Jason loafing around a turn in the road ahead. He bends over pushing with both poles, straightens up while he is sliding, then bends over to push again. He looks like the kind of caterpillar that moves by bending itself up double and straightening itself forward. He's loafing along but he beats the caterpillar's speed. The guys behind me talk and yell.

As Jason goes by he says, "The turnaround is about a quarter mile."

I don't hear anything behind me, so I glance back. The whole pack is standing in the road watching Jason go by, but that doesn't last long. By the time I see the new bridge and the turn-around loop I can hear them right behind me again.

The loghauler is stopped on the loop across the bridge, and beyond the machine the telephone wire and road continue west. As I cross the bridge I see a pile of beams which were sawed in a mill. I think this bridge is being built different from our dam. I don't have time to think very much.

Everyone is lined up around the loop when we snowshoe past and start back to McNally Pond Camp. Someone is running beside me. I hear, "Go, Eddie, go." It's Mom, and the crowd cheers for both of us.

I'm glad we're soon away from the crowd, but two from the pack move up with me. I can hear others. We clatter and crunch along between the tree walls. I hold my chest up and breath deep, but my legs won't move me out ahead again.

Before long I hear the whoosh, whoosh, whoosh of the loghauler engine and everyone in the sleds yelling. I can pick out Mom's screams and Emile's gurgles. I'm proud, but it is costing me numb legs and an iron-spoon taste in my throat. The machine slows to our speed for a mile or so, then the steel treads roll it ahead. Mom is waving to me as it rounds a bend in the road.

The two guys snowshoeing beside me sprint ahead. I didn't think any of us had that much energy left, but the others sprint ahead too. I'm in last place. I think these guys are super men, and they have been playing with me. Now they are serious. I think I'm going to lose the money my crew bet on me, and my neighbors will see me finish last. I think I'm just a kid in a race out of my league, and I wonder why in the world I was dumb enough to do this. I'm going to disappoint Mom and my crew will lose their bet money. Well, I think, at least Jason is doing OK. Hey, I hope, maybe they'll win on Jason. I slow to a long-pace walk, and I wish I'd never come to 30-Mile Depot.

I look at the men ahead of me. Wow. Most have dropped their arms and shoulders. Their heads are flopping from side to side with every stride, and some are staggering and weaving. Hey, I think, these guys aren't super men. They look exhausted, and I still have my form.

I lengthen my stride, move up between two men, and glance at them. Their open mouths, gasping breaths, and squinted eyes show that I still have a chance. I keep my stride, pass others, and I'm in fifth place when I see enough through sweat in my eyes to recognize the big, black log hauler stopped beside McNally Pond Camp.

I wish I hadn't been dumb enough to slow down, and I try to go faster. I see red flashes like the four guys ahead of me are snowshoeing through fire. I hear a long screech, and I don't catch the four guys.

There are people everywhere. I want to fall down, but someone holds me up. Emile gurgles French to me, and Andre says, "We win. Jason win."

The red flashes stop, and the screech stops. It was the log hauler whistle. Someone wipes my face so I can see. It's Mom using her handkerchief, and she is crying.

"Sorry I didn't do better, Mom, but Jason won didn't he?"

"Jason won, and there were no losers in the snowshoe race. I say so, and I am your mother." I guess Mom is crying because she is proud. She wipes her eyes on the same handkerchief. It is probably pretty cruddy.

Mr. Chase shakes my hand. "Thanks and congratulations from the Great Northern Paper Company," he says.

I feel OK again in a few minutes, and as the older competitors recover we shake hands. I have a bunch of new friends, and it doesn't matter that we speak different languages.

People gather around Jason and his skis. My new friends and Mr. Lacroix want to know how anyone can go so fast. My crew and Jimmie's gather to listen, but I back away because I don't like crowds.

Father Belanger and his priest friend are standing apart from the crowd talking and laughing, and Father Belanger accepts money from his friend. He won his bet I guess. They walk over and join the crowd around Jason.

Mom and Mr. Chase are sitting on our tote wagon, and Mom is still crying. She's smiling so she's happy I guess. It's been quite a morning for her.

Wow. Hey, have I got an idea or what. Usually when I have an idea I like to think about it for a while. You know, to see if it's dumb or not. I don't have time to think about this one, but I'm going to give it a shot anyway.

I walk into the crowd and say to Mr. Lacroix, "Andre and Emile made the skis. They did OK, don't you think."

Andre and Emile are soon in the middle, each holding a ski. I guess they are telling everyone how they did it. I grab Jason and pull him out of the crowd.

"I've got an idea, and you go along with it," I tell him.

"Huh?" he says.

17. HEADING TO TOWN FOR CHRISTMAS

"You stay right here," I tell Jason.

I move into the crowd far enough to get Father Belanger's attention, and I motion for him to follow me.

When we join Jason, Father Belanger says, "I need to talk to both of you boys. Jason, a boy from Mr. Jorgensen's town, New Sweden, has skis, and he wants to show how they work at our Winter Field Day. If you ski on my parish team we could add a ski race to the schedule. Now Ed, you've been thinking about this long enough. You're going to snowshoe on my team, too. Right?"

"Hey," Jason says. He's smiling like Father Belanger did when he won his bet.

Before Jason can spoil my plan, I grab his shoulder and close my fingers on a meatless bone like it's my broadaxe handle. His eyes bug out as his smile puckers.

"You're right, Father Belanger," I say. "We've been thinking about it a lot. What we think is that we will both compete for your team ..."

"I knew you would boys. I'm really glad to have you," Father Belanger says. He smiles, and offers his hand for a shake.

"... if you marry Mom and Mr. Chase before Christmas," I say.

When I let off on Jason's shoulder, he smiles again and says, "Hey. Yeah."

Father Belanger's jaw sags so far his mouth isn't big enough to smile and also cover his teeth. "Ed," he says, "I need more time than that."

"Look," I say, "If you agree to do this, Mom and Mr. Chase will ride with you all the way back to Ashland. You've got three days and three nights. If you talk as fast as Jason skis you can do it. Mom will listen. Guaranteed."

"I could get into trouble for this," Father Belanger says.

"Yeah, but we'll win for your team," Jason says.

"Is it a deal?" I ask, and I offer my hand for a handshake.

"OK," he says. "It's a deal." We shake on it to seal the deal. "Excuse me," he says, "I've got to talk to Edna and Roy."

Father Belanger walks over to the tote sled. Soon Mom screams, jumps off the wagon, and kisses the priest on both cheeks. She runs to Jason and me. She is crying but smiling, and she can't say a word. That's not at all like Mom. I give her my bandanna handkerchief.

Mr. Chase and Father Belanger take a few minutes to talk and shake hands with their friends. When we go to Father Belanger's sleigh Mom is first to climb in. Away they go back toward 30-Mile, the priest talking and Mom listening.

Jason goes back into the crowd. I think he wants to make sure he gets his skis back.

My legs are still a little pooped from the race, so I sit on our tote sled to rest. I should feel great. Mom and Mr. Chase will get married soon, and I'm going out to see Janice and the twins. Of course I didn't win, and I'm still disgusted with myself for slacking off in the race. But then again I did OK, and Jason really put on a show. All in all I should feel OK, but I just don't feel great at all. I wonder if I'm sick or something.

Pretty soon the crowd breaks up, and they look happy. Jason carries his skis and poles to our tote sled, and I go say goodbye to Mr. Lacroix and his eleven men who raced. They leave on log hauler sleds with my 30-Mile crew except Andre and Emile. Being the only bachelors in the crew, they will stay to feed and care for the horses.

Jimmie's crew lets their horses out of the stable, grabs their packsacks from their bunk room, and climbs onto our tote sled. With the loose horses following, we head toward 30-Mile. There is a lot of happy whooping and yelling, but I'm dismal.

"Eddie," Andre says as he points to himself and Emile, "we make ski for all Mr. Lacroix scaler. They scale on ski like Jason."

Jason says, "After Christmas they're coming back to McNally Pond Camp for a day so I can show them how I ski."

"Hey," I say to Andre, "Would you show Jason and me how you bend wood and make it stay bent? We want to make skis, too."

"Will do that," Andre says.

With friends like that I ought to be all happy, but I've got a case of nagging miserables.

Jimmie and his crew really get a kick out of watching Jason ski down his favorite hill and step his skis around the turn in the road. Just for the fun of it, Jason skis the rest of the way back to 30-Mile Depot. After winning a six-mile race, he skis for the fun of it. He's quite a kid, and I'm proud of him.

I guess I feel better when we get to 30-Mile. The teamsters put their horses in the hovel with our horses. The lamps are lit in the cook room, the stoves are hot, and Mr. Chase is warming up roast beef and pies and slicing bread. Mom is sitting in her rocking chair listening, and Father Belanger is sitting on a couple of piled up wood cookies talking.

After supper Jason and I do the cookee work, and go to bed in the cook room corner as usual. That's a mistake. Mom and Father Belanger don't shut it off. I wake up at about three in the morning, and I've got to go to the privy right now. I haul my pants and boots on over my long johns and walk right past my mother and the priest to get to the privy. Then I walk past them again on my way back to bed. Embarrassing or what, but they're so interested in what they're talking about that I don't think they even see me.

Come early morning Jason and I slice bacon and bread, Mr. Chase puts pans of leftover beans in the ovens and sets cans of doughnuts on the tables. Mom is bleary eyed, but she starts to help us.

"Mom," I say, "you're supposed to be listening to Father Belanger. We'll do the cooking until you get married."

Mr. Chase chuckles, and Mom smiles and returns to her chair. Hey, I think that's the first time I tell my mother what to do and she does it.

After breakfast, someone hitches up Father Belanger's horse. Mom wraps her long snowshoes in a blanket and piles them under the sleigh seat with packsacks of clothes. Away they go toward 20-Mile with Father Belanger talking and Mom listening.

Andre and Emile say they will do the cookee work so Jason and I load our wangan onto the tote sled with the McNally Pond crew's stuff. Away we go. When we pass the dam the sun is brilliant on the white snow road between tall, green tree walls.

The snow is packed by sled runners and horse hooves, so we walk and it's easy walking. I remember the day I walked in alone. It's more fun to walk with friends because we talk as we walk.

My neighbors tell of things Dad did. They talk of dangerous spring high water log drives and of winter storms with snow so deep it stops cutting for weeks at a time. They tell of experiences with wild animals, and of horses that learn where to go and what to do, so they seldom need a teamster. I'm proud to be one of the men, and I feel great.

I remember that I felt dismal after the race, but as I walk and talk with my neighbors my brain works. I thought the race was the big thing in life, and after the race I thought the big thing was gone. Now I know the race is OK, but it's not the big thing. I'm one of the crew. I'm doing a good job. That's the big thing, and that's why I feel great.

Jason doesn't walk for long. He puts on his skis and loafs. There are a few hills, and we get him to wait until we are part way down before he starts. It's fun to watch the fastest thing in the woods go by.

We build a fire to boil the kettle. We try to stay out of the swirling smoke as we have tea, roast beef sandwiches, and doughnuts. The teamster gives the horses their hay, grain, and water, and gorbeys gather for a handout.

I'm surprised that we get to 20-Mile Depot so soon. The sun is well above the trees and moving west, but I didn't notice because this is a great day.

The 20-Mile crew left this morning, so we have the bunk room to ourselves. Madam Cote has a beef stew for us that kings would fight over. Mr. Chase takes supper for Mom and Father Belanger to the filer's cabin, and the religion lesson goes on I guess. Poor Mom, but I'll bet she's happy, happy, happy.

Come to find out, Madam Cote used to be a logging camp cook. For breakfast, her biscuits make great bacon and jam sandwiches, and her chocolate cake is right up there with her beef stew.

Between 20-Mile and 10-Mile there are pretty good hills, some with curves. Just like yesterday, we get Jason to wait at the top while we go along down to the bottom. It looks like he gets better and faster all the time. He doesn't end up in the woods once.

We take our time nooning and feeding the gorbeys, so the sun is pretty well down when we get to 10-Mile Depot. Father Belanger's sleigh is sitting in front of the dingle. In the cook room the camp-sitters, Mr. and Mrs. LeBlanc, are OK, but Mom, Father Belanger, and Mr. Chase look pretty ragged out. No doubt about that.

"Eddie," Mrs. LeBlanc says while I'm helping her put beans, biscuits, molasses, and pies on the tables for supper, "we are happy that Edna and Roy are going to be married, but they are very tired. Father Belanger keeps talking to Edna. See if you can take him to the bunk room so Edna can sleep here in the cook's corner."

I squeeze in between Mom and Father Belanger on a cook room bench so he has to stop talking to Mom.

"Father Belanger," I whisper, "it looks like you're doing a great job."

He nods his head, but he doesn't smile.

"Look," I whisper, "Mom can learn better if she gets some sleep. OK?"

He nods his head. He leaves the table early, and when I get to the bunk room, he is snoring in the first bunk.

Mr. and Mrs. LeBlanc must have stayed up all night. We have fresh bread and doughnuts with pancakes and bacon for breakfast. As we eat, Father Belanger talks to Mom, and Mom listens. After breakfast the traveling religion class is away toward Ashland.

Our tote sled is not far behind. With only ten miles to go I guess we're going to rest the horses once in a while, skip boiling the kettle, and keep walking. I'm thinking about Janice.

"Hey," Jimmie says at 5-Mile Brook, "here we are. Let's boil the kettle." But the sun is hardly above the trees, and it isn't time to noon-it.

I watch, and maybe my mouth hangs open. The McNally Pond crew whoops like it's party time. Someone gets the fire-blackened bucket, a saw, and an axe from the tote sled. Someone chops a hole in 5-Mile Brook ice and dips out a bucket of water. Two guys up on the crosscut saw, and a cedar log becomes blocks for seats. Someone splits a block into kindling, starts a fire, and before long the bucket of water is boiling tea. Someone comes up with bread, roast beef, tin cups, and a big bag of raisins. Everyone acts like this is a celebration. What, I wonder, is this all about.

Illustration 17-1: *Boiling the Kettle* by Judy Sherman

"Eddie, Jason," Jimmie says, "we've been boiling the kettle here at 5-Mile Brook for thirty years that I know of. Your Dad started nooning-it here about twenty years ago. It's our big-time place for going in and coming out of the woods."

We noon it sitting on wood blocks around the smoky fire. Everyone has a story to tell, and I try to listen to all of them. It's no use. There are at least a half dozen stories going together.

Illustration 17-2: *Gorbey—"The Loggers' Ghost"* by Judy Sherman

"Here they come to visit us," Jimmie says. A shades-of-gray gorbey glides down and lights without fear on the snow among us. We toss scraps of bread to it, and it eats like there will be nothing to eat tomorrow. Other jays come, and we feed them all.

"They are souls of old loggers come to visit us," Jimmie says. I remember that my dad told me that story and about feeding gorbeys.

Hey, I wonder, is that true? Is one of these birds my dad's soul? I know it's just a story, but I can't stop tears. I hope everyone thinks I have campfire smoke in my eyes.

We leave 5-Mile Brook after boiling the kettle, I walk behind the tote sled, and I feel great. I'm a good man like my dad was, and I wonder again why I thought the race was so important. What's really important is I boiled the kettle at 5-Mile Brook. I'm part of the tradition. I'm proud, and I'm going out to see my girlfriend.

Nobody wants to boil the kettle when noontime comes. We rest and feed the horses, but we go on. The sun is still well above the trees when we reach the clearing. We walk on the road between farm fields, past the West End Road, and toward the big white company barn. People are waiting for us there. Mothers and kids yell and scream to us. Little kids run up the road to meet us. Big kids are in school.

Hey, my neighbors are crying. Grown men, loggers, are crying. I remember I didn't want them to see my tears when we boiled the kettle at 5-Mile Brook. They don't care who sees them crying now.

The tote sled stops by the company office near the barn. A noisy, jostling crowd of kids, wives, and loggers swirl like ice chunks tumbling in a rolling, spring-pitch river. I'm glad I'm standing up on the tote sled above the uproar. I don't see Janice, and I remember that there is school today.
I pass packsacks to loggers or wives and give Jason his skis, poles and pack. I grab my pack and snowshoes and step down from the tote sled. I'm thinking I've got to get out of this bedlam.

Someone grabs my jacket and turns me around.

Leonard Hutchins

18. WINTER FIELD DAY

It's Janice. She grabs my shoulders, pulls herself up, and kisses all over my face. We're right in a crowd. People are bumping into us. People see us. They must be laughing at us.

I hug Janice and look around her kisses. Nobody is looking. Nobody cares.

"You grew so much," she says. "I'm so glad you're home. So glad. So glad. How did you do it, Eddie? How did you ever do it?" She lowers herself to stand in front of me, and she smiles up at me. She is dressed in larrigans over running pants, a red and black plaid jacket, a red knit hat and mittens, and she is the most beautiful girl in the world.

"I'm glad to be home, too," I say. I put my arm around her shoulder, and I don't care who sees us. "Now, what did I do?"

"How did you get Father Belanger to agree to marry our Mom and Dad now?"

"Oh, that. Jason and I said we would compete on his Winter Field Day team with you if he would do the wedding."

"Nothing could be better," she says. "Come see what Mom gave me for an early Christmas present." She pulls me out of the crowd to the front of the company barn. The small fish snowshoes are there stuck up in the snow. "They are a lot easier to use than short bear paw snowshoes. Dad said you would show me how you snowshoe."

I usually know more or less where Mom is coming from, but it would be great if I could read her mind. I'd have known when Andre and Emile made them that those fish snowshoes were for Janice.

We strap on our snowshoes and walk to the West End Road. Wow. The road is snow packed by a snow roller, and there are tracks on the rolled snow. Jason's ski tracks are over Father Belanger's horse and sleigh tracks

111

going in and coming out. And can I believe this? Under those tracks are small loghauler tracks.

"Hey," I say, "the company has loghaulers now."

"No," Janice says. "I forgot to write you that they are rolling our road now. They use a new snow car once in a while to bring supplies to the West End School. I rode to school twice in the snow car. It's really fast and neat."

"A snow car?" I say.

In about four seconds my brain overloads and clogs up with questions. How big? What kind of engine does it have? How do they steer it? How fast?

"A snow car?" is all I can ask.

Janice says, "They keep it in a garage over town. We'll go so you can see it someday soon."

"Yeah," I say, "a snow car. I've got to see that."

"Hey," Janice says, "Dad said you did really great in the Madawaska Company race, and Jason put on a show."

"I'll never forget that day," I say, and I hold her hand. We follow Jason's ski track and Father Belanger's sleigh and horse tracks. As we snowshoe through patches of woods and between open farm fields I tell Janice about the snowshoe race, the log hauler, and Mr. Lacroix.

When we reach my house the tracks continue down the road. We stop. The path to our front door is snowed over, and no smoke rises from the chimney.

"Let's go in," Janice says. She puts her arm around my waist.

We go to the woodshed, leave our snowshoes, and go in the kitchen door. Stove, table, chairs, cupboards, and sink are as they always were. The place is quiet. Jason's bunk is on top, all made up. Mine is on the bottom, all made up. Most of our clothes are in the closet. The place is cold.

"Our home is just an old house now," I say.

I remember Dad sitting in front of the stove. I remember Mom putting us to bed. I remember Dingey and Dongie when they were little and sleeping in cribs. Tears come to my eyes, but I can't let Janice see me crying.

"Hey, let's go," I say. "I've got to see Dingey and Dongey."

I walk out of our house ahead of Janice. By the time we have our snowshoes fastened on, out in the yard, my tears are dried up.

Down the road we snowshoe past Janice's house. No path is shoveled. No smoke rises from the chimney. It looks as deserted as our house. She sniffles. I look and see tears on her cheeks.

"Hey, what's wrong?" I ask. I guess she is as sad about her house as I am about mine.

"I'm so happy," she says. "My house has been so big and empty. Now I'll have a mother, two brothers, and two sisters to go with Dad. I am very happy."

Empty houses, I guess, are not all the same.

Farther down the road past the West End School smoke is rising from the chimney at Jimmie's and Cora's place. A path is shoveled to the door. Outside, Father Belanger's horse and sleigh tracks come and go. Jason's ski tracks end where his skis and poles are sticking up in the snow. Inside, the twins are six months bigger, and they sound like the crowd in front of the company barn. Mom and Cora are catching up on six months news and making wedding plans. That helps with the crowd effect. Jason sits in a kitchen chair and grins.

"Eddie," Mom says, "Would you go over and build the fires at Roy's place. We'll have supper there and decide where to stay tonight."

"I'll go with you," Janice says.

We shovel a path to the door and build fires in the kitchen cook stove and a heater stove in the front room. The house soon warms. Soon Mom, the twins, and Jason come with a chicken stew all cooked for supper.

Mr. Chase arrives on snowshoes from the company office where he paid Jimmie's crew. He gives Mom, Jason and me each a brown envelope.

"You boys didn't come into the office for your pay," he says, and he's grinning.

"Forgot about that," I say as I open my envelope. I can hardly believe what I see. I'm holding $184.00 in twenties, tens, and ones. I count it again, and I really have $184.00. A paper lists deductions for boots and clothes I used from the dingle, and I still have $184.00.

Jason has $180.00. He gets less for being cookee, but more for his scaling days, and he doesn't have deductions for clothes.

Mom has $273.00.

We just look at each other. A tear runs down Mom's cheek to the corner of her open mouth.

"Edna," Mr. Chase says, "I hope you're still going to marry me now that you're a rich professional cook." He's still grinning.

Either Mom's brain or her mouth isn't working.

"Yes, she is," Janice says.

Mom functions again. She gives Janice $50.00. "For helping with the girls. Two dollars a week as we agreed," she says.

Janice isn't about to take the $50.00, but it doesn't take long for her to lose her first argument with Mom.

For supper, Cora's chicken stew is as good as Mom's.

We decide to stay with Mr. Chase and Janice. There is a spare bedroom for Jason and me. Janice says she has a big bed, but I'm not sure it's big enough for Janice, Mom, and the girls.

Next morning, Jason and I have to try on wedding clothes Janice bought. She bought the stuff even when she thought the big occasion would be next summer. Jason's clothes are OK. My shirt, suit coat, and outside coat won't make it. We have to fix that right off.

To go to the store in Ashland Janice wears a dress and coat that just about clear her snowshoes. The main road across the bridge is snow roller and sled runner packed, so we leave our snowshoes at the company office and walk. Wow. Can I believe this? The streets in Ashland are plowed for the first time. There is only a skim of packed snow on the dirt. I wonder if they have the plow on a log hauler, a truck or the snow car.

Anyway, so we buy something bigger at the store, and that's it. Right? Not with Janice. I have to go into a room smaller than a privy, put the stuff on, and come out so she can inspect it. The shirt she doesn't like. I don't know why, but in I go with another shirt. Broadaxing logs is more fun.

Can I believe this? She picks me out a necktie, and not just any necktie. One that fits the suit coat, or is it that it matches the coat? Is there a difference? Anyway her hands are flying around tying the necktie when I have a guaranteed great idea. Guaranteed.

"Hey, Janice," I say. "Your hands are about as big as Mom's. How about picking out a ring that fits you?"

"Now, aren't you the thoughtful son," she says.

There are a lot, lot more rings in that store than I suspected. It takes her a half hour or so to pick the ring that Mom will like, and she likes it too. Hey, I'm more pleased with the trip than I thought I'd be. This is going to work.

Hey, I'm soon even more pleased with the trip to town. Janice takes me to the garage where they keep the snow car.

Wow. What a machine. It is small compared to a loghauler, but Janice is right. It is neat. First, it steers front skis with a steering wheel like a loghauler, but the driver sits up on a seat behind a window. There is another seat beside the driver's place, a double seat behind, and a box built over a flat body behind. The box has a back door with a window. Above the front skis there is a compartment for a little gasoline engine. Wow.

"Janice," I say, "this is what we need. I could come out of the woods every weekend to be with you."

Janice smiles. It's not a grin. It's a smile.

That afternoon Janice wears her running pants, and we go out to snowshoe on the road. It is a strange sight to see a girl wearing pants. I don't care. Pants must be better for snowshoeing than a dress.

I think of Emile as we stride along, and I tell her, "See in your mind the push rods on train wheels. Move your snowshoes up, straight forward, down, up, always straight forward, down. See the train wheels in your mind. Head up. Chest and shoulders high. Breathe deep. Look forward. Don't bob your head. Swing your arms and hands straight forward and back like the train piston rod."

"I love it," she says. "This is like snowshoeing on pillows. The long, turned-up fronts don't catch in the snow like short snowshoes do. Hey, all I see is push rods and piston rods. As long as that train goes, I can snowshoe forever." She smiles.

"Maybe you've had enough for today," I say after a half mile or so. "I don't know how many, but we've got races tomorrow."

"High school age snowshoe races are one hundred yards for boys, one hundred yards for girls, one mile for girls, and two miles for boys," she says.

She doesn't wait to catch her breath as she talks. She is in as good condition as I am, and she didn't have Emile to coach her. I think that those races are going to be interesting.

That night, like before the Madawaska Company race, my brain doesn't slow down to sleep. Jason is snoring, and I hear everyone in Janice's room giggling.

Sleep or not, next morning at nine o'clock about all of Ashland is at the station when the train arrives with people and kids from other towns. The place is all crowd and confusion to me, but Father Belanger has things lined up. Everyone walks to the edge of a big field near the train station.

Holding our skis and snowshoes, Jason and I stand away from the crowd. I see church people dressed different so I guess they must be from different kinds of churches. Until that time I think church people, except Father Belanger of course, are a quiet, serious, stern bunch who don't even smile. Not so. These people are having a great time together. A bunch of nuns are everyone's noisy, black and white cheering section.

Wow. I see the pointed front ends of a very long pair of skis and a pole sticking up above the middle of the crowd. As I watch, the skis and pole move toward me. Soon I see a broad shouldered kid who is a whole head taller than me carrying the skis and a pair of bear paw snowshoes. Three men with him make him look small.

When they reach us one of the big men says, "Boys, meet my friends from New Sweden."

Who, I wonder, is this man? I think I recognize him, but….. Yeah. It dawns on me. It's Mr. Jorgensen, the game warden. How, I wonder, does he know us?

"This is Sven Andersen," Mr. Jorgensen introduces us to the big smiling kid. "Sven will snowshoe and ski today."

"Hi," Sven says, and his handshake matches his smile.

For a minute I feel like I'm back at 30-Mile Dam, only the language I don't understand now must be Swedish. No matter. I meet Mr. Andersen and Mr. Bondeson, who is carrying a packsack. As they talk I understand words and phrases, "30-Mile," "Madawaska Company," "Jason," and "ski," in the conversation. Good laughter matches more strong handshakes. I like this Swedish bunch.

Father Belanger announces that the first race of the day is fifty yards for girls, grades one to three. Hey, there are my sisters lining up with a dozen or so others. I'm proud. Janice is behind the starting line, and I can tell that she has coached Martha and Mary well. Some kids are confused, but my sisters take their places, and they are ready to go.

A lady from the black and white cheering section steps in front and to one side of the kids. She raises her arm and says, "OK, now. Are we ready? Are we set?" The kids stop fidgeting and wait. "Go," she yells as she drops her arm.

Hey, I'll tell you what. Down the field laughing and screaming, comes the way to have fun. The kids look like a flock of scrambling, big-footed ducks that can't quite get up enough speed to fly. They keep paddling their snowshoe feet, flapping their arms, and trying. They flap past me, and everyone along the sidelines is yelling so loud I can hardly hear their snowshoes clacking together and crunching on the hard snow. The black and white cheering section picks up the ones that fall and they keep going. They all get blue ribbons at the finish line.

I understand the race, but while all this is going on the Swedish bunch, with Jason following along, is doing something strange. They walk along the race path, scoop up snow, rub it on Sven's skis, rub stuff from Mr. Bondeson's packsack onto the skis, and do it over and over. I don't understand that.

I can't think about that now because Father Belanger announces that the next race is the one hundred yards for high school girls. I stand near the finish line. About twenty girls wearing running pants and sweaters line up on the starting line one hundred yards away. Except Janice, they all have bear paw snowshoes. Also Janice is the smallest girl in the line. Beside her is a girl maybe a foot taller.

I see smoke from the race starter's shotgun, and the competitors stride forward before the bang of the gun reaches me.

19. RACES AND MORE RACES

Janice and the tall girl match strides and lead the pack. The tall girl's strides are a few inches longer than Janice's, and soon Janice is a little behind.

When Janice is close I see her bulging eyes, open nostrils, and grim mouth. She stares up, not straight ahead. Her arms are whirling rather than pumping straight. Wow. She looks fierce, and she has lost her snowshoeing form.

The tall girl's snowshoe catches in a small hole where one of the little girls fell. She falls, Janice wins the race, and the tall girl gets up in time to finish second. The rest of the girls finish in a flurry, and the black and white cheering section mixes happy bedlam into the flurry.

Well, it's mostly happy. I see from the sideline that Janice and the tall girl avoid each other, and in my mind I still see Janice's fierce face.

The boys' one-hundred-yard race is next so I don't have time to talk to Janice. On the starting line we competitors introduce ourselves and shake hands. Sven Andersen and I line up side by side.

We move out when the gun goes off. At about fifty yards I'm ahead, I look back, and Sven is right on my tail. He trips, falls forward, does a summersault, and comes up on his snowshoes beside me. Staggering but still running, he looks at me, shrugs his shoulders, and grins. That is one of the funniest things I've ever seen, and I have to laugh. In about two seconds I'm in last place, and I have to really work to finish near Sven in the middle of the pack.

Mr. Jorgensen and his friends laugh and pat us both on our backs. Win or lose a snowshoe race and it is still just fun for them.

I feel purebred stupid. I shake hands with the competitors, and trade a few good words with the black and white cheering section. Then Janice takes over. She pulls me aside, and the words aren't so good. Win or lose and it is not just fun for her. She says we're racing for a team, and I'm supposed to pay attention. She's not kidding.

I have to talk about her losing her temper and snowshoeing form, but she's in no mood right soon to listen to my words of snowshoe wisdom. I shut up and wait, but I feel bad things in my stomach.

Illustration 19-1: *Sven and Jason Ski Race* by Judy Sherman

After a couple races for young kids, Jason and Sven have a one-hundred-yard ski race to demonstrate the new sport. As far as I know it's the first ski race around here, and everyone wants to see the strange things that game warden Jorgensen uses. I want to see how Jason's short skis and two poles do against Sven's long skis and one long push pole.

As Jason buckles his ski bindings the men with Sven take something from Mr. Bondeson's packsack and rub it onto the bottoms of his skis. What is this I wonder. It seems to me that these Swedish guys do strange things with skis. Anyway, Sven buckles on his skis when the men are finished. Now I notice that something else is strange. One of Sven's skis is shorter than the other.

I don't have time to wonder any more. On the starting line, Jason bends forward and plants his two poles ready to push. Sven stands up straight and grasps his long pole above his head ready to push. Wham. The gun goes off.

In the Madawaska Company race Jason was off by himself, but not here. The two skiers pump along side by side as steady as a pair of steam engine pistons. But in different engines. Jason pushes with a pole every ski stride. Right. Left. Right. Left. Sven rides his long ski and pushes with his short ski like a kid riding a scooter. He makes about three short-ski pushes for every push with his long pole. Wow. Ski poles flail. Skis flap. Snow swirls. People scream. Jason and Sven do not goof off.

From the starting line we see the skiers cross the finish line. The black and white cheering section does their thing, but we can't tell who won. I jog down beside the race course with the three Swedish guys. Janice is standing with Jason, Sven, and Father Belanger. Everyone grins, but nobody knows who won. It was that close.

"You know," Jason says to Sven, "I was sure I would win by forty yards."

"You know," Sven says to Jason, "I was sure I would have to slow down so I wouldn't embarrass you. But look, we'd like to go up in the field and test our waxes while they run the distance races. OK?"

"Well, yeah. OK, but I don't know what you're talking about."

"We'll explain it."

I know I should go with them to learn something from the people who know most about skis. But I've got something more important on my mind right now.

I find Janice, and we walk away from the crowd so we can talk.

"Look," I say, "I'm nervous about you."

"What?"

"You're different when you race."

"How?"

"You looked like you were ugly, lost your temper, and lost your racing form."

"Look, I won."

"OK. OK. You won and I loused up, but those were only one-hundred-yard races. Your next race is a mile. Father Belanger told you not to let your competition win in your head. Right?"

"But I was fighting all the way."

"If you lose your temper, you lose your form, and your competition wins in your head. Right?"

"Hey. Yeah."

Her face looks better, and my stomach feels better.

"Can I have a kiss?"

"Well, not here."

Hey, there's Janice's smile again. She's OK.

After the younger kids have a couple of races, a dozen or so high school girls gather at the starting line for the one-mile race. Father Belanger talks to both Janice and the tall girl, so I guess they both go to the Ashland church and Ashland High School. Standing back, it's easy for me to see more than I could hear if I were close. The two girls think Father Belanger is OK, but the friendship stops there. Period.

I remember that Janice's letters showed how determined she is about racing. This isn't the laughing Janice I went to West End School with. I wonder if she is this way because I snowshoed for the Great Northern Paper Company. Is she doing this just to impress me? I wonder if our talk will help her in the race.

I stop wondering when the starting gun goes off. After a couple hundred yards Father Belanger's girls are shoulder to shoulder in front of the pack and increasing their lead. The tall girl has to lift her knees high to be sure her bear paw snowshoes don't catch in snow. Janice keeps her smooth racing form until the tall girl sprints to a short lead.

Janice is too far away for me to see her face, but her head tips back and wobbles, her arms drop, and her hands flop. She is wasting energy.

I snowshoe to a corner of the field and stand where Janice will see me. When the tall girl comes by I'm amazed that she can lift heavy bear paw snowshoes and keep her stride. Her face shows exhaustion.

A few yards behind, Janice's face is a mask of ugly rage. If she showed exhaustion I'd feel better. I wonder what I did to my girl. But I don't have time to wonder.

Her mask looks at me. I put my finger on my nose then point straight ahead. I move my arms like piston rods and yell, "Whooo. Whooo," like a train whistle.

Wow. Her mask smiles. Her head stops wobbling. Her hands stop flopping. She has her racing form back, and she isn't wasting energy.

The one-mile race is two laps around the field. Early in the second lap Janice passes the tall girl and she keeps her form to finish first going away.

The black and white cheering section helps the competitors walk off their exhaustion, and Janice is all smiles. The tall girl tries not to, but she can't help crying. I remember using heavy bear paw snowshoes at 30-Mile, and I know what a great effort that girl made.

I don't have time to watch Jason and his Swedish friends for very long. They are doing things that look pretty strange to me. There is a little hill in the field. Crouched low side by side and both holding Sven's long pole they start to ski down the hill together. Jason releases the pole and Sven drops it to one side so they are skiing separately. Neither strides with his skis to speed up, but Sven slowly slides ahead of Jason.

OK. My turn again, the boys' two mile is next. Standing on the starting line with maybe two dozen boys, I promise myself that I will not back off like I did in the Madawaska Company race. I will not goof off like I did in the one-hundred-yard race. It's time to do one right.

I try to shut everything but the race from my mind. I have to do this myself, all alone. The starting gun goes off, and I start the race with a faster stride than we kept in the Madawaska Company race. This is a shorter race, so that seems OK.

But I am not alone. Jimmie and his crew are spread out along the race trail. Jason and the Swedes stop doing their strange things on the hill.

They all yell, "Bon Homme. Bon Homme, Eddie. Go. Go."

There is French and Swedish stuff in there too. I guess it all means the same.

Hey, am I proud, or what. I love those guys. But I've got to keep them out of my head.

At the first corner I glance back and I've got a fifty-yard lead. I wonder if I'm going too fast. I remember that Father Belanger warned me about that the first day I ran at 30-Mile. I feel OK, but I slow my stride a little. At the second corner I've got a maybe eighty-yard lead.

What, I wonder is going on? I remember Andre and Emile making my snowshoes, the only pair of lightweight fish snowshoes in this race. I remember that I started training about four months ago with Emile, the best coach in the world. In my mind I hear my 30-Mile crew cheering for me. In my ears I hear Jimmie and my neighbors and the Swedish guys yelling for me.

I guess I'm finally doing a race right, but now I know that I can never snowshoe a race alone. Everyone who ever helped me is with me. Hey, I'm learning.

During the last laps of my race I watch Jason and Sven in the field with their skis. They trade and try each other's equipment. It looks like Jason is learning for me.

I'm thankful for the win. I know, finally, that I gave my best in a race. Also, Father Belanger and Janice are happy. The black and white cheering section is the happiest bunch there—every one of them. I don't like crowds, except that crowd.

The Winter Field Day is over. Competitors and visitors who came on the train walk to the Great Northern Paper Company Hotel for lunch. That place is something great. There is a big dining room and kitchen on the first floor, and a bunch of rooms on the second floor. It has water in pipes, and the privies have flushes. That's handy.

Mom and Mr. Chase are there helping, and I can tell that Mom made the great beef and barley soup. Father Belanger and the cheering section have a ball giving ribbons to competitors from first grade through high school.

Jason comes in late with a can of toboggan paint. He'd skied home for it.

"I traded some toboggan paint to Sven for some of each kind of their ski waxes," Jason tells me as we walk to the train station with our visitors.

"Ski wax?" I ask.

"Look, there's a lot to it. I'll tell you about it when we have time. But I'll tell you this right now. The Swedes know more about skis than we do."

Sven grins.

We go back to the hotel and help wash the dishes so we can all go home sooner.

On our way home Martha and Mary discover they can ski standing behind Jason on his skis. The three of them stay on the road skiing, and the rest of us go inside.

"Well, Mom," Janice says as we take off our coats, "tomorrow you'll really be my Mom, and I'm happy."

Mom smiles. "I'm happy too, Janice," she says. "Things are happening so fast my head is spinning."

"Mom," Janice says, "I want you and Dad to have time to yourselves. After the wedding tomorrow morning how about you newlyweds come here, and the rest of us will stay at your house tomorrow night."

Mom's eyebrows twitch. "No, dear," she says. "I think Roy and I should stay with all of our children."

"Now, Mom...." Janice says.

Mom rests her hands on Janice's shoulders. She looks straight and level into Janice's eyes. "Dear," Mom says, "I just haven't had time to talk to you two." Mom glances at me, then she says to Janice, "You are a splendid and beautiful young woman—not a little girl any more. Eddie," she says to me but she keeps her hands on Janice's shoulders, "you are a splendid and handsome young man if I do say so myself. I ..."

Wow. Hey, I wish I knew this was coming. I don't know what Janice will say. I don't have time to think. I want to get Janice out of this.

"Mom," I say, "Janice and I already talked about this. We're going to be OK."

"Now, Edward ..." Mom says.

"Mom," Janice says, "we think you're too young to be a grandmother any time soon."

Mom's mouth drops open. A little at first, then more.

Mr. Chase listens. He chuckles, then he giggles. Men don't giggle often.

"Edna," Mr. Chase says, "we've got some good kids."

Janice wins the point. Mom says, "OK." She is hugging her almost daughter when Martha and Mary come into the kitchen.

"Jason says you helped Andre and Emile make the skis," Martha says to me.

"Yes, I did," I tell her.

"Snowshoeing is hard," Mary says. "Will you make us a pair of skis tomorrow after we go to the wedding?"

"Hey, look you guys, I haven't got any long boards or tools here. I'd need a place to put the boards in steam to bend the fronts up, and I need to learn to do that right."

Jason comes in taking off his coat. "Jason and I are going to find a place to make skis next summer, and we'll make yours first. Right, Jason?"

"See? That's what I told you," Jason says to the girls.

I guess the girls weren't happy about that outdoors, and they're not happy about it in the house either.

"Jason," I say, "making skis might be a better idea than we thought. More people than game wardens and wood scalers would use skis. Everyone watching you and Sven ski today wanted to be out there with you, and we've got orders for two pair of kids' skis already."

"Make that three orders," Janice says. "And we'd like to have some ski poles like Jason's. And how about if I borrow your skis once in a while until you guys get mine made?" she asks Jason.

"OK," Jason agrees, "but I've got to take those skis back in the woods with me. I haven't got time to scale on snowshoes."

"Ed," Mr. Chase says, "didn't it take you and Andre and Emile only a few hours to make Jason's skis?"

"Yes, but we had steamed and bent toboggan repair boards to start with."

Mr. Chase says, "Toboggan repair boards are standard logging depot items, and we have dozens of them in the warehouse. The tote team took two dozen to Andre and Emile for skis for Mr. Lacroix's scalers. I'll buy six for three pair of skis for the girls. Company policy allows employees to use the shops on weekends."

Wow. Jason's eyes meet mine. Hey. What a deal.

"Look," Jason says to Mr. Chase, "Have you got more toboggan paint? I traded a can to Sven Andersen, the big guy from New Sweden, for some of their ski waxes. I'll pay for it."

"OK," Mr. Chase says, "but if this ski thing goes very far next summer, you boys will have to set up your own shop and business, right? But until then I hope you are both going to be with us at 30-Mile to finish the dam."

"They are," Mom says.

"Yeah. Yeah. Hey, let's go look at the shop," I say to Mr. Chase.

"I think ours is going to be an interesting marriage," Mr. Chase says to Mom as we put our coats back on.

Mom smiles. "Supper will be ready at six," she says.

What a shop. There are wood working tools eyeball deep. Saws, scrapers, shaves, hammers, drills, bits, screwdrivers, chisels, vises, you name it, and it's there. There are lumber racks attached to the walls. Just like Mr.

Chase said, there are dozens of steamed and bent toboggan repair boards on a rack.

"I'm glad the wedding is tomorrow morning so we can make skis in the afternoon," Jason says.

Speaking of weddings, I'll tell you what. There are good days and there are bad days.

And then, there are wedding days.

20. WEDDING DAY

Janice is good with a sewing machine. Her dress and Mom's are blue and white, and the twins' dresses are pink. They look as nice as two does and fawns in spring—different colors of course. So they're happy.

I get into fancy pants, shirt, jacket and coat. And a necktie. I promise myself if I get back to 30-Mile I won't come back out. And shoes. This is winter and I can't wear wool socks. There is room for one pair of paper-thin stockings. For whatever reason I don't have fancy gloves and hat. At least my head and hands feel OK in good knit stuff. Jason looks as miserable as I feel.

Can I believe this? A guy with a company sleigh comes to take us across the bridge to the wedding. I've gone to Ashland in a wagon a few times, but a sleigh? Wow.

The church is pretty big. Not as big as 30-Mile dam, but three or four regular houses could fit inside. It has colored windows.

The sleigh teamster lets Janice and Mr. Chase off at a side door, and we Clarks go in the front door. We're in the back of the church, and there is a walkway to down front with seats on both sides. There are more people in those seats than there were at the Winter Field Day yesterday. I wonder how everyone found out about the wedding so soon.

Jimmie and Cora and some other people are there. The men take our coats. The women comb our hair and fuss over Mom. Everyone in the seats is turned around looking at us. This is the first time I've been in a Catholic church, and I want to run. But I've got to do this for Mom.

Father Belanger, Mr. Chase, and Janice appear down front. There is music, and Martha and Mary skip and hop down to Janice like they do this every day. Cora puts my hand and Jason's in Mom's hands and she steps out of the way. We have to walk all the way, and I don't feel great.

We walk a few steps, and I look at Mom. She is lit up like the colored glass windows with sun shining through. Everyone on both sides of us is smiling, and Janice is down front bouncing on her toes. I feel better.

You know, that wedding is like our eighth grade graduation. I'm looking at Janice, and I have no idea what anyone says. That's OK. When we leave the church we're one family.

I'm not used to style, but it's great to have a sleigh to take us to the company hotel for a wedding lunch. Walking in snow wearing shoes wouldn't be good.

Something else I'm not used to is high school girls. Our family, all seven of us, stand in the hotel dining room. People walk by to say a few good words to us. When a girl comes along, Janice becomes protective. She moves so the girl is far enough from me so I get only a handshake.

On the other end of the family line Jason gathers a cheering section, and they are not wearing black and white. Pretty soon the tall girl who placed second to Janice in the snowshoe races becomes protective. It looks like my little brother has a girlfriend whether he knows it or not. Life is different on this side of the bridge.

Our wedding family sits at a special table for lunch. We just get seated and Mom gets up to go to the kitchen. "I'll help the girls serve lunch," she says.

Three ladies scoot Mom back to our table. "Edna," one lady says, "this is your day, and we are going to do the work." Mom's face is a little red, but I think she wanted to lose that argument.

Our stylish sleigh takes us home after lunch to the Chase house which used to be our next door neighbors' place. I'm happy to change into plain clothes again and be plain us—and all one family, too.

Janice is gathering bread and stuff to take to our house, the Clark house, for supper. I don't have to read Mom's mind to know she's nervous.

"This will be Christmas Eve, and I should be with my children," Mom says, mostly to Janice I think.

"Mom," Janice says, "this is your day. I'm going to feed your kids, including me. We'll be back for breakfast, and I'd like to have bacon, eggs, and toast."

Mom is pretty wide-eyed when we leave for the Clark house for Christmas Eve.

It's strange. When we get to our house the twins rummage around in their room while Janice lays her supper stuff on the cupboard. I build a fire in the stove, and Jason splits wood to fill the woodbox. Jason and I leave for the company shop, and Janice goes out to snowshoe with the twins. The strange part is there are no adults around.

There are always a couple of hostlers in the stable with the horses. The two here this afternoon are old friends. They know we are coming so they have the shop warmed up, coffee brewing, and they sit by the stove to watch us make skis.

We take our time cutting the boards and shaping the front points and foot platforms. Figuring the girls will grow pretty fast, we make their skis shorter than Jason's but maybe a little long for them this year. We drill screw holes and turn every screw in tight through the foot platforms. After we sandpaper the bottoms smooth and attach snowshoe harnesses, we apply a coat of toboggan paint.

"You know," Jason says as we work, "the Swedes make different waxes to put on their skis for different kinds of snow. It's what they put on Sven's skis just before our race."

"Different kinds of snow? All snow is frozen water, isn't it?"

"Yeah, but it freezes different."

"Jason, we're busy. Stop pulling my leg."

"Look, some snow is cold and fluffy. Right?"

"Well, yeah."

"But when it's almost rain, snow is wet and sticky. Right?"

"Yeah."

"When wet, sticky snow refreezes on a cold night it becomes granular. Right?"

"Granular?"

"You know. Like grains of sugar or salt."

"Oh, yeah. Yeah. I never thought about all this."

"Well, the Swedes have. And they mix different waxes for different snow conditions."

"So they told you what they mix to make the waxes. Right?

"Not ever. Never. I really tried to find out, but I'm sure they wouldn't tell even their grandmothers."

"Wow. Did you tell them what's in our toboggan paint?"

"Not on your life, but it doesn't make that much difference. Our paint takes time to dry, but they put their wax on right at race time to match the immediate snow conditions."

"Wow. We've got some catching up to do in this ski business."

"Yeah. But already I know that their waxes smell like a woodshed. Fir, spruce, pine, cedar—stuff that only a beaver would eat. When we use their stuff, we'll learn more. I'll tell you this right now, the sliding friction experiments we did on the hill yesterday showed that if I'd had their wax I'd have won that race."

"I'll tell you what I think. If you two had traded skis, Sven would have won."

Jason grins and says, "It's going to be fun to catch up in this ski business."

The paint takes a while to dry, but the coffee is good and it's good to talk to old friends. When we leave the shop with the skis it would be pitch dark if it weren't for the moon. Down the road in our house the lamp is on the kitchen table, and Janice is sitting facing the stove.

"Look," I say. "The girls have skis for Christmas tomorrow."

Janice turns so the lamp light shows her face. Her eyes are red, wrinkles in her forehead pull her eyebrows too close, her lips are pressed closed, and there are tears on her face. She sees the skis, and she smiles a little.

"Hey," I say, "You're crying. What's wrong?"

"You're so late," she says. "I thought you had an accident. I couldn't go to the shop and leave the girls alone in the house with fire in the stove. I didn't want to wake them up to go tell Mom and Dad you're not home. I didn't know what to do, and you're so late." Her forehead smoothes out a little, and she wipes away tears with her fingers.

"I'm sorry," I say. "I should have thought of that. I'm really sorry." I step toward her, but she turns away, fills three bowls with soup for supper, and sets them on the table.

"I should have thought of it, too," Jason says.

"Look," Janice says, "it's my fault, too. I should have asked when you were coming home. I tell Mom I'm grown up and responsible, and she believes me. Right now I feel like I belong in bed with the twins."

"Good soup," I say. It is, too. Chicken.

"Thanks," Janice says, and she glances at me.

The lamp is close to her, and I can see cry still in her eyes. I think of her bouncing on her toes at the wedding. I'm happy about that. Now she hurts, and I'm not happy.

"Hey," she says as she looks at the skis leaning against the kitchen wall, "you guys worked a long time to make skis for the girls. They are going to be pleased." She smiles, and she is sort of back to herself again.

"Jason," I say, "it's going to be pretty nippy around here if we let the fire go out. I'll stay awake here in the kitchen to stoke it next. We'll trade off after that. OK?"

"Sure," Jason says, and he goes into our bedroom.

"Want to do a fire watch with me?" I ask Janice.

She hesitates. "No," she says, "I better go in with the girls."

She goes into the girls' room, and I watch the fire alone. Jason and I trade fire watch and sleep time all night. On my last turn, sunrise brightens to about kerosene lamp glow.

I blow out the lamp and hear thumps and giggles from the girls' room. "Wait a minute. Wait a minute," Janice says. Pretty soon the door opens and out they come, all dressed in flannel shirts and running pants but with bare feet.

To this day I'm proud of myself. The twins' long hair looks like hay a horse slept on then pawed up loose for breakfast. Janice's hair is shorter and looks like dandelion blossoms gone to seed. Why am I proud? I think my mouth hangs open, but I don't laugh.

Janice pulls the stove oven door down and lays two sticks of stove wood on it. The twins place three chairs in front of the stove. They all sit, rest their heels up on the stove wood, and comb their hair while their feet get warm from the oven. I guess they do that every morning. Soon they all look a lot better.

Things are pretty quiet until Martha notices the skis. Screaming uproar wakes Jason. We adjust ski harnesses to fit the girls' boots while Janice pulls on their coats, hats, and mittens. They clatter out the door, scuff over a layer of chips in the woodshed, and shuffle around the yard—screaming. Mary sees Jason's ski poles, and they each borrow one. Away they go down the road to show their skis to Mom. We strap on skis and snowshoes and follow them, Jason shuffling along without poles.

I see things I'd never imagine. Mom and Mr. Chase are standing—in floor-length nightgowns— in the open kitchen door laughing and watching the girls ski. When they see us they close the door. I look at Janice, and grin. She is red-faced, bug-eyed, and open-mouthed, but somehow she still has room on her face for a grin. This is the first time, for absolute sure, I see Janice grin.

"Did you see them?" Janice asks.

"Nope."

"I didn't either," Jason says.

"Let's wait a few minutes before we go in for breakfast," Janice says.

Down the road a ways by the West End School there is a patch of bushes. We jackknife off and limb out four pretty straight sticks. The girls have ski poles, and Jason gets his poles back.

We go back home to breakfast. Mom and Mr. Chase are dressed, cooking bacon and eggs in fry pans, and browning toast on the stove top between the pans. It smells like breakfast and tastes better. There is a Christmas dinner turkey baking in the oven.

After breakfast Mom is giving everyone the stuff she knit for us, and I've got a problem. Janice keeps looking at me. She's telling me to give Mom her ring, and I'm afraid she's going to spoil my plan. I've got to say something.

"Look, Mom," I say, "Jason and I got you a husband for this Christmas. Do you want us to see about another one next year?"

Everyone has a laugh, and when things slow down again I say to Janice, "Let's go to the school. I haven't seen the place since I left last June."

"Why didn't you give Mom her ring?" Janice says as we buckle on our snowshoes.

Illustration 20-1: *Christmas Breakfast* by Judy Sherman

"I'll see about the ring pretty soon," I say as we jog to the school. Janice grumbles maybe to herself and maybe to me, too. I haven't heard her grumble enough to be sure.

I reach under the school step where I used to keep the key when I was janitor. It's still there, so I unlock the door and we go in. Janice stands an arm's length from me as we look around the room. We see eight years.

"Hey," I say as I point to my initials in my old desk, "do you remember when you sat there so Mom and Mr. Chase wouldn't see them?"

I move away from the desk and Janice walks over and slides her fingers over the letters.

"Yes, I do," she says, and she smiles.

"I owe you for that," I say. "Hop up there again. OK?"

"What?"

"Come on. Just for old time's sake."

"OK"

She hops up, right where she sat last June. I take the ring box from my pocket and offer the ring to her.

"Will you accept a friendship ring from me?"

She stares at the ring. She stares at my face. She stares at the ring again.

"You bought that ring for Mom."

"No. I just said that Mom's hands are about as big as yours."

She smiles. She holds her hands over her mouth. She drops her hands onto her knees.

"I'm afraid," she says.

"What? Are you afraid of me?"

"No. I'm afraid of me."

"Janice, what in the world are you talking about?"

"Look, Eddie, I planned for a month to make love to you when you came out of the woods. That was dumb. If I get pregnant, I'll spoil everything. I'm afraid I'm not mature enough to accept a friendship ring."

"This is a friendship ring, not a wedding ring. Besides, you're a lot more mature than I am."

"You are mature enough to represent the company in a snowshoe race against experienced loggers. Everyone knows 'Bon Homme' Eddie Clark. You heard the men yelling to you during your two-mile Winter Field Day race. You're a good man, and I'm only a freshman school girl."

"Janice, I got discouraged and slacked off for a while in the Madawaska Company race. I might have placed better. I'm not proud of that, so I hope you won't tell everyone."

Janice looks at me with her mouth open a little. I think I should close the ring box and put it back in my pocket. Then I think, hey, that would be slacking off again.

"Janice," I say, "what are you getting for ranks in school?"

"I'm doing OK. A's in four subjects for the first half year. Why?"

"As you know, I don't do so great in school. Maybe some people say I have maturity problems. I'll put up with yours, if you put up with mine."

Janice smiles. "I've got to trust myself," she says. She points the finger beside her right hand little finger at me, and I slide the ring on. We are friends for sure. She slides down off the desk and gives me a kiss.

Leonard Hutchins

21. UNDERSTANDING OBSOLENCE

J anice and I sweep out the schoolhouse door the snow that we tracked in, then hang the key under the steps.

We snowshoe down the road hand in hand, and I'm happy. I have my girlfriend back like she was during our years at West End School only now with a friendship ring. The friendship ring was a good idea, and I'm proud of myself.

Here come Jason and the girls skiing up the road. Jason is carrying a broken ski and pushing himself along with one foot about like Sven skis.

"How did you do that?" I ask.

"Experimenting. I tried Mary's short skis and my long ones on the hill. The long skis hold me up better on soft snow, but the short ones are a lot quicker to turn and easier to use on packed snow. I didn't turn quick enough with these skis, and I hit a stump. How about you help me make another ski?"

"Yeah, OK."

Janice and I turn to go home with Jason. We're too slow for the girls, and they are away on their own.

"You know, Jason," I say, "maybe you ought to have a pair of long skis for scaling on soft snow, and a short pair for packed snow."

"Yeah. Maybe."

I carry the broken ski so Jason can use his ski poles.

"Look at our friendship ring," Janice says. She pulls off her mitten and shows Jason.

"Hey, OK. Looks great," he says and he kisses Janice's cheek.

"Let's hurry so I can show Mom and Dad."

She slides her hand into my mitten and hurries me along.

In the kitchen Mr. Chase closes the oven door after he and Mom check the turkey. Janice smiles and holds her hand out for them to see her ring.

"Oh, my soul," Mom says. She holds a hand over her mouth.

Jason comes in carrying the broken ski. The thump of the closing door is the only sound for a moment.

"Oh, my soul," Mom says again when she sees the ski pieces.

"Mom," Janice says as her smile sags, "It's not a wedding ring. We talked about it. Just a friendship ring is OK, isn't it?"

Mom holds Janice's ring hand, and she says to Jason, "Are you hurt?"

"Nope," he says to Mom. "Sorry I broke my ski," he says to Mr. Chase.

"Janice," Mom says as she holds her wedding ring beside Janice's friendship ring, "our rings are OK for sure. I'm just having a hard time growing up fast enough. Until yesterday, you know, all of my daughters were seven years old."

Hey, this is a new thought. Can adults really have a hard time growing up?

Anyway, I guess this growing up business will happen when it's needed, but right now I've got another problem. I wonder if Emile, Andre, and I should have made Jason's skis stronger so they wouldn't break. Jason, after all, didn't hit the stump hard enough to hurt himself, but his ski still broke.

I place the ski pieces together in front of the stove and try to figure out why the ski broke in front of the harness platform. People get ready for dinner around me. Someone moves the table and chairs. Someone checks stuff on the stove. Someone says something to me, but I'm busy.

Hey, someone takes the ski pieces. My brain leaves the break in the skis and returns to the kitchen.

Jason moves chairs. Janice and Mr. Chase set the table, and Mr. Chase grins at me. Mom carries the ski parts into the parlor, lays them on the carpet, and I go into the parlor. My brain goes back into the broken ski.

In my mind I see Jason's foot pushing down on the harness platform when the curved ski front slides up over the stump. The long ski front puts so much force on the harness platform that the thin toboggan board breaks. I know we should have made the skis different.

I go back to the kitchen, and the girls come in from skiing. On the table is turkey, a dish of gravy, potatoes, carrots, cranberry sauce, and pumpkin pie with whipped cream. And there is a bowl of oranges and apples in the middle of the table. Wow. Mr. Chase says grace, and we eat like the crew at 30-Mile.

"You boys can make another ski for Jason, can't you?" Mr. Chase asks.

"Sure," I say, "but we need to make the foot platforms on the skis longer to reinforce the toboggan board. I'm disgusted with myself for not seeing that in the first place. Is it OK if we use the shop this afternoon?"

"OK," Mr. Chase says. "This is a holiday, and the men are off." Then he adds, "Say, calling me 'Mr. Chase' sounds pretty formal. I don't pretend to take your father's place, but there must be something better for you to call me than 'Mr. Chase.'"

"Janice calls you 'Daddy,' so I will, too," Mary says.

"Me, too," Martha says.

I'm glad my sisters don't have trouble using their mouths. While they're talking, a bunch of Christmases flash through my mind. Christmases were fun while Dad was alive. They were tough the last couple of years. This one is like old times—only different. I remember stopping to noon-it at 5-Mile Brook with Jimmie and the crew. I remember that I tried to hide my tears when Jimmie said gorbeys are dead logger's souls come back to visit. I think of a gorbey and Dad right now, and I feel tears.

"Well, look," Jason says … Good old Jason, I think. He's going to give me a few seconds to get hold of myself … "Everyone in the crew calls you 'Roy.' We're in the crew, so how about if we call you 'Roy?'"

"Yeah," I agree. I fake a cough, take a drink of water, and wipe my eyes.

"Good," Mr. Chase says. No, he's Roy now.

I think I can remember that. I think I've got hold of myself. I think I'll grow up when I need to, but I wonder how many times I have to grow up before it sticks.

Mom says she has enough cookees to help with the dishes after dinner, so Jason and I go to the shop. He scuffs along on one ski rather than use bear paw snowshoes.

We're faster at making skis. It takes only half the afternoon to cut a new ski and attach longer foot platforms to both skis. The new skis are a lot stronger. We paint them, hang them over the stove to dry, and in another hour or so Jason is trying them out on the way home.

Down the road come my three sisters, and Janice is working her snowshoes hard to keep up with the twins on skis.

"Jason," Janice says, "be a kind brother and let me try your skis."

We adjust harnesses so Janice tries Jason's skis and Jason tries Janice's fish snowshoes, each for the first time.

"Hey," Jason says as he jogs ahead of us, "these things sure beat bear paws." Head up, arms swinging straight, snowshoes pumping like drive rods, he moves out.

Janice strides a few times with her skis as she does with snowshoes. Then she pushes with her poles and slides.

"Wow," she says. "This is a whole new world."

Soon she has her poling and striding coordinated, and she catches up to Jason. Jason picks up the pace, and Janice's competitor personality takes over. They are off, Jason standing tall and stretching his stride, Janice bending and poling then standing, reaching ahead and poling again. They are nearly out of sight before Janice gets ahead, and they are still laughing in the yard when the girls and I get home.

"I just can't believe how great skis are," Janice says to me. "You can have your skis back when you make me a pair," she says to Jason. "But I'll tell you what," she says to both of us, "those big wooden blocks on the poles are pretty heavy. Can't you make something lighter?"

"We've been thinking about that." I tell her, "The thing is, we can't figure out how to attach something flat and light to the pole. You see if you put more than a small nail hole in the pole, it makes it weak right where it has to be strong."

"Too bad," Janice says.

Mr. Chase walks the path from the house to the road. Only he's Roy now. Anyway, he looks at Jason's skis.

"The longer foot platform makes a stronger ski, doesn't it?" he says.

"I should have seen that in the first place," I tell him.

"Ed," Roy says, "if we could see a step or two ahead, we could eliminate obsolescence. Skis are a new idea to us, and I think you are doing very well."

"Thanks," I tell Roy as he goes into the house.

"Janice," I say when Roy shuts the door, "what does 'obsolescence' mean?"

"It means not using something because you have something better."

"Yeah," I say. I think of the loghauler and the snow car.

We have leftover turkey for supper because, for sure, that isn't obsolete. I'm getting used to my new family, but Janice doesn't say much during supper. We do the dishes, and she still doesn't say much. I wonder what's on her mind.

After supper she goes to her room and comes back with a bug net. For years I helped her make bug net hoops, and she got A's on every bug collection and report she passed in every year. I never could figure out how she ties knots in string to make the net.

"If we make it smaller it will work," she says.

Jason won't admit that he doesn't know, so I have to ask her, "What in the world are you talking about?"

"We can put a little, round, bug-net snowshoe on a ski pole," she says. "See?" She lays the bug net hoop on the table. "We'll bend the hoop smaller for the outside ring, and I'll tie it to a ski pole with a rope net and wire loop through the pole."

From years of experience I know that Janice can figure things out. Right now I can see the smaller hoop and rope net, but I need to see the wire loop part.

"Let's make a couple," I say.

Soon we have the girls' ski pole sticks, a few feet of woodshed vines to bend into hoops, some wire and clothesline rope, and a few tools on the table. Roy has seen us make bug nets in this kitchen for years so this is no big thing to him. The small round ski pole snowshoe takes shape pretty fast, and Janice makes a second one for a pair.

"What in the world are you two doing?" Mom asks after she watches us for a while.

"She's figured out a way to put a little, light snowshoe on a ski pole," I say.

"What?"

Janice explains the deal to Mom, and Jason nods his head agreeing with Janice.

"I've got another smart daughter," Mom says.

Janice smiles at Mom.

"Janice," Roy says, "I think your ski pole will work as well as the ventilation system Ed put in our cook room last summer."

"And he thought of putting rockers on my flour barrel so I can get flour by myself," Mom says.

Janice smiles again—at me. Kissing my girlfriend right now would taste great, but there's too much family around.

"Mary," I say, "let me borrow your skis, OK? We want to see how the stuff we're making works."

"Don't hit any stumps like Jason did," Mary says.

"I'm going to stay right in the road," I promise her. "Want to ski for a while?" I ask Janice, but she already has on her hat and jacket.

Out in the yard, after the kiss we need, I light the woodshed lantern and adjust Mary's bindings to fit my boots. Winter days are shortest at Christmas time so the sun set is faded to not even a glow. The lantern is pretty dim, but overhead there are a million stars.

"These new poles are a lot lighter," Janice says.

I'm skiing for the first time, but it isn't hard to get my skis and poles working together. "Just like you said," I say to Janice as we ski past the West End School, "skiing is a different world."

"I can hardly believe all of my different worlds," Janice says. "Since you came home this week, I graduated from bear paw to fish snowshoes. I'm going to have skis. Mom and Dad are married—they really are. We are one family living together. And I have your friendship ring. It's like I woke up in a whole different wonderful world."

Skis are far faster than snowshoes, but they are just as awkward when you kiss.

We ski between farm fields and past Jimmie's and Cora's place, but we don't follow the road into thick woods. The trees shade the starlight into blackness.

Janice says as we step-turn our skis to return home, "I'll come here tomorrow to cut little ash trees for more ski poles."

"Jason and I ought to get your skis made tomorrow while you make little snowshoes on the poles," I say. "We'll have all next week to ski before we go back to 30-Mile."

"I don't want to think about that," Janice says.

We stop by the woodshed to take skis off, and Janice says, "Next week is part of Christmas vacation so only the janitor will be at the high school. He'll let us in, and I'll show you our school. OK?"

"Well, maybe we won't have time," I say. I remember the school books at 30-Mile I haven't read.

In the house Mom and Roy are sitting in the parlor, and the girls and Jason are sharing a lamp at the kitchen table. Jason has a book going—of course.

"I hope you don't mind if I borrowed your science book," Jason says to Janice.

"No problem," Janice says. I can tell she's thinking. "Jason," she says, "Next week is part of Christmas vacation so only the janitor will be at the high school. He'll let us in so I'll show you our school. OK?"

"Hey. Yeah. Imagine that. I'm going to see my high school," Jason says. "That will be great, right Ed?"

"Oh, won't that be nice," Mom says from the parlor. "My boys will be in high school."

I can't think of a way out of it. What can I say? Janice Chase thinks fast. That's what.

22. SKIS FOR ROY AND MOM TOO

"Boys," Roy says while we're eating breakfast, "I've got a mountain of year-end reports to do. I'll go to my office with you when you go to the shop."

"Hey," I say to Jason, "How about Roy trying out your skis?"

"Yeah," Jason says.

Roy chews for a while. "You know," he says, "I'd like to do that."

"That sounds like fun," Mom says. "I want to watch you go."

After breakfast the whole family is out front to watch Roy go. While Roy adjusts the ski harnesses to fit his boots, Jason, Janice, and I strap on snowshoes, and the girls buckle on their skis. Mom wraps her apron up over her arms to stay a little warm. The deal isn't as big as company sleighs taking us to the wedding, but it's a change from snowshoes. Roy and Mom wave, and away we go.

Poor Roy. Last night when I skied for the first time I only had one coach. This morning the twins are skiing beside Roy, and Janice and Jason are trotting along on snowshoes beside them. They're all coaching. I'm scuffing along behind, and I'm laughing. This is as funny as seeing Sven Andersen do a forward roll on bear paw snowshoes and come up running.

After a hundred yards or so I guess the three girls are satisfied that Roy will make it. They turn around to go to the woods after ash saplings for ski poles.

When I snowshoe up beside Roy and Jason, Roy says, "You know, boys, I'd like to have a pair of these things. It would be easier and faster to go to the office or over town for groceries or back and forth between the office and the dam at 30-Mile."

"Tell you what," I say. "If you can get us some shop time, we'll make you a pair next week. You'd have to fight with Janice for the pair we're going to make today."

"I'd rather work on getting the shop time. Look, if I can catch Andre in the cook room where he can hear the telephone, I'll come get you so you can talk to him about a longer foot platform for the skis they are making."

"OK."

Roy goes to his office and Jason and I go to the shop. Our hostler friends have the stove going and yesterday's coffee heating.

We do OK with Janice's skis. We know how to cut the skis and the foot platforms, and we know what tools work best. We know how to work together so we make skis faster, and I think every pair we make is better. But the coffee isn't improved.

About noon time we have Janice's finished skis hanging over the stove to dry the toboggan paint. Roy opens the shop door.

Illustration 22-1: *Telephone* by Judy Sherman

"Andre is on the telephone."

I go with Roy. The telephone is a box about as big as your head on the office wall. There is a hole in the box you talk at and a something on a wire you hold to your ear. I remember the thirty miles of wire it took me a long day to walk beside. I wonder how long it takes words to go that far. I feel pretty dumb standing in the office talking to a box and holding something on my ear.

"Andre, this is Ed."

"I guess that you," Andre answers. Wow, I think, the words got there and back already. "Roy say you and Jason do good for Father Belanger in race. We know you both do good every time. Roy say you and Jason twist Father Belanger arm so he marry him to Edna. You and Jason are smart boy. Not many people twist priest arm. Tell Jason will be snowshoe race and ski race for sure next year when Madawaska Company scaler have ski we make. Emile think foot board on ski too short. Ski maybe break. We make foot board longer, OK? We think ski even stronger if thick in middle for foot place and thin on front and back, OK? We try that when you come to 30-Mile, OK?"

He stops talking. I'm supposed to say something. I'm supposed to talk about a longer foot board. He did that. Come on brain, work.

"Eddie?"

"Yeah. Yeah. What you say is OK. Jason did break a ski, and we made longer foot boards. Jason and I think scalers might want two pair of skis. Long ones would hold them up on soft snow, and short ones would be easier to use on packed snow. OK?"

No answer. What is happening? I wonder if the words get there.

"Andre?"

"Wee, wee. I am think. Long and short ski maybe. We talk to scaler. Tell Edna she cook better than Emile. She come back soon."

"OK, Andre. I'll tell Mom."

I give the ear thing to Roy and go back to the shop.

"Well, what did he say?" Jason wants to know.

"Well, let's see …"

"Come on. You just talked to him."

"Well, they already decided to make longer foot boards."

"That makes sense."

"He said we should see what the scalers say about pairs of short and long skis before we make them."

"Yeah."

"He said there will for sure be both a ski and snowshoe race next winter. He wants us to compete again."

"Well, maybe they'll let us out of school long enough to do a race."

"He said Mom is a better cook than Emile."

Jason grins.

"He says maybe we should make skis thick in the middle for a foot platform and tapered to both ends. He and Emile sure know how to make stuff, and that makes sense to me, too. It's a whole different way to make skis, but I guess if we're going to make skis next summer to sell, we've got to consider every idea."

Jason stares at the stove. If I could look in his ear I think I'd see a tapered ski on his brain.

"Hey," I say, "words go to 30-Mile on the telephone wire in no time at all as far as I can tell."

"Yeah. Electrical impulses can travel around the earth in almost no time at all."

"How do you know that?"

"It's in the science book."

"I'm hungry," Roy says when he pushes the shop door open. He looks at Janice's skis. "You're doing better on every pair." He gathers a bunch of leather and some tools from around the shop and puts them into a pack sack. "If I understood Janice's snowshoe on a ski pole idea, I've got what you need to do it. Maybe leather would be stronger than rope. We'll borrow the leather tools and maybe you can make ski poles in the kitchen. I made stuff there, and you and Janice made bug nets there. You can make ski poles there if Edna doesn't mind. Let's go get dinner."

As soon as Roy gets the skis buckled to his boots, he's gone. He's not about to wait for slow pokes on snowshoes. Jason and I each carry one of Janice's skis, and by the time we get home Roy has skied to the West End School and back.

"Wow," he says as he unbuckles his skis.

When we go through the woodshed to the kitchen, Jason and I lean Janice's skis against the wood pile beside a bundle of freshly cut ash saplings. I think that Janice and the girls did OK this morning.

In the kitchen the table is moved to the middle of the room. Along one wall is the big old work bench Janice and I made toys and bug nets on for years. That bench is usually in the woodshed. The tools we used are on the work bench shelves—a draw knife, a half dozen or so wood rasps, different-sized wood planes, C-clamps, saws, a bit brace and set of bits, spoke shaves, and a claw hammer. Janice is draw knifing bumps from a sapling which is C-clamped to the bench. Martha and Mary are shaving bark from saplings with paring knives. Mom is sitting at the table, ear-wide smiling and holding a cup of coffee. There are a couple inches of shavings on the floor.

"I guess Edna doesn't mind if you make ski poles in the kitchen," Roy says.

"Well, it's too cold to make ski poles in the shed," Mom says.

Janice brooms the shavings into a corner while Mom dips beef soup into bowls. Mom makes really good soup. And apple pie, too.

"Say," Roy says after dinner, "How do you think I'd do in a ski race against Janice?"

"Oh," Janice says. "My skis. Did you get my skis done?" She looks in the woodshed, squeals, carries her skis outside, and adjusts her ski harnesses to her boots.

"Some poles," Janice says. "I need some poles. Would you give me two of the sticks we cut this morning?"

"Here," Mom says. She gives Janice her coat, hat, and mittens.

Roy and the twins are ready to go. I give Janice her poles, and there go our first four pair of skis down the road toward the West End School.

Watching from the house we can see that Roy does OK striding with his skis and pushing with his push-cone poles. The twins do OK because they slip along and push with new little snowshoes on their poles. Janice is in big trouble. She has used only poles with push cones. She has no push cones so her ski poles sink into the snow.

Hey, look, I know I shouldn't snicker at my girlfriend, but when Janice is mud ugly at poles and cloud happy with brand new skis she's funny. Besides, Roy slows down for her, and she knows it. I don't let her see me snickering.

Roy borrows Jason's skis again, and the twins ski with him toward the company office.

"I'd like to ski all afternoon, but I can't put up with ski poles that don't work," Janice says as she leans her skis against the wood pile. "Would you bring in a tub of water," she asks me as she selects ash branches from the bundle.

From about the fourth grade on, Janice and I have heated water and soaked vines to bend into bug net hoops. I get the wash tub from the woodshed, pump it about half full of water, and Jason and I set it on the stove to heat. While the water is heating, Mom and I whittle bark from saplings, Janice smoothes them with draw knife and rasp, and Jason reads the science book.

It's easy to bend strips of hot wet vines into hoops about as big as your hand. I wear leather mittens to bend the hot wood into a loop, and Janice ties it with linen thread usually used to sew horse harness.

It's fun to watch an idea become a thing. Instead of using rope, Janice takes Roy's idea and cuts pieces of leather to weave into the wood hoop. She fastens the leather web to the pole with a rivet. The little snowshoe is a lot lighter than a solid wood push cone.

As soon as we have a little round snowshoe on another pole Janice tries out the idea we made into things. From the woodshed door, Mom and I watch her ski to the West End School and back. This time she is cloud happy with both skis and poles.

"Hey," I say. "Teach Mom to ski."

"Yes. Get your coat, Mom."

"Oh, my soul. No. I've never traveled in winter except with horses," Mom says as she scoots into the house.

Janice is not far behind, and she lifts Mom's coat from hooks behind the door.

"Janice, I've never done such a thing," Mom says. She looks downright nervous.

"Mom," Janice says, "Skis aren't just toys. Dad went to work on skis, and you could go over the bridge to town on skis. Now, you said nobody could ever teach you to read, but you can read. Learning to ski is easier than learning to read. Guaranteed." She offers the coat to Mom.

Mom's mouth quivers, but she smiles a little. She puts on her coat, and out they go.

"I'll bet Mom will learn to ski in about five minutes," Jason says.

"Three minutes," I say.

If you don't count the time it takes Janice to adjust Mom's ski bindings, I win. Mom's dress and coat are just clearing her skis as she and Janice, on snowshoes, make their way toward the West End School. I go in to fix more ski poles, and Jason is three or four chapters into the science book.

I'm working on my second pole when they come back, and Mom yells from the road. I open the door to see what she wants.

"Keep water enough in the stew so it won't burn. We're going to the office," she says. "Eddie," she adds, "I just can't believe what I'm doing."

Mom doesn't look quite like she did when Father Belanger told her about her Christmas wedding, but I think her smile is melting snow.

I keep water on the stew and have four little round snowshoes on ski poles when everyone comes home at almost dark.

"Eddie," Mom says, "Isn't it wonderful? We're going to church tomorrow. Right in the middle of winter, and all because I can ski."

I think, whoa. Hey, I went to church once already this winter. Going to church and high school are things to do a lot later. So how do I get out of this? While picking at my bowl of stew I pick the deal that seems sure fire.

"Look, Mom," I say, "You and Roy can't keep borrowing someone's skis. Roy wants us to make him a pair tomorrow, but you might get them if you talk to him right."

Jason and I make skis Sunday. Mom's skis, I'll bet.

23. EXPLORING THE HIGH SCHOOL

"Janice," I say after breakfast Monday morning, "you're going with Mom on her new skis today. Do you think I can keep up with you on snowshoes?"

It doesn't work. Janice, Jason and Mom tell me together that I am going to the high school today.

Hey, at least I tried. Roy grins at me.

"Roy," Mom says. "You take my skis to work this morning. I just have to clean this kitchen. I'll ski with the girls this afternoon. OK?"

That's OK so after breakfast away we go, and I'm the only one on snowshoes. Roy does pretty well skiing to the company office, and I have to work to keep up to him. Janice and Jason are gone down the road and across the bridge to Ashland. It's maybe a mile and a half to the school, and by the time I make it Jason and Janice are inside.

The school isn't as big as the dam we're building at 30-Mile, but it's bigger than the church by quite a bit. It has two stories, a lot of windows, and a path shoveled through the snow to the front door. I stick my snowshoes up in the snow beside the two pairs of skis. The front steps are pretty slippery. Inside, the walls and ceiling are smooth painted plaster. The floor is hardwood boards and as slippery as the front steps.

"Mr. Edwards," Janice says to a big, pretty old man who is sweeping a floor that is already clean, "would it be OK if I show the school to my brothers, Ed and Jason? And do I have to change into a dress? There isn't anyone else here."

Mr. Edwards says, "I guess your running pants will be OK today, Janice. Your brothers? I didn't know Roy Chase had any boys." He looks at Jason, then at me. "Oh, yeah. Roy married Edna."

Mr. Edwards shakes Jason's hand. "Hey Jason, the boys tell me you really showed them how to go in the snowshoe race at McNally Pond. We don't think anyone is going to let you ski in another snowshoe race. And you did good in the Field Day 100-yard ski race. That big Swede kid is strong. How come you traded skis with him out in the field during the 2-mile snowshoe race?"

"Well, he had longer skis than mine, and I wanted to see how they worked. Sven wanted to see how my short skis and poles work."

Mr. Edwards nods his head.

"Bon Homme Eddie Clark," Mr. Edwards says as he shakes my hand and pounds me on my back. "I'm proud to shake hands with the first man to snowshoe for the Great Northern Paper Company in the Madawaska Company race."

I'm about to tell him "Thanks" when tears roll down his cheeks. I look closer and, sure enough, there are tears.

"Mr. Edwards," I ask, "are you OK?"

"Well, I got rheumatism now. I'm too old to work in the woods, but I'd sure like to go back in with Jimmie Roberts' crew next week. Look, I'll get over it. It's just really good to shake hands with good woodsmen."

He pulls a red and black bandanna handkerchief from his pocket and wipes his eyes.

"Now, dear," he says to Janice, "what was it you wanted?"

"Is it OK if I show the school to my brothers?"

"Sure." Then he says to Jason and me, "Roy is a good man. You take care of his little girl."

Janice scoots up a set of steps to the second floor. We slip and slide on the floor, and when we catch up to her she is sitting in a front seat in one of the rooms. Her forehead is on the desk and her hands are fists in her lap.

"Are you sick?" I ask.

"No."

"What's wrong?"

Janice raises her head and rests her chin in her hands. "Look, I feel bad for Mr. Edwards," she says. "He can't work in the woods so he thinks he isn't a good man any more. But do you see what I mean? You guys are good men and famous already. I win two Winter Field Day races, and I'm still 'Roy's little girl.' Nobody cares what girls do."

I lay Janice's hand on the desk and slide my finger over her ring. "I care. Aren't I somebody?" I ask her.

She drops her forehead back onto the desk. This time she's smiling.

"You guys are both somebody, for sure," she says as she stands. "This Christmas time out of the woods is the craziest time of my life. First I'm floating over the trees then I'm back on the ground and I run into a tree. Anyway, this is our language classroom. We all take English, and some take French."

The language room has rows of desks and windows and pictures of Presidents Washington and Lincoln above a blackboard like at the West End School. There is a picture of a pretty bald guy dressed in what looks like old-fashioned clothes. A note on the picture says he is William Shakespeare, and I wonder what he did. There is a picture of a really tall peaked tower. The note says it's the Eiffel tower, but it doesn't say where it is. There are book shelves between and under every window. Hey, I see "Treasure Island". I look for "Tarzan". It's not here. Too bad. There are a bunch of French books. I wish I could come to high school just for French and not bother with the rest of the stuff.

"By the way," Janice says, "You guys haven't sent me any school work to turn in. You're keeping up, aren't you?"

"I finished the algebra book, and I'll have science done this week," Jason says.

"You finished the whole algebra book?"

"Yeah."

"Our class isn't half way through algebra, and I have to work at it. And you're going to finish science this week? Wow. So how are you doing, Eddie?"

"Hey, I'm doing great. I read 'Tarzan' to the crew, and I sure have heard enough of 'Cinderella' and 'Alice's Adventures in Wonderland'. The crew thinks 'Treasure Island' is teaching kids to steal, but I'll tell the teacher a book report anyway. Yeah, I'm doing great."

Janice stands still as a fence post. She just looks at me with her mouth open a little. I know what's coming.

"How are you doing in algebra, science, and history?"

"Well, I'm working you know. And I've been training for the snowshoe race. I'll have more time from now on. Hey, I'll get Jason to help out." I hope a little humor will help, so I say, "Hey, how about you coming to 30-Mile to help me out?"

"Eddie," Janice says … Her voice is nervous as her face … "you have to do it or you'll be a freshman again next year when we're sophomores."

This is typical Janice. When she feels the need she gets to the bottom line fast. I shut up. I don't want to get into a spat with her about I don't want to go to high school anyway.

We go to the next room. There are windows, books, rows of desks, and around the room above the blackboards is a row of two or three dozen pictures. President Washington is on one end, President Lincoln is about in the middle, and I know it's President Coolidge on the other end because I've seen his picture in a newspaper.

Holy smoke, I think. This is the history room, those are all presidents, and if I do history I've got to memorize all of those guys. Hey, I'll stick to squaring logs with a broadaxe.

"This is the history room," Janice says, just like I guessed.

I'm happy to move on to the next room. There are windows, books, rows of desks, blackboards, pictures of Presidents Washington and Lincoln and of two guys dressed in robes. Notes show that one is Euclid and the other is Pythagoras. I wonder if they worked with that guy, Shakespeare.

"This is our math room," Janice says.

"You know," Jason says, "If I knew what I'm going to do next in math maybe the books are here, and I can borrow one."

"Geometry is next after algebra," Janice says. She picks a book from a shelf and gives it to Jason. "Learn that, please. I hear a lot of complaining about geometry, and I'm having trouble with just algebra." Jason sits at a desk and starts reading page one.

"This is the business classroom," Janice says when we go to the next room. There are a bunch of typewriters on the desks. Of course Presidents Washington and Lincoln are up there on the wall. This time they are on either side of a big chart of the push buttons on the typewriter. I think of hunting for the right push button for the letter I want. Just thinking about that hurts.

"The two rooms downstairs," Janice says as we go back down, "are laboratories where we do things we are learning about."

The first room is a kitchen as big as the 30-Mile cook room. There are two cook stoves, three sinks with water faucets, and yards of counter top and cupboards. Instead of a bunch of tables like at 30-Mile there is only one and a bunch of desks. And there are four sewing machines. Can I imagine four sewing machines at 30-Mile?

"This is the domestic science lab," Janice says. "Where girls learn to be good wives," she adds, and she smiles—or that might be a grin.

I stick my head out the door, and there is nobody around. I go back and kiss Janice. She smiles, and I wonder how many girls get kissed in that room. Hey. It's the domestic science lab. Right?

"Come on," she says, and we go to the last room. She opens the door and I can't believe my eyes. The place looks like a dingle without groceries. There is even a block and tackle set hanging on the wall.

"Hey, look," I say, "The guys building sluiceways on the dam use block and tackle sets to lift logs and sluice gates into place."

There are saws, crow bars, wedges, screws, axes, hammers, pails, glass jars with measuring marks on them, little carts, and stuff I don't know about.

"Do you learn how all this stuff works?" I ask Janice.

"One thing at a time."

I go to the door and yell, "Hey, Jason."

"Yeah," comes from upstairs.

"Come down and see this stuff."

Jason clomps downstairs and the clomps echo in hollow rooms. To keep his balance on the slippery floor he walks with his feet apart a little. He has his finger held in the geometry book so he won't lose his place.

"Hey, this place has more stuff than our dingle," he says when he comes into the science lab. "Look at that steam engine piston model." He pushes a part on something and other parts move.

"Be careful. Don't break anything," I tell him.

"This won't break. It works this way."

"How do you know?"

"The science book has a picture of it and a description of how it works. Watch the valve move when the piston reaches the end of its stroke."

He's right. He moves the thing and shows me how the valve directs steam to push the piston back and forth. It makes sense.

"Hey," I say, "that must be how that steam tractor at McNally Pond goes."

"Yeah, it is." He goes to another something. "Hey, wow. This is a model of a four-stroke engine."

"How does it work?"

"I only read that chapter once. The four stroke thing is complicated, but I'll get it figured out."

We keep on looking. A lot of the stuff I have no idea about, but beside that is an axe and a cross-cut saw. I know about them.

"Why do you suppose they have an axe and a cross-cut saw in a science room?" I ask mostly myself.

"Well," Janice says, "a wedge is one of the simple machines, and axes and saws are specialized wedges."

"Yup," Jason says.

"I've got to read that book," I say.

"You know....," Jason says. He is looking at a locked cabinet. On the door of the cabinet is printed: *CHEMICALS—CHEMISTRY CLASS.*

"What?" Janice asks.

"The toboggan paint we're using on our skis wears off pretty quick, and anyway the wax the Swede guys make is better. Do they let people experiment in chemistry class?"

"Yes they do, and sometimes the place stinks so bad I can't eat my lunch."

"Ed," Jason says, "you guys in the crew had better get that dam done next summer. I'm ready to move back to town and start a spare time ski business when we have time off from school."

"Yes," Janice says, "I want to be in on that."

I think to myself that I can work in the woods from fall to the spring high water log drive and make skis during the summer.

"How are you doing?" Mr. Edwards says when he sticks his head in the doorway.

"OK," Janice says. "Thanks for letting me show the place to my brothers."

"Mr. Edwards," Jason says as he holds the geometry book out. His finger is still stuck in it keeping his place. "would it be OK if I take this geometry book to 30-Mile? I finished the algebra book."

Mr. Edwards looks at the book then at Jason maybe three or four times.

"The boys tell me that you're cookee for Edna. Right?"

"Yes."

"Things must have changed in the woods. When I was cookee forty-odd years ago I didn't need a geometry book. Sure. Take it. Just bring it back when you get to be cook and don't need it anymore."

"OK. Thanks. Look, this floor is pretty slippery. Could I have a little of what you put on it to try on my skis? It might make them go better than toboggan paint."

Mr. Edwards says as he goes to a closet, "Yeah. I made a real dumb mistake. I put on floor wax in winter. That stuff is slippery when you have snow or water on your boots." He pours some floor wax from a big can into a bottle he borrows from the science lab. "Try this," he says as he gives it to Jason.

"Thanks," Jason says. He shoves the bottle and geometry book into his coat pocket.

On the way home I wonder if I could take French until I go to work in the woods in the fall and science when I come out in the spring. I think I could stand that much high school, and it might keep Mom happy.

24. SCHOOL AND LIFE LESSONS

Going home from the school, I don't even try to keep up with Janice and Jason. Everyone is sitting down to dinner when I get there.

Roy says, "Those lightweight ski poles are great. I don't think anyone can improve on them."

Mary says, "Well, I think they should have a loop on top like Mom's purse to keep my mittens from slipping."

For the next minute or two the only sound is knives and forks clinking on plates.

"I've been skiing longer than anyone else here, and my little sister tells me how to make ski poles," Jason says. "And she's right, too."

"Well," Roy says, "I take good ideas wherever I find them."

"OK, you get the first set of leather hand loops right after dinner," I say to Mary.

"Hey….," Martha says.

"Look, it will only take a little while. You get the second set before you go skiing this afternoon."

Jason and I rivet leather hand loops onto four sets of poles while Janice does the dishes. To get out of his turn at dishes, Jason tells Janice that if she does the dishes he can learn to use rivets.

Roy goes to the office on Jason's skis, and Mom and the girls ski to Horseback Hill for the afternoon. Jason digests the geometry book, and I get a chance to read about machines in the science book.

Something is wrong.

"Hey, this book is about … What is it? … geology—rocks and rivers," I complain to Jason. "You said this is a machine book."

"That's a general science book, and geology is the first part. Look in the table of contents. Read about simple machines first then go to the engine part."

"What's a table of contents?"

"It's the last part of that book, and it tells you what pages everything is on."

I look. "Hey, that table of contents is a great idea. Yeah, here it is—simple machines. Page 48."

I read, and it's like I am at 30-Mile working on the dam. Lever, inclined plane, block and tackle, wheel and axle, it's all here. Come to find out, a peavey is a lever. And here is a part about friction. I remember that Jason said something about sliding friction.

"Ed," Jason says, "I've got to go back to school to see if I can borrow a ruler, compass, protractor, and triangles to do geometry problems. I didn't know I needed them. I'll take your snowshoes, OK?"

"Yeah."

The door closes as I am reading about figuring mechanical advantage for a set of pulleys—just like they use on the dam sluice gates.

I'm done with the simple machine section when it gets a little dark, so I light a lamp. The steam engine piston is the first part of the engine section.

"Where's Jason?" Janice asks when she comes in. "Hey, can I believe this? Isn't that a school book you're reading? Where are your snowshoes?"

"What?"

Mom comes in. "Where's Jason?"

"Let's see. Yeah. He went back to school."

"Is school in session today?"

"No."

"Well …"

"Let's see. He needs some stuff for geometry."

"Oh, yes," Janice says. "I forgot they use compasses and things."

The twins come in, the kitchen becomes a circus, and Roy is ringmaster when he comes home. It's a fun place but too wild for my brain, so I put the book away.

"Eddie," Mom says while she is cutting baked potatoes and corned beef for hash, "I'm worried. Would you check on Jason?"

"I'll go with you," Janice says.

Beside the woodshed, she holds the kerosene lantern while I adjust Roy's ski bindings to fit my boots. We leave and I carry the lantern and a ski pole in one hand and pole myself along with the other hand. It's so black dark that we can see the road only as far as the lantern glows.

We hear crunch, crunch, crunch of snowshoes.

"I guess Mom is worried again," Jason says from the dark.

"You must have stayed at the school pretty late," I say when he is in the lantern light.

"Only for a few minutes. Mr. Edwards let me take the stuff I needed."

"So how come you didn't come home?"

"I lucked out. When I left the school I met a girl that I talked to at the wedding party. She is taking geometry too, and she said she would help me get started."

"Who?" Janice wants to know.

"Theresa LaPointe. Boy, Janice, Theresa sure bragged you up. Did you know she has nine brothers and sisters? It's tough to do geometry with nine kids around, but her Mom is nice."

"Theresa LaPointe?" Janice says. I do not want a picture of Janice's face right then. "She bragged me up? You were in Theresa LaPointe's house?"

"Hey, her place is right beside the school, and we didn't do anything wrong. She said her Mom sassed her for envying you. She said you were first to wear running pants, you have fancy snowshoes and beat her in the Christmas Field Day races, and this morning she saw us on our skis. That's when she mouthed off, and her Mom got on her case. She promised her Mom that she would apologize to you, so how about being nice to her? She's OK. Her Mom said I could come back to do more geometry."

I look at Janice again, and her face is the mean mask that twists my stomach.

"What's for supper?" Jason asks.

"Corned beef hash," I tell him when my mouth works again. I guess Janice's brain can't handle that question right now.

"Yeah."

During supper, Mom and the twins detail their afternoon ski trip for Roy. I don't think anyone notices that Janice and I don't talk.

I'm thinking. There are a lot of times that changed me. Dad's funeral. Kissing Janice the first time. Mom thanking Janice for teaching her to read. Walking to 30-Mile. Reading the first page of "Tarzan" to my crew. Seeing a steam log hauler. The Madawaska Company snowshoe race. Mom's wedding. Giving Janice a friendship ring. Right now, my little brother has a girlfriend, and he is fighting for her. Right now, Janice's mean mask sometimes tells me there is something wrong inside of her. I don't like this change in my girlfriend.

We're doing the supper dishes, and Janice says, "Let's ski for a while."

I borrow Mom's skis, and we slide toward the West End School far enough to talk in the dark.

"Do you know Theresa LaPointe?" I ask.

"She hates me. Last year as a freshman, no girl in school could beat her in a race. At the Summer Field Day I beat her in the quarter mile, and I was just out of eighth grade. She is the tall girl who placed second behind me in the one-hundred-yard and -mile races at the Winter Field Day. Come to think of it, she spent a lot of time with Jason at the wedding party. She is two years older than Jason, and she must be a whole head taller."

"Jason isn't old enough to have a girlfriend," I say.

No answer. It's too dark for me to see Janice's face, but I can feel her smile. Yeah, that's a dumb thing to say. Janice has been my girlfriend since maybe before first grade.

"Can this Theresa really do geometry?"

"She earned all A's last year. We are the only two in school who have all A's this year, and I am not about to let her get ahead of me."

"Yeah," I say. What else can I say?

Theresa isn't all that's new. When Janice and I return home, Janice and Mom talk skiing. I'm not sure who thought of it first, but Mom is willing to try a pair of running pants. Only at night, she says. She isn't about to let Cora and Jimmie see her in pants.

Next morning Jason does geometry, and I try to follow a science book description of how a four-stroke engine works. Mom and Janice giggle and make running pants with the sewing machine. I do OK with the engine details until my mother comes out of the bedroom wearing pants. My mother. Can I believe my mother is wearing pants?

"I just love them," Mom says. "And I just love you for having courage enough to be the first girl to wear running pants in races. I'll be the first mother in ski pants."

Mom fidgets around the kitchen a while. She has Janice hold a mirror so she can see herself in her new outfit. She gets another mirror so she can see the back of her new outfit.

"Jason, dear, could I borrow your skis?" Mom asks.

"Yeah," Jason is adjusting his compass, and he doesn't need skis.

"Come on," Mom says to Janice, "I don't care who sees me. Let's go ski."

I watch what looks like two sets of twins ski toward West End School, and the kitchen is quiet enough for me to try the four-stroke engine idea again. I get how and when the valves work, but something called a carburetor I don't understand.

Wow, time goes by. I hear Roy laughing and a lot of giggling. Dinner isn't on. I glance out the window, and I'm proud. There are five of my family out in the road on five pairs of skis. But dinner isn't on. I'm slicing bacon when Mom comes in and takes a pan of left-over corned beef hash from the oven. I ought to know that Mom always has our meals in mind.

"Do you need your skis this afternoon?" Roy asks Jason after dinner.

"No. You use them."

Soon the five skiers are on their ways.

"Let me borrow your snowshoes," Jason says.

"Yeah. Where are you going? How come you didn't keep your skis?"

"I'm going across the bridge to do geometry with Theresa, and I can just imagine everyone discussing that, so I lent Roy the skis. I'll be home before everyone else, and you don't have to let the cat out of the bag about where I go. OK?"

"Yeah. Sure. OK."

So I keep house, put wood in the stove when it needs it, and read the science book. Just as he plans, Jason is home before everyone else, and nobody except me knows he was gone. This goes on every afternoon all week.

I read the book all week. A lot of things I know about are in the book, but who would believe that there are male and female plants? And glaciers were here. Now I know how some house-sized rocks got way out in the woods where they don't seem to belong. It doesn't seem right that the sun is closer to Earth in winter. And plants and animals are classified according to how their parts grow. It would make more sense to me to classify animals according to how they taste.

I do better with the book than I do sleeping nights. I want to get back to 30-Mile to see how Andre and Emile are doing with skis. I want to finish the cribwork on the dam. I want to have fun listening to my crew hash over my school books at night. But I don't want to leave Janice. I keep remembering her mean mask, and I know there is something wrong.

Sunday comes and I can't think of a way out of church. I'll tell you what, being English and working with a French-speaking crew is easy. Everyone knows what everyone does, and a glance or movement now and then is all the talk we need. A Catholic Mass is something else. I don't know what anyone does, I don't know how to do it anyway, and there is a strange language involved. I wish I'd tried harder to stay home.

For a while, watching the after-Mass show outside the church is fun and worth the bad time in church. There is no mistaking tall Theresa LaPointe and her family. Jason can't do a thing to prevent Mrs. LaPointe from holding him with her arm over his shoulder. She tells Mom how nice it is to have Jason studying with Theresa. I wonder if Mom ever found out anything about me that bugged out her eyes like that. Martha and Mary don't care if they don't know the LaPointe kids. They have fun anyway. I recognize Mr. LaPointe as one of the hostlers, and he and Roy talk as old friends.

Janice and Theresa talk but not as old friends. They walk far enough away so I have to watch body language, and it is not fun. If I saw Janice's mean expression on a guy working in my dam crew, I'd worry. During her races Janice looked like that. I remember her laughing, always laughing, when we raced around the West End School. Something is wrong, and I have a sick feeling in my stomach.

Theresa talks, and Janice's jaw drops a little. Theresa says more and

Janice's eyes open from slits to round. Theresa doesn't talk any more, and Janice's face looks almost as bug-eyed as Mom's did a minute ago. Janice speaks, and she looks OK. What, I wonder, happened? I still don't feel good.

Here comes Mom with Mrs. LaPointe to meet Theresa.

Sunday afternoon I don't feel great as we pack our stuff to go to 30-Mile next morning. When we're done, Janice and I go out to snowshoe and be together.

"Janice," I say, "do you want me to stay home?"

"What?"

"Look, I'm nervous. You look ugly when you are around Theresa. Are you OK?"

We go maybe fifty yards before she says, "You're serious, aren't you?"

"Of course I'm serious. The snowshoe race is over, and now I'm only one guy in the crew. They don't need me."

In another hundred yards or so she says, "When I louse up, I do it well. I decide to make love with you, and I don't want to think what that could do to us. I get in a cat fight at school, and I don't even guess that might mess up my family, too.

"Look," I say, "I'll go to school with you if that will help."

"Look, Eddie, Dad needs you at the dam. You do good work, and the men really like your reading. Dad told me that."

"Well …"

"I'm carrying all A's, and I'm still dumb. Eddie, I'm OK. Theresa and I are OK now. At first I thought she was lying to Jason, but now I know she wasn't. You go finish the dam, and I'll help Cora with Martha and Mary."

"OK. Yeah. You're OK, but I don't think you're dumb."

There are times when I need to kiss my girlfriend, but we're right in front of Jimmie's and Cora's place.

25. BACK TO CAMP

Next morning after breakfast we dump all the water in the house because the place will be frozen until spring. Jimmie and Cora come, and we pile our pack sacks on a toboggan. Mom and the twins get weepy.

Janice tells the girls, "I'm going to school on my skis, so I'll be home soon after school. We'll have time to ski. Take my clothes with you to Cora's place. OK?" She helps each twin slip pack sack straps over their shoulders.

"OK," they agree, and they leave with Cora.

"Janice," Mom says as she buckles on a pair of bear paw snowshoes from the woodshed, "I'll be too busy for skis at 30-Mile. Do you think Theresa would like to borrow them?"

Janice blinks and glances at me. "I'm sure she would. I'll talk to her today," she says as I pull our toboggan toward the company office.

In front of the office, horses are hitched to the tote sled and the McNally Pond Camp sled. That has long seats attached along each side. A cool breeze swirls smoke from the chimney around men, women, and kids in the yard. After Jason and I pile our packs, skis, and snowshoes on the tote sled I stand with my arm over Janice's shoulder.

"Oh, My soul," Mom says. She is looking at Janice and me, and at Jason—and there is Theresa with him. "I came here as a girl to see my man off to the woods. Now my children are here. Am I that old?"

I guess that Theresa came to the office when her father came to work in the stable.

"No, Mom," Janice says. "We're just starting young." She hugs me.

"You can't fool me, girl. I came here when I was your age."

We leave sitting on the sled seats, and Theresa snowshoes beside Janice on their way across the bridge to school. I think about Jason and

157

Theresa, and I feel old. Jason is my kid brother, and he has a girlfriend older than Janice.

After listening to sled runners squeak on packed snow, I'm sure I would rather walk than ride to 30-Mile. However, boiling the kettle with a logging crew and the local gorbeys at 5-Mile Brook is more fun than walking. You just don't find cedar smoke, hot tea, sandwiches, and loggers' stories even on a fancy hotel menu.

Hot tea and sandwich in hand, Mom sits on a cedar block like the woods queen she is. She trades stories, laughs, and smiles. I wonder if she knows that Dad used to boil the kettle here. She is happy now, and I am happy for her.

It's about the middle of the afternoon when we arrive at 10-Mile Depot. I see piles and piles of four-foot-long logs beside the river waiting to be pushed into spring high water. Loggers who came in yesterday are in the bunk room. Anxious to get back to doing something they love, they sharpen their axes.

Mom helps Mrs. LeBlanc with supper. Codfish chowder, biscuits, and molasses cake served in a cook room make me feel at home in the woods. The same stuff wouldn't taste the same outside, but I wouldn't tell Mom that. Jason and I do the cookee work for Mrs. LeBlanc after supper.

"Do one of you boys have a book you could read for us?" Roy asks.

"I've got my geometry book," Jason says. He's grinning.

"Yeah. Well maybe something with a little more story in it would be better," Roy says. He is also grinning. "Hey, can you tell the crew the 'Tarzan' book," he says to me.

This is a good idea, but I can't remember exactly how it all goes. Reading a book is a lot easier than remembering it. I do the best I can, and when Tarzan has grown up enough to give his famous yell, Jason does Tarzan proud. I never saw grown men laugh so hard. Books are fun even in logging camps.

Next day the ten miles to 20-Mile Depot is a short day, but to go to 30-Mile Depot with loaded sleds would be too hard on the horses. Only a few of the crew are back from Christmas in Quebec, so the bunk room isn't very crowded. Mom pitches in with Madam Cote to put supper on. Madam Cote makes pea soup that speaks perfect English and pure French. Guaranteed. And she put four biscuit-pan sized chocolate cakes on the tables—with frosting.

After supper Jason and I cookee, and Mom does the book thing with "Alice's Adventures in Wonderland". She has the story about memorized. She does French well enough so the guys from Quebec follow the story, and she slides enough English in to keep the rest of us with her. Soon there is an English and French uproar about whether or not any sensible rabbit would dig a hole that big. I laugh so hard I have to make a quick trip to the privy.

We arrive at 30-Mile Depot at about noon the next day. Snow has nearly filled the dam crib and drifted against the sluice gates. I guess that we are going to shovel a long time before we can make progress on the job. I feel pretty dismal about that.

Andre and Emile are not in the blacksmith shop, but Jason and I hop off the sled to see how the ski project is coming. Wow. Those guys have not been loafing. Standing against a lumber rack are twelve pairs of skis as long as Jason's, complete with bindings and all painted with toboggan paint. A shorter pair on the work bench, tapered both front and back from the center foot platform, are nearly finished. I don't feel at all dismal about that.

We walk to the depot in the bobsled runner track to help unload the camp wangan from the tote sled. Our crew has returned from Quebec so the wangan is already stored in the dingle. Our pack sacks, my snowshoes, and Jason's skis are on the platform and Andre and Emile are discussing the little round snowshoes on Jason's ski poles.

"You have good Christmas?" Andre says as we shake hands.

"Yeah. Great."

"You have good thought." He points to a ski pole snowshoe.

"My girlfriend thought of that."

"We need her work in blacksmith shop," he says and he grins as we carry our wangan into the cook room.

Our crew and Jimmie's crew crowd the place, but Andre and Emile have enough beef stew, roast beef, bread, pie, and gingerbread to go around. Nothing less will do but Mom and Roy sit with the crews for a wedding celebration dinner. Mom looks happier than she did at the hotel wedding celebration in town.

After the celebration Jimmie borrows a pair of fresh horses, and his crew leaves for McNally Pond. Mom and Roy use a toboggan to move their wangan into the old filer's cabin, and I pitch in to help Jason with a pile of dishes. Andre comes in and makes sure I can get on with "Treasure Island" if the crew carries water and splits the wood.

At supper time the men show Mom new family pictures. The bulletin board is soon pretty well covered with pictures.

While I read in the bunk room that evening it seems like we had never left camp for Christmas in town. I don't read much about the *Hispaniola* when Andre and Emile talk French to the crew for quite a while. Andre says to me, "We tell about go to France on troop ship to fight in Great War. Many men. Little space. Seasick. Very, very bad time."

I read about Ben Gunn, the pirate marooned on Treasure Island for three years. When Andre translates to French, Alcide talks for a while, and the crew laughs. Andre says, "Alcide build camp in woods one summer. Lost from camp only three days. Many mosquitoes and very lonesome.

Almost hungry enough to eat porcupine raw. Alcide hope Ben Gunn have fire to cook."

Next day is snow-shovel day. Believe that. Jacques, Alcide and I clean out the log hewing beds, but we don't have as much snow to move as the guys working on the sluice gates.

That night I'm glad to be reading in the bunk room. Outside, the wind really howls.

I read about shooting the *Hispaniola's* cannon at the stockade. Again Andre and Emile talk a long time. Andre pulls up his shirt and shows a scar. Everybody listens. Nobody smiles.

Andre says, "Old cannon shoot iron ball. Does not explode. Cannon shells in Great War explode in trench. Little pieces very bad." He points to his scar.

That night in my bunk I think a long time. Andre and Emile are good men in the woods. Also they can make anything. Now I know they are veterans of the Great War. Miss Rogers said that was the War to End All Wars. I am proud to be friends with men I respect. Because of them, Jason and I will not have to sail on a troop ship and face cannons.

Next day is snow-shovel day all over again because the night wind blew the snow back where it was. We hew only a couple of logs for the crew to fit into the sluice gates, and we don't do much better for another week.

But we make progress with "Treasure Island". My crew is delighted to learn that the pirates get their due—nothing. Except John Silver, of course. They want John to show up at 30-Mile looking for a cook's job. They have a place in the dam for John—way down bottom under the rocks. They are flat disgusted with Jim because Jim thinks taking stolen stuff is an honorable way to make a living. They want the boy to come looking for a cookee job. Edna and Jason will show Jim what work is. For sure.

The morning after we finish "Treasure Island" I'm shoveling snow and chips from our log bed. Wind is drifting snow in about as fast as I'm shoveling it out.

Roy comes by and says, "Ed, I hear you've done it with "Treasure Island". I sure hope you've got another book."

"Yeah. I've got United States History, General Science, 'Robinson Crusoe', 'Tom Sawyer', and Algebra I. Let's pretend I don't have History and Algebra. I read Janice's General Science book last week, and some of it is a lot like working here on the dam. Why?"

"Well, we're in the worst weeks of winter, and we're going to be snowed off the job a lot. These men are workers, and they'll get restless loafing. I want to keep them here until we can dynamite rocks this spring. There will be plenty to do then, and you're reading now is more help than you might think."

"Glad to help," I say. I remember that Janice spoke of me reading to the crew.

"Look, we'll lose the crew in a week if you read science, history, or algebra. 'Tom Sawyer' might be as good as 'Alice's Adventures in Wonderland' I suppose, but I think 'Robinson Crusoe' is the way to go. OK?"

"Yeah."

"You know …," Roy says, and he turns his back to the wind while he's thinking. "I can't remember why. It's been twenty-five years or so since I read 'Robinson Crusoe'. I remember that, for some reason, it's a hard read. Look, why don't you take this afternoon to read ahead a little bit? Pay is the same."

"Yeah. Well, OK."

Roy goes on his way, and I stand with my mouth open staring at nothing. Can I believe this? My boss wants me to read a school book—and I get paid for it.

After dinner the crew leaves for the dam, and I dig "Robinson Crusoe" out from under my bunk. I think this will be a fun time with Jason, and I say nothing as I clear dishes off a dining table under a lamp.

"Hey," Jason says, "aren't you going to work?"

"Yeah."

"Well, what are you here for?"

"I'm going to work."

I got him. Jason stands there with his mouth open and his head cocked to one side.

"Eddie," Mom says, "what is going on?"

"I'm going to start reading a new book tonight, and Roy says I should take time to read ahead."

"You're getting paid to read a school book?" Jason says.

"Hey, you do your math on company time. Besides, you get paid for skiing every time you scale wood. I'm just trying to catch up to you."

I grin at Jason then try "Robinson Crusoe", page one. Something is wrong. I look at other pages, and something really is wrong.

"Hey, I say. They didn't print this book right."

"Maybe you've got it upside down," Jason says.

"I've got it right side up, but the sentences are as long as paragraphs, and the paragraphs would make chapters. Besides, different people say things in the same paragraph, and there are no quotation marks."

"Naw," Jason says. He wipes his hands on his pants and comes over to see the book.

"Hey," he says, "you're right."

I turn back and we read the little part before the story.

"Look," I say. "This says 'Robinson Crusoe' was first published in

1719. Let's see, that's two hundred and ..."

"Seven years ago," Jason says.

"I guess they didn't write then the way we do now. I've got to just straighten it out as I go, and remember it to tell the crew."

Mom is over by the stoves, and Jason whispers to me, "You be sure you do remember it so you can tell me, too. I've got to write a report on it, and I can do a whole high school math program in the time it would take me to read 'Robinson Crusoe'."

So I turn the lamp wick up a little and start. There are a jillion parts—words, phrases, and sentences. Commas, semicolons, periods, and question marks. Only now and again there is a new paragraph. Wow. Quotation marks would sure help straighten this mess out.

Picking "Robinson Crusoe" apart is like picking fly specks out of pepper.

26. SKIS FOR LACROIX SCALERS

After supper I take "Robinson Crusoe" into the bunk room, but I don't get onto the story right away.

"This book have stolen treasure?" Andre asks.

"I don't know. I haven't read it all yet."

"This book have big white rabbit?"

"I don't think so."

"Tarzan in book?"

"Nope. This story is about ships and islands, and it starts in 1651."

The crew hashes that over for a few minutes.

"Long time. Maybe long as four grandfathers live," Andre says.

I start telling the story. "So this guy Robinson Crusoe decides to go to sea as a sailor and trader to make his living. His old mother and father are sad. They want him to run the family farm, go to school, and take care of them."

Every man in the crew takes part in a discussion, and I can see they agree on something.

Andre says, "We like that. Work in woods is like sail on ocean. What you have in brain is what you have to do."

I think yes, I understand that too. I guess I was born with woods work in my brain, and that is what I have to do. I think I'm here in the bunk room to tell my crew a story, and my crew tells me how my brain works. I like these guys.

"Anyway," I say, "Robinson had some bad luck and some good luck. His ship sank in a storm, but he survived. He went on another ship and did some buying here and selling there. He made a lot of money which he put in a bank."

During that discussion, the wind outside sounds like it could sink a ship. When it blows just right, smoke puffs from the stove. I can tell that my crew agrees about something again, and Mr. Lacroix is part of it.

Andre says, "Robinson is good man for all. Bad luck find everyone, but man who keep working hard have good luck and earn money. Mr. Lacroix earn money and hire many people. This is good for all."

The next day is Sunday. It's Jason's day to scale for Jimmie, and I don't like the storm. I decide I'll go with Jason, but Roy telephones Jimmie. They call off the scaling, so during the morning I read more of "Robinson Crusoe".

I look up from my book, and … Can I believe this? Mom is reading our United States history book to herself. While ovens of bread and pies are baking Mom is really into it. Look, this is a big improvement. She isn't reading "Cinderella" out loud.

During the afternoon I tell that Robinson's ship is captured and he is made a slave. His captors own Robinson. As Andre tells the story I watch my crew turn from the good natured people I know to fighting ugly. Never less than five yell at once. This goes on and on, but they are all agreeing on whatever they are yelling about. I'm confused. It takes a while for Andre to quiet the bunk room down so he can catch me up.

Andre says, "We think no man can own other man. Never, never, never. When we are little boys, old people tell us about black folks come to Canada on Underground Railroad. They are slave in United States then free in Canada. You know Underground Railroad and slave, Eddie?"

"No."

"You learn about slave, Eddie. Everyone learn. Then no more slave." Andre points his finger at me as he speaks. I, for sure, know that he means what he says.

"Yeah. Yeah. OK."

I remember that Miss Rogers never pointed her finger that way when she gave me an assignment.

Wind and snow keep us off the job for days. The men get bored, and Mom keeps pails of tea and coffee on a stove for them and doughnuts and pies on a table. They shovel snow from the firewood log pile and work up a bunch of stove wood for Jason. We have a lot of "Robinson Crusoe" time so I read ahead.

I tell my friends that the slave, Robinson, works hard for his master, and the master begins to trust his slave and gives Robinson more freedom. One day Robinson and a slave boy steal a small boat and escape.

Discussion time. The crew decides it is OK for Robinson to steal the boat to gain his freedom because he shouldn't be a slave. It is good of Robinson to take the boy to freedom.

Robinson sells the boat.

The crew decides that is OK because the owner didn't pay Robinson for all the work he did while he was a slave. Robinson is a good man. He can work at 30-Mile anytime.

At the next story time I go on with the book. I tell the crew that Robinson sells the slave boy to a new owner.

Wow. There is rowdy, rowdy discussion. "Whoa. Hold up," Andre says. "Robinson know better than that. He doesn't like be slave, but he sells boy. If Robinson come to 30-Mile he clean stables with his hands. Eat hay with horses."

Wednesday is tote sled day, and I wait for a letter from Janice like I have for too long. Deep, drifting snow is still too much for the team so again no letter comes. I wonder if Janice skis to school during storms, and I wonder how Janice and Theresa are getting along. I'd like to talk to Janice on the telephone, but the company doesn't allow personal calls. I miss Janice. I'm lonesome—but I'm not about to say so.

Except during story time, Emile and Andre work in the blacksmith shop. One day they bring a pair of skis and shoulder-high ski poles to the cook room where I'm reading ahead about Robinson.

"We have two little push pole made for all scaler," Andre tells me as he gives me a ski pole.

Wow. They sure do. The pole has a leather hand loop on the top and a small round snowshoe near the bottom. It also has a steel point sticking out of the bottom end.

Andre slides a finger over a steel point. "Some time is slippery crust on snow," he says. "Pick point stick in snow crust like stick in log on river drive. Do not slip."

I hold the ski pole and stare at it for a while. Some jewelry is made to wear, but this is made to use. It looks as great as the axe these guys brought me when I was cookee. I think that Jason, Janice, and I have to do this well if we want to sell skis and poles. I wish I had a pair of these poles to send out to Janice. Anyway, I guess I'm standing there with my mouth open.

"You like push pole?" Andre says.

"Yeah. I sure do."

Emile hands me one of the skis he's carrying. It is one piece of wood tapered from a thick foot platform to the turned up front and flat back. There is no weak place in this ski like a toboggan board with a screwed-on foot platform. I wonder how long it took them to shave the tapers with wood planes then steam and turn up the fronts. The ski belongs in the museum with the axe and ski pole, and I wonder if we will ever be able to match such high-quality work. My mouth must be open again.

"Ski OK?" Andre asks.

"It's better than OK," I tell him.

Jason has a bunch of pots and pans going in the sink, and I carry skis and poles across the cook room.

"Hey," I say.

He glances at the skis. "Mom," he says as he wipes his hands on his pants, "I'll be right back."

On the snow-covered dingle platform he adjusts the ski bindings to his boots and steps off into wind and swirling snow. He strides with his skis, pushes the little ski pole snowshoes into the soft snow, and soon disappears into a tumbling snow cloud.

"Whoopie deeeee," he yells as he skis back out of the cloud and steps up onto the dingle platform. His face is a snow mask, and his snow-covered hair looks like a scruffy white hat.

Mom sticks her head out the door to see what is going on, and I guess it's the white hair that does it. You know how mothers are. Mom unloads on me, Andre, and Emile. Emile doesn't understand the English, but he knows for sure that Mom thinks we ought to know better than let her boy ski without a hat and jacket.

But as soon as Mom wipes Jason's face and hair with her apron, she calms down—sort of. Before he goes back to his dishes Jason tells us that the tapered skis feel really strong and the poles are perfect. Andre and Emile smile. Then they leave for the bunk room where Mom won't get them again.

It seems like it takes forever because storms come one after another, but the bad weather eventually blows itself out. Now the sun on the white snow is so bright it hurts my eyes. While we shovel snow and hew logs I have to stop once in a while to close my eyes. I'll never wish for snow again.

There is so much discussion about Robinson when I tell the story in the bunk room that it doesn't take much reading time to stay ahead. Robinson uses the money from selling the boat and the boy to buy a plantation in South America.

Everyone in the bunkroom tells everyone else, all at once of course, then Andre tells me that Robinson is just plain stupid. He leaves home because he doesn't want to run the family farm. He follows the sea as he wants to. Now he buys a plantation. The dummy should have stayed home and cared for his parents. I agree all the way on that.

One morning after it had stopped snowing for a few days Roy says to me, "The snow has settled enough so horses can break a road to McNally Pond Camp. The log hauler is bringing the Lacroix scalers there today to pick up their skis and learn about skiing. If you want to go with Jason, Andre, and Emile, I'll cookee for Edna today, OK?"

OK for sure. I agree to that deal.

It's a good trip. We have boxes for seats on the bobsled, and the trees along the road shade the snow and cut the glare. At the camp it's great to meet the old guys again who snowshoed in the race. I think those guys will forever consider Jason and me their sons—or maybe grandsons.

I stand aside and watch Andre, Emile, and Jason talk skiing with my old friends. I think that my place is, for sure, in the woods with these guys. They are all good men. I think again that there must be a way to do a little high school work in the summer to keep Mom happy. I wonder if I can find a French teacher next summer.

Meeting my old friends again is so great that I hardly notice the huge, black, smoking, steaming, log hauler stopped beside the cook room. The new skiers adjust their ski bindings to their boots, slide away on the log hauler road, and I snowshoe to the machine and marvel again. In my mind I see the steam piston model in the science laboratory. In front of me is a real steam piston, and I know how the valves work inside.

Hey, whoa. The piston rod slides, and big steel treads move. I jump back and look up at the engineer's window. A guy smiles at me and points at the turn-around loop around the camp buildings. He yells something in French to the guy out front who steers the thing. He pushes a stick, tons of steel rumbles forward, and he motions for me to follow.

I have to believe this because I'm watching it, and it works just like the science book says. The piston rod slips back and forth, and steel treads turn, squeaking, clunking, and squealing. Smoke and steam whoosh, whoosh, whoosh from the smokestack on top of the thing. I feel like a mouse running beside a bear. I know that machine is more powerful than a whole herd of bears.

"Mercy," I tell him when we return to the starting place. He nods and smiles. I will never forget what I saw.

Jason and the guys with new skis slide back to camp. I guess that I might be looking at more skis than anywhere this side of Sweden, wherever that is. The new skiers all talk French at once. I don't understand much French, but I know they think skis are here in the woods to stay. Emile gurgles to them about the pair of tapered skis, and Andre gives them a couple cartons of toboggan paint.

"Mercy," they say. They shake our hands, pat us on our backs, and away they go on the log hauler sled. I am proud to be friends with that outfit.

I wish my New Sweden friend, Sven Anderson, were here. He'd like my French friends, all those skis, and that marvelous machine.

After dinner Jason scales wood for Jimmie's crew on the tapered skis. He says they work great.

Of course on the way home Jason tries the tapered skis on his favorite hill and the curve at the bottom. He does great, but something is different when he makes the curve. Instead of stepping his skis around the corner he somehow makes the skis slew. He is really whizzing, and Andre and Emile watch with their mouths open. When we catch up to him, he lays his skis on the bobsled then sits on a box beside me.

"Jason," Andre says, "you hit tree. Edna have no cookee."

"Yeah. I'll keep that in mind," Jason says to Andre, and he grins. "You know something," he says to me, "I could cut a corner better if I had better control of my skis. We need special ski boots that lock onto the skis."

I feel my brain rattle. When we make skis and poles that I think are perfect, someone thinks of something better. Every time. What is the word Roy used? Obsolete. I wonder if there is anything about skis that isn't obsolete before you finish making it.

"Use calk boot," Andre says to Jason.

"Huh?" Jason says.

"Boot calk stick in wood. Do not slip. We put little holes in ski for calk to fit. We screw boot to ski. You turn boot. Ski turn, too. OK?"

Jason looks at me. I guess he wants to know if Andre knows what he is talking about. Imagine that. I don't know about this calk boot and ski thing, but Andre and Emile are never wrong. Also, I remember that Roy said he takes good ideas wherever he finds them. I nod an OK to Jason.

"Yeah," Jason says to Andre. "That will work great. Thanks."

We arrive at 30-Mile. Wow. There in front of the dingle is the tote sled.

27. LETTERS AND LESSONS

Roy is standing on the dingle porch checking paperwork as some of the crew carries our groceries inside.

In the cookroom Mom is sitting in her rocking chair reading a newspaper.

"Look. Come see what I have," she says when we come in.

I'm looking for a letter from Janice, but I go to see whatever it is Mom wants to show me.

"Eddie, I can read now, and I'm working. I subscribed to the newspaper for us." She has a big envelope, and I guess it's the newspaper envelope. "Look, Eddie. Doesn't that look grand? I owe this to Janice for teaching me to read, and to you for making Father Belanger marry Roy and me at Christmas time." Mom goes weepy, sticks the envelope under her arm, and pulls a handkerchief from her apron pocket. She hugs me and wipes her eyes. "I want you to know, Eddie, that I think you are a fine son."

"Now Mom, that's not what you said when Jason was skiing in the snow."

"That was then, and this is now."

She gives me the envelope, and the address is

> Mr. and Mrs. Roy Chase
> Great Northern Paper Company
> Ashland, Maine

"That is the first time I've been Mrs. Roy Chase. I'm going to keep that envelope forever, Eddie, and I'm going to read the newspaper forever. I've got to know what is going on because I'm going to vote. Can you imagine that, Eddie?" Mom goes back to her handkerchief. "Women can vote now. I'm going to vote, and I don't care if some men don't like it."

"Haven't women always voted?"

"No, Eddie. Women have voted only for a few years now. I have never voted because I couldn't read a ballot. I'm going to read about what President Coolidge is doing, and I can read a ballot, and I'll vote depending on what I read.

And something else, Eddie, Janice said I should read the United States History book so I will understand the newspapers better. I'm doing that."

My brain doesn't absorb that all right off. All I can think is Janice is a lot smarter than I am, but a few years ago she couldn't vote even if she were old enough. That doesn't make sense.

But my brain finally jiggles this history deal into a plan. Mom is reading the book. I'll get her to tell me about it, and if I can pass a test she'll think I'm a student for sure. Hey, does that make sense, or what?

Yeah. Let's see. I'm looking for a letter from Janice.

"Hey, Mom," I say.

"Janice's letters are on your bunk."

That also makes sense. I walk over, and Jason is sitting up on his bunk reading something.

"Are you doing geometry again?"

"Nope. Letter from Theresa."

My brain wobbles again. I know Jason and Theresa have a thing going, but Jason isn't old enough to get letters from a girl—is he? Jason has changed. Mom has changed. Janice has changed. Well, I think, that's the way it is. I don't need to change.

It's been a month since the tote sled could make it to 30-Mile so I have four letters from Janice. I sort them out and read the last one first. She's lonesome, and she thinks the snow makes the woods a thirty-mile wall between us.

In the third letter she says she is doing OK in school, and Theresa is a big help with algebra. Hey, that's a great change. I remember how awful Janice looked when she snowshoed against Theresa and when she squared off with Theresa after church.

The second letter says she is disappointed that the tote sled couldn't make it in deep snow.

The first letter says she and Theresa are friends now, and Theresa is ashamed that she was jealous. Theresa loves Mom's skis, and Theresa is going to write to Mom. The twins are doing great with their new skis. So I'm glad things are better with Janice.

Roy is busy with the tote sled stuff so Jason and I wash a set of pots and pans for Mom. I read a little more of "Robinson" while I eat supper, and I guess the crew will want to hang Robinson.

I have the crew figured right. Robinson makes a deal with his neighboring plantation owners. He will take a ship to Africa and trade for a whole boatload of slaves to be divided among the plantations. Hanging is one of the more gentle things the crew wants to do to Robinson. In fact, they want to borrow the Queen of Hearts' executioner from the "Alice in Wonderland" story.

Two good things happen. First, we have an early rainstorm. We don't have to shovel rain like we do snow, and the rain melts some of our snow. Second, Robinson is shipwrecked alone on an island on his trip to Africa. He doesn't get any slaves.

We think it serves him right.

However, over the next weeks Robinson does better on his island than we do on our dam. Robinson builds a raft and moves clothes, guns, nails, food, sail cloth, and even money from the ship to his island. He works on a home and fortress combined. Our dam is too dangerous to work on because it's covered with layers of ice and snow.

As the story goes on, we at 30-Mile Depot decide that we are a lot better off than Robinson. We have only a little while to wait to get on with our job, but Robinson is on the island for who knows how long. He digs up a garden spot and plants a few seeds.

One morning I'm reading ahead about Robinson when Andre and Emile come into the cook room with a pair of calked boots screwed to the tapered skis. On the dingle platform Jason laces his foot into one boot OK, but the screws hold that foot to the ski so tight he can't kneel down to lace his other boot. I lace it for him.

The packed snow is pretty hard, and Jason skis toward the dam. He controls the skis to slew back and forth across the road, but he stands straight up instead of bending forward to push with his poles. Something doesn't look right. He stops at the blacksmith shop and beckons for us to join him.

When we get there, he says, "I can make the skis go where I want, but I've got to lift my heel to bend my knees. Can you take the screws out of the boot heels?" That doesn't take long, and Jason uses his skis and poles better than ever. But to take off his skis, he has to take off the boots too.

We guess there has to be a better ski setup, but Jason does great scaling the McNally Pond Camp wood on what he has. I go with him on his first skis. On the way home Jason slips down the hill and flits around the turn like a bird picking bugs out of the air. I think too late. Skis are a lot faster on ice-crusted snow than on soft snow, and long skis with floppy harnesses are hard to control—especially when you don't have much experience. Into the pucker brush I go where Jason made it on his first ski trip, and bushes rip my jacket.

"Jason," I say on our way home, "we need one kind of skis and bindings for going on flat snow and a different setup for skiing on hills. Right?"

"Yeah. Maybe we'll have to learn to make special ski boots and bindings, too," he says.

A half mile or so later he says, "Say, do you think people would buy special ski boots and bindings?"

"That doesn't seem likely to me, but we can try this stuff when we have time. Now I've got to get on with reading about Robinson."

That night I tell about Robinson catching wild goats and making a pasture for them. He also hews off the sides of a log to make a board. Then he hollows out half a log and makes a boat, but the boat is too far from the water and too heavy to move.

After the crew grumbles a while Andre says, "If Robinson stay home on farm he don't have to catch wild goat. He could use sword like froe to split log, and Robinson is dumb to make boat he can't use. Pretty stupid."

I tell that Robinson walks all over his Island, and there are no other people. But one day Robinson sees a man's bare foot print much larger than his. Later Robinson finds a cannibal picnic spot. There are human skulls, hands, feet, bones, and a fire pit.

My crew surprises me. Instead of uproar there is a pretty calm discussion. Andre says, "Robinson be careful. Cannibal eat him. Cannibal not bad people. They do what they learn. Like we learn to eat animal. Cannibal not so bad as soldiers kill prisoners of war for nothing." Andre closes his eyes and his forehead pulls into wrinkles. He shakes his head. I'm glad I can't see what he's remembering.

I go back into the cook room, and there sits Mom reading the history book.

"Eddie," Mom says, "I'm reading about all of the colonies now. It's interesting."

Here's my chance.

"Great, Mom," I say. "How about you tell me about it."

In about twenty minutes Mom tells me what would be two or three weeks of school assignments. This is the way to go to high school. I have to remember to check in with Mom now and then to get the rest.

The next morning is warm. The crew scrapes slushy snow off the melting ice in front of the dingle and drives two horseshoe stakes into the frozen ground. I read Robinson in the cook room while they pitch a few games. I hear them laugh and cheer once in a while.

After dinner while I'm reading, the crew digs their bear paw snowshoes out and sloshes through the slush to look at the dam. At supper time Andre tells me that we can work again in a couple of weeks—if the rock drill comes and if dynamite breaks the ledge into rocks we can handle.

That night before I tell more about Robinson the men hang their wet boots from drying racks over the stove. I guess that the fire pit where the cannibals cooked their lunch on Robinson's island smells better than the bunk room.

Anyway, I tell that Robinson is doing OK with farm goats and crops after twenty years or so. The cannibals come back once in a while, but Robinson hides from them. He always thinks of escaping from the island, and he decides that he should have stayed on his Brazil plantation and waited for his few slaves to multiply.

Andre tells them, and I expect the uproar.

After things quiet down, Andre says, "This Robinson very bad. Good man not allow little new baby to be slave. We want Robinson on island forever."

I tell them that Robinson rescues a prisoner from cannibals and names him Friday. Friday learns some English. Right off, Robinson teaches Friday that he must eat goats and not people.

Andre says, "That is good for Friday. Many goats on island. Only one Robinson."

I tell that Friday isn't too interested in clothes, but he learns to use tools very well. He and Robinson make a boat.

The crew has a good laugh, and Andre says, "Me and Emile use Friday in blacksmith shop. We find pants for him in dingle."

The crew is still chuckling about Friday's pants when Roy comes in and says something in French. The crew splits a seam. Roy says to me, "Our rock drill will be here in a few days."

Wow. Hey. I cheer with my crew, and that's the end of Robinson tonight. This is a time I wish I knew French. I know my crew is hashing over our spring work, and all I can do is cheer with them.

So I go back to the cook room, and Mom is reading the United States History book again. She tells me about our Revolutionary War. I listen hard, and I try to keep the dates straight.

Late next morning I'm reading ahead in "Robinson", and the crew is out front pitching horseshoes. I hear a lot of laughing and yelling, more than just for a game of horseshoes. In the door comes Jimmie Roberts and the rest of our Ashland neighbors from McNally Pond Camp. It dawns on me that they are going out for the summer. Come to think about it, they have to go out before the snow and ice melts and the road becomes squishy mud for a month or so.

I'm high when I talk to the neighbors about their families and summer jobs. I'm down when I remember I can't go out to see Janice until we finish the dam. Yeah. Janice. I've got to write her a letter because there will be no tote sled trips during mud season.

I write Janice about Mom planning to vote and reading our history book. I tell her about Jason's tapered skis and screwed-on calked boots. I tell her that we're ready to get on with the dam. I tell her I'm feeling great, but that's a lie. I want to go out with Jimmie and the neighbors. Mom, Roy, and Jason also have letters for Jimmie to take.

I help Mom and Jason set an early dinner for the neighbors. When Jimmie and the crew leave after dinner their horse's hooves and sled runners sink deep into soft ice and slush. I want to go, too.

That night I tell the crew that cannibals come to the island again with prisoners for dinner. Robinson has taught Friday to use guns, and they rescue two prisoners. That isn't a big deal. Next, after nearly thirty years, comes an English ship that had been captured by some of the ship's crew in a mutiny.

That is a big deal, and my crew wants all the details. The mutineers are going to put the captain and two other good guys on the island and sail away, but there are some trustworthy men among the mutineers. Robinson and Friday trick the mutineers and win the ship back for the captain.

Andre says, "This time Robinson do something right. We guess will go home where he belong."

Next morning at breakfast, Andre says, "We wonder about Robinson. You tell us this morning?"

"Tell you what," I say, "I'll come to the bunk room and read a little and tell you that much. You can talk that over while I'm reading more. OK?"

"OK."

That works OK. Robinson takes Friday to England. I read and tell that Robinson is nearly broke in England. The crew says they understand that. He goes to his plantation in Brazil and finds that it has done great over the years. He's rich. The crew says that doesn't happen in Quebec. He sells his plantation, goes back to England, and gets married. The crew says it's about time he acted like a man. The Robinson family has two sons and a daughter, and the crew thinks that is a pretty good start on a family.

When we go to the cook room for dinner Roy says, "10-Mile Depot called. The rock drill is there."

28. ROCK DRILL ARRIVES

We give Roy a big cheer for his good news. During dinner I know my crewmates are talking about the dam because I understand a French word now and then. Once again I wonder if I can find a French teacher this summer when school is closed.

"Eddie," Andre says, "Robinson OK now with wife and little ones. You read and we play horseshoe this afternoon. After supper you tell how many more little ones Robinson have. OK?"

"OK."

It doesn't turn out that way. Robinson's wife dies, and he is restless. He wonders how things are going on his island. I guess the crew will complain about that, and after supper I find I am right.

"Too bad," Andre says. "Mother die. Little ones need father more. Robinson need stay home."

I tell them that Robinson places his kids with a housekeeper and provides for their schooling when they grow up. He buys a bunch of stuff for his island and sails away. I guess the crew will complain again, and they sure do.

"Robinson not good father," Andre says. "Leave little ones is bad as own slave. Little ones his. Should take care of little ones right. Stay away from little ones years and years too long."

Next morning I have trouble reading ahead in "Robinson". I keep thinking of the rock drill. I don't know what it looks like, but I know it's coming on a bobsled.

I pitch horseshoes with the crew in the afternoon, but I take time to listen to Mom tell about the Louisiana Purchase and people moving west across the Mississippi River. Mom is all enthused.

Anyway, after supper I tell the crew that a storm blows Robinson's ship off course a long ways north to cold weather and snow. Then the wind stops blowing. Robinson complains that the ship stays still for three weeks.

The crew looks pretty bored as they talk that over.

"Not a big thing," Andre says. "Sometime, like right now, we don't work longer than that because of snow. Robinson should stay home with little ones anyway."

The story goes on. When the wind blows again, Robinson's ship chances to find a burning ship. The crew and passengers are in small boats and nearly frozen when he rescues them. He finds that they are Quebec French people on a trip to France. Robinson takes them to Newfoundland so they can take a ship home to Quebec. He will not accept pay for helping them.

A mental midget could see the change in my crew when Andre tells them.

"We have Robinson all wrong," Andre says. "Maybe Robinson do little mistake now and then. We do, too. Robinson save our grandparents. He is hero, for sure."

At breakfast next morning Roy tells us, "The rock drill made it to 20-Mile yesterday. They plan to be here at 30-Mile today." That makes breakfast extra great.

"Ed," Roy says as he sits beside me for breakfast, "let's go look at that ledge outcrop this morning."

"Great," I say, "I'm getting a little tired of 'Robinson'."

We ski down the road and find that a good bit of the snow has melted, but the outcrop is still under eight or ten inches.

"You know," I say, "If we shoveled that snow off we wouldn't have to wait for it to melt. Today, I'd rather shovel snow than read about Robinson."

So back we go to get the crew, and like me they have loafed long enough. They toss the horseshoes on the dingle porch, pick up shovels, and snowshoe back to the outcrop. By noon we have rock showing on a place as big as a couple of baseball diamonds. In the afternoon we have about twice as much bare rock, and we dig the rock carts out of the snow.

We see two bobsleds coming up the road, the tote sled and the drill.

I'm all for setting the drill up right now so I can see how it works. The teamsters and the two guys with the rock drill are looking for supper, so supper it is.

I get a letter from Janice dated April 12, 1926. She is mostly OK. The twins ski a lot, but they let their schoolmates use the skis during recess and lunch time. Janice often eats her lunch at Theresa's place. School is going OK (that means all As). She is the only one in her class with a friendship ring.

But she isn't all OK. She says she was lonesome for my letters when snow kept the tote team out of the woods for a month. She says the teamster tells her this will be the last trip in the woods until the snow melts and the road mud dries up. Maybe that will be six weeks or so. She wants us to get the dam finished soon so I can come home. I agree with her on that.

After supper I tell some "Robinson Crusoe" to our crew and the rock drill men. The new guys tell us they came from Italy to build the Great Northern Paper Company mill. They do English about like Andre, but it doesn't matter what language we use. Robinson's story and our work on the dam is the same for everyone.

Robinson takes a bunch of tools and a boat to his island. The people there are doing pretty well. They take the boat Robinson brought for them to a neighboring island and bring people back. When Robinson leaves, the island is like the early American colonies Mom told me about. When I leave to write to Janice, our crew is catching the rock drill guys up on "Robinson".

I write Janice that the rock drill arrived, and we are going to help set it up tomorrow. I tell her we want to get on with the dam, and we're not going to waste any time. I ask her to be sure and write when the tote wagon can come in after mud season. I tell her I love her, but I don't tell her I'm lonesome and I'd like to go out with the tote team tomorrow.

Next morning I learn that a four-cycle gasoline engine is the biggest part of the rock drill set-up. Its bigger than the engine in the snow car. I remember the model in the science lab and the description in the science book so I know sort of how it works. The rock drill guys let me crank it, and it goes when they turn on the electricity part. It chug, chug, chugs, and the exhaust really stinks.

If I understand the science book right, a crank shaft turns twice for every chug. It turns a drive wheel fast like you wouldn't believe. Someday I want to take one of those things apart and really understand it.

Anyway, they run a belt from the engine drive wheel to an air compressor, and an air hose from the compressor to a rock drill. They put a crow-bar sized bit in the drill, and the thing drives a hole in rock ledge faster than I'd believe. The drill rattles, clatters, and bangs so I can't even hear the engine chugging.

The crew goes back to the dam and we shovel snow from where the first rocks will go. Wow. It's great to be back to work.

About the middle of the morning one of the rock drill guys carries a couple of drill bits to Emile's blacksmith shop. At noon time I walk to the cook room with Andre and Emile, and there is something wrong. Usually Emile gurgles a stream of French, but today he doesn't say a word. He looks sad like someone shot his dog or something.

"Is something wrong?" I ask Andre.

"I talk to Roy," he says.

When we go in for dinner, Andre, Emile, and Roy stay on the dingle and talk for a few minutes. When they come in, Roy sits beside me.

"Would you help Emile in the blacksmith shop?" Roy asks me.

"Sure," I agree. So I go with Emile and Andre after dinner.

Andre says, "Emile have chlorine gas one day in Great War. Could not see and talk for long time. Only see and talk little bit now. Emile have to see right color to temper steel rock drill bit. He try and try this morning. Nothing work for him. I have tool to fix. You learn to temper rock drill bit. OK?"

"OK," I tell him. "Say, Emile looks sad. What's wrong?"

"Emile cannot see to temper steel any more. He think he not 'Bon Homme'."

"What? Hey, wait a minute," I say. "You and Emile made my snowshoes and Mom's little snowshoes. Emile coached me. I'd have been last in the big race without Emile, and my girlfriend won two races with the little snowshoes. You guys made Mom a chair. You make skis and everything else. You're both 'Bon Homme'. OK?"

Andre talks to Emile for a while, and Emile smiles again.

That afternoon Emile picks out a glass marble from a ton of stuff on the bench. The marble color is somewhere in there between pink, red, and yellow.

Emile gives me the marble, and Andre says, "Heat drill bit white hot in forge, and hammer on anvil to four-side point. Hot steel change color as cool. That color," he points to the marble, "you dip in oil." He points to a bucket of oil beside the anvil. "How you use forge Emile show you."

A blacksmith forge is a special kind of stove which burns coal and has an air blower called a bellows. You pump the bellows with one hand. With a set of long tongs you hold the steel drill bit in the fire with the other hand. The more you pump the hotter the fire gets. It's not Mom's cook stove. It runs so hot it would burn a frying pan of bacon in no time—then melt the pan.

A forge takes some getting used to. I melt the end of one bit, and next time I don't make it hot enough to hammer the point. My blacksmith's hammer is about twice as heavy as a carpenter's nail hammer. Emile works a forge and bellows all day long, but in a half hour or so my hammer arm is so tired I have to switch hands.

After a few mistakes I make a four-sided point right. I pump the bellows and reheat it white hot. As it cools the color changes, and I hold the hot bit near the marble waiting for a match. There. The colors match. The hot steel spizzles and spuzzles when I dip it in the oil.

The snow on the road past the dam and to the rock outcrop is so packed that I can walk and carry the bit. The rock drill guys have quite a few holes drilled in the rock, and they try my sharpened bit. It's OK, I'm proud, but I have four dull bits to carry back to the forge.

By noontime my arms feel as floppy as wet towels, and eating dinner is embarrassing. I have to hold my eating arm with the other hand so I can put a forkful of dinner in my mouth. But when it's time for Mom's pie my arms are sort of working OK again.

"Eddie," Andre says after dinner, "You do bit then take little rest, OK?"

That works, and I sharpen six bits in the afternoon.

Telling about Robinson is the last thing I want to do that night, but the crew wants to know if Robinson is smart enough to go home when he leaves his island. Robinson isn't. He stays on a merchant ship and trades here and there. He makes good money, but the crew goes ashore and destroys a local religious symbol. There is big trouble and the sailors kill many innocent people. Robinson gives them such a hard time about killing innocent people that they put him off the ship at the next port.

After the discussion, Andre tells me, "Robinson right. Breaking idol is like burning church. Killing innocent people always wrong. So Robinson right, but have no ship. What does he do now we find out next time, OK?"

Next morning I feel like a new guy—for a while. At least I sharpen as many bits as the machine uses.

That night I tell that Robinson finds a partner, buys another ship, and trades here and there for all sorts of stuff including opium. He makes more money than he can believe.

The discussion is a lot of growling. "This is bad money," Andre tells me. "Opium is dope. Bad, bad for people. Robinson hurt many people for bad money. We work at 30-Mile for good, honest money. Robinson wrong."

I don't know about this stuff, opium, but every one of my crew and the new Italian guys think it's no good for sure. I believe them.

Next morning we're busy. Andre replaces broken snow shovel handles, and Emile and I trade off using the forge. Emile heats and bends a new set of horseshoes for one of the horses. I sharpen rock drill bits.

WHOOOMM.

The shop door bangs against the frame. The poor horse jumps, prances, and squeals in terror. Andre and Emile dive under the work bench. For a moment I stand at the forge probably bug-eyed. Then I grab the horse's bridle to calm the animal.

I look outdoors to see what happened. A cloud of smoke and dust rises down the road toward the rock outcrop, and I guess it was dynamite.

Back in the shop Andre and Emile roll out from under the bench and stand up. Their faces are wide-eyed and drop-jawed. They shake so bad they have to hold onto the bench to stand up. This is Andre and Emile, the guys who fear nothing—well, maybe. They look like kids cornered by a huge animal. Why, I wonder? It was only a noise.

They lean on the bench and talk French.

Andre says, "We sorry, Eddie. We do not like to be like little child. We think German artillery in France. Now we know dynamite. We sorry, Eddie."

"It's OK. OK for sure," I tell them. "I'm sorry it happened. I'll get the rock guys to let us know when they are going do that. It's OK."

"You don't say we act like little child. OK?" Andre says.

"OK," I tell my friends.

As I hammer on the next drill bit, I think again that Jason and I owe these guys big. They helped win the Great War, the War to End all Wars. They carry the scars not only on their bodies but in their minds too. Because of them, Jason and I will never fight in a war. I wipe tears from my eyes so I can see the color of the hot steel and the marble.

29. ROCK FOR THE DAM CRIB

When the rock drill guys walk by toward the cook room we join them.

"Hey, would you let us know when you're going to set that stuff off?" I ask.

"Yeah. OK," They say. "Sorry. We'll do that."

After dinner 30-Mile Depot looks like last summer. Teamsters lead horses out of the hovel and hitch them to rock carts.

Andre, Emile, and I go with the carts to see how the dynamite works on the rock outcrop. There are pieces of rock ledge all over place, and the teamsters load their carts in almost no time at all. The engine chug, chugs, and the rock drill rattles and bangs as the rock drill guys drive more dynamite holes in the ledge.

Roy joins us when we walk back to the dam and watch teamsters dump rocks into the log crib.

"You're idea is working," he says to me.

"Huh?"

"You thought of trying dynamite."

"Oh, yeah. Hey, I'll try anything to get this dam finished."

So back I go to sharpen drill bits in the blacksmith shop. The days are pretty warm now, and it's good to leave the door open to get rid of stray forge smoke and watch rock carts go by. I don't have much time to read in the cook room, so I bring the Robinson book to the blacksmith shop. I read when I'm resting my arms between sharpening rock drills.

Soon the book gets pretty cruddy and I guess I'll have to buy it from school, but maybe it's worth it. Andre wants to know every little bit I read, and he talks it over with Emile. They tell it to the crew at night, and they don't need me in the bunk room at all.

"That's OK."

I listen to Mom tell about the California gold rush, the Underground Railroad, and the Civil War. She says that farmers worked hard to move west and plow new farms, and she thinks that building the railroads was a great thing. The more history Mom tells me, the more I think I might read the book—someday.

Illustration 29-1: *Building McNally Pond Dam* by Judy Sherman

Every morning Andre tells me what the crew thinks about Robinson. "Stupid, stupid, stupid," he says about Robinson's long, long caravan trip across China. Of course, Robinson trades and makes money all the way. "Robinson already rich. Should go home with little ones."

Spring moves along, and as the days get warmer the snow and ice melt. That's good. But the frost in the road melts. That's bad. Soft spots turn into mud holes, and the rock cart guys have to dump in rocks and gravel to stiffen them up. One mud hole spreads into the next, and they keep dumping in rocks. But there is only a half mile or so of road between the dam and ledge, and soon it all gets pretty solid. The best part is that while the road improves the log crib fills fast.

Day after day I watch from the blacksmith shop, and it looks like the crew is building a beaver dam. As the crib fills with rocks, the crew faces the upstream side with dozens of beams we broadaxed square last fall and winter. Beavers build their dams with sticks and sometimes pretty big logs. The rock cart guys haul mud and gravel to cover the beams and hold back the water. Beavers cover their sticks and logs with mud—just like our dam.

But sometimes a late snowstorm keeps us off the job, and it doesn't seem like we will ever finish the dam. And for sure, sometimes I wonder if there are numbers enough for all the pages in the "Robinson Crusoe" book.

I'm happy for sure when I do finally finish "Robinson". His caravan goes across Russia after he gets out of China. He spends a winter in Siberia. He does some stupid things (I think, anyway), but he always makes money. He gets back to England in 1705, and he is an old man.

I go to the bunk room to hear what the crew thinks. Andre keeps me and the two Italian guys caught up in English with the French conversation.

Andre says, "Robinson waste his life—almost. He save some Quebec people, but he leave old mom and dad. He make people slave. He kill people. He leave his little ones. He never happy. We work at 30-Mile Depot. Be happy."

Before I leave Andre says, "Now Eddie, we have little more work on dam. You have more book?"

"Yeah. I have a book about Tom Sawyer. OK?"

"This Tom Sawyer, he dumb like Robinson Crusoe?"

"Don't know. I'll bring the book to the blacksmith shop to read tomorrow. We'll see, OK?"

"OK."

I go into the cook room, and there sits Mom rocking with her history book in her lap like it's a family treasure. I help Jason fill the woodbox, and he sacks out.

Mom tells me about people moving to the West Coast in caravans of Conestoga wagons. The people plow farms and connect roads to the wagon trails. Railroads go to the Pacific Ocean. She tells about better roads for cars and trucks. I see tears in her eyes when she tells about the Great War.

"Eddie," Mom says, "I'm going to be part of our history."

"What are you going to do?"

"Like I told you, I'm going to vote. I'm going to be part of it."

"Mom," I say, "you've been part of it for quite a while. You're doing OK with five kids. That's five citizens. Isn't that part of it?"

Mom smiles. "Yes, I suppose it is," she says. "I never thought of it that way, but I'm still going to vote."

Mom gives me a kiss. I guess that I'll pass a history test if I get to take one. I decide I'm going to buy that book for Mom.

Day after day the road past the blacksmith shop dries a little more. Pretty soon it's as hard as it was when I walked in last summer.

From the road, day after day, I look down into snow-covered Rocky Brook gorge. The brook first appears as a wet strip of slushy snow. Over time, pools of darker water appear here and there. Soon the pools flow and once again become Rocky Brook. It flows through the dam rocks and logs until the rock cart guys stop the holes with dozens of loads of gravel and mud. Now it collects into a bigger and bigger pool above the dam.

Except for snow days the dam project goes OK, and it's fun to work in the crew—especially in the blacksmith shop. I guess I sharpen hundreds of drill bits. Every time before the dynamite guys set off a charge they tell us. Those Italian guys are 'Bon Homme'.

Between drill bits I read "Tom Sawyer"—an OK read. The guy who wrote it used quotation marks. I tell some of the story to Andre, and he laughs at the fence whitewashing deal Tom pulls off with his friends. Emile gets the story, and he laughs.

"That Tom," Andre says, "I don't think I keep up with him for son. Be fun to watch him as neighbor kid. That Aunt Polly, she have place in heaven for bring up Tom."

I tell about Tom can't remember his Bible verses. Andre and Emile laugh again.

"Protestant and Catholic all same," Andre says. "We don't remember catechism. And we tell you what, Eddie, nun is harder on boy than Aunt Polly."

I tell that Tom's big bug bites the dog right in church, the dog yowls and that does it for church that Sunday.

Before he talks to Emile, Andre says, "Long time ago I see Emile let squirrel go in church. It run all over altar. Priest send altar boy after little food and water for squirrel—keep right on with Mass."

He catches Emile up on the dog in church story, and Emile does another laugh.

Day after day the Tom Sawyer story goes OK, I sharpen drill bits, and the dam crib fills with rocks fast. When the crib is full, the dynamite guys are done their job. One morning they take their kids' pictures from the bulletin board and thank Mom for her cooking. The road is dry and they can't go out on bobsleds, so Roy lends them a wagon. They leave with their drill rig to put it on the train in Ashland.

The day they leave the first tote wagon after mud season arrives. Janice's letter is dated May 31 and it's all happy—sort of. She writes that the people in the office say the dam will be done in a week or so. That's the happy part. She writes that we'll be out for the last week of school, and Jason and I can take final tests for the year. That's the sort-of part. I can't imagine what will happen, so I don't even try.

I write to Janice.

Dear Janice,

It's hard to believe that the dam is about done. I'm proud to help Roy and do something useful. I feel that we are different people. Last year we were kids in school, but this year we have done something adult.

I know you said you are just a freshman school girl, but you are more. You mothered the twins this year so Mom could cook for a whole crew. That's not just babysitting. Roy said you made this whole thing work, and he is right.

See you soon. Be happy with me. I love you.
Eddie

"Jason," I say, "I'm in big trouble. You've got to teach me a year's algebra in a couple of weeks."

"Yeah," Jason says. "Theresa writes that I can take tests when we go out. Now let's see, I did algebra and geometry and I read the science book. Mom might be the best history teacher in the world. I can do something with 'Tarzan' and 'Alice's Adventures in Wonderland' and, for sure, 'Cinderella', but you've got to catch me up on the rest."

"OK. It's going to take us three days to walk out. I'll do 'Treasure Island' and 'Tom Sawyer' in a day, and that leaves two days for 'Robinson Crusoe'."

"How come two days for one book?"

"Look, just be thankful you don't have to read it. OK?"

So I get my hands washed while I'm helping Jason with pots and pans, and we start on algebra. I'll tell you what, reading Robinson is easy pickings compared to this stuff. But I make some progress. Who would think that you can use a letter to represent a number? Jason doesn't let me goof off. Doing a year's worth of algebra (more or less) in two weeks is the way to go. Suffering two weeks is enough.

One night I'm having a bad time with quadratic equations. I guess my brain needs some time out so I get an idea to work on. The thing is, Mom might be the key that keeps me working in the woods. She is proud of her cooking job, and if she gets a job next winter in the woods and I do OK at high school this year—maybe she'll go for this same deal again. Good idea, so I go back to quadratic equations.

It's pretty late, and we hear roars of laughter from the bunk room. Jason and I go in. Andre had told about Tom Sawyer feeding his medicine to his cat, and the cat goes nuts.

"We remember something we do," Andre says to us. "Alcide help friends lean big plank up on barn roof of mean farmer. They push farmer's wagon up and leave on ridgepole. Farmer pretty ugly." He points at Alcide and the crew laughs again.

"Jacques push over outhouse with crabby man inside." Jacques stands and bows for another laugh.

"Horse come down road all peaceful. Emile jump out of ditch and pop open umbrella in front of horse. Horse run away. Farmer catch Emile. Not good for Emile." Emile gets the laugh.

"With Emile I set outhouse on front porch roof of big rich house. Emile safe this time. No one find out." Emile and Andre get another laugh.

When we go back to the cook room it's too late for more algebra. I'm in my bunk and I think that somehow I've got to come back to work with these great guys again next winter.

Next morning Jimmie's crew stops on their way out for the summer. Come noon, the cook room sounds like some kind of madhouse. Mom is a busy, happy queen. We're proud when the visitors are impressed with our dam job. They wave on their way down the road. I think of Janice, and I wish I were going out with them.

But our turn is coming soon.

30. SAYING *GOODBYE* TO BEST FRIENDS

The rock drill is gone, so I don't have any drill bits to sharpen. Today I'm cookee again while Jason scales the last of the wood at McNally Pond Camp.

I soon guess that Mom is wise to my plan to have her read my United States history. While she's cooking she keeps poking dates and presidents at me.

By the middle of the afternoon the cook room is ready for supper so I walk up to the dam. The pool above the dam looks as big as a lake, and it's up to the lower sluiceway. As I watch the crew test the gates I remember broad axing the gate planks. The men lift and drop the big doors with block and tackle, and the gates work great. They leave the gates closed so the dam will fill with water overnight.

While walking back to the cook room, I remember walking in last year. Our dam was only a few base logs in a muddy ditch across Rocky Brook gorge, and I am proud of our dam.

Like before I sharpened drill bits, I go in the bunk room after supper. Doing "Tom Sawyer" for a great bunch of friends is more fun than doing "Robinson". I tell about Tom playing Robin Hood and robbers, and the crew remembers the way it was when they were kids.

Andre says, "We Royal Canadian Mounted Police, and we catch fur thief. Every time."

I tell them about Tom and his friends running away to play pirates. After a while the whole town thinks the boys are dead, plans a memorial funeral, and the boys wait to walk in on their funeral.

The crew talks, laughs, and chuckles. Heads shake, no, and nod, yes. Eyes roll.

"We do not do that," Andre says. "No. No. We have to live with nun teacher after funeral does not happen. Maybe we be in real funeral."

Next morning we make short work of breakfast, head for the dam, and Mom and Jason join us. We walk out on the dam, and it's great to see. The pond is so high it trickles over the sluice gates. Roy nods his head to Jacques and Alcide, and they pull the block and tackle rope to open the top gate.

Wow. A river of water thunders into the gorge. Little trees and big bushes downstream bend like grass under the rushing, tumbling, rolling force. I raise my arms and yell. Everyone yells but the booming, churning water is all I hear. The men open the lower gate and two rivers compete for room to tumble down the gorge. Big trees along the banks bend in the force. As the pond empties the rushing river slows to a gentle waterfall, and I hear happy yells and laughing. Everyone shakes everyone's hand, and Mom hugs more guys than she did at her wedding lunch.

It's over, we did it, and it's time to go home. I leave with Mom and the crew to walk back to the cook room. Roy stays on the dam so I go back.

"We did it," I say.

"Yeah, we did."

"Is it as good as you expected?"

"Yeah. This is the best dam I've ever seen. It will do for a couple of years."

"A couple of years? It looks to me like it will do forever."

"Well, Ed," Roy says as he pats the upper sluice gate post, "I guess it would do about forever, but now we know it's obsolete. We'll use it to drive the wood close by, but log haulers will move everything else."

I guess I stand there with my mouth open. I know what Roy said, but I can hardly believe he said it. I look at his face to see if he's kidding me, and he isn't.

"When we planned this dam," Roy says, "we didn't know what log haulers would do. We found that out at the Christmas snowshoe race, didn't we?"

I guess I answer him, but I'm not sure. My brain tries to think of everything at once, and nothing, nothing, nothing makes sense. Roy goes back to the depot, and I help the crew pick up a few stray tools and return them to the dingle.

In the cook room Roy gives every man a pay envelope and handshake. The men take their family pictures from Mom's bulletin board. They have a few good words with the cook, and shake hands with Jason and me. Carrying their packs, my friends leave in small groups heading west toward McNally Pond Camp, Clayton Lake, and Quebec.

Emile talks to Andre, and Andre says to Jason and me, "Emile say you both run two, three time every week. Sometime long, slow. Sometime short, fast. Every week. We see you in Clayton Lake race next winter. OK?

Roy says, "It's all set up, Andre. We'll see you there."

We shake hands, and I can't talk. Two of my best friends are leaving, and I feel like I've lost control of my life. I hope they don't see tears in my eyes. As my hero friends walk out the cook room door, I look under my bunk to see if I've left anything. There is the walking stick I used the day I walked in. By the time I fish it out I've got my tears under control.

My brain is in no shape to argue with Mom or Roy about me and high school next year so I help pack our wangan, including Mom's rocking chair of course, onto a wagon. We take down Mom's bulletin board planks, make sure the stove fires are out, and nail the planks across the doors to keep bears out.

"Boys," Mom says as we hop onto the wagon, "Roy and I have something to tell you. We have new jobs. Roy is the new Ashland Superintendent for Great Northern Paper Company. I can read recipes and menus now, and I am the new cook at the company hotel."

My brain is so bent this morning that I can't fit that into anything, but I agree with Jason that Mom and Roy are doing OK, for sure.

When we leave 30-Mile Depot the sun east of the dam looks tree-top high, and it glints along the telephone wires. As we pass the dam Mom and Jason have all sorts of great things to say about it, but Roy and I don't even glance sideways. All I can think is we built a dam the company doesn't need. I'm glad I've got a teaching job on the way home so I won't have to think much about the dam.

Mom and Roy are doing OK on the wagon seat because it has springs under it, but bouncing on a wagon body is not the place to teach high school literature. Jason and I walk behind, and I do "Treasure Island" first. Jason says this is a great story, but he thinks whoever wrote it can tell it better than I can. He's going to read it when he has time after we do the tests.

Walking and eating ham sandwiches and donuts for dinner slows down my teaching, but I still have time for "Tom Sawyer". I tell Jason the story. He says someone ought to straighten the kid out and put him to work—at a job the kid has to do himself. Jason also says if he's really looking for something to do sometime, he might read the book.

At 20-Mile Mom and Madam Cote sit up nearly all night talking. Roy talks to Mr. Cote about riding a horse in once in a while to check on 30-Mile Depot and McNally Pond Camp. There are no camp sitters there because the camps are so far in the woods.

Next morning on the way to 10-Mile Depot I start telling "Robinson Crusoe" to Jason. Jason thinks Robinson is OK until he sails after a load of people for plantation slaves. Like the 30-Mile crew he thinks Robinson deserves to be shipwrecked on his island.

At 10-Mile Depot Mom and Roy have fun talking to our Ashland neighbors, Mr. and Mrs. LeBlanc. Our neighbors have all sorts of compliments for Mom and Roy on their new jobs. I have time to think about that, and I guess those new jobs really are a good thing for my family. But Mom won't be working in the woods, and she is for sure going to push high school at me.

Next morning on the way to 5-Mile Brook I talk Jason through the rest of "Robinson". He says it's a good enough story, but maybe someone should shorten it up. And use quotation marks too, just so I won't complain so much.

Before we get to 5-Mile Brook we hear a rumble or roar. It can't be thunder because there isn't a cloud in the sky. We round a curve in the road and there are two trucks, a tractor with a push blade on front, and half a dozen men. There is a new bridge over the brook. The push blade tractor is roaring and pushing gravel over the old kettle-boiling fire pit. The place where my Dad and generations of loggers boiled the kettle and traded stories is gone.

I'm ugly, sad, disgusted, and disappointed. But this new bridge seems OK with everyone else. It won't do any good for me to mouth off about losing Dad's old nooning place. I look for gorbeys, dead loggers' souls, and there are none. I feel like I did when Andre and Emile walked out of the cook room. I lost something big.

Roy steps down from the wagon, talks to the men, and looks at the new bridge. The huge, square beams are mill sawed. I think the mill probably sawed all the bridge beams square and smooth in the time it would take me to broad axe one.

"Ed," Roy says as we cross the bridge, "our new bridges have to support trucks and log haulers. Before long, we'll be driving machines to 30-Mile in a morning."

"Yeah," I say. I don't look under the bridge because I know there aren't any trout there. But I guess they might come back when the road crew stops banging around.

The road between 5-Mile Brook and town has gravel in the ruts and wet spots. It is as good as some town roads, so Jason and I sit on the back of the wagon and ride.

As we bounce along I try to make sense of what is happening in my life. We spend a year building a good dam, and it's obsolete. Log haulers move wood better. Better bridges support heavy machines which are faster and stronger than storybook flying horses. I'll never have to walk to 30-Mile Depot again, and before long I might be able to come out of the woods for Sundays with Janice. I remember the snow car.

I think this is like making skis. We make what seems like the best idea, and someone thinks of something better. So we need to think of the better idea first. How do we do that? I think of Jason standing in front of the chemicals closet in the science lab at school. He asked about doing experiments to find the best ski paint. I remember all the stuff in that lab I didn't know about. I wonder if maybe there are ideas in there that would mean better skis and maybe even better ways to work in the woods.

I can hardly believe what I'm thinking. For the first time in my life I'm wondering if I should go to high school to learn something. I'm not going to tell anyone about that.

We have a lot of wangan on the wagon, so when we get to the West End Road Roy drives the team to our house. The twins are in the yard and they come running. Theresa comes running from the house with Janice. For an instant I remember the awful look on Janice's face when she had the tiff with Theresa. For sure that is past because they're all smiles. Hey, it's great to be home with my girlfriend.

The girls can cook. Their pot roast is really good. After dinner Jason and Theresa drive the horses and wagon to the company stables, and Jason walks his girlfriend home.

Janice and I go for a walk to be together for a while. Because this is Saturday and there are no kids in West End School we go in. We sit in our old seats in the back corners of the room, and for a long time we say nothing.

Then Janice says, "This is our starting place."

"Huh?"

"We started school here, you got your 30-Mile Depot job here at graduation last year, and I got my friendship ring here last Christmas. I wish we could make skis here."

"Yeah."

"For sure, we'd be in big trouble if we tried that, but we'll find a place to make skis somewhere. First things first. Are you ready for your freshman final exams next week?"

"I can't even guess, but I think it's going to be a different world," I say.

Leonard Hutchins

31. HIGH SCHOOL EXAMS

It's Monday morning. I can't believe I'm doing this. Last year I got the cookee job that I thought would keep me out of high school. Not only that, I got better jobs that paid real logger's wages. But here I am walking to high school, and I'm wearing a necktie. Mom won.

But look. Theresa is waiting at the company office so she can walk across the bridge with us to Ashland and high school. I remember the look on my girl's face when she hated Theresa, but it's all smiles and giggles now. So walking to high school isn't all bad. I hold my girl's hand and Jason holds Theresa's.

Before we get to the school the girls stop.

"We better tell you about the school rules," Janice says.

"Rules?" Jason says.

"No fighting, no yelling, and no physical contact," Theresa says.

"Physical contact?" I ask.

"No kissing, hugging or holding hands," Janice says, and our girls pull their hands from ours, "until we're walking home," she adds.

Being at high school is something else. There were more people at the Winter Field Day, but there was a whole field to get out of the crowd. Here everyone stands in two bunches in front of the front door—girls and boys. There is no place to go. I feel like a stick of wood in a woodpile.

But I know the guys who worked on farms with me before I went to the woods to work. We talk. I talk to the guys who snowshoed in Winter Field Day races. Everyone wants to talk to Jason about his skis. Look, this crowd isn't as bad as I expected.

"Good morning Mr. Andersen," someone says, and the talking stops.

Here is a big blond guy dressed in a white shirt, black necktie, and black suit. It seems to me I've seen this guy before. And here comes Janice right into the middle of the crowd of boys.

"Mr. Andersen, these are my brothers, Eddie and Jason Clark. This is our principal and math teacher, Mr. Andersen," Janice says.

"Glad to meet you, boys," Mr. Andersen says, and he smiles as we shake hands.

"Math teacher," Jason says. "Look, is it OK if I take both the geometry and algebra tests? I'd like to know how I did."

Mr. Andersen's mouth drops open a little.

"You did both algebra and geometry in one year?" a guy in the crowd says.

Here comes Theresa. "Yes, he did," she says.

The girls' crowd follows Theresa into the boys crowd, and everyone looks at Mr. Andersen.

"Well," Mr. Andersen says. He looks around the crowd. "Come into the office, boys. I don't think I should do student interviews with the whole student body looking on."

"Boys," Mr. Andersen says as he gives us chairs in the office, "you are high school correspondence experiments. Miss Rogers said you were good students. Father Belanger borrowed books for you last fall. Mr. Edwards told me he lent a geometry book and tools at Christmas time. Father Belanger, after visits to your camp, assured me that you were reading your books to the crew and doing your homework. Theresa and Janice told me that your letters to them showed good school progress. However …"

Mr. Andersen looks at us—from one to the other—two or three times. Again I think I've seen this guy before, but what is he thinking right now?

"… we did not receive a single piece of homework correspondence from either of you."

"Oh, oh," Jason says.

I don't think in words. All I see in my mind is Mom's face if we have to tell her we don't take the tests. There is a frown, and there are tears.

"Mr. Andersen," I say, "look, we were busy working, but we did the school stuff. Honest. We can prove it. We've got to take those tests. How about giving us a chance? OK?"

I can't believe what I'm doing. For a whole year I tried to get out of high school. Here I am fighting to get into high school.

Mr. Andersen keeps looking at us—from one to the other. I know I've seen this guy before.

He says, "If you don't take the tests, we won't know if the experiment worked, will we?"

"Yeah. Yeah," I say. "We won't know."

"No. No," Jason says. "We won't know."

"Jason," Mr. Andersen says, "your geometry test and the history test are both to be given this morning. Take the geometry test first, and if you need more time for the history test you can finish during lunchtime."

"Ya hooo," I scream.

"Theresa said you're not supposed to yell in school," Jason says.

I glance at Mr. Andersen, and he grins. Wow. I've seen that grin before. Sven Andersen. Sven grinned like that when he did a forward roll on snowshoes in the one-hundred-yard race and came up running.

"Mr. Andersen, do you know Sven Andersen from New Sweden?" I ask.

"He's my nephew."

"Hey," Jason says, "you're a Swede. You must know how to make ski wax."

Mr. Andersen laughs until he cries.

"Look," Jason says, "I'll bet you do. I need to take chemistry next year so you can help me with ski wax experiments. OK? We're going to make skis, you know."

"Boys," Mr. Andersen says when he gets his tears wiped away, "I need to see your test results."

"He's not a hard guy to get along with," Jason says as we leave the office.

"He hasn't seen our test results yet," I tell him.

Jason goes to the geometry test with Theresa, and I go with Janice to the history room. The teacher, Miss Simpson, gives us test papers, and she sits down. I feel like I did when the log hauler steam whistle blew to start the snowshoe race. This is the start of a long haul.

OK. I go through the test and answer about half the questions, the ones I think I know. This won't make it. I go over the questions again, and I really try to remember what Mom told me in the 30-Mile camp kitchen. I get a few more answers, but this still won't pass—for sure. I've been in school less than an hour, and I'm in trouble already.

While I'm thinking I stare at the row of presidents' pictures up on the wall. There is old George Washington on the left and Abe Lincoln in the middle and...wow, do I get an idea or what. Those pictures are in order, and I know some of them. Hey, by matching the pictures with what I remember, I remember a little more. I might make this yet.

While I'm sweating presidents, in comes Jason. He's finished his geometry test and he starts history. We finish the history test at about the same time. When the bell rings for lunchtime, in comes Theresa with her bag lunch. She tells Jason he got an A. She does too, of course.

"Miss Simpson," I say during our bag lunch time, "could I buy our history book for my mother?"

"Huh?" Miss Simpson says as she looks up at me from correcting our tests. "I mean what?"

Janice says, "I taught Mom to read last year, so now Mom can vote. She read the history book all winter so she would better understand how to vote. I want to pay half on the book because Mom really likes it. OK?"

Miss Simpson's eyes flick from Janice to me a few times. She says as she takes a book from a shelf behind her desk and gives it to me, "I'll talk to Mr. Anderson about selling the history book. Your mother is my kind of woman. This is a civics book, and I will lend it to her for the summer."

"Thanks," I say. "By the way, did I pass?"

Miss Simpson gives our test papers to us. Janice has an A, Jason has an A (He spent more time in the 30-Mile kitchen with Mom and the history book than I did.), and I made it. Mom is a super teacher. I get a C. Am I happy or what?

However, afternoon is English test time. I read the instructions. "Write no more than two-page book reports about two books." OK, I understand that. "Writing will be graded 15% each on grammar, syntax, sentence structure, paragraph structure, and essay construction. Literary interpretation of the book will be graded 25%."

What is this? Just when I get started with a C in U.S. history my high school career is ending here in this room. That's about guaranteed.

I have to do something. I think to myself that I just finished "Tom Sawyer", so maybe I remember that best. I write some about the story and what my Quebec crew said about it. The report might not be great, but remembering the crew is fun.

But when I pull a stupid, I do it fancy. I decide to write a report on "Robinson Crusoe". I remember the story. I remember what the crew said about it. I write and write and write. There is all but no end to "Robinson Crusoe". Hey, paper has two sides. It will still be two pages if I write on the backs too. Everyone else is done. They all fidget around waiting for me. When the bell rings, Miss Phelps takes my paper, and I don't even have Robinson off his island yet. Well, at least Miss Phelps won't have our tests graded until the day we turn our books in after the tests.

When we get home that afternoon, Mom gets her civics book. Hey, just like Christmas.

No Christmas for me. I dream all night that Miss Phelps and the cannibals on Robinson's island roast me over a cannibal fire pit.

Next morning I learn that Jason is a very good Algebra teacher. Also, I'm sure that doing a year's algebra in two weeks just before the test is the way to go. You don't have time to forget so much. I get another C. That's at least two passes for four subjects. Happy. Happy. Happy. Janice and Jason? An A each. What else?

That afternoon is science test time. Science makes more sense than other stuff so I remember quite a bit of even the geology and biology parts. I don't think I do the simple machines and engines parts like other people.

Most everybody learns from the book and answers the question. When the question is about a wedge, my mind sees Alcide twitching his fingers teaching me to use a broad axe. Remembering that steam log hauler answers every steam engine question. I think I can hear the chug, chug, chug of the rock drill engine as I do the four-cycle engine part of the test. I wish I were back at 30-Mile until I look across the room and see my beautiful girlfriend.

My girl and my brother do just as I expect—each earns an A in science. I do better than I expect. I get a B. Can I believe this? All winter I sweat going to high school, and I pass three courses. Look, high school can be done.

Well, I don't know about the English part. I dream about showing Miss Phelps the cruddy "Tom Sawyer" and "Robinson Crusoe" books. I dream that I also have coal dust smooches all over my face and clothes as I stand in front of her and the whole class. The class laughs at me. I'll tell you what. It's more fun to be roasted in a cannibal fire pit.

Book day comes, and English class comes. I get a D. There are red notes on every sentence. D must be flunking because Janice's eyes bug out and her mouth drops open when I show her. And that's not all.

"Edward," Miss Phelps says, "I do not approve of correspondence courses for English. If I could have discussed your writing with you, one on one, side by side, shoulder to shoulder, during the year I'm sure you would have done much better. However, I must say that your literary interpretation shows great maturity."

"Thank you, Ma'am," I say. "But I guess I have to admit that my mature literary interpretation comes from my crew. Some of them are grandfathers."

"I don't understand."

"Well, Ma'am, my crew can't read. Now that doesn't mean they're stupid. They just didn't have time to go to school. Most speak only French and I don't. Only one, Andre Cyr, also speaks English. Now things get pretty boring in a lumber camp, especially when you're snowed off the job for weeks. I read my school books to Andre or told him the story in English, and he told the story to the crew in French. They hashed it over, and I got their book interpretation back from Andre."

Something is happening. Miss Phelps' eyes bug out and her mouth drops open like Janice's. What, I wonder is this? Well, now that I'm in trouble anyway, I guess I might as well get the cruddy book thing over with too.

"Look, Ma'am," I say as I lay the two dusty, smooched books on Miss Phelps desk, "I guess I need to pay for these books. I'm sorry I got them dirty, but I was working in the blacksmith shop when I needed to read them. You see, I got a little time off now and then to read. Like I say, I'm sorry I got them dirty. Look, something else, too. I've got to learn French so I can talk with my crew. Do you teach in the summertime?"

Miss Phelps' face, still bug eyed and drop jawed, doesn't change. She stares at the books. She stares up into my eyes. She doesn't blink. She doesn't smile.

Sooner or later, I'm not sure when, Miss Phelps' face works again. And she picks the books up.

"Eddie," Miss Phelps says. Her eyes aren't bugged now, she is sort of smiling, and her voice isn't as crisp as it was. "I will cherish these books. I have a trip planned for this summer. You will be here in school next fall, won't you?"

"Well....but....look, Miss Phelps," I say.

"Eddie, give me your test paper," she says.

I give her the paper. She writes something on it and gives it back to me. There is another D hitched to the bottom of the first one. It's a B now. I show it to Janice, and she jumps up from her seat and runs up beside me.

Miss Phelps says, "I will catch you up on your writing skills and teach you French when you are a sophomore next fall. You will be here in school next fall, won't you?"

"Yes, he will," Janice says as she takes my test paper. "I'm going to show this B to Mom, and we will get him back to school. Guaranteed."

I'm not sure how many things can crowd into your brain at once. I hear my crew arguing over "Robinson Crusoe", and I can't understand them. I hear my crew laughing with me when I measure logs in French— sort of. I see the log hauler at the snowshoe race, and I remember the steam piston model in the school science room. I see the engine in the snow car, and I think maybe there is a mechanic's shop manual in the school library. I look at Janice. She is in my brain, and she is also standing right there, my real, beautiful girl.

"Yeah. OK. I'll be here. Guaranteed," I say.

On the way out of the schoolhouse I think that I must be a pretty good English teacher even if I can't write for nothing. Jason gets an A and it only took me a couple of days on the way out of the woods to teach him about the books. I wish I could write like him. Well, maybe I'll learn next year.

I'm carrying the history book I bought for Mom. Mr. Andersen is out front of the school telling everyone to have a good summer and he'll see us all next fall. "And by the way," he says to us as we walk by, "local high school principals are working to have a high school winter sports program next winter. Father Belanger's Winter Field Day got something started."

"Hey, yeah," Jason says. "I'll make ski wax for the team in the chemistry lab. OK?"

Mr. Andersen grins. "According to the school schedule, Jason, your science course will be biology. Maybe we can work in an extra project, but I can't be sure yet."

"Look, you're Swedish," Jason says. "I know for sure I'll be making ski wax in the lab next year. And when you see Sven, tell him I'm going to beat him skiing. OK?"

"See you all next fall, folks," Mr. Andersen says. He grins again.

School is over, and Jason goes to Theresa's place with her. As Janice and I walk across the bridge, a truck loaded with school desks and chairs drives by toward Ashland.

"Hey," Janice says, "That's the West End School stuff."

Janice lifts her dress enough so she won't step on it, and we run—all the way to the West End School. The door is unlocked, and the room is empty. No furniture.

We run home. The twins sit at the kitchen table snuffling and sniveling.

"They took our school," Mary says.

Mom says, "The snow roller and new snow car worked so well on our road last winter that they are going to take students to the big town school in the snow car."

Janice sits and snivels with the girls.

"What are they going to do with the schoolhouse?" I ask.

"Well it's on land they leased from Roy, and it's not worth moving. It looks like Roy has a schoolhouse."

The word "obsolete" flashes in my mind, then pictures. Work benches, tools, a steam pipe, racks of beautiful skis and poles.

Janice and I walk back to the school, and she stands where the stove used to be.

"Janice," I say, "you wished we could make skis in the school. We're going to get your wish."

"But I didn't want them to close the school." She's still sniveling.

Girls are strange sometimes.

Leonard Hutchins

ABOUT THE AUTHOR

Born in Fort Fairfield, Aroostook County ("The County"), Maine, Leonard Hutchins graduated from Fort Fairfield High School in 1948. During his years at the University of Maine, 1948–1954, in the Army, 1952–1954, and teaching at Brownville Junction High School and Hampden Academy, 1954–1962, he noted that County people have a thing, a nuance. He was pleased to return home to The County to teach at Ashland Community High School, 1962–1980.

Home indeed. His "kids" explained with pride their home and history—and sent their parents to parent-teacher meetings so he would get a better picture (not kidding, this happened). The parents sometimes brought neighbors to fill him in. The anecdotes filled newspaper and magazine articles. Over the years, this information took shape as "Bon Homme". Grateful, Leonard adds, "For all of my Ashland students and their older friends, THANK YOU."

Leonard Hutchins

ABOUT THE ILLUSTRATOR

Aroostook County Artist Judy Sherman was raised and still lives in OxBow, Maine, a rural plantation with approximately 55 residents. The beauty of this little place is astounding—the wild animals, wildflowers, birds, and fantastic sunsets. It is more than any photographer/artist needs for a canvas. Judy was "always a doodler" but with the urging of her husband she took art lessons from a local artist during the summer of 1988, and has been hooked ever since. Judy uses acrylic medium for most of her paintings. Although she loves nature, Judy also paints landscapes, still life, florals, and will try anything to bring her illustrations to life. Most of her work is on a commission basis.

Over the years, Judy has received many awards for her work. She has also donated many pieces or prints of her artwork to local fundraisers such as the local Masonic Lodge, Ashland Fish & Game, Northern Maine Veterans Memorial Cemetery, Elks Club, Rotary, MPBN Great TV Auction and more. Judy has taught acrylic medium for Adult Ed at the Ashland District School for several years.

Since 1981, Judy has owned and operated her own business in OxBow. Her Deep In The Woods Gift Shop features quality Maine-made arts and crafts. Christmas is her busiest season as she and husband Steven have a Christmas tree farm and maintain about 15,000 balsam fir trees.

Judy has created illustrations for Leonard Hutchins in the past including his two "tall tales" books, "Gram, is He Telling Me the Truth" and "Legends & Lore". When asked if she would like to illustrate this novel, Judy got excited and her research began. Judy says, "It was a lot of hard BUT fun work. I enjoyed every aspect of it from the research to the many sketches to make it come together. I hope you enjoy it as much as I did."

Illustrator Judy Sherman thanks Ed Chase for allowing her to take pictures at the Ashland Logging Museum to be used as references for her paintings. She also thanks friends and family for their assistance and especially thanks her husband Steven for all his help and expertise.

The inspiration for Judy's illustrations came from the following:

Chapter 2-1 (Page 9) *Heading to 30-Mile Depot*—Her imagination.

Chapter 3-1 (Page 16) *Lumber Camp at 30-Mile Depot*—Ashland Logging Museum.

Chapter 3-2 (Page 18) *The Cook at 30-Mile Depot*—Ella Weeks of Masardis gave Judy a copy of an old photograph of Charlie Thompson, cook at Weeksboro Mill, taken around 1896. The dinnerware is from that photo and Charlie's stance is also used. "However," Judy said, "The description of the cook in 'Bon Homme' came from me. Charlie Thompson was a much happier cook, I think."

Chapter 7-1 (Page 41) *Jason Does the Tarzan Yell*—Her imagination.

Chapter 7-2 (Page 43) *Hewing Logs*—The result of online research, a photograph of Gib Gagnon from the book "Portage Lake: History and Hearsay Early Years to 2009", and Steve Sherman's broadaxe.

Chapter 12-1 (Page 72) *Discovering the Outcrop*—Her imagination.

Chapter 12-2 (Page 75) *Larrigans*—A concoction of several photos and the author's description.

Chapter 12-3 (Page 76) *Calked Boots*—Ashland Logging Museum; replacing the quilt with one Judy's grandmother, Eldora Grass, made for her brother in the early 1950s.

Chapter 16-1 (Page 100) *The Race*—Research of log haulers for design and the author's description of the race.

Chapter 17-1 (Page 107) *Boiling the Kettle*—For the two attending the fire and coffee pot, Judy used old photos of her Dad Brian Grass cooking over an open fire and her Uncle Merle Grass boiling the kettle while beaver trapping years and years ago. Judy adds, "It's funny that when Steven got home from work, I showed him the painting and said I didn't know if there were any mountains like that there or not, but I put some in. His reply was, 'Well, that's Rocky Brook Mountain!'"

Chapter 17-2 (Page 108) *Gorbey—"The Loggers' Ghost"*—Personal photo.

Chapter 19-1 (Page 118) *Sven and Jason Ski Race*—Her imagination.

Chapter 20-1 (Page 130) *Christmas Breakfast*—Personal childhood memories of cooking toast on her family's old cook stove in OxBow.

Chapter 22-1 (Page 140) *Telephone*—Ashland Logging Museum.

Chapter 29-1 (Page 182) *Building McNally Pond Dam*—Historical photos.

"Bon Homme" is available for sale on the web at amazon.com and at the Deep In The Woods Gift Shop, OxBow, Maine.
(207) 435-6171

Leonard Hutchins

Made in the USA
Charleston, SC
07 February 2014